"Every type of energy has positive and negative charges," Zhou Tzu said quietly.

"The ideal situation is one where a balance between the two is established and maintained."

"Yin and yang," Kane murmured. He eyed the general keenly. "And you represented the balance?"

"With the cooperation of the Devi-Naga, of course."

"And of course," Kane replied sarcastically, "the balance has now tipped into the negative."

"I'm glad you understand."

"I think I do," said Kane flatly. "You said it was a chess game, right?"

Zhou Tzu nodded.

"And you expect us to join the game."

"I see no other option." The man sounded genuinely regretful. "Not if you wish to be reunited with your friends."

"What pieces do Nora and I represent in the warlord's gambit?" Kane snapped. "Knights or pawns?"

General Zhou Tzu smiled faintly, a slightly amused, almost pitying smile. "I expect you will prove that to me once we begin our journey downriver. But you may take some solace in the fact that I do not intend to sacrifice you needlessly."

Other titles in this series:

James Axler
Outlanders

EVIL ABYSS

A GOLD EAGLE BOOK FROM
WORLDWIDE®

TORONTO • NEW YORK • LONDON
AMSTERDAM • PARIS • SYDNEY • HAMBURG
STOCKHOLM • ATHENS • TOKYO • MILAN
MADRID • WARSAW • BUDAPEST • AUCKLAND

For Robert Culp and Chuang Tzu.
Both of them inspirations.

First edition February 2005

ISBN 0-373-63845-0

EVIL ABYSS

Special thanks to Mark Ellis for his contribution to the Outlanders concept, developed for Gold Eagle.

Printed in U.S.A.

Together we visit the land of the ancient hero
Majesty that endures eternal among the
   rivers and mountains
Courts of stone and mossy walls that
   live on in the mist and the rain.
A thousand reeds sing and sway in the fluttering wind
Or is it the flags of old, still lingering?

                            —Hoàng Quý

The Road to Outlands—
From Secret Government Files to the Future

Almost two hundred years after the global holocaust, Kane, a former Magistrate of Cobaltville, often thought the world had been lucky to survive at all after a nuclear device detonated in the Russian embassy in Washington, D.C. The aftermath— forever known as skydark—reshaped continents and turned civilization into ashes.

Nearly depopulated, America became the Deathlands— poisoned by radiation, home to chaos and mutated life forms. Feudal rule reappeared in the form of baronies, while remote outposts clung to a brutish existence.

What eventually helped shape this wasteland were the redoubts, the secret preholocaust military installations with stores of weapons, and the home of gateways, the locational matter-transfer facilities. Some of the redoubts hid clues that had once fed wild theories of government cover-ups and alien visitations.

Rearmed from redoubt stockpiles, the barons consolidated their power and reclaimed technology for the villes. Their power, supported by some invisible authority, extended beyond their fortified walls to what was now called the Outlands. It was here that the rootstock of humanity survived, living with hellzones and chemical storms, hounded by Magistrates.

In the villes, rigid laws were enforced—to atone for the sins of the past and prepare the way for a better future. That was the barons' public credo and their right-to-rule.

Kane, along with friend and fellow Magistrate Grant, had upheld that claim until a fateful Outlands expedition. A displaced piece of technology…a question to a keeper of the archives…a vague clue about alien masters—and their world shifted radically. Suddenly, Brigid Baptiste, the archivist, faced summary execution, and Grant a quick termination. For Kane there was forgiveness if he pledged his unquestioning allegiance to Baron Cobalt and his unknown masters and abandoned his friends.

But that allegiance would make him support a mysterious and alien power and deny loyalty and friends. Then what else was there?

Kane had been brought up solely to serve the ville. Brigid's only link with her family was her mother's red-gold hair, green eyes and supple form. Grant's clues to his lineage were his ebony skin and powerful physique. But Domi, she of the white hair, was an Outlander pressed into sexual servitude in Cobaltville. She at least knew her roots and was a reminder to the exiles that the outcasts belonged in the human family.

Parents, friends, community—the very rootedness of humanity was denied. With no continuity, there was no forward momentum to the future. And that was the crux—when Kane began to wonder if there *was* a future.

For Kane, it wouldn't do. So the only way was out—way, way out.

After their escape, they found shelter at the forgotten Cerberus redoubt headed by Lakesh, a scientist, Cobaltville's head archivist, and secret opponent of the barons.

With their past turned into a lie, their future threatened, only one thing was left to give meaning to the outcasts. The hunger for freedom, the will to resist the hostile influences. And perhaps, by opposing, end them.

Prologue

Northern Cambodia

Flat palm leaves, the rich color of emerald, drooped over Zhou Tzu's face. He gazed up at the ruby-red droplets glistening on the tips, appreciating the contrast of color. Then a fat drop of blood fell from a frond and splattered warmly against his forehead. Except to narrow his eyes, he didn't move.

His skull throbbed, as if hammers pounded away at the bone. A vibration, like that of a musical note refusing to fade hummed against his eardrums. Absently he wondered whose blood daubed the foliage, whether it was his own or that of his men.

In his nostrils burned the chemical stink of high explosive. A heavy umbrella of smoke hovered over the crater punched in the center of the jungle clearing. It slowly drifted away, pushed by a humid breeze, but he followed its path with only his eyes. He didn't turn his head. Dazed as he was, he instinctively remained motionless.

Zhou Tzu's face and khaki clothing were the hue of the mudflat in which he lay. He didn't stir for fear of breaking the illusion he was only a slime-covered log half-submerged in the muck. Over the hum echoing in his head, he heard the moist sucking sound of feet slogging through the mire and the murmur of male voices speaking in the Khmer dialect. One announced loudly, his tone suggesting more outrage than surprise, "This one is alive!"

A bubbling moan at the very edges of audibility reached him. It was drowned out by a voice, as sharp as a whip crack, demanding, "Where is your general? Where is Zhou Tzu?"

He heard no response, but he did hear the meaty smack of a hand striking flesh. "Can you hear me, pig? Where is General Zhou Tzu?"

The response, when it came, was so low Zhou Tzu's ears barely registered it but he recognized the voice as that of Chaksi, his second lieutenant. Chaksi had celebrated his fourteenth birthday only two days earlier. The sound of another slap was followed by a gasped-out obscenity from the youth. An instant later came a door-slamming bang. A guttural voice snarled, "Little bastard. Find a suitable tree. Make an example of this one."

Zhou Tzu knew Colonel Puyang's voice just as he knew it was the colonel who had administered the head shot to Chaksi with his beloved Tokarev pistol. Stomach muscles knotting with adrenalin, Zhou struggled against the almost insane urge to burst up from the bog and attack the patrol but he had only a *piha-kaetta* dagger as weapon. His subgun had been damaged by the explosion. He had been walking point when the world blew up in a blaze of flame, heat and mud barely ten feet ahead of him. He couldn't be sure if the explosion had been due to a warhead fired from an airborne *vimana*, or from a buried mine, but at the moment he cared very little one way or the other.

Through the haze of his fogged perceptions and stunned eardrums, Zhou barely understood that Colonel Puyang's patrol had violated the border between his territory and that of the Devi-Naga. Blinking up at the little beads of crimson dangling on the tips of the palm fronds over his head, he wondered again how much of the blood had been splashed there by the four men comprising his escort.

As the patrol moved on, checking the other bodies, Zhou Tzu continued to lie motionless in the marsh surrounding the vast lake of Tonle Sap. His right leg and rib cage throbbed fiercely but he dared not move. Dark shapes shifted against the blaze of the afternoon sun. Zhou watched through slitted lids as six men stepped into his range of vision.

Colonel Puyang caught and held his attention. He was a large man with the beginnings of a paunch swelling against the green-gray uniform tunic. Worked in gold thread, both sleeves bore the overlapping-scale design of an officer in the elite Cobra Guard. Perched on his skull was a gold-hued helmet fashioned to resemble the hooded head of a king cobra, one of the great Naga who had, according to legend, created the land of Kambujadesa and the city of Angkor Thom.

Beneath the helmet's overhang, meant to suggest the upper jaw and snout of a serpent, Puyang's face was that of the Vetala, the two-visaged demon of legend. The left half of the face was normal, but the other half was no face at all—rather it was a raw red cicatrix. The maimed tissue was knitted into a network of scar tissue that reached down beneath his chin and around to the right ear. The colonel's eye was still there, and although it glared with a milky blue-white hatred, it did not see.

Colonel Puyang's disfigurement was a silent testimony of why he hunted Zhou Tzu so relentlessly, regardless of borders or pacts. Some years before, Zhou had given the man two faces to symbolize his treachery.

A scarlet plume, a symbol of his rank, fluttered from the crest of Puyang's helmet. His men were similarly uniformed, although their helmets were unadorned and their tunics didn't carry the scale design. All of them carried spindly KM-50 subguns, a carryover from the long-ago reign of the Khmer Rouge.

A Cobra guard used the barrel of his weapon to push aside a clump of foliage. He exclaimed, "Colonel! There is another one of the general's men alive!"

Zhou Tzu recognized the man they dragged from the underbrush as Mongpa, a young man who had served him for three years. A wet, dark red stain spread across the front of his olive-drab tunic, and the crimson froth flecking his lips indicated a punctured lung. Two of the Cobra guards held the man up before the colonel, who demanded harshly, "Is there any point in asking you about General Zhou Tzu?"

The young man shook his head dazedly as if he didn't understand the question. Puyang spat out an obscenity and slammed the frame of the Tokarev flat against the left side of Mongpa's jaw. A little spurt of blood burst from his slack lips.

"You are not worth a bullet," Puyang growled, drawing a two-foot-long *poignard* from a canvas hip scabbard.

The highly polished blade flashed in the afternoon sunlight as the point crunched through Mongpa's chest. The two troopers pushed the young man forward to meet Puyang's thrust, and the triangular point slid out of his back very near his spine. Even at that distance, Zhou Tzu heard the grate of steel against bone.

Colonel Puyang whipped the blade free with an angry flourish, a flat ribbon of liquid crimson trailing after it. As Mongpa sagged in the grips of the troopers, his head bowing, Puyang raised the knife and brought it down edge first, in a swift, practiced stroke.

The razor-keen steel of the blade sheared through Mongpa's neck, severing tissue, muscle, blood vessels and bone. His head dropped to the marshy ground with a moist thud and rolled like an awkward ball.

The Cobra guards laughed in their appreciation and admiration of the decapitation performed by their commanding officer. They allowed Mongpa's body to fall to the muddy ground, where it twitched in postmortem spasms for a few moments.

Reaching down, Colonel Puyang picked up the head by a handful of hair and stated loudly, "It's not Zhou Tzu's head, but it will suffice to provide an object lesson to those who defy her holiness, the Devi Kumudvati, the Naga princess."

The colonel swaggered into the jungle, swinging Mongpa's head as if he were carrying a basket by its handle. "Let us keep searching."

Zhou Tzu didn't move, not even when the laughing voices and slogging sounds of the Cobra guards' progress faded away completely. He knew that Puyang had spoken strictly for his benefit, in the chance he might be hiding within earshot and creep out when the patrol seemed to be gone. The colonel would probably leave a trooper in vicinity to make sure. Zhou Tzu would practice the same tactic were the situation reversed.

A heavy, deafening silence fell over the jungle. Somewhere close by a tree frog chirped inquisitively. Squinting up between the sheltering fronds, he glimpsed three white egrets soaring overhead, their curve-beaked heads at the ends of elongated necks peering down at the scene of the ambush. Zhou Tzu knew that carrion feeders would soon be winging their way toward the feast.

The hot yellow disk of the Asian sun slowly darkened at the edges as heavy clouds scudded across the sky, heralding the approach of one of the season's frequent storms. By degrees, the sun was swallowed by huge black thunderheads. Cloud mountains massed in the west, and a crooked finger of lightning arced across them. Almost automatically, Zhou Tzu counted the seconds. When the thick humid air shivered to a clap of thunder, he estimated the storm front was less than two miles away and moving very fast.

He continued to lie still, listening but hearing nothing but the chittering of monkeys and the clacking screech of tropical birds. The buzz of flies winging over and settling on the bodies of his men to drink the blood oozing into the mud reached his ears. He knew it was already turning gummy and dark brown, especially in such intense heat. The equally high humidity would prevent the blood from drying for some hours, and the odor was sure to draw scavengers larger than flies. He hoped the rain arrived before that.

Zhou Tzu drifted in and out of wakefulness or consciousness—he wasn't sure which during his brief periods of lucidity. He couldn't understand what would have driven the Devi-Naga to break the truce. It was possible Colonel Puyang had acted on his own, without the approval or knowledge of Kumudvati.

He and the princess were enemies true enough, the last members of rival dynasties continuing a thousand-year-old struggle to claim lordship over Phnom Kuleh and Angkor Thom. However, they had always observed the rules of warfare as laid down by the Seven Serpent Princes and honoring a truce was paramount. He had only met her face-to-face on one occasion, and that had been at least fifteen years ago.

Since both of their opposing positions were due to birthrights, they were obligated to participate in an exchange-of-essences ceremony, a ritual that extended back to the first meeting of Ye-liu, the dragon princess and the great hero Kaundinya. He remembered very little of it and he assumed she didn't, either, since both of them were aswim in a sea of opiates. He couldn't even recall what she looked like, since her face had been veiled.

Regardless of what either one them remembered, the ceremony was a symbolic replay of the first truce struck between Naga and man. Without it, Cambodia and the Khmer empire could not have been built. For Kumudvati to violate the substance of the truce was the same as spitting upon the spirit of the ancient ritual.

A stiff wind rattled the leaves of the underbrush and the fronds of the banyan trees. The sky rolled with thunderclaps and flashed with bolts of lightning. The storm front swept in even more swiftly and fiercely than Zhou Tzu had calculated.

Wind-driven sheets of refreshingly cold rain fell, first in scattered showers then in a torrential downpour. Gusts of wind tore at the tree line and the palm fronds hanging over Zhou Tzu were beaten down by the deluge. Streams of water poured over his upturned face, washing away the mixture of crusted mud and dried blood. When he inhaled some of it, he was forced to raise his head from the mire to keep from choking to death.

Zhou decided the time had come to return to life. Setting his teeth on a groan, he heaved himself out of the sucking grip of the bog. He staggered to his feet and nearly fell. His head swam with vertigo and his stomach lurched. Only the cool kiss of rainwater kept him conscious, rinsing his uniform and hair of clotted mud.

When he was fairly certain he would not faint, General Zhou Tzu straightened to his full height, tugging at the hem of his uniform tunic to straighten it. He winced at the flare of pain in his rib cage. Raising his right hand he briefly eyed the long flat blade of the *pihakaetta* dagger. The downpour swiftly cleansed it of sludge and slime.

Moving slowly and carefully, alert for any signs of movement in the undergrowth, Zhou Tzu crept away from the site of the massacre, favoring his stiff right knee. Squinting through the shifting veil of water, he looked for the path Colonel Puyang had followed. Despite the dim light he found it—a narrow animal trail cutting between two tangled walls of vegetation. He gained strength with every step as his mind cleared. His lips compressed in the determination to track down Puyang and execute him for the barbaric manner in which he had put Mongpa and Chaksi to death.

Zhou Tzu wasn't horrified by the deaths of his men— in his years as hereditary warlord of Phnom Kuleh, he had witnessed many people, soldiers and civilians alike, die in every conceivable way. But during the period of the truce he had observed with the Devi-Naga, deaths had been few. There had been no massacres.

Despite the pain in his right side and leg, Zhou Tzu walked with his spine straight, his carriage erect. He was a soldier, not a criminal, and he wouldn't skulk through the jungle, especially in his own ancestral territory, like a fugitive.

Zhou Tzu was tall for a Cambodian, nearly six feet, slender of build and long limbed. He attributed his height and build to his Chinese heritage. He wore his sleek blue-black hair long in the tradition of the ancient Khmer kings, knotted at his nape and held in place by a clasp made of a tiger's claw.

Using one hand to shield his eyes from the downpour, Zhou Tzu walked warily through the undergrowth. When lightning lit up the sky, he glimpsed a helmeted figure huddled miserably under the leafy canopy of a prana tree. As Zhou had suspected, the colonel had posted a sentry in the vicinity of the ambush, but the soldier was more concerned with staying dry.

Zhou Tzu took a breath, held it for a moment then sidled forward, making sure he stayed on the outer edge of the Cobra guard's peripheral vision. The racket of rain and wind-whipped foliage covered any sound he made as he crept up behind the soldier. Zhou struck quickly, his left hand slapping around the man's mouth and the same moment he drove the point of his dagger up under the protective fan of the helmet. He slid the blade into the base of the trooper's skull, severing the nerves and stabbing deep into the brain proper.

The Cobra guard died quickly and painlessly and very nearly bloodlessly. Mongpa's death had been far more agonizing. Twisting the handle of the dagger to free it from the man's skull, Zhou Tzu lowered his body to the ground. He wasn't a sadist. He always preferred to give an enemy an easy death, if possible.

Quickly he stripped the soldier of his weapon and ammo. He checked the chamber of the KM-50 to make sure a round filled the spout. The harness with the extra magazines went over his shoulder and, subgun held at hip level, he moved on. The rain abated for a few seconds then poured down hard again. Water dripped from the limbs of trees and down the back of his neck.

After a few minutes the wind died down to no more than an intermittent breeze. The rain slacked off to a steady drizzle. Lightning still arced across the sky, but the heart of the storm had moved away. The humidity rising in its wake was oppressive. Little streamers of mist curled up from the ground. The setting sun peeked out from behind the thick fleece of cloud cover, casting a sullen scarlet glow against the distant thunderheads.

Zhou Tzu eyed the position of the sun apprehensively. Within half an hour, full dark would settle over the jungle and the Magickers would be abroad in the night—or so the old village shamans claimed. Despite his anger and desire for vengeance, Zhou permitted himself a very small but very sour smile.

Still, as he followed the animal trail, he grew more alert for glimpses of shadowy, hooded figures. The Magickers were reputed to be a dark brotherhood of sorcerers who sought to claim and channel the eldritch energies hidden within the walls of Angkor Wat. They wished to subvert natural law to serve their own black purposes, or so the village shamans claimed. Zhou Tzu was not quite sure what the shamans meant by that, but he knew the towers of Angkor often shimmered with a luminosity that seemed something more than a trick of the light.

The Magickers themselves viewed both Zhou Tzu and the Devi-Naga as impediments to that quest. To them, it made little difference who controlled the territory or what ideology they espoused. As far as the Magickers were concerned both factions were the same and were hated with equal ferocity.

Lifting his gaze up to the tree line, he could barely discern the outline of the pinnacled towers of Angkor Wat. The distance was deceptive—many miles of fields, paddies and canals lay between him and the sprawling complex of temples and tombs claimed by Kumudvati.

Sweat rivered down Zhou Tzu's face as he walked through the dense mass of dark green, the somber verdant hue relieved by brilliant blossoms of flowering plants. Brightly feathered birds sang and screeched from the trees. Twice snakes and lizards slithered out of his path. Once he heard the hoarse cough of a tiger but the great cat was not close by. If it had scented the patrol, the tiger had probably decided the party was too strong to attack.

The sinking sun left bands of molten yellow and seething orange along the horizon, providing just enough illumination for Zhou to see the green-hued walls of the ancient Ta Som temple. Time and the merciless hands of the elements had etched deep scars and grooves in the low sandstone walls surrounding the temple grounds. A giant fig tree, with roots thicker than his thighs, spread out over the smiling, lichen-encrusted face of a massive likeness of a kneeling Buddha that arose from the courtyard. Paving slabs were cracked and upended. Between them roots, grass, weeds and saplings had forced their way.

The architecture of the temple was ornate, the facade swarming with sculptures and carvings depicting dancers, many-armed gods and multiheaded demons. Giant stone faces of slumbering Buddhas smiled down from the sides of the building.

Zhou Tzu paused, hidden by the flowering foliage, his eyes sweeping the temple's grounds for any sign of Puyang's patrol. A sudden shifting of shadow, of a paler shade of dark than the gathering blackness, made his shoulders stiffen. A chill finger seemed to stroke the base of his spine and he repressed a shudder.

A gray-robed figure slunk across the courtyard of Ta Som, moving stealthily and silently. Although the figure was too far away for him to see a face, there was no mistaking the robe or the glimpse of the smooth, hairless head. It was a Magicker, apparently intent on performing some arcane ritual within the temple itself. But as far as Zhou knew, all the galleries inside the main structure were empty, containing nothing but shadows and the accumulated detritus of many centuries of neglect.

Zhou Tzu had just started to step toward the temple grounds when he heard a faint crunch, as of a foot treading upon a twig. Instantly he sank to his knees, silently enduring the flare of pain from his rib cage and knee joint. He waited breathlessly for another sound, realizing either a tiger or even one of the ravenous dragons that terrorized the region could be tracking the Magicker. His many years as a guerrilla fighter and hunter had honed his senses to such an uncanny degree of sharpness he sometimes fancied he could hear sounds before they were made.

He knew a human had stepped upon the stick. An animal would have continued tramping along, not caring about the noise. Then, nearly twenty yards to his left, the gloom between a copses of silk-cotton trees disgorged Puyang's patrol of Cobra guards. All of them walked lightly on the balls of their feet.

Zhou Tzu's throat constricted in sudden fear but he realized after a panicky half second that the colonel and his troopers were not stalking him. Their attention was fixed on the temple. He guessed they had found the tracks made by the Magicker and decided trailing him was more important than searching further for General Zhou Tzu.

To capture one of the elusive sorcerers would be almost as great a coup as killing or apprehending the Khmer warlord. At the very least an imprisoned Magicker could be tortured into offering up a clue as to the location of his order's hidden stronghold.

As the patrol crept closer to the temple, Zhou drove the blade of his dagger into the ground, to make sure it did not reflect any light. The irony of being betrayed by the very instrument of his vengeance upon the vicious colonel would be the type of cruel jest to become legend.

He watched the approach of the patrol through a screen of leaves. The Cobra guards entered the courtyard through a crumbled section of wall. Suddenly Colonel Puyang rocked to a halt and gestured imperiously for the men behind him to do the same. The commanding officer of the Cobra Guard gazed intently toward the gaping dark doorway of the temple.

Shifting position, Zhou Tzu followed the colonel's intent gaze. To his astonishment, he saw the Magicker stumbling from the temple, nearly falling in an almost frantic sprint to escape. At the same time his ears registered a faint, high-pitched whine so far on the edges of audibility that he couldn't really be certain he heard it.

The air around the temple opening pulsed like the beating of a gigantic, invisible heart. From within it flashed a hazy, blurred shimmer of light, more like a ripple of energy than a glow.

Zhou Tzu gazed at it, frozen in place, spellbound. The ripple of light expanded into a gushing borealis, spreading out over the temple courtyard. A thready pulse of vibration suddenly tickled his skin, and shadows crawled over the ground moving in fitful jerks and leaps.

Then a brilliant yellow nova erupted from within the temple, followed by darkness so total that for a moment Zhou feared he was blind. He knew the rods and cones of his optic nerves had been overstressed by the blaze of light, so he squeezed his eyes shut, still seeing afterimages of the flare.

After a few seconds he carefully opened his eyes, gazing toward the temple—and his breath seized in his lungs. Three figures stood in the doorway, and he felt his jaw drop open in astonishment. Two of the figures were undeniably female, the third one a man.

One of the females strode forward a few paces, walking with a swift, almost mannish stride. She was a tall woman with a fair complexion and big feline-slanted eyes the color of polished jade. A high forehead gave the impression of a probing intellect, whereas her wide mouth with the full underlip hinted at an appreciation of the sensual.

A mane of red-gold hair fell in loose waves almost to her waist. She wore a black bodysuit that showed off her willowy figure to full advantage. Her body was slender with a flat belly, rounded hips and taut, long legs. Her arms rippled with hard, toned muscle. There was an air of assurance about her, even of superiority that Zhou Tzu didn't care for.

The man was long limbed and lanky of build. He wore a white, zippered bodysuit. Pale blond hair was brushed back from a receding hairline. He wore black-rimmed eyeglasses and his cheeks appeared to be pitted with acne scars.

The second woman was dressed identically to the man, but upon seeing her Zhou Tzu felt as if his dagger had been driven into his own heart. Petite of build, slender and small waisted, black lustrous hair framed her face with a cluster of waves. Curls and clouds.

Her face was a perfect heart, the complexion the rich hue that reminded him of fresh cream. Her wide mouth was moist and superbly colored with scarlet, the nose straight and haughty, the blue-shadowed eyes were wide-set, but narrowed as she gazed around.

Zhou Tzu found himself staring at her, entranced, noting absently the lithe quality of her limbs. Her slim and graceful body denoted breeding, he thought, even nobility. She moved with dignity and poise, like a princess.

The taller woman with the sunset-colored mane spoke softly over her shoulder to the bespectacled man.

Zhou didn't immediately recognize the language, but after a moment he realized she had spoken English. She said, "It's awfully hot."

The man chuckled and replied softly but with a wry humor, "Yeah, but it's a *dry* heat."

Gripping the KM-50, Zhou Tzu tried very hard to control his breathing. His thought processes felt frozen. He couldn't even speculate on the true nature of the vision his eyes transmitted to this brain. From whence the strangers had come and how was beyond his ability to imagine.

A rustle of underbrush drew his attention away from the three people. Colonel Puyang and his patrol moved forward, fanning out to surround the temple in a classic pincer maneuver. At the same time, Zhou caught a blur of movement from the corner of his right eye. He glimpsed the Magicker gliding toward the three people in the doorway, body bent almost double, shaved head thrust forward as if he were an animal and scented a particularly appetizing—and rare—meal.

Zhou swallowed a sigh and slowly arose, pulling his dagger free of the ground with one hand and holding the subgun across his chest with the other. He had no idea if the three strangers were friends, foes, demons or divine, but he intended to keep them out of the grip of his enemies.

General Zhou Tzu couldn't imagine what possible use the Devi-Naga or the Magickers would have for them—and that was why he intended to claim at least one of the three visitors for himself.

Chapter 1

Ragnarville, the state formerly known as Minnesota

The imposing mass of monolithic structures that carried Baron Ragnar's name rose from the top of the high, cold hill, casting its dark shadow over the fields of snow, slush and ice. Each of the ville's walls stood high in a defiant thrust of mortared stone and forged steel, offering impregnable buttresses of protection.

At each intersecting corner of the walls protruded a Vulcan-Phalanx gun tower. Powerful spotlights raked the immediate area outside the walls, leaving nothing hidden from the glare. The hillocks surrounding the walls were kept cleared of vegetation.

As in all the fortified villes a narrow roadbed of crushed gravel led up to the main gate, passing two checkpoint stations. The first, at the mouth of the road, was a small concrete-block cupola, manned only by a single Magistrate. Past the cupola, pyramid-shaped "dragon's teeth" obstacles made of reinforced concrete lined both sides of the path. Five feet tall and weighing a thousand pounds each, they were designed to break the tracks or axles of any assault vehicle trying to cross them.

A dozen yards before the gate, stone blockhouses bracketed either side of the road. Within them were electrically controlled GEC Miniguns, capable of firing 6000 5.56 mm rounds per minute. Past the blockhouses was the main gate itself—twenty feet wide by fifteen high, with two-foot-thick rock crete sheathed by cross-braced iron. The portal was opened by buried system of huge gears and cables.

One of the official reasons for fortifying the villes was a century-old fear—or paranoid delusion—of a foreign invasion from other nuke-scarred nations. Then there had been the threat of mutie clans, like the vicious stickies, unifying and sweeping across the country. As with the fear of a foreign invasion, a war waged by the muties had no foundation, but the threat alone burned so brightly in the collective minds of the architects of the baronial system that a major early aspect of the Program of Unification had been a campaign of genocide against mutie settlements in ville territories.

Inside the walls stretched the complex of spired Enclaves. Each of the four towers were linked to the others by pedestrian bridges. Few of the windows in the towers showed any light so there was little to indicate that the interconnecting network of stone columns, enclosed walkways, shops and promenades was where nearly four thousand people made their homes.

In the Enclaves, the people who worked for the ville administrators enjoyed lavish apartments, all the bounty of those favored by the baron. Seen from above, the Enclave towers formed a latticework of intersected circles, all connected to the center of the circle, from which rose the Administrative Monolith. The massive round column of white rock crete jutted three hundred feet into the sky, standing proud and haughty and cold, symbolizing to all and sundry that order had replaced the barbarism of post-skydark America.

Every level of the tower was designed to fulfill a specific capacity. E Level was a general construction and manufacturing facility, D Level was devoted to the preservation, preparation and distribution of food, and C Level held the Magistrate Division. On B Level lay the Historical Archives, a combination of library, museum and computer center. The level was stocked with almost five hundred thousand books, discovered and restored over the past ninety-five years, not to mention an incredibly varied array of predark artifacts. The work of the Administrators was conducted on the highest level, Alpha Level.

Far below the Enclaves light peeped up from dark streets of the Tartarus Pits. This sector of Ragnarville was a seething melting pot, where outlanders and slaggers lived in planned ghettos. The muddy lanes and paths swarmed with cheap labor, living in ramshackle squats and hovels. Most of them were leftover workers' quarters from the time of the ville's construction, nearly a century before.

Random movement between the Enclaves and Pits was tightly controlled—only a Magistrate on official business could enter the Pits, and only a Pit dweller with a legitimate work order could even approach the cellar of an Enclave tower.

In layout and design Ragnarville was virtually identical in form and function to the other eight baronies consolidated by the Program of Unification, but the frontier ville also possessed enough differences to stake out its own pocket of individuality.

The land was cold and gloomy even in high summer. Snow still clung in glistening white patches to the northern faces of hills and bluffs. The chem storms and geological catastrophes that had once ravaged all of the central United States had spared the northernmost reaches of the continent from widespread devastation but the weather became locked in a near permanent deep freeze.

It was almost always cold in Ragnarville, particularly in the ramshackle huts, shops and squats of Tartarus. At the moment, Kane felt comfortably warm but he was also drunk. But he wasn't as drunk as he looked.

Boss Klaw had generously supplied him with drink after drink and Kane pretended not to notice how the bartender filled Klaw's glass with nine-tenths water while Kane's was nine-tenths home-brewed whiskey. What neither the Pit boss nor the bartender of the Grifter's Gristle tavern knew that when Kane set his mind to it, he could handle more liquor than just about any man alive—with the possible exception of his partner, Grant.

Boss Klaw clapped him on the shoulder, her thin lips twisting in an unconvincing attempt at an affectionate smile. "Drink up, Kane. I owe you big."

Kane returned her smile over the rim of his glass. "For what?"

Boss Klaw brayed out a laugh and turned to the pair of strong-arms standing on either side of her. One was heavyset, dark eyed and scar faced. His hunched shoulders sloped down like those of an ape. The other man was blond, smaller, wiry-looking, but hardly more than a teenager. She had introduced them as Nero and Crip, respectively.

Despite their physical dissimilarities both of them wore ankle-length greatcoats. Neither of them seemed amused when she asked, "Can you believe this bastard? 'For what?' he asks. The man is a comedian."

Klaw's voice was melodic, sonorous, completely at odds with her appearance. She was very broad and very short, under five feet tall, but the hands she used to grip her glass and clap Kane's shoulder were huge. Metal thimbles capped four fingers of her right hand, light glinting from the curved steel spurs tipping them.

A massive head, the size and shape of a pumpkin and matted with fiery red hair, squatted between her broad shoulders. The skin of her cheeks bore a blue maplike pattern of broken blood vessels.

As the Pit boss of Ragnarville, Klaw didn't feel the need to pay much attention to her appearance. The power she wielded was important, not her looks. Despite the ruthless treatment of the Pit dwellers, one constant in all of the nine villes was a Pit boss. By no means an official title or position, Pit bosses nevertheless served a purpose of varying degrees of importance, depending on the ville.

Part crime lords, part information conduits and part procurers of luxuries, most barons tolerated Pit bosses as long as they knew and kept their place. If they maintained a certain order among the seething masses in Tartarus, Magistrates were inclined to look the other way if they engaged in limited black-marketeering, or the elimination of troublesome elements.

Fixing her yellow eyes on Kane's face, Boss Klaw leaned forward, acrid whiskey breath searing his nostrils. He managed to keep from recoiling and maintained his smile. Deliberately slurring her words to sound far more intoxicated than she was, Klaw declared, "I have to admit I was surprised when word reached me that the infamous Kane wanted to talk to me."

"Infamous?" he echoed with mock innocence. "Me?"

"Kane the infamous renegade," Boss Klaw declared stentorially, as if she were reciting a list of job qualifications. "Kane the infamous insurrectionist. Kane the infamous baron blaster. And I know damn good and well you had something to do with blasting Barch."

Kane nodded. "I may have had a little something to do with it, but only a little." He pinched the air between thumb and forefinger. "Only a teensy-weensy bit."

"So he *is* dead." Klaw gazed at him steadily, waiting for either a denial or a confirmation.

"What do you think?" Kane demanded. "The son of a bitch hasn't shown up back here after—what's it been?—nearly two years. Yeah, I think you can safely assume Barch is most thoroughly dead."

Boss Klaw nodded as if satisfied. "I figured he had to be but I wanted to hear it from you. It's been a long time in coming, but you have my thanks. With the baron himself dead, things have been a little unsettled here. I didn't need to worry about Barch coming back on top of everything else."

When Kane didn't respond, Klaw lowered her voice to a conspiratorial whisper. "Do you still deny killing Baron Ragnar?"

"Why shouldn't I?" he countered. "It's the truth. He was assassinated by the same force that killed Barch."

Kane didn't bother elaborating. A computer-generated hologram had actually killed Baron Ragnar, but the story was too convoluted to tell at the moment—not to mention that, unknown to her, Boss Klaw had a personal connection to the assassin.

After the death of the baron, the administrator of the Magistrate Division tried to take over the barony, but his ambition was checkmated by the very instrument he had used in his attempt to gain power.

In the subsequent power vacuum, Ragnarville had been governed by the small group of baronial councilors and bureaucrats known as the Trust. Like the Tartarus Pits, every ville had a version of the Trust. The organization, if it could be called that, was the only face-to-face contact allowed with the barons, and the barons were the only contacts permitted by the Archon Directorate. All of them had been told that secret societies like the Trust had their roots in ancient Egypt, Babylon, Mesopotamia, Greece and even Sumeria. Throughout humankind's history, secret covenants with the entities known as Archons were struck by kings, princes and even presidents.

The Trust was formed more or less as the protectors of the Directorate, and its oath revolved around a single theme—the presence of the Directorate must not be revealed to humanity. If the Directorate became known, if the technological marvels they had designed became accessible, if the truth behind the nukecaust filtered down to the people, then humankind would no doubt retaliate with a concerted effort to wipe them out. Or the Directorate would be forced to visit another holocaust upon the face of the earth, simply as a measure of self-preservation.

The members of the Ragnarville Trust had factionalized, and it wasn't until the advent of the imperator that the volatile political situation stabilized. But now the climate had acquired a new and potentially even more dangerous element.

"Whatever happened," Boss Klaw said, "I owe you big time."

"I was hoping you'd feel that way," Kane replied.

"Is that why you're here, after all this time?" Boss Klaw's wild, untrimmed eyebrows arched quizzically. "To call in the marker?"

Kane shrugged. "I hear you've acquired a new possession. I'm here to sort of convince you to trade up."

Boss Klaw's little eyes narrowed. "Take a tip from me, Kane. Don't start the haggling with that item. Believe me, there's way too much at stake for me to give her up."

The corner of Kane's mouth lifted in a humorless smile. "In my opinion, you have too much at stake to keep her imprisoned here."

Klaw blinked him owlishly. "Who are you to make a claim like that, Kane?"

"You know damn well." All the casual good humor disappeared from Kane's tone. "You've got spies and intel pipelines running all through the Outlands just like I have. You know the group I represent has been reaching out to the Roamer bands, trying to organize them."

Boss Klaw's little eyes glinted shrewdly. "So I've heard."

He nodded. "Just like I've heard you're holding Thoraldson's daughter hostage. I've cut a deal with him to bring her back."

"Kane, you may have a glib tongue and be a handsome enough rogue," Klaw said with a dour smile, "but that's not enough for me."

Kane offered a hard-edged grin. "And don't start thinking empty flattery is enough for me."

In truth, some women found Kane handsome, at least in a rough-hewn manner. Tall and rangy, he carried most of his muscle mass in his upper body above a slim waist which lent him a marked resemblance to a wolf. His longish dark hair, a shade between black and chestnut-brown, held sun-streaked highlights. His skin was lightly bronzed from exposure to the elements. A thin hairline scar stretched diagonally like a white thread across his left cheek. Steely blue-gray eyes glinted above high, almost regal cheekbones.

He was dressed as a Farer in scuffed and zippered road leathers that had faded to rust-brown at knee and elbow. A fourteen-inch-long combat knife rode in a canvas scabbard inside his right boot. A long-barreled Smith & Wesson Model 59 autoblaster was snugged in a military-style flapped shoulder holster beneath the battered black jacket.

Kane normally preferred to carry his Sin Eater, the 9 mm handblaster that served as the chief sign of office of the Magistrates. But his penetration of the Ragnarville territory depended largely on not calling attention to himself. Although he may not have been quite as notorious as Boss Klaw implied, the name of Kane was a curse among the Magistrate Divisions of all the villes.

As it was, he still felt surprise he was able to smuggle weapons into the Tartarus Pits at all. Security had been shockingly lax at all the checkpoints.

Klaw smiled in a fashion she probably hoped was coquettish. Kane didn't allow the surge of revulsion he felt to show on his face as she said, "I'm not trying to flatter you, my boy. You're too wise for that. And I'm too wise to be buffaloed."

"Yes, you are," he agreed earnestly. "And I'm not trying to. I'm making you a reasonable proposition. Let me take Ayn home to her father. He'll let bygones be bygones."

Leaning forward, Boss Klaw dropped her voice. "You don't know what I have going on out there. It's more important than Thoraldson's daughter or his goodwill. I can cut you in for a percentage."

Kane pretended to think the offer over for a moment. Then he shook his head. "Whatever operation you're staging on Thoraldson's turf won't keep it safe by holding his kid for ransom."

"I'm not holding the little bitch for ransom," Klaw shot back, forgetting to slur her words. "She's my protection from him and his men until I'm done out there. Once I've completed everything and got what I want, I'll give her back to the old bandit, safe and sound. He and his crew could even benefit in the long run if he leaves us alone."

"I don't know if he'll buy that," Kane said dubiously. "Roamers aren't businessmen as a general rule."

He had spoken an understatement. Roamers. For the most part, Roamer bands were nomadic outlaws but they used resistance to baronial authority as a justification for their raids. Alf Thoraldson was of a slightly different breed of Roamer in that he had staked out a large section of the Ragnarville area Outlands as his own, citing an ancestral connection. Of course, he had never presented the claim to the baron or his representatives since he would have been executed just on general principles.

Boss Klaw sighed and idly dragged her hook-tipped fingers across the surface of the table, adding to its collection of deep gouges. Kane remembered when he had first met the woman, she described the metal spurs as symbols of her name and power.

She had further claimed to have used them to blind, scar and flay a number of enemies. To illustrate her boast, she often wore a belt made of intertwined strips of dried and cured human skin. Kane didn't know if she was wearing the belt today but he figured she was, if nothing else but to hold up her baggy khaki trousers.

Patiently Klaw said, "All you have to do is walk out of here and tell Thoraldson his little Aynny will be safe as long as he doesn't interfere with me or the people I'm doing business with. I've got to take advantage of the window of opportunity while it lasts—the Mags are too busy dealing with domestic strife right here in the ville to patrol the Outland territories. But that situation won't last forever."

Kane shook his head. "As much as I wish I could do that, I can't. See, I have to take advantage of a window of opportunity myself. Thoraldson has a lot of influence with other Roamer gangs. If I do this for him, he'll talk to the other groups for me."

"Talk to them for what?" Boss Klaw demanded. "Do you really think you can build an army from that scum disciplined enough to take on baronial forces? You're not *that* drunk, are you?"

"I'm not looking to build an army," Kane retorted sharply. "But I can maybe work out a nonaggression pact where the Roamers won't interfere with what I and the people represent have planned for the Outlands."

Boss Klaw eyed him keenly. "Which is?"

"You tell me what you're up to, and I might tell you what we're up to."

Klaw snorted. "I never figured you for an idealist, Kane. I thought you were a pragmatist like me. I combine opportunity with profit. Thoraldson can understand that a hell of a lot easier than he can understand you trying to organize the Roamers."

Calmly but coldly, Kane declared, "I came here to bring Ayn home. I won't leave without at least talking to her." He nodded toward the young, wiry strong-arm. "Send him to fetch her."

Klaw scowled. "Don't be an idiot. Do you think I'd keep her here in the Gristle?"

"As a matter of fact," he answered, "I do."

Klaw blew out another sigh, this one exasperated. "I don't want trouble with you."

"Good. Then bring the kid to me."

Boss Klaw hesitated. "I've got partners to answer to, Kane."

Skeptically he inquired, "What partners?"

"They're of the silent variety."

"And probably of the nonexistent variety, too."

Klaw licked her lips and looked around the room apprehensively. The Grifter's Gristle was nearly full. Around forty or fifty people, most of them rough-looking men, stood at the bar or were seated at the crude wooden tables. Behind the bar, bottles of whiskey and other liquors from scavenger's trades were racked side by side with homegrown popskull and moonshine. The bartender was a lean and leathery rat of a man with a luxuriant black mustache. He swept the people in the tavern with contemptuous eyes, as if he hated the very people who kept him in business.

The tavern's interior was lit by kerosene lanterns hanging from ceiling hooks. Buckets of sand were placed against the walls between the tables, just in case a fire broke out.

Tobacco smoke, like streamers of filthy lace, hung above the crowd. The tavern was longer than it was wide with only one visible exit and entrance, although a short flight of stairs on far wall ran up to a wooden door placed eight feet or so above the floor. A fat man in dirty coveralls sat on a three-legged stool at the bottom of the steps. He absently fondled a naked machete that lay across his knees and watched the crowd with dark, expressionless eyes.

Turning back to Kane, Boss Klaw asked quietly, "You've heard of the Millennial Consortium?"

Kane hadn't, but he could guess by the name that it referred to a group of organized traders who plied their trade selling predark relics to the various villes. The baronies hired their own traders, who in turn controlled the supply routes and made a profit that was plowed back into expanding or finding new supply routes. Various trader groups had been combining resources for the past year or so, forming consortiums and absorbing the independent operators. The consortiums employed and fed people in the Outlands, giving them a sense of security that had once been the sole province of the barons before the Imperator War. There were some critics, Kane knew, who compared the trader consortiums to the barons and talked of them with just as much ill favor.

"Yes," Kane lied. "I've heard of them."

"Then you know how powerful they are," Klaw said. "They're my partners, my backers in this enterprise. So I suggest you go tell Thoraldson his girl is safe with me. Once he hears the millennialists are involved, he'll understand."

"I don't think he will." Kane kept his voice pitched to a low, unemotional level. "I think if I go back to him empty-handed, he'll try to chop my head off and I'll have to chop off his. Either way, I won't be able to strike the deal I'm after."

Boss Klaw's lips writhed, peeling back over her discolored teeth. "Goddammit, if you keep hounding me about this, he won't have the opportunity—*I'll* chop your head off!"

Kane took a sip of his drink, placed the glass on the table and let his right hand stray down, out of sight. "Gee," he said mildly, "what was all that about you owing me big?"

Klaw glared at him. "I'll give you anything you want but I won't go against the Millennial Consortium. Now, do you drop the subject or do I have to get rough with you?"

Kane presented the image of seriously pondering the question. After a few thoughtful moments, he said casually, "I think you're going to have to get rough."

Boss Klaw stared and he met her stare, alert for any change in her eyes. She whispered hoarsely, "Your choice, Kane."

The talon-tipped fingers of her right hand crooked, and she shifted position in her chair. As her hand rose from the tabletop, Kane's right arm blurred in a practiced explosion of reflexes and coordination. Metal gleamed briefly in the lantern light.

The point of the combat knife in his fist pierced the back of Boss Klaw's hand, the razor-sharp blade slicing through the palm and sinking an inch deep into the table. Her splayed, spur-tipped fingers contorted like the fluttering legs of a fat beetle transfixed to a board.

"The way I see it," Kane said in the same mild tone, "it's more in the way of *your* choice."

Chapter 2

Boss Klaw compressed her lips tightly, bottling up the scream of pain and rage. Her eyes narrowed to slits, but she remained seated. Maintaining his grip on the Nylex handle of the blued tungsten-steel blade, Kane drew his autopistol with his other hand. He swept its bore from left to right between the two strong-arms.

Quietly he asked, "This rough enough for you?"

The woman's face screwed up but she didn't utter so much as a groan. Tears of pain glistened in her eyes. The strong-arms looked from the gun to Klaw and back to the gun again.

"Tell your boys to get rid of their hardware," Kane suggested.

When Klaw didn't immediately respond, Kane waggled the knife blade slightly from side to side. The woman's lips went white with the new pain and she husked out, "Nero, Crip—do as the man says."

The two men exchanged swift, uneasy glances, then their hands disappeared beneath their voluminous coats. Weapons began clattering and thudding onto the floorboards at their feet. Kane counted at least four knives, two cudgels, a set of brass knuckles, a knotted garrote and two small-caliber revolvers.

The sight of the firearms surprised Kane. During his

many years as a Magistrate, insuring that the denizens of Tartarus were unarmed was a standard duty. Although one of the first priorities of the Program of Unification was the disarmament of the people, books and diagrams survived the sweeps. Self-styled gunsmiths continued to forge weapons, though blasters more complicated than black-powder muzzle loaders was beyond their capacities.

Apparently upon the deaths of both Baron Ragnar and Barch, the pretender to the title, Boss Klaw had tapped a new pipeline of contraband into the Pits. On a strictly professional level, Kane felt annoyed by how the Mag Division of Ragnarville had become so sloppy but by the same token, if it hadn't he would not have been able to virtually stroll into the barony unmolested, pretending to be part of a Farer trading caravan.

Crip and Nero raised their hands and Crip declared flatly, "That's it."

Kane nodded to them politely. "Thank you. Now step back."

The strong-arms did so, their faces as impassive as stone.

Whipping the knife free from the tabletop and Boss Klaw's hand, Kane stated matter-of-factly, "Now you and I are going upstairs to find Ayn Thoraldson."

"Right." Boss Klaw cradled her punctured hand, examining it with a frown. Although blood seeped from the palm and the back of it, the wound was not serious. Kane had known where and how to place the blade with a minimum of damage to the metacarpal bones and the nerve ganglia. She didn't seem grateful for his expertise, however. She took a strip of cloth from her robe-garment and bound it around her hand.

Sullenly, Klaw said, "You won't get out of here alive—I promise you that."

Slowly she rose and Kane did the same, standing up to his full height of six feet one inch. Flashing his teeth in a wolfish grin, he said, "Keep in mind that whatever happens to me will happen to you."

Kane lightly touched the carmined tip of the long blade against the back of the Pit boss's neck. Keeping Nero and Crip covered with the Colt autopistol, he prodded Klaw with the knife and she shuffled forward toward the rear wall.

They had not taken five steps before Nero put two fingers in his mouth and produced a shrill whistle. Almost immediately half a dozen of the thugs seated at the tables knocked chairs over in their haste to get to their feet. Kane figured they were Klaw's personal entourage. Although most of them were in various stages of inebriation, they saw an interloper holding a gun and a knife on the Pit boss and they began to close in at an ominous gait.

Kane didn't even look at them. He kept Klaw moving toward the short flight of stairs by the judicious pressure of his knife blade. A bearded, begrimed man reached over the bar and snatched up a full, unopened whiskey bottle. Raising it by the neck as though it were a bludgeon, he snarled through browned snaggleteeth, "Turn 'er loose!"

"Easy there, Ike. He's got a gun on the boss," Crip said.

Ike acted as if he hadn't heard as he took lurching steps toward Kane, shaking the whiskey bottle threateningly. Lean and leathery, his face disfigured by old radiation burns, the man looked like a former scavenger who had spent far too many years working too close to hot spots. He had probably skulked into the Tartarus Pits with a bogus ID chip paid for with his life savings.

Now the man was drunk, as well as stupid, if he thought a relatively sober, armed man would back down from a bottle. But Kane knew if he shot the man, he could very well so enrage the other patrons they would rush him from all directions.

As Pit dwellers, they might not particularly like Boss Klaw but Pit residents tended to be very clannish in their loyalties, for mutual protection if for nothing else. For a second, Kane toyed with the notion of announcing to the tavern at large who he was, but his pedigree as a former Magistrate could easily outweigh his reputation as a baron-hunted, baron-hated outlaw.

More people began standing up from tables, turning away from the bar. Seamed faces twisted in angry surprise, fists knotted, voices raised in profane queries.

Kane tapped the back of Boss Klaw's neck with the knife. "Tell them to back off."

Tone rich with cruel amusement, Klaw retorted, "*You* tell them, Kane. You think you're in charge, right?"

Kane didn't answer, tension coiling in the pit of his stomach like a length of wet rope, his nape hairs tingling at the sound of chair legs scraping back, shuffling feet and outraged muttering.

"I thought Mags—even ex-Mags—were trained to be always prepared," Klaw continued tauntingly. "Didn't you have a backup plan before you waltzed into the lion's den?"

Eyeing the man with the bottle but keeping his gun on Nero and Crip, Kane replied absently, "As a point of fact, I had two of them."

"Turn 'er loose, I sez!" Screeching, the bearded man lunged forward, bottle held high to deliver a smashing blow with it on Kane's head. Kane didn't flinch.

The sound of the shot was like a muted thunderclap, the concussive force of it pressing painfully against eardrums. The bottle in the man's hand dissolved in a spray of liquor. Flying splinters of glass stung his face and he screamed, flinging away the sheared stump of the bottle's neck and clapping a hand over the blood-oozing gash in his cheek. The mustachioed bartender dropped out of sight.

The scarred man gaped in silent, openmouthed astonishment at Kane, his eyes wild with accusatory wonder of how he had managed to shoot the bottle out of his hand without aiming or even pointing the gun at him.

"Hey," Kane told him defensively. "Don't blame me…blame my backup plan."

The patrons of the Grifter's Gristle milled around uncertainly, expressions registering their fear and confusion. A small figure suddenly sprang atop a corner table.

"Everybody please stand still!"

The voice was high, sharp and undeniably female. The girl who stood atop the table was petite, her diminutive frame draped by a ragged poncho-type garment. She tossed the strips of fabric over her shoulders, revealing a petite but exquisitely formed figure despite the unflattering Farer garb she wore.

Her hollow-cheeked face was the color of bone, her eyes the bright hue of polished rubies. Her short-cut hair circled her head with a spike-tipped white crown. One of the genetic quirks of the nukecaust aftermath was a rise in the albino population, particularly down south in bayou country. Albinos weren't exactly rare anywhere else, but they were hardly commonplace, so she made a striking sight.

Crip murmured incredulously, "I don't believe this shit."

The girl grinned down at him wickedly. She had a big automatic pistol in her small hands, and there was a hard gleam in her bloodred eyes.

"Who the hell is that?" Boss Klaw demanded.

"Like I said," Kane answered, "my backup plan. One of two."

Kane pushed the woman forward, straight-arming the astounded scar-faced man out of his path. "Move aside, putrid."

The bartender suddenly rose from behind the bar with a hollow-bored shotgun in his arms. He pointed it not at Kane but at the albino girl, since she was a much easier target.

Another gunshot cracked and the man crashed backward, an expression of surprise stamped on his mustachioed face. Blood spurted from a blue-rimmed hole in the center of his forehead. The rear of his skull broke open, and a slurry of bone chips and brain matter splattered the bottle racks behind him.

As the man sank, his finger spasmed on the trigger and the bore of his weapon erupted with flame and buckshot. A number of bottles on the racks danced, shattered and flew apart in fragments and geysers of liquor.

From a table opposite the one on which the white wraith of a girl stood loomed a figure who looked gigantic in the lantern light. A massive-shouldered and -chested man swept the patrons of the Grifter's Gristle with the long barrel of a .44 Magnum Colt revolver.

He stood four inches over six feet, and much of his coffee-brown face was cast into shadow by the broad brim of an old felt fedora. Gray threads showed at the temples his short curly black hair. A gunfighter's mustache curved fiercely around his lips, and the ends drooped halfway to his chin. He was dressed in standard Farer wear—patched denim jeans and leather hip jacket over a khaki shirt. High-laced jump boots rose nearly to his knees.

"You!" Boss Klaw blurted incredulously. "Grant!"

"Me," Grant agreed, his voice a genial, lionlike rumble. "The second part of the backup plan. I would have been the first part, but Domi was faster getting out of her chair than I was."

"Well," Kane said kindly, "she's much younger and a lot more spry."

Sourly, Klaw murmured, "I should've known. Kane and Grant, Grant and Kane. The billing varies, but where there's one, the other is around someplace."

"What about me?" Domi demanded peevishly, training the sights of her Detonics Combat Master on the fat man with the machete. "Don't I rate a credit?"

Boss Klaw acted as if the questions were rhetorical. Kane pricked her lightly with the point of his blade, but she only stiffened, refusing to move. Between clenched teeth, she spat, "Three of you instead of one. Big fucking deal. You're still outnumbered and outgunned."

Her last word seemed to be a signal for the men scattered around the barroom to swing into action. A variety of guns came into view, feet scraped along the floor-boards, lips hissed curses as at least a dozen men spread out in a semicircle, blocking the path to the stairs.

"Guns, guns, guns," Kane said laconically. "I don't believe I've ever seen so damn many in a ville before. Your Mag Division must be seriously asleep at the switch."

"Or," Grant ventured darkly, "seriously on the take."

"Maybe a combination," Klaw said. "Doesn't matter, does it? I'm counting at least twelve to your three."

"Me, too," Domi chirped cheerfully. "But like you said—big fucking deal."

Her left hand darted under her poncho and came out gripping a metal-shelled orb, the size and shape of an apple. The people in the tavern instantly recognized it as a hand grenade. As they watched, struck dumb by sudden shock, Domi inserted her thumb into the ring and snatched it away. Only her fingers pressing down on the spoon kept the striker from igniting the fuse.

With an engaging smile, Domi displayed the grenade and how she held it as Kane announced breezily, "As you can see, our model holds an M-33 fragmentation grenade. Equipped with four-second fuse delay and the explosive power of a kilo and a quarter of TNT, the M-33 will most definitely renovate this quaint establishment.

"Observe how our model, if she should happen to be shot, would naturally drop the grenade. If that unfortu-nate eventuality does occur, there would be a very, very big boom."

"And," Domi added, eyes bright with malice, "if any of you pieces of shit should try to get the drop on my friends instead of me, I'll drop this and we'll all go to Hell together."

"And wouldn't that be a damn shame," Grant commented grimly. "Because I really hate to travel."

A fearful silence fell over the tavern for a second, then a hoarse male voice said, "Bitch'll never do it—all of 'em are just bluffin'!"

Another voice, inspired by terror and a touch of awe, broke in, "Oh, no, she ain't. I know who they are now! They're the ones who chilled Baron Ragnar!"

The anger and fear in the eyes of the assembled Pit dwellers changed to surprised admiration. Kane didn't feel the time was appropriate to correct the misapprehension about the culprits behind the baron's assassination, so he declared confidently, "That's right. We're the baron blasters you've heard so much about. Who wants to interfere with us?"

The term "baron blasters" was old, deriving from the warriors who staged a violent resistance against the institution of the unification program nearly a century before. Neither Kane nor Grant enjoyed having the appellation applied to them—their ville upbringing still lurked close to the surface, and they had been taught that the so-called baron blasters were worse than outlaws, but were instead agents of chaos, terrorists incarnate.

Regardless, the reputations of Grant and Kane had grown too awesome, too frightful for even the most courageous Pit dweller in the Grifter's Gristle to want to trifle with them. Everybody who lived in the twilight world of any Tartarus Pit in any barony had heard tales of them. No two men over the past two hundred years had reputations to equal theirs, even if it was an open question of just how many of the stories were based in truth and how many of them were overblown fable.

But one thing the Ragnarville Pit dwellers were certain of—the three devils in their midst would not die easily. They would indeed take as many of the blastermen to Hell with them as they could. And the thugs, thieves, plug-uglies, strong-arms and smugglers in the Grifter's Gristle did not want to die.

So they stood stock-still with lowered guns as Kane pushed his way across the room, using Boss Klaw to clear a path to the stairs. The fat man on the stool lifted his machete at their approach, but Domi called out, "Drop the sticker, porky."

His eyes slid sideways to the ghost-girl on the table, then back to Klaw, who inclined her head in a short nod. The man laid the machete on the floor and placed his hands on his knees.

They paused at the foot of the stairs and Kane nudged Klaw up them. "Ladies first."

She grunted. "And dead men last."

"Very whimsical."

At the closed door at the head of the stairs, Kane propelled Boss Klaw against it by a shove in the small of her back. Her not inconsiderable weight slammed it open. Beyond the doorway a dimly lit corridor stretched to another closed door at the far end. The walls and ceiling were of poorly nailed together squares of wood and Kane guessed the accessway was a relatively new addition, probably extending to a storehouse.

The door at the end suddenly opened, and the outline of a man appeared. Despite the poor light, Kane glimpsed him putting a subgun to a shoulder. Boss Klaw uttered a frightened squawk and dropped flat to the floor at the same instant the barrel of subgun lipped a flickering spear point of flame. The staccato hammering filled the confines of the corridor.

The stream of bullets swept high, peeling long splinters from the ceiling. Little showers of sawdust sprinkled down. By the time the blasterman adjusted his sights, Kane squeezed the trigger of the S&W. The recoil was light, allowing for a quick recovery and a fast second shot if one was necessary.

It wasn't. The report of the single shot was louder than what he had grown accustomed to with his Sin Eater, but the wad of lead that caught the blasterman dead center was just as lethal. He didn't cry out, he just left his feet, staggering backward into the room behind him.

Kane started to speak, but a second figure appeared in the doorway, reaching down to pull the subgun from his companion's dead hands. Kane squeezed off another round, but the man ducked back out of sight then almost instantly reappeared to fire a long burst down the hallway.

His aim was a bit more accurate than his predecessor's—Kane felt two jarring blows, one against his left bicep and the other against his upper left thigh. Stumbling backward under the double impacts, he returned the fire but knew he missed. Biting back a curse, he adjusted his aim.

"You nailed him!" Boss Klaw shrilled from where she cowered on the floor. She turned her head toward the tavern and bellowed, "Kill 'em all!"

Chapter 3

Grant whirled toward the drumming of autofire. A brief hailstorm of bullets spewed through the open door and pounded into the ceiling. Crying out in angry alarm, people dropped flat to the floor, showered by wood particles. One of the lanterns hanging from a rafter was set to swinging dangerously by a near miss.

Domi crouched low on the table but continued to hold the grenade high over her head, grinning affably at the tense and watchful Pit dwellers huddled together on the floor.

Holding his revolver in a two-fisted grip, Grant swept the barrel back and forth menacingly, just in case any of the patrons of the Grifter's Gristle summoned up enough nerve to rush him. The staccato hammering of a second burst from a subgun echoed through the tavern, followed by two hand-clapping shots. Then came Boss Klaw's infuriated screech of "You nailed him! Kill 'em all!"

Grant didn't hesitate—he bulled his way toward the stairs, stomping on several men crouched in his path, his 240-plus pounds slamming them hard to the floor and driving the air from their lungs.

The overalled fat man made a frantic grab for his machete but Grant reached him in one swift bound, crashing the long barrel of the Magnum gun against the side of his head. The cracking of bone sounded almost as loud as the individual gunshots floating through the door at the head of the stairs.

His scalp laid open and pouring blood, the man staggered to the side as though he were rolling out of bed. He hit the floor heavily. The slamming impact of at least 325 pounds of deadweight hitting the floor nearly overwhelmed the cracking reports of Kane's automatic pistol. Dust squirted up between the planks.

Over his shoulder, Grant snapped to Domi, "Any of them move, light this place up."

Grant sprang up the stairs taking the sagging risers three at a time. He joined Kane just inside the doorway, nearly stepping on the supine body of Boss Klaw. Wincing, Kane massaged his left bicep. "Son of a bitch tagged me with a lucky shot before I got him."

Grant eyed the sleeve of his friend's jacket, noting the bullet tear but seeing no blood. "He didn't get penetration?"

Grimacing, Kane shook his head. "No, but it still hurts like hell. I'm surprised the bone isn't broken."

"It's like I've been saying," Grant retorted flatly, glancing down the hallway at the two bodies sprawled in the doorway, "sometimes our Mag armor is the best choice of wardrobe."

"Except when we don't want to call attention to ourselves, which we would have when we hooked up with the Farer train." Kane looked out into the tavern and the blaster men stirring, rising from the floor but making no aggressive moves.

"Stay here with the boss lady," Kane said, stepping over her, trying to ignore the twinge of pain in his left thigh.

Grant noticed how he favored the leg and said, "Let me handle it."

Kane shook his head. "Negative. You know I always need to finish what I start, even if it doesn't make a damn bit of sense."

Staying close to the left-hand wall, Kane fired twice through the clapboard framing both sides of the far doorway to discourage anyone who might be lurking to catch him unawares. Although his left arm and leg ached fiercely, he knew he had gotten off extremely fortunate.

Underneath the road leathers, Kane's body was encased in a one piece skintight garment he had christened a shadow suit. Grant and Domi wore duplicates of the black garb. The coveralls had become important items in the Cerberus ordnance and arsenal over the past few months. Ever since they absconded with the suits from Redoubt Yankee on Thunder Isle, the suits had proved their worth and their superiority to the polycarbonate Magistrate armor, if for nothing else than their internal subsystems.

Manufactured with a technique known in predark days as electrospin lacing, the electrically charged polymer particles formed a dense web of form-fitting fibers. Composed of a compiled weave of spider silk, Monocrys and Spectra fabrics, the garments were essentially a single-crystal metallic microfiber with a very dense molecular structure.

The outer Monocrys sheathing went opaque when exposed to radiation, and the Kevlar and Spectra layers provided protection against blunt trauma. The spider silk allowed flexibility, but it traded protection from firearms for freedom of movement.

The inner layer was lined by carbon nanotubes only a nanometer wide, rolled-up sheets of graphite with a tensile strength greater than steel. The suits were almost impossible to tear, and dense and elastic enough to deflect arrows and knives, but unlike the Mag exoskeletons, a large-caliber bullet could penetrate them. Kane guessed the bullets fired by the subgun hadn't been of a sufficiently high caliber.

When he reached the doorway, he discovered his guess had been correct. Carefully easing his body through the opening, he stepped over the two bodies leaking fluids onto the plank floor. One of them held an M-16 autorifle in his arms.

Reaching down, Kane tugged it from his nerveless fingers, surprised by its excellent condition. The weapon looked as if it had just rolled off the assembly line—or was stolen from the Cerberus armory. Briefly he wondered if all the firearms he had seen in the Grifter's Gristle were part of the Outlands enterprise Klaw had alluded to.

Quickly, he checked over the M-16, popping the magazine free and counting the rounds it held. There were fourteen bullets remaining in the clip, which he reinserted. The autorifle's rate of fire was 700 rounds per minute, but its bullets didn't possess the penetration power to breach his shadow suit unless the strike was dead-on. Holstering his pistol, Kane reset the M-16's selector switch to fire in semiautomatic mode.

Another passageway stretched off to the right. There were doors on either side. He assumed he was in Boss Klaw's personal suite, which contained living quarters for her strong-arms and lieutenants—and hopefully, her guests.

Kane tried each door as he came to it, standing to one side, turning the knob and flinging it open. He peered into three rooms in such a fashion, and they were all unoccupied and sparsely furnished.

As he reached the fourth door, he heard a shuffling of feet from the other side of it, a muffled murmuring of voices—one of them was unmistakably feminine. For a few seconds, Kane contemplated which weapon would be the most effective, then he gently placed the M-16 on the floor stock first and leaned it against wall in such a way he could grab it quickly.

Keeping to the left side of the doorway, Kane unholstered his S&W Model 59, reached out, turned the knob and pushed the door open. Before it had swung fully ajar, a fusillade of gunfire burst out, the rounds perforating the opposite wall, smashing holes in wood.

Kane dropped flat onto his stomach and wormed forward just enough so he could peer around the molding of the frame. He glimpsed two men in a dimly lit room. Both had shaggy hair but were fairly young. One of them held an Uzi and the other held a slender blond girl, his arms crossed possessively around her waist. She struggled, crying out, "No—!"

The man holding Ayn Thoraldson saw him and called a wordless warning to his partner. The warning came a half second too late. Kane squeezed off two shots, the cracking reports sounding brutally loud. One .45-caliber slug took the Uzi man high in the stomach, right at his diaphragm, the kinetic shock folding him double.

The second shot, fired a little more carefully, struck the other man full in the face—barely an inch above the crown of the girl's head. The man flailed backward, a crimson liquid tendril squirting from just beneath his right eye. The girl screamed as he dragged her down to the floor with him. They fell heavily, with her atop him.

The man with the Uzi, mouth opening and closing like a landed trout's, tried to straighten, but the pain of his belly wound kept him doubled over. Blood foamed from his lips as he gaspingly aligned the bore of the sub-gun with Kane's head.

Kane shot him a second time, an up-from-under directly through the chest. The bullet crushed the man's clavicle and ripped both lungs apart. The hammer blow to his upper body jerked him erect, slamming him against the wall. He slid down it, leaving a wet, red smear to commemorate the exit wound.

Kane came to his feet as Ayn Thoraldson disentangled herself from the dead man's hands. She was a slim-waisted girl of about sixteen with unruly blond hair billowing about her blue-eyed face. She wore little more than a diaphanous dressing gown, but jewels glittered at her throat and wrists.

Staring wide-eyed at the Uzi man, she husked out, "You killed him."

Kane gave her a swift visual inspection, wondering if she were in shock. "Well," he said quietly, "sort of."

Ayn swayed, eyelids fluttering. Kane grabbed her by the upper arm and shook her. "This isn't the time to faint, kid. You're all right."

Her eyes opened wide, darting first to the dead man then back to Kane's face. They took on a gimlet-hard sheen as she said, in a high, aspirated whisper, "You killed him, you bastard. *You killed my Vend!*"

The last four words came out as a keening shriek of

fury. She clawed at Kane's face with sharp, lacquered fingernails. He was so surprised he didn't react until he felt the pain of her nails raking across his cheek, inflicting blood-oozing scratches.

"You killed my Vend!" Ayn shrilled again. "My husband!"

Kane grappled with her, too surprised to speak. He didn't know whether to restrain her, coldcock her or run. Before he could make up his mind, the entire room shook from a tremendous concussion. The floor shuddered, then plaster and dust sifted down from the ceiling.

Setting his teeth on a groan of dismay, Kane knew instantly what had happened—and who was responsible.

DOMI ANNOUNCED loudly, "Every one of you assholes who's packing—get rid of your hardware. Throw 'em over there."

She jabbed the barrel of her autoblaster toward a relatively clear space between the far end of the bar and the foot of the stairs. Domi knew the command was essentially futile, more for show than anything else. Only the people who carried their guns in the open would be inclined to comply, but a demonstration of who was in charge was necessary, particularly with the intimidating figure of Grant out of sight.

None of the people arrayed around the table obeyed. Men looked up at her furtively, then cast anxious glances over their shoulders at the stairway and the open doorway.

"Do it, you pieces of shit!" Domi shouted, sweeping the room with her fierce crimson eyes. She raised the grenade high over her head. "My fingers are getting tired."

Faces blanched and guns began thudding and clattering to the floor. Domi watched, but felt only a little satisfied. She knew if much more time passed the Pit dwellers would grow edgy and less compliant. Suddenly, the stuttering of autofire floated out of the open door at the head of the stairs. The staccato rhythm ended, punctuated by three door-slamming bangs.

Reflexively, Domi's head swiveled in the direction of the noise. She considered joining Grant, but a whip-cracking concussion caused her to jump. She felt and heard a thump of displaced air near her right ear. Instinctively she bent her knees, eyes and gun barrel questing for a target.

She glimpsed a dirty-faced man crouching near the end of the bar. In his hand he held an ugly little revolver of unidentifiable make, but its barrel was so short it could easily be concealed in the palm of his hand. It was the type of gun made strictly for cowardly murders at very close range with shots fired into the backs of heads.

The range at which he had fired was nearly thirty feet, so the fact the shot had come so close to Domi was an impressive display of marksmanship. She showed her admiration by squeezing the trigger of her Combat Master. The heavy bullet struck the man in the left shoulder, knocking him backward. His finger constricted on the trigger of his little pistol, and the round, fired upward, struck a ceiling lamp. The glass of the reservoir shattered and a sheet of burning kerosene cascaded down.

The people huddled on the floor screamed and lurched to their feet, a few of them beating desperately at the flames falling onto their threadbare clothing. They milled around, bowling one another off their feet before turning en masse to stampede for the exit. Bodies crashed into the table atop which Domi stood, nearly jarring her from it.

Arms windmilling, she fought to regain her balance—and to maintain her grasp on the grenade and the gun. Before she could recover her footing, the entire table tilted rearward. The soles of her boots scrabbled frantically on the surface, then she realized someone had deliberately tipped over the table.

Domi toppled from it, screaming a curse. She hit the floor gracelessly, on her left side, the impact loosening her grip on the grenade. All she could see was a forest of feet and legs around her. She was kicked, trampled and stepped on. She tried to use her Combat Master as a club, but a foot dropped down in a hard stomp, trapping her left wrist between the rough leather sole of a boot and the floor. The man was heavy. Numbness shot up her arm to her elbow.

Domi glanced up, recognizing one of Boss Klaw's strong-arms, Crip. He ground his heel into her wrist, the expression on his face one of delighted malevolence. Desperately, Domi raised her pistol but a kick delivered from behind her sent the weapon flying from her hand. Her fingers loosened around the grenade and a hand darted down to snatch it.

Teeth bared in a silent snarl, Domi summoned all her strength and flipped the grenade out of her hand. The metal-shelled orb rolled across the floor. Instantly, Crip lifted his foot from her wrist and cried out hoarsely. With alarmed shouts, the people around her started to run.

Heaving herself up from the floor, Domi shoulder-rolled swiftly behind the overturned table, huddling there between the legs. For once she was happy with her small stature since she was able to conceal her entire body behind the thick slab of wood.

The grenade rolled only a few feet before detonating with a brutal thunderclap. A hell flower bloomed, petals of flame curving and spreading outward. Spewing from the end of every petal was a rain of shrapnel, ripping into bodies, walls, bottles. Fragments rattled violently against the tabletop behind which Domi had taken cover. It felt as if a work gang were pounding on it with sledgehammers. The rolling echoes of the explosion faded, replaced by screams of men in agony.

Cautiously, Domi rose to a half crouch. She counted three tattered and blood-slicked bodies crumpled in various places on the floor. A man lay half-prone against the wall, face buried in his hands as he rocked in agony.

The grenade's explosion had shattered several more oil lamps, and flames licked eagerly at the old wooden furnishings of the Grifter's Gristle. All of the Tartarus Pits in any of the villes were virtually tinderboxes in the wettest of weather, and the tavern was no exception. Within seconds, fire raced along the floor, the walls catching the sparks almost hungrily. A haze of eye-stinging, throat-closing smoke filled the building. The buckets of sand weren't sufficient to extinguish the flames.

The crowd herded toward the door, a howling panicky rush that bowled people off their feet and trampled them as the air fogged with astringent vapors. Domi stayed behind the table until the main mass of the crowd had passed, then she eased her way out. She shouted Grant's name but her voice was absorbed by the cacophony of terror.

The lurid glare of the spreading flames tinted the tavern with hellish hues. Almost the entire taproom was ablaze. The heat of the fires beat upon her face as she made her way toward the staircase. She narrowed her eyes against the smoke and glimpsed her Combat Master lying almost at her feet. As she bent to pick it up, the strong-arm called Nero lunged out of the smoke, arms outstretched.

His expression was bestial, painted a lobster-red due to the second-degree burns inflicted by the flapping tongues of flame. Blood from a scalp wound slid down the left side of his face. With a lumbering charge, the man was upon Domi, hands reaching for her neck. Domi leaped nimbly aside. With a bellow of rage, Nero whirled and lunged again.

It was a one-sided battle, since Nero outweighed Domi by over a hundred pounds. Only the albino girl's quick feet and lightning-fast reflexes saved her from being instantly overpowered. Nero wheezed due to smoke inhalation and his eyes watered, so Domi was able to retreat, duck and dodge.

But the dense smoke smarted in her eyes, as well, blurring her vision. The heat seemed to sear her lungs at every gasping breath. Domi flung a quick glance in the direction of the door at the head of the stairs but saw only drifts of black, spark-shot smoke.

Fire licked out at her right side and she cursed, twisting away. Behind her and to her left, walls hemmed her in. His burned, scarred face split by a grin of malicious triumph, Nero closed in. He had successfully maneuvered her into a corner. He planted his legs wide, flinging out his arms to keep her from darting to one side or the other.

Domi abruptly dropped flat and swiftly belly-crawled between the man's splayed legs. Mouthing a venomous curse, Nero tried to grab her, but his fingers only grazed her heel. He spun just as Domi sprang to her feet.

A challenging smile creased her face, and firelight glinted from the nine-inch-long serrated knife blade in her right fist. Nero blinked at her, first in confusion, then with homicidal rage. His fists clenched and unclenched as he debated the wisdom of trying to outmuscle the outlander girl again. Domi decided the issue by pursuing her lips and blowing him a contemptuous kiss.

A growl humming in his bull throat, Nero charged in again. Domi flexed her knees and thrust the knife forward in a swift lunge, all of her body thrown into the blow, her arm locked straight at the elbow and the shoulder.

The tip of the blade slid under Nero's chin and entered his throat. Domi maintained its position as she spun on the ball of her left foot, dragging the knife with her and opening the flesh in a red-rimmed slash. She whipped the blade free and scarlet fountained from the man's severed jugular. Nero's hands went to his neck as if to staunch the flow of blood, and he staggered blindly in a circle. Crimson spewed from between his fingers, and he cried out gurglingly. He stumbled, then plunged directly into the inferno.

Domi paid no more attention to him—the heat of the fire was almost unbearable, and the smoke nearly impenetrable. It took her by the throat and triggered a coughing fit. She dropped to all fours, head almost at floor level, seeking a breath of untainted air. She didn't find it, but through smoke-bleared eyes she did find her

Detonics Combat Master again. She quickly returned it to its holster, choosing to keep her knife unsheathed.

The weapon was her only memento of the six months she'd spent as Guana Teague's sex slave in the Tartarus Pits of Cobaltville. She had sold herself into slavery in an effort to get a piece of the good life available to ville dwellers, but she had never risen any further than Cobaltville's Tartarus Pits. She ended her term of slavery by cutting the monstrous Teague's throat with the blade, saving Grant's life in the same impulsive act.

Domi wasn't sure how much good it would do her at this point, but if she was going to die, she would feel better with the knife in her hand.

Chapter 4

Flames were already roaring with blast-furnace intensity in the tavern when Kane joined Grant and Boss Klaw at the doorway. They shielded their eyes from the plumes of smoke and showers of embers floating up toward them.

Kane held the spitting, cursing Ayn Thoraldson in a hammerlock in one hand and in the other he gripped the M-16. "What the hell is going on?" he demanded.

"Those sons of bitches rushed Domi." Grant snarled out the words. "Started a fire. I don't see her, so I'm going down there—"

Kane released Ayn and grabbed a handful of Grant's jacket sleeve. "Like hell you are! We can't get out that way."

Grant jerked free. "What do you figure we should do, then?"

Fixing his pale eyes on Klaw's heavy-jowled face, Kane said, "There's another way out of here." He didn't ask a question; he made a statement.

Klaw nodded, gesturing down the hallway. "Back in the room where you found Ayn."

As the woman spoke, Grant holstered his weapon and shrugged off his jacket. Whipping off his hat, he draped it over his head and upper shoulders, swiftly knotting the sleeves at his throat. He snatched the M-16 from a startled Kane, who asked, "What do you think you're doing?"

"Just what I said—I'm going down there to find Domi."

He gave Kane no chance to argue, but he paused long enough to touch his right index finger to his nose and snap it away in the wry "one percent" salute. It was a private gesture he and Kane had developed during their years as hard-contact Magistrates and was reserved for undertakings with small ratios of success. Kane returned the salute, and Grant plunged down the stairs, into the billowing wall of smoke.

Ayn glared at Grant's retreating back, then at Kane and hissed, "I hope he dies."

Turning to face Klaw, Kane snapped, "Why didn't you tell me she was here of her own accord?"

Klaw's lips twisted. "I told you there was more to this than you knew."

Kane spun Ayn and hustled her back down the hall. She was light, perhaps 110 pounds, small boned with a firmly fleshed body. Her face wasn't beautiful or even pretty but a striking in-between, at the same time tough yet vulnerable. It was the face of a fighter accustomed to taking a beating but never giving up.

Ayn resisted being pushed, slapping back at him. "Don't touch me! You don't have the right!"

"The right?" Kane growled. "You ran away from your father, you weren't kidnapped. Do you have any idea of the lives you've put in jeopardy? How many actually died?"

Ayn muttered something sullen and indistinct.

"A spoiled little bitch like you isn't the worth the men I killed to get you."

"You killed my husband," Ayn shot back furiously. "He was trying to protect me and you killed him!"

"Shut up." Kane's tone held an iron edge.

In a voice sibilant with spiteful amusement, Boss Klaw said, "I warned you, Kane, that you didn't know the score. Some things just aren't what they seem. Thoraldson used you."

Kane gave her an over-the-shoulder, bare-toothed glare. He was barely able to refrain from pistol-whipping the smirking woman. "You can shut up, too."

They entered the room where the two men he had shot still lay, blood spreading out in pools around them. Klaw glanced down at the man with the Uzi still in his hands and said bleakly, "Vend was a millennialist rep…a nice kid. His section chief won't be too happy when he hears you killed him."

Kane didn't answer. He said to Ayn, "Get some traveling clothes on. It's cold outside."

She snorted in derision and went to the closet. "What else is new? Me and Vend were going down south, once his reassignment was approved."

Bending over the dead man, Kane felt a surge of sickness at how young he looked. Kane doubted he was much over eighteen, if that. As he pried the Uzi from his fingers, the lamplight winked dully on a small brass button pinned to his shirt.

Pushing his denim jacket's lapel aside, Kane saw a cheap, machine-stamped disk of base metal. The image it bore was the stylized representation of a standing, featureless man holding a cornucopia, a horn of plenty in his left hand and a sword in his right, both crossed over his chest. No words were imprinted on it.

Kane unpinned it and slipped the button into a pocket. Standing, he said to Boss Klaw, "Show me the way out of here."

Klaw marched across the room to a corner and inserted her hook-tipped index finger into an almost invisible seam. At a quick tug, a wide panel swung open on tiny hinges, revealing a cross-barred window. Chill air, redolent with the mixed odors of open cesspits, rotting garbage and smoke blew into the room.

Kane stepped up to the window, peering between the bars at the alley, about fifteen feet below. It thronged with people, most of them coughing patrons who had escaped the tavern. A series of staple-shaped metal rungs was bolted to the wall. Shrouds of smoke floating on the breeze stung his eyes.

Tapping a padlock on the security bars with the spiked nose of the Uzi, Kane asked, "How do you get this open?"

"You unlock it," Boss Klaw retorted flatly. "With a key."

"Use it."

Her yellow, red-netted eyes stared at him blankly. "Why should I do anything to help you? You stabbed me, you've killed my friends, probably fucked up my deal with the Millennial Consortium, set my place on fire—"

She broke off when Kane arched a challenging eyebrow at her, lifting the pistol meaningfully. She snorted derisively. "You think threatening to kill me will get me to cooperate?"

"You could look at it as paying off the marker," he suggested blandly. "You're the one who said you owe me big-time, remember?"

Boss Klaw's brow furrowed as she thought that over, then she scowled in frustration and dug around in a pocket. She produced a small key and inserted it into the lock. "We're even after this, Kane."

"Whatever you say, Boss." He glanced toward the closet. "You ready, kid?"

Ayn Thoraldson appeared, sniffling and dabbing at her eyes. She had donned corduroy trousers and a heavy woolen sweater. To Klaw, she said plaintively, "I don't want to go back to Daddy. Can't you do something?"

Boss Klaw hugged her, patting the back of her head. "Not right now I can't." She turned her head, spearing Kane with an icy glare as she added, "But that could change."

Kane ignored her, pulling the cross-barred framework away from the window. A gun fired from the alley below and he ducked back. Pushing Ayn against the wall, Klaw barked out a laugh. "There's some folks who feel *you* owe *them,* Kane, instead of the other way around."

"Tell them to stand down," Kane snapped.

Klaw shook her head. "Not even if I could. Like I just told you, we're even."

Kane leveled the pistol at her. She swallowed but didn't flinch. Then he spun toward the window, squeezing off three rounds. Three of the people in the alley cried out, slapping at themselves. One of them dropped, clutching at his hip. He dragged himself into the shadows.

Pulling Ayn Thoraldson over to the window, he said, "Start climbing. I'll follow and cover you."

"Cover *me?*" she echoed spitefully. "They won't be shooting at *me*—I can tell you that!"

Boss Klaw chuckled mirthlessly. "I can tell you that, too."

Defiantly, Ayn folded her arms over her breasts. "I'm not going to make it easy for you, you widow-making bastard!"

Kane gazed at her steadily, then holstered his pistol. He nodded toward the smoke pouring into the room from the hallway. "It's the only way out of here. The fire will reach us in about five minutes or less. If you prefer to stay here and burn rather than go back with me to your father, go right ahead."

Ayn chewed her lower lip nervously and cast a questioning look at Boss Klaw. The woman shrugged in resignation. "He's got a point, sweetheart. We can't stay here."

Ayn looked toward the body of Vend and a sob caught in her throat. Then, as she stepped toward the window, she murmured fervently to Kane, "I hate you. I hope you die."

"Take a number," he replied gruffly.

THE HEAT SEEMED to sear Grant's lungs with every breath as he crept down the stairway. Protecting his face with the jacket also inhibited his vision, so he couldn't see much even if plumes of smoke weren't boiling up from all points. "Domi!" he bellowed.

He paused at the foot of the stairs and squinted around. The entire tavern looked like a wall of billowing black smoke laced with lurid, bloodred tongues of flame. Sparks and embers swirled in artless patterns around him, stinging his face and hands. "Domi!" he called out again.

He inhaled an acrid tendril of smoke, and a coughing fit bent him double. As he gaspingly tried to regain his breath, he barely heard the faint, strangulated voice almost at his feet. "Here…over here…"

Knuckling his streaming eyes, he shuffled forward and glimpsed Domi lying prone on the floor, lifting her head and gazing around unfocusedly. She coughed and choked. Her knife lay on the floor between her hands.

Grant slapped out the sparks dancing on the hem of her poncho and heaved her up, cradling her childlike body in his arms, despite the encumbrance of the M-16. He picked up her knife in the process, knowing how much it meant to her. He slid it into his belt.

As the girl wheezed against his chest, Grant looked around through slitted, sweat-and-smoke-stung eyes. They were almost surrounded by leaping flames. He turned back toward the stairway, hearing glass crack and shatter. The heat had broken the liquor bottles behind the bar and ignited the volatile fluids leaking out with a loud *pop*. Trails of blue fire streaked swiftly across the floorboards, feeding the flames of the fierce conflagration and whirling up to cut off his path to the stairs.

Grant bit back a groan of despair. He realized that in such an inferno the minutes of life could be counted on the fingers of one hand. He shifted position to a point comparatively free of flame and quietly, bitterly chuckled to himself. He saw no way out.

Chapter 5

Although Grant knew the means and moment of a man's death could not be anticipated, and that when the time came it would most likely not be glorious, he hadn't envisioned burning to death in a pesthole tavern with Domi in his arms. He couldn't help but wonder, if only for a second, how Shizuka would react when she received the news.

The concept brought him short, and a cold fist of determination knotted with painful tightness in the center of his chest. He would be damned if he and Domi would die in Ragnarville's Tartarus Pits. The Pits of Cobaltville hadn't claimed either one of them, thought they had tried, and wouldn't allow the late and unlamented Baron Ragnar's version of the place to accomplish the task.

He stepped to an area that was not yet thoroughly ablaze and swiftly studied the nearest wall. He found a small strip where the wood, though smoldering and glowing, was not afire. He edged as close to it as he could, manipulating the M-16 with difficulty since Domi sagged limply within the cradle of his arms.

Holding the autorifle at hip level, he pressed down the trigger, stitching a human-sized oval into a wall. Little gouts of sparking, rotten wood mushroomed up, like a series of miniature explosions. When the firing pin snapped loudly on a dry chamber, he dropped the M-16 and covered Domi's head with the tail of her poncho.

Tucking his chin against his shoulder, Grant sprang forward through the wreath of fire and hurled his entire weight against the wall. The bullet perforations broke away, and the section burst outward in a scattering of glowing, emberlike splinters. He fell to the ground, cushioning Domi as best he could.

Hair singed and wisps of smoke curling from his clothing, he staggered to his feet. Bruised and breathless he picked up Domi and carried her away from the smoke-belching building. He bulled his way through a milling throng of people, but none of them paid him any attention. They congregated at the mouth of the alley that ran parallel to the Grifter's Gristle. He didn't know why, and at the moment he wasn't inclined to find out.

Domi stirred fitfully in his arms and murmured something indistinct. The fresh air had revived her and she coughed, squirming to be put down. Grant stopped by a wooden fence. "Can you stand?" he husked out.

"Think so." Her voice sounded hoarse, the tissues raw and abraded from the heat and smoke inhalation. "Are you all right?"

"Think so."

Grant sat her down atop an overturned barrel and for a moment the two of them simply breathed deeply, reveling in the cold air, despite its malodorous quality. Gray and black smudges contrasted sharply against Domi's white complexion and with a wrinkled nose, she fingered the scorched ends of her hair.

Suddenly she clapped a hand to the empty knife sheath at her waist and almost wailed, "Oh, no—"

Grant pulled her knife from his belt and presented it to her pommel first. Wryly he said, "Couldn't let you lose that. It looms large in both our legends."

She blinked at him in confusion but said gratefully, "Thanks."

Before he could reply, the staccato rattling of auto-fire emanated from the alley. Hand on the butt of his Magnum pistol, he stepped cautiously into its mouth, peering through the hazy murk. He saw half a dozen or more men scattering in a panic and taking cover. Several of them were armed.

Lifting his gaze, he saw Kane hanging on to metal rungs bolted to the wall, keeping an Uzi trained on the alley below. Ayn Thoraldson crouched under the foot of the ladder. Boss Klaw appeared in the window just above Kane, her stumpy legs groping fitfully for footholds on the uppermost rung. Smoke curled all around her.

A shaggy-haired shape shifted in a wedge of shadow cast by a heap of garbage, raising his head and arm just enough to draw a bead on Kane with a handgun. The pistol was small, but the range was short enough for him to score a hit with little skill. Grant recognized him as Crip, one of Boss Klaw's strong-arms.

Grant drew the Magnum pistol and swiftly lined Crip up in its sights, holding the heavy weapon out in front of him with both hands. He called, "Hey, Crip, what're you doing with that popgun?"

The young man whirled, the look of slack-jawed surprise on his face so comical that Grant almost laughed. Then the expression of surprise was replaced by a mask of homicidal, bare-toothed ferocity. He squeezed off a wild shot, a little spurt of flame stabbing through the shadows. Almost at the same instant, Grant squeezed the trigger of his pistol.

The full-throated boom of the report sounded like a thunderclap in the alley. The gun bucked in his hands. The steel-jacked bullet hit Crip with the force of a sledgehammer, lifting him completely off his feet and dropping him dead five feet away, blood spewing in a liquid banner from his chest.

The other men lurking in the alley gaped at Grant with shocked, frightened eyes, fisting their small pistols. They looked like toys in comparison to the big Colt.

"Anybody else?" Grant demanded loudly.

The men scuttled away swiftly, the gloom and the smoke seeming to swallow them up. Evidently Crip had been the rallying point, the organizer and with him dead they saw little reason to continue the hostilities.

Grant, joined by Domi, who had her own pistol in hand, reached the foot of the ladder just Kane jumped down into the alley. He glanced at them incuriously and said with studied nonchalance, "I see you two made it."

"Don't we always?" Domi countered waspishly.

Assuming the question was rhetorical, Kane didn't answer. He drew Ayn away from the ladder, saying, "This is Thoraldson's daughter…the one we came to rescue. Except she didn't want or need to be rescued."

Domi eyed her a little superciliously. "Why not?"

Ayn said sharply, "Why do you care?"

The albino shrugged. "I don't. I was only asking to be polite."

Boss Klaw descended clumsily, her face red and her respiration labored. She glanced over at Crip's corpse and then at Grant's Magnum pistol. She spat angrily,

"You two bastards have just about ruined my life in the last ten minutes."

"Then it's to your advantage to get us out of here," Grant rumbled. "Preferably with nobody else trying to set us on fire or shoot us."

Boss Klaw glared at him with loathing. "How do you figure to get out of the Pits, let alone the ville, without one or the other happening?"

Kane regarded her with a cold, stitched-on smile. "Glad you asked. You've been such a help to us so far, I think we can rely on you to arrange for us a quick and quiet method out of Ragnarville and into Thoraldson's territory."

Klaw's flesh-bagged eyes slitted with barely repressed rage. "What the hell makes you think I have the resources to pull off something like that?"

"*You* made me think that," Kane countered. "If you've got a big operation underway in the Outlands it stands to reason you'd have some method of getting to it, right?"

Grant raised a quizzical eyebrow. "Big operation?"

"If fat old Guana Teague over in Cobaltville was able to own a vehicle," Kane continued, "right under the noses of the barons and the Mags, no less, I'm betting you have something better…especially since everything has gone to hell here, governing wise."

He paused and added in a soft tone, silky with a threat, "In fact, I wouldn't be surprised if what you have was provided by a Mag." He held up the Uzi. "Like this."

Although Klaw's expression remained as immobile as if her face were carved out of wood, Kane caught the almost imperceptible quiver of her eyelids. "So," he went on, "you're going to take us to where your transportation is kept. And you're going to give us the lend of it with your blessing."

The Pit boss drew herself up haughtily. "And if I don't?"

Within a heartbeat, three pistol barrels were trained on her head. "Oh," she murmured, shoulders sagging. "That."

"Yeah," Domi chirped. "That." Favoring Ayn with a slit-eyed stare, she added, "And that goes for you, too."

Head bowed, Boss Klaw turned and began trudging through the maze of back alleys, side lanes and foot paths. The smell of burning wood and smoke overlaid all the other redolent stenches. The few people they encountered didn't appear concerned about the Grifter's Gristle burning down, although they heard a few muttered worries about the fire spreading to other hovels. The inferno of the tavern and the adjacent apartments smeared the dark sky with a glow that could probably be seen from any point in Tartarus. The orange-and-yellow stain hung above the rooftops like a miniature aurora borealis.

Grant, Kane, Ayn Thoraldson and Domi followed Boss Klaw through narrow alleys that twisted between ramshackle buildings, past squalid shacks and shanties. As in the Pits in any ville, there were no main avenues, only muddy streets that were guttered down the center for drainage. All of them were thick with the droppings of mules, horses, pigs and probably humans.

After several minutes of wending their way through the stinking labyrinth, the five people reached a narrow wooden footpath, a channel that cut its way from the outer limits of Tartarus proper to a walled compound that surrounded the Administrative Monolith.

The flat-topped column of white rock crete jutted three hundred feet above the muck of the Tartarus Pits. Light poured out of the slit-shaped windows on each level, a silent signal and warning to all residents of the barony without a baron that the divisions of the ville still labored, regardless of the hour.

The wooden pathway they followed was strictly forbidden to anyone but Magistrates. Vid spy-eyes affixed to posts at regular intervals made sure no Pit denizen planted a dirty foot on it. Nothing could be done to avoid the surveillance, so Kane, Grant and Domi pretended the spy-eyes didn't exist. But to be on the safe side, he cast aside the Uzi, since he had emptied the clip and whispered to Grant and Domi to make sure their own pistols were out of sight.

The path jogged to the right and dead-ended at a metal gate set in the center of the wall. Boss Klaw, acting as if she were suffering the torments of the damned, groaning and murmuring painfully under her breath, tapped in a numerical sequence on the keypad beside the gate.

With a grinding of gears, the portal squeaked to one side. She stepped through it, and the four people followed her into the vehicle depot of Ragnarville's Magistrate Division. Arrayed within it, parked beneath a protective overhang, were two Land Rovers, an APC and four Sandcats. The ville's rolling stock didn't seem like much, but then much of it had probably been depleted during the Imperator War. Without a baron to make a formal request to Sam, the ordnance hadn't been replaced.

"Hey!" rasped an annoyed male voice. "What the hell is goin' on here?"

A burly black man pushed his way between the two Land Rovers, his leather belt jingling with various hand tools. A stub of foul-smelling cigar jutted out of the corner of his mouth. Kane kept his S&W held behind his back and indicated with nods to Grant and Domi they should do the same. The man wasn't a Mag, but only a mechanic, a service attendant.

"It's okay, Jason," Boss Klaw called. "It's only me."

Despite the grime and grease caked on his face, Kane saw the expression of relieved recognition replace that of apprehensive suspicion. "I wasn't expecting you, Francine."

"Francine?" Kane whispered incredulously. "You're on a first-name basis with the Mag Division mechanic and your name is *Francine*?"

Jason's eyes flitted suspiciously from Kane to Grant to Domi to Ayn then back to Klaw. Grant and Kane did their best not to look like themselves, the notorious renegade Magistrates from Cobaltville. Nearly two years before, during the height of the cooperative search among all the baronies, pix of Kane, Grant and Brigid Baptiste had been circulated throughout all the ville territories.

Since the advent of the imperator, the search had been called off, presumably because Sam knew exactly where to find them. However, that didn't mean someone like Jason would forget their likenesses if he had seen the pix.

"Who're you?" Jason demanded of Kane. He had drawn the mechanic's attention by whispering to Boss Klaw.

Kane saw he carried a "chicken switch" alarm box

on his tool belt. One touch of the button and the compound would be automatically locked and, within a minute or less, swarming with Magistrates.

When Boss Klaw didn't offer an explanation for their presence and identity, Kane said, almost on impulse, "We're with the consortium."

When Jason's eyes narrowed in suspicion, Kane reached inside his pocket and produced the button he had taken from Vend's body. The mechanic gave it a swift, cursory examination. "Benedict Snow's crew, huh?"

Kane nodded, noticing how Jason's demeanor had become considerably more relaxed. "What can I do for you?"

Once more Boss Klaw seemed disinclined to speak up, so Grant surreptitiously nudged her in the back. Flatly, she said, "We need a Cat. I've got business out at the site."

Jason's thick eyebrows rose. "Kind of late to be going out there, ain't it?"

"It's an emergency," Klaw stated.

The mechanic gazed her questioningly, then over at Ayn and shrugged. "Okay. I just finished servicing one. C'mon, I'll get you the keys."

He turned and marched quickly toward a lighted area beneath the overhang. They followed him into a workshop, illuminated poorly by overhead naked lightbulbs. It was filled with heavy trestle tables, tools, chain vises, band saws and drill presses. Parked on a concrete slab, both of its gull-wing doors open, was a Sandcat.

The vehicle was known by assorted names: fast attack vehicle, armored personnel carrier or simply a wag, but was most often referred to as a Sandcat. Built to serve as an FAV rather than a means of long-distance ground transportation, a pair of flat, retractable tracks supported the Sandcat's low-slung, blunt-lined chassis. The armored topside gun turret held a pair of USMG-73 heavy machine guns.

The Cat's armor was composed of a ceramic-armaglass bond, which shielded against both intense and ambient radiation. The topside turret appeared to be a transparent half dome, but at the touch of a button microcircuitry would engage, feeding an electric impulse to the chemically treated armaglass bubble.

It would instantly become opaque when exposed to energy-based weapons, such as particle-beam emitters—not that there was much chance of encountering such weapons. Like most everything else used by the Magistrate Divisions, the Sandcat was based on an existing predark framework, built to participate in a ground war that was never fought.

Jason's gait quickened as he walked around the rear of the vehicle. He spoke far more loudly than was necessary. "The keys are back here so hold on a sec and I'll grab 'em and bring them to you—"

Kane didn't need what his sixth sense, what he called his point man's sense to let him know Jason couldn't be trusted. He brought his autopistol around from behind his back. Grant and Domi followed suit with their own weapons.

Jason reappeared, but not with keys in hand. Instead he gripped a Magistrate Division-issue subgun, a Copperhead. Less than two feet long, with a 700-round-per-minute rate of fire, the ammunition clip held fifteen 4.85 mm steel-jacketed rounds. The grip and trigger unit were placed in front of the breech in the bullpup design, allowing for one-handed use. An optical image intensifier scope and laser autotargeter were fitted on the top of the frame. The Copperhead's low recoil allowed it to be fired in a long, devastating full-auto burst that emptied it in less than five seconds.

Domi made a grab for Boss Klaw but she was remarkably agile and fleet of foot for a woman of her frame. She lunged for cover on the opposite side of the Sandcat, shrieking, "Kill 'em! They're Kane and Grant! *Kill 'em!*"

Domi wrestled Ayn Thoraldson forward, jamming the bore of her Combat Master hard against the side of her head, invoking a cry of pain from the girl. "Shut up," Domi spat. "You die first."

Jason blinked in surprise as if he were trying to process a new concept. He squinted at Kane, then toward Grant. He lowered the barrel of the Copperhead.

"What are you waiting for, you idiot?" Klaw screeched, coming out from behind the Cat. She waved her injured right hand. "They stabbed me, burned down the Gristle, killed my strong-arms!"

Jason continued to gaze steadily at Grant and Kane, chewing meditatively on his cigar. Then a smile spread slowly across his dark features, and he let the Copperhead dangle at the end of his right arm. "I'm sure they had good reasons, Francine."

Klaw bleated a wordless squawk of total astonishment. Kane could barely restrain himself from doing the same. He, Grant and Domi eyed the man warily, keeping their guns trained on him.

"Yeah, I thought you two looked familiar," Jason

commented pleasantly. "Grant and Kane, the badasses that scare the biggest badasses shitless, the barons' worst nightmare. Always wanted to meet you—you done some wild-ass shit."

Neither Kane nor Grant doubted tales of their actions had spread far, but more than likely legend had cloaked the truth, fable supplanting fact.

"You looking to collect the bounty on our heads?" Domi challenged, sounding a little irritated she had not been included in the "worst nightmare" appellation applied to her male colleagues.

Jason laughed uproariously as if Domi's question was the funniest thing he'd heard in a long time. "Hell, whatever bounty you three are worth ain't as valuable as what I got goin' on here. Thanks to you, getting rid of Baron Ragnar and Barch, I pretty much have the run of the entire division. I owe you big."

"We've heard that before," Grant rumbled. "Prove it."

With his left hand he tossed a set of keys to Grant, who snatched them out of the air. "Take the Cat with my thanks."

Kane arched a questioning eyebrow. "Won't your division commander miss it?"

Jason shrugged. "Eventually, mebbe. But he never comes down here. 'Sides, I'll just tell him a couple of boys from the Millennial Consortium requisitioned it. That'll keep him from asking too many questions."

Kane's own questions about the consortium and its apparently deep involvement with both the high and low ends of Ragnarville's society were nearly all-consuming. But he forced down his curiosity and holstered his Sin Eater. Domi released Ayn, who rubbed at the red imprint of the Combat Master's muzzle on her temple. The look she gave Domi was not one of admiration.

Boss Klaw lumbered around the front of the Sandcat, almost too overcome with frustrated fury to speak. She managed to sputter at Kane, "You ever come back here—" She didn't finish the threat.

As Kane passed her, he patted her cheek and said with a quiet but severe mockery, "Now, you see how it's done, Francine? When Jason says he owes us big, he proves it to us. That's the difference between a Mag and a slagger."

They climbed into the Cat, Grant sliding into the pilot's chair. Kane sat down beside him, while Domi and Ayn climbed into the back. Before Grant pulled the door shut, Jason leaned down and said earnestly, "Not every Mag is against you. You're an inspiration to some of us."

"I'll try to remember that the next time you Mags start shooting at us," Grant said grimly.

Jason grinned around the cigar. "Hell, even *I've* shot at you. And I ain't a bad shot. Think about it."

He slammed the door shut, and Grant keyed the powerful engine to roaring life. He sat for a long moment, hands on the horseshoe-shaped wheel, staring out through the ob port.

"Let's go," Kane said impatiently. "Why are we sitting here?"

A smile quirked the corner of Grant's mouth under his mustache. "I'm doing what Jason said." He glanced sideways at Kane and said, "I'm thinking about it. Mebbe you should, too."

Kane felt the pressure of Ayn Thoraldson's hate-filled glare against the back of his head and sighed. "Yeah, just starting to think period might to do me some good."

Chapter 6

Mohandas Lakesh Singh stared over the lip of the precipice without really seeing what lay at the bottom—not that there was much to actually look at.

The sky over the craggy cliffs was a heavy, leaden gray, despite the midmorning hour. The sudden rain shower had finally stopped, and the mountain air smelled clean and fresh. The rich scent of wet grassy meadows and groves of trees rolled up from the foothills below.

Standing on the rutted asphalt-covered plateau, Lakesh faced a deep abyss that plummeted straight down a thousand feet or more. At one time, steel guardrails had bordered the lip of the road, but only a few rusted metal stanchions remained. Although he couldn't see them, Lakesh knew the skeletons of several vehicles rested at the bottom of the chasm. They had laid there since the nuclear holocaust or the subsequent skydark, weathering all the seasons that came after, like monuments to predark desperation.

Also down there, completely invisible among the rocks bordering the stream, lay the three pieces of the Chintamani Stone, the Shining Trapezohedron. In a moment of impulsive self-righteousness, an act Lakesh still bitterly resented, Kane had dumped them down there like so much garbage. More than once he had contemplated climbing down the cliff face to search for them. But not only would the effort be exceptionally hazardous, it would also be futile. Even if he managed to retrieve the three black stones, he would never be permitted to put their dimensional-rifting properties to use again.

He shivered in the cold air. Although autumn had yet to give way to winter, the mornings were still chilly at such a high altitude. Lakesh seemed particularly susceptible to cold temperatures, and he wasn't sure if it was due to being born in the tropical climate of Kashmir or was a metabolic carryover from the 148 years, three months and thirteen days he'd spent in cryostasis. Although it made no scientific sense, he had been susceptible to cold ever since.

He glanced up at the gray Montana sky. For a generation following the nuclear holocaust of 2001, the sky had been gray twenty-four hours a day. The worldwide atomic explosions had filled the atmosphere with inestimable tons of dust and debris, severely diminishing the amount of sunlight reaching Earth. The thirty-year-long nuclear winter, the skydark, had caused many of the survivors of the nukecaust to freeze to death in the long night.

The shadows on the plateau were no less deep and dark than those that covered the entire world during the nuclear winter, a quality Lakesh always found appropriate, since the Cerberus redoubt was built into a peak of the Montana mountain range known colloquially as the Darks. Long ago, in the centuries preceding the apocalypse, the mountains had been known as the Bitterroot Range. In the generations since the nukecaust, a sinister mythology had been ascribed to the mountains, with their mysteriously shadowed forests and hell-deep, dangerous ravines.

The road leading down from Cerberus to the foothills was little more than a cracked and twisted asphalt ribbon, skirting yawning chasms and cliffs. Acres of the mountainsides had collapsed during the nuke-triggered earthquakes nearly two centuries ago. The wilderness area was virtually unpopulated. The nearest settlement was nearly a hundred miles away, and it consisted of a small band of Indians, Sioux and Cheyenne.

Lakesh turned away, massaging his throbbing temples, hoping the headache was only stress induced and not the symptoms of a condition far more serious. If there were any solutions to the worries assailing him, they didn't lie within the abyss.

The scraps of a chain-link fence enclosing the entrance to the Cerberus redoubt clinked in the breeze. When Cerberus was built in the mid-1990s, no expense had been spared to make the installation a masterpiece of impenetrability. The trilevel, thirty-acre facility had come through the nukecaust in good condition. Its radiation shielding was still intact, and an elaborate system of heat-sensing warning devices, night-vision vid cameras and motion-trigger alarms surrounded the plateau that concealed it.

When Lakesh had reactivated the installation some thirty years before, the repairs he made had been minor, primarily cosmetic in nature. Over a period of time, he had added a security system to the plateau surrounding the redoubt. He had been forced to work in secret and completely alone, so the upgrades had taken several years to complete.

Planted within rocky clefts of the mountain peak and concealed by camouflage netting were the uplinks with an orbiting Vela-class reconnaissance satellite, and a Comsat. It could be safely assumed that no one or nothing could approach Cerberus undetected by land or by air—not that he expected anyone to make the attempt, particularly overland. In the unlikely instance of an organized assault against the installation, an electronic force field energized with particles of antimatter could be activated at the touch of a button.

In one way it was the most recent addition to the Cerberus security systems, but in another way, one of the oldest. The plateau had originally been protected by the energy shield but at some point over the past century, it had come to be deactivated. With the help of Brewster Philboyd, the force-field emitter had been repaired and put back into service.

Recessed within the rock face of the mountain peak was a fifteen-foot-high, twenty-two-foot-wide sec door. Vanadium alloy gleamed beneath peeling paint. The gate opened like an accordion, folding to one side, and was operated by a punched-in code and a hidden lever control. One of its panels was partially ajar, allowing light from the interior to spill out. It faintly illuminated the area where the plateau debouched into the higher slopes, and gleamed off the white headstones marking eleven grave sites.

The fabricated markers bore only last names: Cotta, Rouch, Adrian, Davis. Seven of them were new, inscribed with the names of the Moon base émigrés who had died defending Cerberus from the incursion staged by the mad god, Maccan, and his followers. Two of the graves didn't hold remains at all. Adrian and Davis had died years ago in Mongolia at the hands of the Tushe Gun, and their bodies had never been recovered.

Lakesh wondered gloomily how many more such austere markers Farrell would fashion in the redoubt's workshop before the work of Cerberus was done. At the moment he feared three new stones would need to be made in the very near future, inscribed with the names Philboyd, Pennick and Baptiste.

Lakesh sighed, realizing he had been grousing alone in the dusk long enough. Slowly, reluctantly, he walked toward the sec door. Cerberus had been built over two hundred years ago as the seat of Project Cerberus, and all design and construction specs were aimed at making Cerberus a viable, impenetrable community of at least a hundred people.

Although there were still fewer than that now, the installation currently held more people than had been stationed there since the last days of the twentieth century. For most of the permanent residents, time was measured by the controlled dimming and brightening of lights to simulate sunrise and sunset.

When the day-shift lighting had automatically switched on, the desire to get out in the fresh air had become a compulsion, despite the rain shower. As a young genius, Lakesh had spent most of his youth laboring within the walls of installations much like Cerberus, only rarely venturing into nature.

During his late teens he had been recruited, duped into serving the web of treachery that had been the Totality Concept. His brilliance in the fields of quantum physics and cybernetics eventually earned him the overseer position of Project Cerberus, the subdivision that dealt with matter-transmission through hyperdimensional channels. Without him, there would have never been the quantum mat-trans inducer process, otherwise known as the Cerberus gateway network—or, he reflected sourly, never such a thing as the interphaser, which very well might have caused the deaths of three of the redoubt's valued personnel. And in the instance of Brigid Baptiste, perhaps the loss of the closest thing he had to a daughter.

Clenching his teeth and fists, Lakesh stepped through the open sec door panel and marched purposefully down the twenty-foot-wide main corridor. The floors and walls were sheathed by dully gleaming vanadium alloy. The high rock roof was supported by curving arches of thick metal.

A large illustration of a three-headed, froth-mouthed black hound was rendered in lurid colors on the wall near the sec door control lever. Underneath the image, in an ornately overdone Gothic script, was written the single word: Cerberus.

The artist had been one of the enlisted men assigned to the redoubt toward the end of twentieth century. Lakesh hadn't bothered to remove the illustration, partly because the paint was indelible and partly because the ferocious guardian of the gateway to Hades seemed an appropriate totem and code name for the project devoted to ripping open gates in the quantum field.

He caught a glimpse of himself in one of the polished wall panels. Although distorted, he saw a reflection of a well-built man of medium height, with thick, glossy, black hair, an unlined dark olive complexion and a long, aquiline nose. He looked no older than fifty, despite a few strands of gray streaking through his temples. He resembled a middle-aged man of East Indian extraction in reasonably good health. In reality, he was just a year or so shy of celebrating his 250th birthday. His good health was on loan and could disappear at the whim of Sam, the imperator.

He still remembered with startling clarity what Sam had said to him as he writhed in pain across the corridor floor of the Scorpia Prime's fortress: "I will concede my defeat on this occasion, Mohandas, but it's only a small move in a far larger game. But I'm the game master, and it's up to me whether I'll keep you alive to contend against me another day, or kill you at a whim. I have plenty of time to make up my mind."

Months before, upon their initial meeting, Sam had restored Lakesh's physical condition to that of a man in his midforties by what, at the time, seemed to be a miraculous laying on of hands. Then, Lakesh's eyes had been covered by thick lenses, a hearing aid inserted in one ear and he resembled a hunched-over, spindly old scarecrow who appeared to be fighting the grave for every hour he remained on the planet.

At the time Sam claimed he had increased Lakesh's production of two antioxidant enzymes, catalase and superoxide dismutase, and boosted up his alkylglycerol level to the point where the aging process was for all intents and purposes reversed.

Sam had accomplished it, but it was not until recently Lakesh learned the precise methodology—when he laid his hands on Lakesh, he had injected nanomachines into his body. The nanites were programmed to recognize and destroy the dangerous replicators, whether they were bacteria, cancer cells or viruses. Sam's nanites performed selective destruction on the genes of DNA cells, removing the part that caused aging.

The nanites stimulated the metabolism by resetting cellular control mechanisms, but the results of a recent medical examination had shown that the nanites in Lakesh's body were now inert. They no longer worked to maintain his metabolism at its restored levels. If Sam had exerted control over them, he had either relinquished it on his own accord as a way to punish him or the influence was broken for another reason. Regardless of the reasons, DeFore's prognosis was that Lakesh would begin to age, but at an accelerated rate.

He had no choice but to agree with her gloomy diagnosis. The worst-case scenario she offered had him back to his prerestoration physical condition inside of a year. The absolutely best-case situation would be one where he simply began to age normally from the point the nanites stopped functioning, but he knew that was an unrealistic hope at best and a delusion at worst.

Without the help of Sam's nanomachines, his body simply couldn't maintain its present state. In fact, the possibility existed that his cardiovascular system wouldn't be able to withstand the strain of rapid aging and would shut down.

But until that day, he told himself, he would still try to control his own personal world within a world that the Cerberus command center represented.

The command center was a long, vault-walled, high-ceilinged room filled with orderly rows of comp terminals and stations. The central control complex had five dedicated and eight shared subprocessors, all linked to the mainframe behind the far wall. Two hundred years ago, it had been an advanced model, carrying experimental, error-correcting microchips of such a tiny size that they even reacted to quantum fluctuations. Biochip technology had been employed when it was built, protein molecules sandwiched between microscopic glass-and-metal circuits.

On the opposite side of the operations center, an anteroom held the eight-foot-tall mat-trans chamber, rising from an elevated platform. Upright slabs of translucent, brown-hued armaglass formed six walls around it. Armaglass was manufactured in the last decades of the twentieth century from a special compound that plasticized and combined the properties of steel and glass. It was used as walls in the jump chambers to confine quantum-energy overspills.

Lakesh glanced over his shoulder at the indicator lights of the huge Mercator relief map of the world that spanned one entire wall. Pinpoints of light shone steadily in almost every country, connected by a thin, glowing pattern of lines. They represented the Cerberus network, the locations of all functioning gateway units across the planet. None of the tiny lights blinked, so no indexed mat-trans was currently in use.

Monitor screens flashed incomprehensible images and streams of data in machine talk. Only Donald Bry, Mariah Falk and Quavell were present in the redoubt's nerve center. In the wake of the recent assault on the redoubt, some of the operational functions of the installation had been restored only to nominal levels. Although the major repairs had been completed, a few of the subsystems had yet to be thoroughly debugged.

Lakesh wasn't concerned about those, however. Coming to stand beside Quavell, who was seated before the biolink medical monitor, he asked gruffly, "Status?"

Chapter 7

The inhumanly large, crystal-blue eyes of Quavell regarded him placidly. She tilted her head slightly as she shifted in her chair, trying to find a comfortable position. Her eyes dominated a face of chiseled, elfin loveliness. If not for the grave austerity of her expression, she would have been beautiful. White-blond hair the texture of silk threads fell from her domed skull and curled inward at her slender shoulders.

Under five feet tall, her small, fragile form was encased in a silvery-gray, skintight bodysuit. It only accentuated the distended condition of her belly and the slenderness of her limbs. The material of the one-piece garment was a synthetic polymer with a high degree of elasticity, and it provided adequate support for her gravid condition.

"There has been very little change since the last time you inquired," she responded crisply. Lakesh thought he detected a patronizing note in her soft, childlike voice, but he attributed his sensitivity to lingering resentment against the hybrids. "As you can see, Domi, Grant and Kane are in very close proximity to Redoubt Tango. They actually could be within it by now."

She nodded to the monitor she sat before. On the screen he saw an aerial topographical map of the state of Minnesota. Superimposed over it flashed three icons. The telemetry transmitted from Kane's, Grant's and Domi's subdermal biolink transponders scrolled in a drop-down window across the top of the screen. The computer systems recorded every byte of data sent to the Comsat and directed it to the redoubt's hidden antenna array. Sophisticated scanning filters combed through the telemetric signals using special human biological encoding.

The digital data stream was then routed to another console through the locational program, to precisely isolate the team's present position in time and space. The program considered and discarded thousands of possibilities within milliseconds.

All of the icons glowed a steady green, which indicated everyone was in good health.

"And if they are indeed within the redoubt proper," Quavell continued, "then they should be returning here in very short order."

Redoubt Tango was one of the many of the Totality Concept–related installations buried within subterranean military complexes all over the United States. The official designations of the redoubts had been based on the old international radio code, as in "Tango" representing the letter *T.* The official title of the Cerberus facility was Redoubt Bravo.

Before the apocalypse, only a handful of people knew the redoubts even existed, and only half a handful knew all their locations. That knowledge had been lost after the nukecaust, rediscovered a century later, then jealously, ruthlessly guarded.

Even before the nukecaust, the purposes of the redoubts and the Cerberus gateways were classified at the highest secret level. Lakesh knew the mania for secrecy was justified. A device that could transport matter—like nuclear devices—was a more important weapon than the atomic weapons themselves. If a state of war existed, it was theoretically possible to invade the enemy nation and pour in troops, tanks, personnel carriers and whatever weapons tactics indicated.

Lakesh tried to focus on the less destructive applications of the gateways. Given wide use, the mat-trans could eliminate long-haul transportation of goods and even turn international travel into no more daunting a journey than opening and closing a door. He realized, of course, that many decades, perhaps even a century, would pass before the gateway units would be accepted by the public for tourist traffic. The transit phase was so unnerving that wide public acceptance was probably an impossibility.

Eventually, Lakesh hoped, the gateways would primarily be used for space exploration, replacing cumbersome, slow-moving shuttles that were restricted to the closer planets of the solar system.

But with the interphaser, the applications widened even beyond that. Jumping from any point on Earth, it was possible to establish a base anywhere on Earth and conceivably on the other planets, if corresponding vortex nodes could be matched up within the gateway and interphaser's targeting computers.

Even then, the mystery of the origin of the technology that made the entire system viable haunted Lakesh. It would be many years before he came across the shocking fact that although the integral components were of terrestrial origin, they were constructed under the auspices of a nonhuman intelligence—or at least, nonhuman as defined by late-twentieth-century standards. Nearly two centuries would pass before Lakesh learned the entire story, or a version of it.

"As for the interphaser test team," Bry said from the main operations console, "the status is still the same as it's been for the last seventy-five hours. No signal."

Lakesh definitely detected an impatient note in Bry's tone. He turned toward the small man with rounded shoulders and copper-colored hair. The man sat before a big VGA monitor screen, a four-foot square of ground glass. His fingers clattered over a keyboard like a concert pianist performing an intricate sonata.

As the leading tech of the redoubt, Bry usually oversaw all the away missions that involved using the Cerberus network. He had made no secret of his antipathy toward the interphaser, which circumvented the entire gateway process.

Lakesh started to retort, then changed his mind. Getting testy with Bry wouldn't change the situation or ease his burden of guilt. Sometimes he felt as if guilt motivated and colored his every action, trapping him in an eternal, suffocating sense of responsibility for the entire world. The interphaser had initially been conceived as a method to set right everything that he unwittingly helped to go so horribly wrong as a dupe of the Totality Concept.

The interphaser was the third version of a device that evolved from Project Cerberus. Over two years before, he had constructed a small device based on the same scientific principle as the mat-trans inducers, an interphaser designed to interact with naturally occurring quantum vortices. Theoretically, the interphaser opened dimensional rifts much like the gateways, but instead of the rifts being pathways through linear space, Lakesh had envisioned them as a method to travel through the gaps in normal space-time.

The interphaser hadn't functioned according to its design, and was lost on its first mission. Much later, a situation arose that showed him the wisdom of building a second, improved model.

A mission a few months ago had brought Brigid Baptiste, Kane and Grant to a Totality Concept installation, the primary Operation Chronos facility. They assumed the installation had been uninhabited and forgotten since the nukecaust of two centuries before. Only much later did they find out the place was inhabited by an old enemy, the brilliant but deranged dwarf, Sindri.

He told them during his investigation of the installation, he had discovered a special encoded program that was linked to, but separate from, Chronos. It was code-named Parallax Points. Sindri was far more interested in the workings of the temporal dilator than the Parallax Points program, but his tampering with the technology caused it to overload and reach critical mass, resulting in a violent meltdown of its energy core.

Lakesh learned that the Parallax Points program was actually a map, a geodetic index, of all the vortex points on the planet. This discovery inspired him to rebuild the interphaser, even though decrypting the program was laborious and time-consuming. Each newly discovered set of coordinates was fed into the interphaser's targeting computer.

With the new data, the interphaser became more than a miniaturized version of a gateway unit, even though it employed much of the same hardware and operating principles. The mat-trans gateways functioned by tapping into the quantum stream, the invisible pathways that crisscrossed outside of perceived physical space, and terminating in wormholes.

The interphaser interacted with the energy within a naturally occurring vortex and caused a temporary overlapping of two dimensions. The vortex then became an intersection point, a discontinuous quantum jump, beyond relativistic space-time.

Evidence indicated there were many vortex nodes, centers of intense energy, located in the same proximity on each of the planets of the solar system, and those points correlated to vortex centers on Earth. The power points of the planet, places which naturally generated specific types of energy, possessed both positive and projective frequencies, and others were negative and receptive. He referred to the positive energy as prana, which was an old Sanskrit term meaning the "world soul."

Lakesh knew some ancient civilizations were aware of these symmetrical geoenergies and constructed monuments over the vortex points in order to manipulate them. Once the interphaser was put into use, Lakesh hoped the Cerberus redoubt would revert to its original purpose—not a sanctuary for exiles or the headquarters of a resistance against the tyranny of the barons, but a facility dedicated to unfathoming the eternal mysteries of space and time.

Unfortunately, the second interphaser had been lost during a recent mission to Mars. Brigid Baptiste and

Brewster Philboyd had assiduously labored over the past few weeks to construct a third one, but with expanded capabilities. They had completed Interphaser Version 2.5 only in the past week or so.

"Not that it matters," Bry continued, "but I never trusted those damn interphasers anyway."

"Yes, yes, I know," replied Lakesh with a studied indifference. "You must have informed me of your mistrust about a dozen times."

Bry snorted in disdain and returned his attention to his computer station. Lakesh repressed a smile. He felt a little sorry for the man. Over the past couple of years, Bry had learned the hard way the meaning of Einstein's statement that "physics had lost its walls."

Einstein was obliquely calling to the attention of all physicists what philosophers had always known to be true, that the boundaries between space and time carried a large subjective element. Men either created these differences unconsciously for themselves and by their own power or that invisible creatures called gods created the differences so that men might live by them.

Quavell said in her lilting voice, "So we've finally ruled out either interference or a major malfunction in the transponders as the culprit?"

"I don't think we should rule out anything," stated a throaty female voice.

Turning, Lakesh saw Reba DeFore, the resident medic of the redoubt, striding up the aisle. "Neither do I," Lakesh replied.

DeFore came to Quavell's elbow and frowned at the icons representing Grant, Domi and Kane. "I knew it wasn't wise for Brigid to make the test-phase jump without Kane and Grant being here as backup. You should've stopped her."

Buxom and stocky, DeFore wore the one-piece white bodysuit common throughout the installation as something of a uniform. Her complexion was a deep, smooth bronze color which contrasted sharply with the uniform and her intricately braided, ash-blond hair.

Lakesh matched the woman's frown with one of his own. Their relationship was often awkward, despite the fact she was one of his first recruits. The tension between them had grown more pronounced over the past few months due to his association with the imperator.

"The interphaser was completed," Lakesh declared, his affected tone of weariness suggesting that the topic had been discussed more than once. "You know as well as I that I don't have the authority to forbid anyone to do or not to do anything here."

DeFore didn't react to his oblique and slightly bitter reference to the fact he had been unseated quite some time ago from his position as final arbiter of policy and plans.

"Dearest Brigid and friend Philboyd felt the time was ripe for a test," he went on. "This particular version of the interphaser was more of their creation than mine, so I couldn't have prevented them even on ownership grounds."

Mariah Falk spoke up from the enviro-ops console. "I think Philboyd talked Brigid into it. He was anxious to go on a mission without Kane being involved. She must've suspected that and asked Nora to go along as a chaperone."

Nonplussed, Lakesh turned to stare at the woman. "Surely you're joking."

"Of course I am," she replied with a laugh. Mariah, like Brewster Philboyd and Nora Pennick was an evacuee from the Manitius Moon base. An attractive woman in her late forties, her short chestnut-brown hair was threaded with gray. Deep creases curved out from either side of her nose to the corners of her mouth. Brown eyes bracketed by laugh lines gazed over at him, twinkling with amusement.

"Nora volunteered to go because she thought she might be of some use," Mariah said. "And because she was very curious about the workings of the interphaser."

DeFore wasn't amused. Crossing her arms over her breasts, she said stubbornly, "I just don't know why they couldn't have waited until Grant and Kane got back and not left us shorthanded."

Most of the people who lived in the Cerberus redoubt regardless of their specialized skills, acted in the capacity of support personnel. They worked rotating shifts, eight hours a day, seven days a week. For the most part, their work was the routine maintenance and monitoring of the installation's environmental systems, the satellite data feed and the security network.

However, everyone was given at least a superficial understanding of all the redoubt's systems so they could pinch-hit in times of emergency. Fortunately, such a time had never arrived but still and all, the installation was woefully understaffed. Their small numbers had been a source of constant worry to Lakesh, but with the arrival of the Moon base personnel, there was a larger pool of talent from which to draw.

Grant and Kane were exempt from cross training inasmuch as they served as the enforcement arm of Cerberus and undertook far and away the lion's share of the risks. On their downtime between missions they made sure all the ordnance in the armory was in good condition and occasionally tuned up the vehicles in the depot.

Brigid Baptiste, due to her eidetic memory, was the most exemplary member of the redoubt's permanent staff since she could step into any vacancy. However, her gifts were a two-edged sword inasmuch as those selfsame polymath skills made her an indispensable addition to away missions.

"There is another perspective," Quavell interjected quietly. "Kane, Grant and Domi could have postponed their mission until the first phase jump was completed."

DeFore cast her a slightly reproachful glance. "This isn't a game of Mother May I or a matter of who goes first. It's a matter of maintaining certain safety and security protocols. The Ragnarville mission was much more time sensitive."

She turned toward Bry. "Right?"

Almost reluctantly, he nodded. "Right. At least that was the evaluation based on what we heard over the voyeur channel."

Bry employed his personal vernacular for the eavesdropping system he had developed through the communications linkup with the Comsat. It was the same system and same satellite they used to track the telemetry from the subcutaneous transponders implanted within the Cerberus personnel.

Bry had worked on the system for a long time and finally established an undetectable method of patching into the wireless communications channels all of the baronies used. The success rate wasn't one hundred percent, but he had been able to listen in on a number of baron-sanctioned operations in the Outlands. He monitored different frequencies on a daily basis, but he paid particular attention to the one used by the Ragnarville Magistrate Division. Ever since Baron Ragnar's assassination, the ville had been in a state of flux.

Ten days before, Bry had learned of the abduction of Ayn Thoraldson by Boss Klaw. Kane didn't want to pass up the opportunity to strike an alliance with one of the largest and most organized Roamer gangs in the country and so he and Grant had concocted the plan to rescue Alf Thoraldson's daughter and return her to him, assuming Boss Klaw would be willing to strike a deal with them.

The outcome of the assumption and mission was still an unknown to the Cerberus personnel, but if nothing else, the away team had survived it. Lakesh feared that might be more than could be said for the test-jump team.

"All we really know at this juncture," Quavell stated stolidly, "is that three days ago our instruments registered Brigid, Dr. Philboyd and Dr. Pennick arriving in Southeast Asia, Cambodia to be precise. The transponder signals lasted long enough for us to lock in their locations before we stopped receiving them."

The calm, matter-of-fact manner in which the hybrid described the incident didn't hint at the frantic reactions and near panic that both Lakesh and Bry experienced when they watched the icons of the three people simply wink out. There had been no preliminary pixelization, no image flutter, no flashing. For one second the signals were received as strong and as steady as if the members of the jump team stood out in the corridor. In the next second, the icons vanished from the monitor screen as if they had never been displayed there at all.

Lakesh took a certain cold consolation in the fact that because the telemetry ceased simultaneously and so quickly, he doubted a sudden and unexpected death had befallen all three people at the same exact instant.

Bry hooked a thumb over his shoulder toward the Mercator map. "There are no indexed gateway units anywhere near Cambodia, so the only way to retrieve them is with another interphaser, which somebody would have to build…or with the TAV, which conveniently only Grant, Kane and Philboyd are rated to pilot."

"So what's the damn plan, then?" DeFore demanded with asperity.

"You can always sit here and find new ways to ascribe blame," Mariah said flatly. "You seem to be enjoying that."

DeFore swung toward her, eyes glinting in sudden anger, mouth opening to voice a profane rejoinder. Before she could speak, a sound like a fierce rushing wind emanated from the jump room. The noise climbed in pitch and rose in volume. Bright lights flashed behind the eight-foot-tall slabs of brown-hued armaglass, swelling in intensity and in tandem with the hurricane noise.

Lakesh spun around to consult the Mercator map. When he saw the flashing yellow bulb that represented Redoubt Tango he experienced a surge of relief so overwhelming his knees grew momentarily weak.

"Incoming jumpers," Bry reported unnecessarily.

Chapter 8

First the entire universe seemed to explode in a blaze of force. From the hyperdimensional nonspace through which they had been traveling, Kane, Domi and Grant fell through one bottomless abyss after another. There was a microinstant of nonexistence, then a sharp, wrenching shock and their senses returned.

Kane stared up at the pattern of hexagonal silver disks on the ceiling and realized the gateway transit had been successful.

Trying to focus through the last of the mist wisping over his eyes, Kane silently endured the nausea churning and rolling in his stomach. He knew if he waited it out, he wouldn't vomit, but it would take another minute to regain his emotional equilibrium. No human being, no matter how thoroughly briefed in advance, could expect to remain unflappable on a hyperdimensional trip through the mat-trans gateway.

By stepping into the armaglass-enclosed chamber, one second a person was in the relativistic here, surrounded by glowing mist, and in the next second, all eternity seemed to cave in. Perceptions changed, time jumped and for a heart-stopping instant, the cosmos at large seemed to stand still. Then the traveler was wherever the transmitter had been programmed to send him or her. Whatever else, a trip through the gateway was unsettling to the mind, to the nerves and to the soul itself, as Kane had personal reason to know.

Still, the overland journey from Ragnarville to the rendezvous near Redoubt Tango had been far more unpleasant. All four people were keyed-up, tense and on edge. Ayn refused to answer any questions about Vend or the Millennial Consortium. All she did was cry and tell whoever spoke to her to go to hell.

Kane couldn't really blame her, despite doubting the depth of her love for Vend. Regardless of whether the girl had truly been devoted to the man, the circumstances of his death evoked too many unpleasant memories of a similar incident well over a year ago, when he shot and killed a woman whom he perceived was threatening Brigid Baptiste. But in this case, although he felt he hadn't been given much choice in the matter, he also felt he had been maneuvered into acting as assassin.

The route to meet Alf Thoraldson was over exceptionally rugged terrain. Although Minnesota had been spared direct strikes during the nuclear conflagration of two centuries before, skydark had turned the state into a virtual deep-freeze covering a hundred thousand square miles. Redoubt Tango itself was located about thirty-five miles to the southwest of Ragnarville. Fittingly, the Tango installation had served as a research center into new forms and applications of cryonic science.

Thoraldson and his Roamers had agreed to wait for them a few miles north of the redoubt. The Roamers knew the installation existed but they didn't know how to overcome the security lock and enter the place. Grant and Kane felt it would be tactically unwise to let them in on the secret.

When the Sandcat topped a rise, Grant pointed out two fires burning in the postdawn dark, providing the only light on the dark plain. A group of people moved about between the fires, trying to keep themselves warm in the below-freezing temperatures. A makeshift corral had been erected near the site containing a remuda of about two dozen horses. An old pickup truck was parked near them.

At the sight and sound of the Sandcat's approach, no one in the camp ran, but the men all formed a fairly impressive skirmish line, brandishing a variety of weapons, from simple spears to rifles. Alf Thoraldson's Roamer gang wasn't quite as barbaric and wild-looking as some they had encountered, but they were a rough-looking crowd, nevertheless—bearded, wild-haired, wearing a variety of rags, furs and even cloaks crudely cut and stitched from carpets.

All of them had the same feral, predatory look as Le Loup Garou's band of Roamers Kane and Grant had caused to be buried beneath a C-4-triggered avalanche a couple of years before. Born into a raw, wild world, Roamers were accustomed to living on the edge of death. Grim necessity had taught them the skills to survive, even thrive in the postnuke environment. They may have been the great-great-great-grandchildren of civilized men and women, but they had no choice but to embrace lives of semibarbarism.

Thoraldson himself apparently set the fashion standard. A man of about the same height and build as Grant, he was a few years older. A dark blond beard clothed the lower half of his face. A medal of polished iron inscribed with indecipherable runes hung from his right ear, stretching out the lobe. His buckskin tunic and leggings were fringed and beaded. A long-handled tomahawk hung from his wide belt, and riding high on his right hip was a SIG-Sauer P-226 pistol.

Neither Grant nor Kane could even guess at where the man might have found such an unusual handgun. Dangling from a leather tie attached to the bottom of the holster were human scalps, the hair of all textures and colors. Kane counted seven of them.

As Grant and Kane disembarked, Thoraldson regarded them dispassionately with hooded, heavy-lidded eyes. His face and hands were covered by a network of old scar tracings, mementos from his lifelong war against nature, against hardship and the forces of the villes. His eyes held the pale gray color of ice, and their frostiness did not thaw even when Ayn climbed out of the Sandcat and approached him.

Without preamble, Thoraldson said in his gravelly voice, "You brought her back just like you said. You get to keep your heads."

Kane sensed Grant tensing up, due to apprehension or anger, but he chose not to respond, either verbally or with a show of weapons. Ayn stood before her father, head bowed but the expression on her face was anything but contrite.

Putting one blunt, crooked finger under her chin, Thoraldson lifted the girl's head so she stared directly into his eyes. They gazed at each other in silence for a long moment, then Thoraldson whipped his hand from beneath her chin and slapped her face. She went staggering toward a fire.

Kane lunged forward, catching the girl before she fell into it. Glaring at Thoraldson, he snapped, "I can't say much for the Roamer welcome-home customs."

The man's bewhiskered lips curled in a sneer. "Don't interfere, sec man."

Kane felt the back of his neck heating with a flush of anger. "Sec man" was an obsolete term dating back to preunification days when self-styled barons formed their own private armies to safeguard their territories. It was still applied to Magistrates in the far hinterlands beyond the villes, mainly by Roamers and Farers.

"Don't give me orders, you lying slag-ass bastard," he shot back.

Ayn Thoraldson jerked away from Kane's touch as if his hands contaminated her. Rubbing the reddened side of her face, she stumbled toward a knot of people. A middle-aged woman reached out for her, enfolding her in her arms and hustling her away.

"What do you mean by calling me a liar?" Thoraldson demanded. "Speak up!"

It required a conscious effort of will on Kane's part to keep from drawing his pistol and planting a bullet in the man's forehead. He might not have been a Magistrate any longer, but his ingrained Mag pride was offended by the Roamer's arrogance. He felt the old Magistrate sense of righteous superiority rise up in him. "Don't call me a sec man," he shot back.

Thoraldson's frosty eyes darted from Kane to Grant. Both of them kept their weapons leathered but the Roamer chieftain knew such a condition could be reversed in an eye blink.

He nodded brusquely. "Fair enough. But you called me a liar."

"Actually," Kane replied smoothly, "my exact words were 'lying slag-ass bastard.' But I suppose we can split the difference since you probably know who your daddy was."

Thoraldson scowled. "You have any idea of how close to death you are?" His hand brushed the scalps hanging from his pistol's holster.

"Actually," Kane said again, "I think that should be *my* line."

He gestured with his left hand, and the topside bubble turret of the Sandcat revolved, the perforated barrel of one of the big USMG-73s aligning itself with Thoraldson's upper body. Domi's white-haired head was barely visible behind the armaglass.

Thoraldson's eyes flickered briefly with surprise, then anger which was quickly veiled. Hooking his thumbs into his belt, he rocked lightly on the balls of his feet. In a more relaxed tone, he said, "So Ayn told you she hadn't been kidnapped."

"And that she was married," Grant put in.

"What did that little mucksucker Vend have to say for himself?" Thoraldson asked contemptuously.

"Not much," Kane answered. "I shot and killed him before we could talk."

Thoraldson snorted out a laugh. "The little prick is dead? Thanks, Kane—you're back in my good graces again."

In a rumbling, lionlike growl of menace, Grant said, "But you top *our* shit-list, shit-head. What's the real story?"

Thoraldson shrugged. "The Millennial Consortium approached me about a year ago, wanting my permission to dig around in some old caves and Indian mounds. Their barter was good, so I let 'em. Then one of 'em got too friendly with Ayn."

"Vend," Kane stated.

"Vend," Alf Thoraldson confirmed. "I told the kid's section chief, a hardcase named Snow, that the deal was off and to haul ass out of here."

"But instead," Grant ventured, "Vend hauled ass to Ragnarville with Ayn. The consortium told you that unless you left them alone, you'd never see her again."

Thoraldson nodded. "That's about the general shape and size of it. I had my own plans for the girl. I promised her hand in marriage to old Demero. She didn't like the idea and that's why she ran off with Vend."

"Who's old Demero?" Kane asked.

"Chief of the Thief River Falls Roamers. Ayn's been betrothed to him since she was eight."

Kane shook his head in disgust. "So you just used us so we'd fetch her back against her will and arrange for a pretty terminal annulment from Vend. My 'lying slag-ass bastard' comment still stands...you lying slag-ass bastard."

Thoraldson's eyes flashed with sudden fury. Slapping his broad chest with a hand, he roared, "My daughter ain't got no right to do what she done! As for usin' you to bring her back—what the fuck are you plannin' for me and mine but to use us?"

Kane struggled to tamp down his own rising rage. "To act as intermediaries, not as assassins, that's what the fuck we're planning."

"Which I already took care of with old Demero," Thoraldson countered harshly. "Now he owes you, too. Everybody got what they wanted, so you got no call to get on the muscle with me."

Kane bit back a profane comeback, realizing with a sickening sense of humiliation that the Roamer chieftain was right. Even though he and his friends had been played and used as pawns, the mission objective had been reached.

Repressing a sigh, he asked, "Where are the millennialists operating?"

Thoraldson gestured vaguely southward. "Some place called Carver's Cave."

"What are they doing there?" Grant asked.

"I don't know," Thoraldson replied with gruff impatience, as if the matter were of no importance. "They didn't tell me. Paid me not to ask. So what about our own business? What do you want my clan to do?"

Kane inhaled a deep breath, winching slightly as the chill air bit at his lips. "Spread the word among all the Roamer clans. Cerberus wants to be afforded safe passage through all of their territories."

Bushy brows knitting at the bridge of his nose, Alf Thoraldson demanded, "What the hell does that mean?"

Flatly, Grant replied, "It means that if Roamers see strangers in their territories, particularly if they're in vehicles, not to attack them. If they identify themselves as being from Cerberus, then they're to be allowed to pass unmolested."

Thoraldson's eyebrows did not lift but he grunted. "Bargain."

He thrust out his right hand, and after a thoughtful

few seconds, Kane took it, stoically enduring the painful crushing pressure the Roamer chief applied to it. He took Grant's hand and Kane saw him grimace when he tried the same trick and instead had it done to him.

Thoraldson swept his frosty gaze over Kane and Grant and said simply, "You have my word."

Kane didn't ask him further questions about the Millennial Consortium or Carver's Cave. He was by now accustomed to the frustration of dealing with mysteries on an almost daily basis.

One mystery that had never been solved was how someone could begin a mat-trans journey standing up and almost always end it by lying on their back. Kane turned his head to look at the armaglass walls. These were colored a rich earth-brown tone, not red, so he knew the jump from Redoubt Tango was successful. No matter how many gateway transits he had made in the past two-plus years, he was always pleasantly surprised when he realized he was still alive and whole.

Intellectually, he knew the mat-trans energies transformed organic and inorganic matter to digital information, transmitted it through a hyperdimensional quantum path and reassembled it in a receiver unit. Emotionally, the experience felt like a fleeting brush with death, or worse than death. It was nonexistence, at least for a nanosecond of time. Often the only way a jumper could be sure a transit had been initiated at all was by the color of the armaglass walls.

All of the official Cerberus gateway units in mat-trans network were color-coded so authorized jumpers could tell at a glance into which redoubt they had materialized.

Despite the fact it seemed an inefficient method of

differentiating one installation from another, only personnel holding color-coded security clearances were allowed to make use of the system. Inasmuch as their use was restricted to a select few of the units, it was fairly easy for them to memorize which color designated what redoubt.

Domi and Grant stirred on the floor plates as Kane pushed himself up, leaning against the wall. Grant levered himself to his feet, swaying on unsteady legs before straightening. He extended a hand to Domi, who affected not to notice it as she rose.

"I hope Brigid has gotten the new interphaser working," she said. "Traveling by that spoils you for the mat-trans."

When Grant snorted, she muttered, "Far as I'm concerned, anyhow."

Kane reached for the wedge-shaped handle of the door. "She said it was ready to be tested before we left."

The heavy slab of armaglass swung open on counterbalanced hinges, and Kane stepped down from the elevated platform—and stared directly into the hollow bore of a subgun held by Lakesh.

Chapter 9

The weapon Lakesh sighted down was one of the small SA-80 subguns from the armory. All of the Cerberus exiles were required to become reasonably proficient with firearms, and the lightweight "point and shoot" subguns were the easiest for the firearm challenged to handle.

He lowered the SA-80 immediately upon recognizing the three people. They weren't surprised to be greeted by a gun—after the mad Maccan's murderous incursion into the redoubt, it had become standard protocol to have an armed guard standing by during a gateway materialization.

Domi stepped down from the elevated platform and embraced Lakesh tightly. He hugged her in return, placing the SA-80 on the long table which served as the ready room's sole piece of furniture.

"Missed you," she whispered.

"Likewise, darlingest one," he replied softly. He stroked the back of her head, then his nose wrinkled. "You smell like smoke…and is your hair burned?"

The girl pushed away from him, touching with the browned tips of her hair. Laughingly, she answered, "Got a little singed in Ragnarville."

"Both of us did," Grant stated flatly, his expression neutral.

Lakesh's eyes widened and he took Domi by the shoulders, turning her this way and that, examining her. "You're not hurt, are you?"

"No," declared Kane in as flat a tone as the one Grant had adopted, "*we're* not."

Glancing his way, Lakesh smiled crookedly at Kane's sarcasm. "What was the outcome of the mission, friend Kane?"

Kane shrugged out of his jacket. "We broke even, as usual. Learned a few interesting tidbits, but other than that, we had no big wins, no big losses."

As they started toward the operations center, Lakesh said quietly, "We might be facing rather big losses here."

The comment stopped Grant and Kane in their tracks. They turned to face Lakesh, eyes quizzical and troubled. "What do you mean by that?" Grant asked.

Sighing, Lakesh tugged at his long nose. "Brigid, Brewster Philboyd and Nora Pennick are missing."

"Missing?" Grant echoed. "From where and how?"

"From here," Lakesh answered. "But we know where they were three days ago."

Kane swung on Lakesh. "Three days? They've been missing for *three* days?"

Lakesh only nodded.

"Where were they three days ago?" Grant demanded.

"Cambodia."

For a long, tense tick of time, no one spoke. Then Grant half snarled in disbelief, "*Cambodia?* How the hell did they get there?"

"The interphaser," Lakesh replied. "Brigid and Brewster felt the time was past for a test. They programmed an unindexed set of Parallax Point coordinates into its targeting computer, then left from here—" he nodded toward the mat-trans chamber "—and materialized in Cambodia. Within a minute or so, the transponder signals simply stopped."

"Stopped," Grant repeated, a dangerous, challenging edge to his voice. "Stopped how? Do you mean their life signs ceased?"

"We don't think so," DeFore announced from the doorway between the ready room and the command center. "The biolink readings indicated the three of them were in perfect health. No stress readings, no spikes in heart rate or blood pressure. One second we received the telemetry strong and clear and in the next second—" she snapped the fingers of her right hand "—poof. Gone."

Kane arched his eyebrows at the medic, not allowing the cold fingers of dread closing around his heart to be evident in his voice. "They just ceased transmitting or was our ability to receive the signals somehow impaired?"

Lakesh shook his head. "It was more like a jar had been dropped over them, cutting off the transmissions of all three people all at the same time. There was no preliminary ebbing or a degradation in the strength of the signal."

"Where's Cambodia?" Domi asked, lines of worry creasing her forehead.

"Southeast Asia," Lakesh said. "Halfway around the world from here."

Domi made a wordless exclamation of angry confusion. "Why they go there?"

Under stress, the girl reverted to the abbreviated pattern of Outland speech.

"To test the Parallax Points data," Lakesh told her

soothingly. "Benchmarking, like we've been doing for the past few months."

"And you're sure the new interphaser didn't malfunction?" Grant inquired. "Like materializing them inside of a mountain?"

Lakesh opened his mouth to reply, closed it, then shook his head in frustration. "I'm not sure of anything."

Kane said nothing, but he knew that an analogical computer built into the interphaser automatically scanned and selected vortex nodes above solid ground. The device had worked fine on all their previous phase transits—they had never materialized either in a lake or an ocean or underground.

Months before, he, Brigid and Grant had undergone several weeks of hard training in the use of the second version of the interphaser on short hops, selecting vortex points near the redoubt. Near at least in the sense that if they couldn't make the return trip through a quantum channel they could conceivably walk back to the installation.

Before the device had been destroyed on Mars, they began to make jumps very afield from Cerberus, to the Moon and to the Australian outback. Many details of exactly how the machine worked that remained mysteries to Kane, but he preferred to leave the brain-battering intricacies of quantum physics to Lakesh and Brigid.

Grant was not so patient with Lakesh's admission that he had no definitive answer whether the interphaser could have been the culprit behind the jump team's disappearance. Normally phlegmatic in the face of adversity, the big man exuded agitation like an aura of static electricity.

Harshly, he declared, "You made the damn thing in

the first place, Lakesh, just like you made the damn mattrans units when you ran Project Cerberus. You were the first human being who was ever transmitted by the things. If you don't know everything about matter transmission and wormholes, then who the hell would?"

Lakesh glared at him, swallowing down his anger. Although the aim of Project Cerberus was the conversion of matter to energy and back again by reducing organic and inorganic substances to encoded information, the primary stumbling block to actually achieving the goal was the sheer quantity of information that had to be encoded.

Scientists had labored over a way to make this possible for nearly fifty years, financed by black funds funneled away from other government projects. Project Cerberus, like all the other Totality Concept researches, was classified above top secret. A few high government officials knew it existed, as did members of the Joint Chiefs of Staff of the military. The secrecy was believed to be more than important; it was considered to be almost a religion.

After much research, matter transmission had been found to be absolutely impossible to achieve by the employment of relativistic physics. Only quantum physics, coupled with quantum mechanics, had made it work beyond a couple of prototypes which transported steel balls only a few feet across a room. But even those crude early models could not have functioned at all without the basic components which predated the Totality Concept.

Lakesh experienced a scientific and metaphysical epiphany and made the breakthrough. Under his guidance, the quantum interphase mat-trans inducers opened a rift in the hyperdimensional quantum stream, between a relativistic here and there. The Cerberus technology did more than beam matter from one spot in linear space to another. It reduced organic and inorganic material to digital information and transmitted it along hyperdimensional pathways on a carrier wave.

In 1989, Lakesh had been the first successful long-distance matter transfer of a human subject, traveling a hundred yards from a prototype gateway chamber to a receiving booth. That initial success was replicated many times, and with the replication came the modifications and improvements of the quantum interphase mat-trans inducers, reaching the point where they were manufactured in modular form.

"As I explained to you more than once," Lakesh bit out, "the interphaser is not a junior, portable version of a mat-trans. The interphaser interacts with the energy within a naturally occurring vortex node and initiates a temporary overlapping of two dimensions. The vortex becomes an intersection point, a discontinuous quantum jump, beyond relativistic space-time."

Kane nodded. "And one of those discontinuous quantum jumps dropped three of our people in Cambodia. Can you at least give us an idea of *where* in Cambodia they might be found?"

Lakesh waved toward Bry at the master ops console. "That's what we've been trying to ascertain for days. Mr. Bry is presently coaxing the Vela to transmit images from the vicinity of the great lake of Tonle Sap."

"Not just coaxing," Bry called from the adjoining room. "Got them."

"Why do you think they ended up there?" Grant asked brusquely, pushing past Lakesh and DeFore and entering the central control complex.

Lakesh frowned at the big man's back. "We were able to correlate their biolink telemetry with the GPS aboard the Comsat, which was then bounced over to the Vela. Besides, it's the logical destination."

"How so?" Kane inquired, following Grant into the operations center.

Lakesh trailed after him. "Because of the Angkor temple city. Almost all holy sites of the ancient world were constructed at the intersection points of geomantic energy...vortex nodes."

Kane nodded in recollection. "Right. Not that I understand it, but I remember you talking about it."

They joined Grant at the main ops console, standing behind Bry. Kane nodded to Quavell and Mariah as he entered, although he felt the usual quiver of unease whenever he was in Quavell's company, under the scrutiny of her huge blue eyes, as chillingly placid as the surface of a frozen lake.

Bry's skinny fingers played over the keyboard, inputting a numerical sequence. Across the right side of the screen scrolled a constant stream of figures, symbols and numbers. The screen was dark, yet it swarmed with little points and pixels of brightness. Then, near the bottom edge a curving sweep of blue-green began to appear. Triumphantly, he announced, "They said it couldn't be done, but I done did it. Ladies and gentlemen, I give you Cambodia."

Kane and Grant exchanged weary glances and head shakes. Lakesh repressed a smile. No one could really blame the man for preening a little. After all, it was his year's worth of hard work—as well many failures—that allowed Cerberus to at long last gain control of the two still functioning satellites in Earth orbit.

Although most satellites had been little more than free-floating scrap metal for well over a century, Cerberus had always possessed the proper electronic ears and eyes to receive the transmissions from at least two them. One was of the Vela reconnaissance class which carried narrow-band multispectral scanners. It could detect the electromagnetic radiation reflected by every object on Earth, including subsurface geomagnetic waves. The scanner was tied into an extremely high resolution photographic relay system.

The other satellite to which the redoubt was uplinked was a Comsat, which for many months was used primarily to keep track of Cerberus personnel by their subcutaneous transponders when they were out in the field. Everyone in the installation had been injected with the transponders, which transmitted heart rate, respiration, blood count and brain-wave patterns. Based on organic nanotechnology, the transponder was a nonharmful radioactive chemical which bound itself to an individual's glucose and the middle layers of the epidermis.

The telemetric signal was relayed to the redoubt by the Comsat, and directed down to the redoubt's hidden antenna array on the mountain peak, which in turn transferred it to the Cerberus computer systems.

Bry manipulated the computer's mouse, and the image transmitted from the Vela suddenly dominated the big screen. The view tightened and more details began to show. A low mountain range broke the far horizon and a vast rain forest appeared as a sea of undulating greenery surrounding the dark oval of an immense body of water. The banks were crowded with rattan palms and the bone-white trunks of trees. Here and there on its surface were the oblong shapes of boats, and what appeared to be villages were scattered along the banks.

"Tonle Sap," Lakesh said quietly. "In the summer, excess water from the Mekong River backs up into the lake which expands to cover an area larger than Utah's great Salt Lake. The trees are palmaceae, cypress and fromager."

Eyeing the image on the screen, Kane reflected that the jungle appeared to cover thousands of square miles with a brooding wilderness. Kane found the image inexplicably ominous.

That sense grew more pronounced when he saw ruins rising above the treetops. He knew instantly the ruins were relics of another, forgotten age predating the nukecaust. They thrust jagged pinnacles into the sky from the squarely cut lines of walled enclosures. For many miles the complex of ruins stretched in a breathtaking sweep of intricately carved esplanades, megalithic walls and heaps of tumbledown masonry.

In midst of the jungle terrain, the towers rose like the masts of buried sailing ships. The numbers in the measurement window gave the height of the satellite image as twenty thousand feet.

"The region was known as Phnom Kuleh," Lakesh announced in a voice softened by awe. "The Angkor plain and one of the wonders of the predark world."

Leaning over Bry's shoulder, Lakesh worked the

keys and the image on the screen changed. The jungle country leaped toward them. "I'll see if we can't get a better shot of Angkor Wat, the most magnificent of the structures."

The perspective on the screen changed, rushing downward, through a sky flecked with scraps of white clouds. The plummet halted, over a place that was flat and bare, but held a complex of stone buildings in the center of it. The range readout gave the altitude as a little over five thousand feet.

The image was blurred, slightly out of focus, but Kane saw a series of small outlying constructions arranged in a circle around the dark bulk of a larger building. A high wall reared out of the foliage surrounding a looming, sprawling black structure that resembled a half-squashed ziggurat. Shadowy, terraced pinnacles rose from all four corners.

"That's a huge place," Grant murmured.

"Angkor Wat," Lakesh said. "The summit of Khmer architectural achievement. It's actually a temple-tomb, erected in the twelfth century, built on the foundation of far older structures—"

He broke off and leaned forward, squinting at the screen. "What's going on here?"

A shimmering effect, as of heat waves rising from a sunbaked road, seemed to ripple out from the tops of the towers. The shimmer expanded until it seemed to form a canopy over the gargantuan complex.

By now, Domi, DeFore, Quavell and Mariah Falk had all gathered around the monitor screen, gazing at the images with keen interest. Bry reached for the mouse, saying, "Let me try to clean up the picture."

He tapped the button, but the blurry quality seemed to increase. "Other way," Lakesh told him absently.

"I know how to do this," Bry retorted waspishly.

Kane caught a suggestion of movement around the structures, of people moving to and fro. Suddenly, shades of bright color bloomed up from the central structure like the petals of an unimaginably huge flower. Whorls of red, white, yellow, green, cyan, blue and even violet spread out across the ruins, almost as if they were spewed from the towers.

The palette of colors almost completely filled the image area of the monitor screen. The picture fluttered, black jagged lines shooting through it. Then it dissolved in a burst of pixels.

"Dammit, Donald," DeFore snapped sharply. "What've you done?"

"Nothing!" Bry countered defensively, working both the mouse and keyboard in tandem. "We lost the signal."

Quavell said quietly, "The pattern suggests a burst of electromagnetic radiation. It blinded the satellite."

Lakesh frowned, straightening. "I don't believe I've ever seen anything quite like that before."

"The timing seems suspiciously convenient," Mariah commented dourly.

Lakesh nodded. "I concur. Mr. Bry, give us a playback."

Bry dutifully complied with request. Lakesh studied the whorls and waves of color spreading up from the structures and said, "There's definitely a pattern there."

"What kind?" Kane asked.

"What's known in earth-energy studies as *cursus,* after the Latin for 'racecourse.'"

"And what does that mean?" Grant demanded impatiently.

Still gazing fixedly at the screen, Lakesh answered, "Sacred architecture around the world—cathedrals, temples, mosques, stupas, pagodas—is designed to join Heaven and Earth. The great Asian sites of Borobadur in Indonesia and the once magnificent Nalanda University in India are three-dimensional mandalas of the four directions, and monumental examples of joining Heaven and Earth by design."

"Geomancy," Quavell said.

Lakesh turned toward her. "Exactly. As a form of study, geomancy has its roots in the Temple of Solomon and was developed by the Greek mystery schoolteachers over three thousand years ago. The knowledge and skills were used in the construction of the great cathedrals in Europe during the Middle Ages. It was then regarded as superstition by the church administration and it all but disappeared."

Mariah Falk ventured, "I thought the whole study of channeling earth energies, ley lines and so forth was pretty much discredited by physical scientists by the end of the twentieth century."

Lakesh shook his head. "Not so much discredited as reevaluated. The scientists who studied the phenomenon concluded that the ancient observations about grid lines and *cursuses* were explained to the dominant cultures via myths…or scholarly pursuits such as sacred geometry. Ancient knowledge from past civilizations may have seemed like superstition to many people in later civilizations, but is this superstition just logic interpreted by different senses that most people don't use today? As with all specialist studies. they have their experts who contribute much to the understanding of any particular discipline. Lao Tse and Pythagoras immediately spring to mind."

"What springs to *my* mind," Kane said, a steel edge in his voice, "is what any of this has to do with the disappearance of our people—and how we can get them back."

Lakesh gave him a fleeting, jittery smile. "I need some time to collect my thoughts on that matter. If you and friend Grant would care to clean up and rest a bit, perhaps have a bite to eat, then join me back here in an hour, I might be able to offer a few suggestions."

Chapter 10

Kane turned on the faucet and a spray of water jetted from the nozzle. He adjusted the showerhead to shoot out a needlelike rain.

When the water temperature was almost too hot to tolerate, he stepped into the cubicle. He used a liquid-soap dispenser affixed to the wall to work a lather all over his body, even making a shampoo of it for his hair. Although his left arm and hip bore blue-black contusions from the bullet strikes, they weren't particularly painful.

The bathroom filled quickly with billowing clouds of steam, and he contented himself with luxuriating beneath the driving jets of hot water, letting them soothe the muscle ache. He focused on that, not wanting to think about might what befall Brigid, Philboyd and Nora. After a few minutes he adjusted the faucet, and streams of cold, clear water gushed down and rinsed the soap from his body.

He watched the water drain away, down into a natural limestone filtration system built under the redoubt. Once it passed through and the chemicals leached out, the water was routed back into the complex's water supply. He wished his worries could drain away so easily.

Stepping out of the shower, Kane wiped the condensation from the mirror and critically eyed the reflection staring sullenly back at him. It was a face that had once laughed a lot, had liked carousing with his fellow Mags and had gazed out at the world with prideful eyes.

The face had forgotten all those things now, the memories of his youth subsumed by the history of violence scattered all over his lean, long-muscled body. He saw the stellate scars of bullet punctures, the thin and jagged white lines of edged steel that had sliced into his flesh. Turning, he looked at the swirling weal of a long-ago burn between his shoulder blades. It was from an injury he had sustained in the Black Gobi two years before, when he rescued Brigid from the Tushe Gun's genetic mingler.

He had shielded her unconscious body from the mingler's wild energy discharges with his own. Only the tough, Kevlar-weave coat he'd worn at the time saved his life. Brigid had suffered wounds of her own, far subtler and emotionally devastating. Her exposure to the energy of the mingler and to an unknown wavelength of radiation had rendered her barren.

Toweling his hair and face dry, he entered the bedroom and took a pair of jeans and a black T-shirt from the closet. They were articles of predark clothing he had found hermetically sealed in one of the storage rooms. He preferred them to the bodysuits. He tried to maintain a patient, calm manner as he walked around his quarters and dressed, hoping he would actually begin to feel that way.

Fear for Brigid's safety filled his mind, and his stomach slipped sideways. He sat on the edge of the bed, breathing deeply, closing his eyes and striving to achieve the "Mag mind." It was a technique that emptied his consciousness of all nonessentials and allowed his instincts to rise to the fore. He'd been trained to do it while a Cobaltville Magistrate and had called on it to handle the pain of injuries or deal with physical exhaustion. But now he couldn't reach it. His concentration was scattered in all directions.

Kane wasn't sure if it was due to the nagging pains of the injuries inflicted by the bullets, or whether he was simply emotionally drained. When he closed his eyes, he kept seeing Ayn Thoraldson's husband, Vend, lying dead and bloodied on the floor, like a vid tape on continuous replay.

Intellectually he accepted the fact that the young man had given him no choice, but emotionally was a different matter altogether. He struggled with the humiliating knowledge he had been manipulated by Alf Thoraldson, used as a pawn to carry out a vengeful, vindictive agenda. He couldn't help but wonder how Brigid would have analyzed the situation if she'd been along.

He shook his head, battling the tentacles of dread and panic that threatened to engulf his reason. Most of the time he shied away from scrutinizing his feelings for Brigid Baptiste. They were as deep as they were complicated, and the unspoken bond between them was an issue neither one discussed, even after all this time.

From the very first time he met her he was affected by the energy Brigid radiated, a force intangible, yet one that triggered a melancholy longing in his soul. That strange, sad longing only deepened after a bout of jump sickness both of them suffered during a mat-trans jump to Russia. The main symptoms of jump sickness were vivid, almost real hallucinations.

He and Brigid had shared the same hallucination, but both knew on a visceral, primal level it hadn't been gateway-transit-triggered delirium, but a revelation that they were joined by chains of fate, their destinies linked. Images from that vision spun in the depths of his memory. He saw Baptiste, a beautiful captive dragged at the stirrup of a Norman lord's horse and as he tried to cut her free, he was struck down by the bone-shattering fall of spiked mace.

They never spoke of it, though Kane often wondered if that spiritual bond was the primary reason he had sacrificed everything he had attained as a Magistrate to save her from execution. The possibility confused him, made him feel defensive and insecure. That insecurity was one reason he always addressed her as Baptiste, almost never by her first name so as to maintain a certain formal distance between them. But that distance shrank every day.

During the op to the British Isles, when Kane had protested to Morrigan that there was nothing between him and Brigid, the Irish telepath had laughed at him. She'd said, "Oh, yes, there is. Between you two, there is much to forgive, much to understand. Much to live through. Always together…she is your *anam-chara*."

In ancient Gaelic, Kane learned, *anam-chara* meant "soul friend."

He wasn't sure if believed that, but he knew he always felt comfortable with Brigid Baptiste, despite their many quarrels. He was at ease with her in a way that was similar, yet markedly different than his relationship with

Grant. He found her intelligence, her iron resolve, her wellspring of compassion and the way she had always refused to be intimidated by him not just stimulating but inspiring. She was a complete person, her heart, mind and spirit balanced and demanding of respect.

Kane found the thought of losing that person too horrifying to contemplate, not just because of the vacuum she would leave in the Cerberus personnel, but because of the void her absence would leave in his soul. The memory of the kiss he'd given her when they'd taken the jump back in time to the eve of the nukecaust drifted across his mind. It was no surprise that he should remember the kiss, but the intensity of emotion associated with it shook him.

He also recalled with startling clarity what the Sister Fand of the third lost Earth had whispered to him about Brigid Baptiste: "The lady is your saving grace. Trust the bond that belongs between you. The gift of the *anam-chara* is strong. She protects you from damnation—she is your credential."

Although most, if not all the details of his visits to the three parallel planes of reality were now misty fragments, he remembered those words as if they'd been deliberately imprinted in his mind.

Kane shook his head furiously to drive out the recollections of the past so he could focus on the present. He had seen Brigid injured before, he argued with himself. She had even gone missing and been imprisoned in the past. But she had always recovered, or escaped or been rescued.

Brigid Baptiste was one of the toughest human beings he had ever met. For a woman who had been trained to be an academic, an archivist, and had never strayed more than ten miles from the sheltering walls of Cobaltville, her resiliency and resourcefulness never failed to impress him. Over the past couple of years, she had left her tracks in the most distant and alien of climes and breasted very deep, very dangerous waters.

Both he and Brigid had come a very long way, in distances that couldn't be measured in mere miles, from the night of their first meeting in the residential Enclaves of Cobaltville. As a sixteen-year veteran of the Magistrate Division, Kane was accustomed to danger and hardship, but it was nothing compared to what he, Brigid and Grant had exposed themselves to since their exile.

Kane propped his chin on his fist, memory skittering back to a day, a little over two years ago, when he had sat in the same place and contemplated putting the bore of his Sin Eater to his head. Of course, he had been suffering from a severe case of shock, having just escaped Cobaltville, learned the back story of the nukecaust and been introduced to Balam, a representative of the so-called Archon Directorate. His entire life and belief system had been revealed as a lie, a construct, a fabrication. He and Grant were left with two options—die or reinvent themselves.

Reinvention of the human identity was something that had never occurred to him before. Like Grant, he had been a Magistrate, sanctioned both legally and spiritually to enforce the laws of the barons and arrest the flood tide of chaos by any means necessary.

Though he had often entertained doubts about his life path, his identity seemed inviolate. It took him months to understand and finally accept that his identity had derived from his role as a Mag and both were lost to him forever. What took its place was forged in the crucible of horror, life risk, self-discovery and a commitment to a cause greater than mere physical survival.

A knock sounded at his door, a familiar three-sequence rap, and he repressed a groan. He called, "It's open, Domi."

The girl pushed open the door and strolled in, her petite form swathed in a white terry-cloth robe. She had made an effort to scrub away the smoke smudges and soot from her face. The angry red streaks of burns showed brightly against her hands and right cheek. They were more unsightly than serious. If not for the pallor of her complexion, they probably would have been barely visible.

Without preamble Domi said, "Need to talk to you. And my shower isn't working."

Kane gestured to the bathroom. "Help yourself."

Domi walked in and after a moment, he heard the sound of a shower.

"Hey," she called out.

Kane went to the doorway and stood. Domi stepped under the water flowing from the showerhead, picking up a sponge and soap. His eyes dwelt on her compact, perfectly proportioned body. He had never known a woman so unconscious of her body. She had a way of wearing nudity as if it were clothes. Despite the scars marring the pearly perfection of her skin, particularly the one shaped like a starburst on her right shoulder, Domi was beautiful in a wild way, mustang beautiful.

Her body was a liquid, symmetrical flow of curving lines, with small, pert breasts rising to sharp nipples, and a flat, hard-muscled stomach extending down to the flare of her hips.

He had seen her naked before—the entire redoubt had, particularly during her first few weeks at Cerberus. The outlander girl wasn't accustomed to wearing clothes unless temperatures demanded them, and then only the skimpiest concessions to weather, not modesty.

"You'll be taking a Manta to that Cambodia place?" she asked.

Kane shrugged, leaning against the door frame, crossing his arms over his chest. "Flying there is the most efficient way. Walking around the Pacific seems a little impractical."

Domi didn't smile. "You expect Grant to go with you?"

Kane blinked at her, realizing that he hadn't thought that far ahead. "I doubt either one of us would fit in the jump seat we installed," he replied. "I suppose I could ask him if he wants to try it."

"I wish you wouldn't," she stated.

Kane felt his eyebrows knit in a frown. "Why not?"

Domi titled her head back and let the water flow down over her body. "Because you know he'll say yes, no matter what."

Kane gazed at her in silence for a moment. He felt puzzled by her comment and he let that be detectable in his tone. "Yes, I'm sure he will. What else would he do?"

"Go back to New Edo and Shizuka for a little bit of time. They've been separated for quite a while now."

"They've been apart longer than this before," Kane pointed out.

Domi turned off the shower, stepped out and dried herself with a big bath towel. She shook her head, sighed and nibbled at her underlip. Her white lashes, looking like pine needles dusted with snow, veiled her eyes.

"What?" he prodded.

In a desperate burst, Domi said, "Got a bad feeling. Something's on the wind—something nasty is on its way. Grant already damn near died saving my life from the fire. No point in him pushing his luck again until he has no choice. He should spend some time with Shizuka. That's what he was hoping to do when we got back."

Kane eyed her challengingly. "Did he tell you that?"

She shrugged into her robe and pushed past him, leaving the bathroom. "He didn't need to. I could tell by how upset he got when Lakesh told him what happened. Take me with you instead."

Kane realized Domi spoke the truth. Grant's reaction to the news of the missing people was definitely extreme for him. Rather than agree with her, he asked bluntly, "Wouldn't you rather stay here with Lakesh? Haven't you missed him?"

Domi gestured in the direction of the command center. "My life, your life, Lakesh's life is all part of Cerberus. Grant's life is following a different path now. It's not fair to keep pulling him back to Cerberus if he wants—needs—to go someplace else. I'll go with you, not him."

He felt surprised by Domi's compassion toward Grant and experienced a quiver of unease by her readiness to accompany him into dark territory. A year or so ago during a mission to Utah, he and Domi had shared a room and she made it clear she wouldn't be averse to sharing more than that with him. He had dashed cold water on her amorous advance by reminding her of her devotion to Grant. That had been the end of it, and he'd never mentioned the incident to anyone, not to Brigid and certainly not to Grant.

Not too long ago on Thunder Isle, after the two of them barely escaped the depredations of a crazed Daspletosaurus, Domi had expressed a desire for him. At the time, he had attributed her arousal to a natural jubilation they had survived the carnosaur's attack. He hadn't followed up on her invitation, if she had extended one.

Now he wondered if he should have accepted it. He remembered Domi's wild behavior when she believed Grant had rejected her love in favor of Shizuka. Without Grant as the mitigating influence, the authority figure, what little self-restraint the girl ever practiced was completely discarded. All her bottled-up passions were unleashed, but turned from love to violence.

Her shame, her mad desire for vicarious revenge against Grant, had been unbottled during the mission to Area 51 and set in motion a dramatic sequence of events, the fallout of which Cerberus was still dealing with. The presence of the pregnant Quavell was a case in point.

Kane presumed that since Domi and Lakesh had entered into an apparently exclusive relationship, she had recovered from her heartbreak over losing Grant to Shizuka and the resentment she had harbored against the man. Although Grant had never treated her badly, certainly never abused her physically or emotionally, she felt she had never earned his respect—or his love. Since hoping to one day gain his love was no longer a mitigating influence on her behavior, Domi had, for a couple of months, discarded the little self-restraint she had practiced in the past. Grant ceased to be an authority figure in her mind.

But Kane also knew the depth of Grant's love for the girl, and the guilt he felt about treating her as less than a fully-developed human being, and more as an empty-headed stereotype. In many ways, guilt was the whole foundation of the ville society.

For the past ninety-plus years, it was beaten into the descendants of the survivors of the nukecaust that when judgment day arrived, humanity was rightly punished. Therefore, people were encouraged to tolerate, even welcome, a world of unremitting ordeals, conflict and death, because humanity had ruined the world; therefore the punishment was deserved.

Love among humans was the hardest bond to break, so people were conditioned to believe that since all humans were intrinsically evil, to love another one was to love evil. That way, all human beings forever remained strangers to one another.

Both Kane and Grant had been conditioned to believe that, as they had so many other spurious beliefs. But he recalled what Domi had said to him in Area 51: "You and Grant didn't stay what you were. I don't have to stay what I am."

Nor had she. She apparently admired the way Grant and Shizuka were still determined to spend a couple of days together a month, despite their respective duties, which kept them apart most of the time.

Until just a few weeks ago, it had been Grant's intent to leave Cerberus altogether and live in the little island monarchy of New Edo with Shizuka, particularly after the arrival of the Manitius Base personnel and

Quavell. But after being captured and tortured by the sadistic Baroness Beausoliel, Grant realized the struggle remained essentially the same; there were just new players on the field.

The war itself would go on and would never end, unless he took an active hand in it, regardless of his love for Shizuka and Domi's apparent devotion to Lakesh—a concept Kane still found a little disconcerting. However, he was in no position to make judgments, or even to comment on it. Domi's loves were as tempestuous as her hatreds. Unlike himself, Grant and Brigid, the only life path Domi abandoned when she joined Cerberus was the marginal existence of an outlander, and later, as Guana Teague's sex slave.

Sighing, Kane slipped on his other shoe and stood. "I think you might have a point, Domi. There might not be any real reason for Grant to go with me on this op…even though I'm sure he'll disagree. He'll probably insist on being the one to fly there while I sit it out here."

Domi smiled wanly. "He's too damn big to sit on. Probably be a good idea not to mention any of this to him until it's too late for him to do anything about it."

Kane returned her smile with a wry one of his own. "Pretty scheming for a little Outland girl."

For a second, Domi's smile faltered. "I've learned from the best, remember?"

Kane didn't answer. He knew to whom she referred. He moved toward the door, saying only, "Let's go get something to eat."

Chapter 11

The massive city walls rose from the plain, looming high with intricately constructed towers. Made of blocks of a green-stained sandstone, some walls were completely overgrown with flowering vines and huge roots. A few sections were so eroded they had fallen altogether. The great pillars of a gate reared from the underbrush, flanked by three-headed elephants of stone. Beyond them stretched roofless arches and crumbling buildings containing nothing but empty galleries. Everywhere there was sculpture, some of it in low relief, some freestanding and of colossal size, depicting men, women, gods and bird-headed creatures. Many broken statues lay on the ground, their features screened by the merciless sproutings of the jungle.

"What are we looking at, Lakesh?" Grant rumbled impatiently, arms folded over his broad chest. Like Kane, he wore a T-shirt and jeans.

"Images of Angkor Thom, the capital of the Khmer empire," Lakesh answered, eyes glued to the images flickering across the big monitor screen he sat before. "I pulled these visuals from the database. Obviously they date back to the twentieth century."

"Obviously," Mariah Falk said wryly. As one of the Moon base émigrés, Mariah had been born in the twentieth century but spent most of the twenty-first and twenty-second centuries in a form of cryogenic stasis.

She, Grant, Domi and Kane stood behind Lakesh at the main operations station, watching as more scenes of lichen-encrusted temples and statues passed over the screen. Angkor Thom was enormous, and Kane tried to picture it when it was in its glory, a city blazing splendidly with light and color and bustling with life. But judging by the images downloaded from the database, only brooding silence and the encroaching jungle filled the streets and shattered buildings.

Despite the bright sunshine, the city seemed shadowy, dim, with a lost look to it as though the universe had forgotten about it long ago. Cunningly sculpted reliefs were everywhere the camera panned, allowing glimpses of cavorting, bare-breasted dancing girls, the clash of stone armies and balustrades crafted in the form of seven-headed cobras.

A huge building surrounded by carved terraces and galleries appeared. A broad avenue ran inward toward it from a gate. Clusters of square towers rose from all sides, each one bearing huge stone faces that were foreboding of aspect.

"The Bayon temple," Lakesh said as if that meant something. "The faces are popularly thought to represent the Buddhist divinity Lokeshvara."

The avenue widened inside the walls, opening into a vast courtyard filled with ruins and tangles of green. Disturbed by the cinematographer, multicolored birds took wing and flapped over great blocks of sandstone and granite that had fallen from the buildings.

"I presume," Kane commented with a studied indifference, "that you'll get around to telling us who built the place sooner or later."

"The Khmer," Lakesh responded crisply.

"And who the hell are they?" Grant demanded.

"That's a good question, friend Grant, one that was never satisfactorily explained. The only written records of the Khmer culture were put down by one Tcheou-Ta-Quan, who was in the service of the emperor of China in 1296 A.D. The Khmers have completely disappeared from the face of the earth."

"But," Kane interposed wearily, "they left behind legends and myths and all those kind of fairy tales you love so much."

Lakesh swiveled his chair just enough to favor Kane with a reproachful stare. "Those 'fairy tales' have proved to have their foundation in fact more than once, as you know from firsthand—and painful—experience."

Kane met his stare, then smiled ruefully. "Point taken. Pray proceed."

Lakesh turned to face the screen again and tapped a key. An aerial topographical map appeared in a drop-down window above the image of the overgrown temple.

In the brisk, scholarly tone Kane had finally learned to tolerate after so much time, Lakesh stated, "Modern Cambodia is tucked into a small corner of mainland Southeast Asia, squeezed on the west and north by Thailand and on the east by Vietnam. Its heart is the cul-de-sac of the great Mekong River, whose waters flowing from the north at some times of the year are so great in volume that the channels of the Mekong Delta cannot handle the flow, and the waters back up to the northwest into the great lake of Tonle Sap.

"In ancient times, this region was inhabited by people speaking an ancestor of the modern Cambodian language. The people and their language was known as Khmer. Little is known about the Khmer in prehistoric times, even as late as the first century B.C. It seems clear that there were scattered groups in the region living in tiny cleared pockets of cultivated land on the edges of the floodplains along the major rivers, in the western portion of the Mekong Delta, in the Phnom Penh region, to the northwest of the great lake. It was the primary agricultural center of the entire region."

Domi, who was usually very tolerant of Lakesh's tendency to turn everything into an academic lecture, asked crossly, "What does that have to do with our missing people?"

He chuckled. "Believe it or not, I *am* getting to that, darlingest one. Because the livelihoods of the early Khmers depended so heavily upon the regularity of the seasons—especially the southwest monsoon that each year, from June to November, brought the rains that fed their rice crops—the early Khmer were at some pains to attune their lives to the celestial calendar. They worked out a means to measure precisely the duration of the solar year so that farmers would know when to plant.

"The Khmer lived very close to the lakes and river, in pretty waterlogged or soggy country. Their main communications were along the rivers and streams, in boats large and small, and many of the spirits whom they propitiated were water spirits of one sort or another, especially the Naga, or water serpents. Folk legend traces the very foundation of the country back to the marriage of a foreigner and a female Naga, whose father was the king of a waterlogged country."

"Here we go," Grant announced with a flat, tired exasperation. "Serpents, snakes, dragons. This is all going to tie into the goddamn Annunaki, isn't it?"

Before Lakesh could reply, Kane said, "I thought the Naga were a tribe of serpent worshipers in Assam, not reptile people themselves."

Lakesh said, "Obviously they took their name from the Naga myths, like so many other cultures. And of course the Naga myths derived from the Annunaki."

In a soft, disgusted voice, Grant muttered, "What doesn't."

The Cerberus warriors had contended with the ancient alien reptilian race known as the Annunaki for quite some time, or at least contended with their descendants, the so-called Archons. Both races were responsible for—or guilty of—influencing most human cultures since before the dawn of recorded history.

The Annunaki were the serpent kings, the dragon lords of Mesopotamian legend. They provided the basis of much culturally diverse ancient folklore in which a godlike reptilian race figured prominently. They established serpents as having special places in most spiritual traditions where they symbolized either good or evil.

The Annunaki came to Earth nearly a half a million years before from the planet Nibiru, a world in the solar system, but one that orbited a considerable astronomical distance away from the Sun, returning to the vicinity of Earth only once every 3,600 years.

A highly developed race with a natural gift for organization, the Annunaki viewed Earth as a vast treasure trove of natural resources, upon which their technology depended. As labor was their scarcest commodity, the Annunaki's chief scientist, Enki, set about redesigning Earth's primitive inhabitants into models of maximized potentials.

The Annunaki remolded the indigenous protohumans, grading them at rough intellectual levels, and classifying them by physique, agility and dexterity. After much trial and error, a perfect specimen was attained and served as the template for succeeding generations. But during the creation process a myriad of monstrosities was also birthed, which gave rise to the legends of the cyclops, the centaur and the giant.

The early generations of slave labor were encouraged to breed, so each successive descendant would be superior to the first. The human brain improved and technical skills grew, along with cogent thoughts and the ability to deal with abstract concepts.

After thousands of years, the human slave race rebelled against the Annunaki, who failed to notice the expansion of cognition on the part of their servants. By the time they did, Earth had become an unprofitable enterprise. Although the Annunaki were essentially a peaceful people, Enki's cruel half brother, Enlil, arranged for a catastrophe to destroy their labor force. The catastrophe was recorded in ancient texts, and even cultural memories, as the Flood. The Annunaki departed to their home world of Nibiru, determining to wait for another three and a half millennia before venturing forth to Earth again.

Mariah asked, "What's the difference between the Naga and the Annunaki?"

"Cosmetic, mainly," Lakesh replied. "Like the Annunaki, the Naga allegedly came from other realms. But, unlike them, according to both Hindu and Buddhist lore, the Naga were reputed to be half human and half reptile."

"Ugh," Domi murmured, repressing a shudder. "Like them Imperial Dragoons we met over in England."

Lakesh gave her a crooked smile. "Actually, though it might seem like a singularly unattractive combination, the Naga were supposed to be an extremely handsome race. The Naga maidens were so wise and beautiful that a mortal male counted himself fortunate if she took him for a lover or a husband."

"Doesn't much sound like the Annunaki legends so far," Grant observed.

"There are a few disconcerting similarities," Lakesh said. "Although most Naga were benevolent toward humankind, there were a few who were violently antagonistic. One, by the name of Naga-Sanniya, hated humans so much, later generations turned him into the prince of a pantheon of demons."

Angling quizzical eyebrows at both Kane and Grant, he commented dryly, "I'm sure that has a familiar ring."

"It does," Kane agreed. "That corresponds roughly with the story of Enlil. Are you saying the Annunaki built the Khmer empire?"

Lakesh tugged absently at his nose. "There's much room for interpretation, friend Kane. According to one version of the myth, a Hindu brahman named Kaundinya, armed with a magical bow, appeared one day off the shore of Cambodia. A female Naga, a dragon princess paddled out to meet him. Kaundinya shot an arrow into her boat. This action frightened the princess into marrying him. Before the marriage, Kaundinya gave her clothes to wear and her father, the dragon king, built them a capital city and named the country 'Kambuja'—Cambodia."

Grant said quietly, "I'm not going to reject out of hand the possibility of the Annunaki having a hand—or claw—in building the damn place. But you still haven't explained how it's relevant to our reason for being here—retrieving our people."

Lakesh manipulated the mouse and the image on the screen vanished, to be replaced by a grid schematic. Certain squares glowed red. Luminous straight lines stretched from the red glowing squares, connecting them all in a confusing, crisscrossing webwork.

"The Khmers loved squares and straight lines in their architecture," Lakesh announced. "They divided their public buildings into hollow squares, sometimes dividing them into a series of smaller squares by cruciform structures. These squares and subsquares are made up of long galleries. Towers were erected at the center and one at each corner of the larger hollow squares. Each enclosure was terraced, so that each inner square is higher than the one surrounding it, giving the whole thing a resemblance to a pyramid."

He swiveled his chair to expectantly scan the faces of the people around him. After a moment, he asked with some asperity, "Do none of you have an idea of where I'm going with this?"

Mariah Falk leaned forward, eyes narrowed as she inspected the image on the screen. She ventured, "The entire city complex, when each of the sites are connected, forms a huge mandala."

"Exactly!" Lakesh exclaimed. "And does that mean anything to any of you?"

Kane resisted the urge to glance over at Grant to see if the word meant anything to him. Then he repressed the much stronger urge to tell Lakesh in very profane language to knock off the academic performance and get to the point.

"Shit," Domi muttered sullenly.

Lakesh glanced toward her, eyebrows rising. "What?"

"I said 'shit,'" she snapped. "As in it means shit to me. And to the rest of us, too. Wasting our time here, Lakesh."

"Yeah," Grant rumbled peevishly. "Just tell us what a mandala is supposed to be so we can get on with whatever we're here to get on with."

In an aggrieved tone, Lakesh said, "Mandalas are symbols that are used as a potent means of altering consciousness, especially by practitioners of Buddhist tantra. Mandalas are usually divided into four quadrants but the entire image represents the palace of the central deity of the universe. Angkor was built according to these principles.

"All of its monuments and temples have encoded in them a message or a recognition of a different kind of reality, an awareness based on knowing how we make our life passage in this universe, and the insights and enlightened states of mind that come about as a result of paying attention to the spiritual journey of our souls."

Mariah frowned. "Lakesh, at first I thought I knew where you were going with this. But now you've lost me completely."

"He *never* had me," Kane stated sourly.

Lakesh ignored Kane's remark. "A mandala is also an esoteric method of focusing and generating energy. What kind of energy were we discussing only an hour ago?"

"Electromagnetic," Domi said. "So?"

"Earth energies," Mariah blurted, comprehension dawning in her eyes. "You're talking about ley lines, aren't you?"

Lakesh smiled in relief. "Yes, finally. Now we're on the same page."

Before any of them could dispute his claim or opine that it was premature, Lakesh returned his attention to the keyboard. "Ley lines is the term applied to a vast network of straight lines connecting power points or sacred places of the ancient landscape. All of you know my belief about people throughout prehistoric times mapping the energy in this lines and siting their monuments at intersection points.

"I postulate that the ancient Khmer built Angkor Thom to interact with the high earth energies in the region. They existed in a cause-and-effect relationship with it. Most of the buildings are erected upon convergences of the ley lines. The entire plain is a hub of geomagnetic energy."

"That sounds like sheer straw-grasping speculation to me," Kane said doubtfully.

Lakesh smiled. "Straw-grasping I might be guilty of. But I dispute your claim of sheer speculation. Astronomically all the structures have built-in positions for lunar and solar observation. The sun itself was so important to the builders of the temples that solar movement regulates the position of the bas-reliefs. It is not surprising that Angkor integrates astronomy, the calendar and religion since the priest-architects who constructed the temple conceived of all three as a unity. To the ancient Khmers, astronomy was a sacred science."

"As it was to any number of cultures," Mariah offered. "From the Mayans to the Sumerians."

Lakesh nodded in agreement. "The expression of calendrical, astronomical and cosmological themes within the dimensions of Angkor raises an important question. Was this purely a Cambodian innovation or had Angkor's architects learned of the practice from an even earlier source representing a tradition that was practiced elsewhere?"

"Like the Naga," Grant suggested. "Or the Annunkai. Could the Khmers have learned the art of geomancy from them, too?"

"Perhaps," Lakesh replied genially. "I'm playing back the satellite transmission right before we lost the telemetry. I've slowed it down considerably as you can see, and I've run it through a thermal line scan filter to pick up energy signatures."

Grant and Kane stepped forward, watching the familiar events unfold again on the screen. With the speed of the sequence slowed, they were able to make out more details of the temple Lakesh called Angkor Wat. It almost looked as if it had been carved out of a single crag of rock that broke the flatness of the tableland on it which it stood.

All of the visible surfaces were covered with a multitude of intricate carvings and frescoes and squatting stone giants. The tapering tops of the towers took the form of lotus buds. Low down at their base they saw openings where pale lights glimmered. They could see now people moving about the buildings.

"Here we go," Lakesh announced.

A shimmering haze, more like a barely visible distortion, suddenly emanated from the tops of the towers, seeming to spring from one to another. Even with the speed of the playback slowed to a virtual, the motion was so fast they barely caught it. At normal transmission speed, the phenomenon was too quick to be seen with the unaided eye.

As they watched, the distortion expanded, making sweeping pirouettes back and forth and around the pinnacles. It fluctuated, stretched, almost appearing to tremble, then it fanned, forming a semiopaque tent with the towers serving as pegs. At the center of the energy pattern, a great swirling whorl arose, like a maelstrom. It bulged upward as if it were a membrane being pushed below. It gushed into the sky—and the image on the screen broke up as it had the first time.

No one spoke for a long, tense, tick of time. At length, Lakesh intoned reflectively, "Does that phenomenon suggest anything of note to anyone?"

Mariah grunted thoughtfully. "If the building is a nexus point of geomagnetic energy, then it could have been a release, a venting of sorts."

Lakesh nodded. "I concur. Whether it releases the energy as a wave or intermittent bursts, there's no way we can know."

"Just like," Kane put in, "if the venting is controlled or a natural event, like a geyser."

"If it's powerful enough to blind our satellite," Grant said grimly, "it sure as hell could blank out the transponder signals."

Lakesh hesitated before answering, then nodded. "That would be my guess, as well. It's the logical conclusion."

"Could it have the same qualities as a dampening field?" Kane inquired.

Lakesh pursed his lips, pondering the question. "Possibly. But geomancy is the manipulation of constant earth energies. I don't perceive a way they could be used to generate a field that inhibits the transformation of energy. The variable factors to create and maintain such a field would be too—" He paused, groping for a word.

"Variable?" Grant supplied.

Lakesh chuckled. "Exactly. It's remotely possible that the geomagnetic field is generated at will, but I tend to doubt that's the case. If on the outside chance it is, the potential for a truly dreadful weapon is locked up within the ancient kingdom of the Khmers."

Grant sighed, then swept Kane and Domi with a dark, penetrating gaze. "There's a matter we're going to have settle first—the means of actually getting to the 'ancient kingdom of the Khmers.' We only have the one TAV here at present—and the jump seat we installed is barely big enough for Domi, let alone a full grown man. And only me and Kane are rated to fly the thing."

Lakesh turned in his chair, regarding Grant appraisingly. "What do you suggest, friend Grant?"

The big man lifted the broad yoke of his shoulders in a shrug and pointed to Kane, then tapped his chest with a thumb. "Me and Kane draw straws about who goes and who stays. It's the only fair way to do it."

"And," Kane asked wryly, "will the winner get to go or get to stay here?"

Grant's lips quirked in a rueful smile beneath his

mustache. "I suppose that's something else we're going to have to settle, isn't it?"

Kane stared at him in silence for a few seconds, then said, deadpan, "Yes. Yes, it is."

Chapter 12

The flight went smoothly until Kane made his second flyover of the Angkor plain. Then the Manta began to have trouble.

The journey from Montana at slightly under the transatmospheric vehicle's maximum cruising speed of Mach 25 had been uneventful, boring even. Once the destination coordinates were input into the onboard navigational computer and the GPS lock achieved with the Comsat, Kane did little more than watch as the vast blue tapestry of the Pacific Ocean blurred by so quickly waves and islands became mere patterns of contrasting texture and color.

At an altitude of thirty thousand feet, Kane wasn't too concerned with accidentally overshooting his objection or colliding with another aircraft. Because of the 250-mile-per-hour winds that once swept regularly over the rad-ravaged face of America, aerial travel had been very slow to make a comeback. Unpredictable geothermals in the hell zones and chem storms had quadrupled the hazards of flying. Even the Deathbird gunships in use by the Mag Divisions had only been pressed into service thirty or so years ago.

The TAV, although sheathed in bronze-hued metal, held the general shape and configuration of a seagoing manta ray; it was little more than flattened wedges with wings. Intricate geometric designs covered almost the entire exterior surface. Deeply inscribed into the hull were interlocking swirling glyphs, cup and spiral symbols and even elaborate cuneiform markings. The composition of the hull, although it appeared to be of a burnished bronze alloy, was a material far tougher and more resilient.

The craft had no external apparatus at all, no ailerons, no fins and no airfoils. The cockpit was almost invisible, little more than an elongated symmetrical oval hump in the exact center of the sleek topside fuselage. The Manta's wingspan measured out to twenty yards, and the fuselage was around fifteen feet long. A short tail assembly was tipped by an ace-of-spades-shaped rudder.

A small fleet of the transatmospheric craft had been found on the Manitius Moon base. Of Annunaki manufacture, they were in pristine condition, despite their great age. Powered by two different kinds of engines, a ramjet and solid-fuel pulse detonation air spikes, the Manta ships could fly in a vacuum and in an atmosphere. The Manta transatmospheric vehicle wasn't an experimental craft, but an example of a technology that was mastered by a race when humanity still cowered in trees from saber-tooth tigers.

Grant and Kane had easily learned to pilot the ships, since they handled superficially like the Deathbirds the two men had flown when they were Cobaltville Magistrates. But they learned that when they were flying in space, the Mantas did not handle like winged aircraft within an atmosphere.

A pilot could select velocity, angle, attitude and other complex factors dictated by standard avionics, but space flight relied on a completely different set of principles. It called for the maximum manipulation of gravity, trajectory, relative velocities and plain old luck. Despite all the computer-calculated course programming, both men discovered quickly that successfully piloting the TAV through space was more by God than by grace. Skill had almost nothing to do with it.

Kane wore a bronze-colored helmet with a full-face visor. The helmet itself attached to the headrest of the pilot's chair. A pair of tubes stretched from the rear to an oxygen tank at the back of the ejection seat. The helmet and chair were of one piece, a self-contained unit.

The instrument panel was almost shocking in its simplicity. The controls consisted primarily of a joystick, altimeter and fuel gauges. All the labeling was in English. But the interior curve of the helmet's visor swarmed with CGI icons of sensor scopes, range finders and various indicators.

All the HUD icons and indictors showed green, and so Kane had plenty of time to think—and to worry. He couldn't help but smile in recollection of his last sight of Grant, standing out on the improvised launch pad as the Manta lifted off at shortly before midnight, propelled upward by the vectored-thrust ramjets.

Grant had been bellowing profanities, first into the grit-laden backwash kicked up by the thrusters, then into a handheld transcomm unit. His voice, transmitted into the confines of Kane's helmet, was the deafening roar of an outraged lion.

"You tricky bastard!" Grant raged. "You drew the short straw! You lost!"

"Oh, sorry," Kane replied with bland innocence. "I was confused. I thought if I lost that meant I *had* to go."

"You know damn well what the deal was!" Grant yelled. "Get back down here—"

Kane glanced down and saw Domi struggling over the embankment to join Grant. She had her Detonics Combat Master in her right hand. He engaged the pulse detonation engines, and the Manta hurled across the sky like an artillery shell. Whatever else Grant had to say was swallowed up by the sonic boom. Within seconds, the TAV was out of the transcomm's range.

Kane didn't feel too badly about tricking his partner and Domi. He easily imagined the type of obscene and imaginative vituperation the girl spat out. But he knew he would feel a lot worse if something happened to either one of them on the op and he had to break the news to Lakesh or Shizuka. He would miss their presence, regardless, particularly that of Grant.

When two men worked together for as long as they had, often balancing on the knife edge between life and death, they relied on each other implicitly. Without Grant along, Kane felt distinctly like a trapeze artist performing dangerous stunts without a net.

But unlike him, Grant had not chosen the life of an exile, an insurrectionist. He had sacrificed everything that gave his life a degree of sense to help Kane and Brigid escape from Cobaltville. Even after all the time that had elapsed since that day, now seeming to be very long ago, Kane still felt responsible for what the man had given up and what he had suffered since then in the war against the hybrid barons.

But old habits died very hard. Kane and Grant had been partners for nearly fifteen years, and it was part and parcel of Magistrate Division conditioning to always back a partner's play.

The Magistrate Divisions were formed as a complex police machine that demanded instant obedience to its edicts and to which there was no possible protest. Magistrates were a highly conservative, duty-bound group. The customs of enforcing the law and obeying orders were ingrained almost from birth.

The Magistrates submitted themselves to a grim and unyielding discipline, because they believed it was necessary to reverse the flood tide of chaos and restore order to postholocaust America. As Magistrates, the courses their lives followed had been charted before their births. They had exchanged personal hopes, dreams and desires for a life of service. They were destined to live, fight and die, usually violently.

All Magistrates followed a patrilineal tradition, assuming the duties and positions of their fathers. They didn't have given names, each taking the surname of the father, as though the first Magistrate to bear the name were the same man as the last.

The originators of the Magistrate Divisions had believed that only surnames, family names, engendered a sense of obligation to the duties of their ancestors' office, insuring that subsequent generations never lost touch with their hereditary roles as enforcers. Last names became badges of social distinction, almost titles.

Over the past ninety years, both the oligarchy of barons and the Mags who served them had taken on a fearful, almost legendary aspect. For most of their adult lives, both Kane and Grant had been part of that legend, cogs in a merciless machine. They had been through the dehumanizing cruelty of Magistrate training, yet they had somehow, almost miraculously, managed to retain their humanity.

Now, for the past two years, they had exercised their humanity by doing their very best to not just dismantle the machine, but to utterly destroy it and scatter the pieces to the four corners of the world. They had devoted themselves to the work of Cerberus.

But the situation in Cerberus had changed dramatically over the past couple of months, particularly after the arrival of the Manitius base personnel and the pregnant hybrid woman Quavell. If Quavell really did carry Kane's child, then the entire dynamic of the struggle against the tyranny of the barons had changed.

The barons—the hybridized god-kings who had inherited Earth from their human cousins, whom they scorned as "apekin"—actually represented the final phase of human evolution. They referred to themselves as "new humans" and empowered themselves to control not only their immediate environment, but also the evolution of other species.

The barons did so by planning and creating wholesale alterations in living organisms, changing evolutionary patterns to suit themselves. They considered the pinnacle of evolutionary achievement was themselves, the barons, as high above ordinary hybrids, who were bred as a servant class, as the hybrids were above mere humans.

Despite how mad the entire tale of Archon-human hybrids seemed initially, Kane grew comfortable with it and eased into hating the hybrid dynasty and the baronial oligarchy. He woke up hating the hybrids and the barons and went to bed hating the hybrids and barons.

Then he learned his hatred was not only pointless, but also pretty much without basis. The Archons existed only as a fabricated cover story created two centuries before and expanded with each succeeding generation. It was all a ruse, bits of truth mixed in with outrageous fiction. Only a single so-called Archon existed on Earth, and that was Balam, who had been the redoubt's resident prisoner for more than three and a half years.

Balam claimed the Archon Directorate was an appellation created by the predark governments. Lakesh referred to it as the Oz Effect, wherein a single vulnerable entity created the illusion of being the representative of an all-powerful body.

Even more shocking than that revelation was Balam's assertion that he and his folk were humans, not alien, but alienated. Kane still didn't know how much to believe. But if nothing else, he no longer subscribed to the fatalistic belief that the human race had had its day and only extinction lay ahead. Balam had indicated that was not true, but was instead another control mechanism. New and old humans would have to learn to share the planet with each other if either group was to have a destiny.

But even by crossbreeding with humanity, the hybrids were still markedly different from humankind. However, as Quavell pointed out, different was not the same as alien. She herself confessed that her own race viewed humans as savages, little more than bloodthirsty apes who were incapable of transcending their roots as killers. She had other experiences with humans, as well, specifically with Kane.

A mission to Archuleta Mesa biomedical facility had inadvertently wiped out the genetic-engineering division of the vast facility. What remained of the place, both in personnel and machinery, was transferred to the much larger Area 51 facility. The necessary equipment and raw material to implement procreation had yet to be installed. Baron Cobalt had unilaterally decided that the conventional means of conception was the only option to keep the hybrid race alive.

Since the baron held Kane responsible for pushing the hybrid race to the brink of extinction, he made it his task to repopulate it, as well. Kane wasn't the first human male to be pressed into service. There had been other men before him, but they had performed unsatisfactorily, due to their terror of the hybrids.

Kane's sense of surprise was still fresh when he recollected how Quavell, during one of their scheduled periods of copulation, confided to him that not every hybrid agreed with the baronial policy toward humanity. He was even more surprised when she helped him and Domi escape. Both of them were forced to reassess everything they thought they knew about the barons, about the hybrids.

According to Quavell, she had made the long overland trip from Area 51 in a stolen Sandcat, all alone. She traveled as far as the foothills of the Bitterroot Range to the encampment of Sky Dog. The shaman brought her the rest of the way to the mountain peak on horseback.

Both Kane and Lakesh were still skeptical of certain details of her story, particularly how she knew the location of the redoubt. She offered only a vague explanation about learning of it from either Kane or Domi during their period of imprisonment in Dreamland.

She had refused to name which one of them actually made the revelation. Neither Kane nor Domi admitted to telling her or anyone else about Cerberus. Still and all, Quavell had provided them with information about the current state of the baronies following the Imperator War, although few details could be confirmed.

Quavell's presence in the redoubt made Kane distinctly uncomfortable, since the entire situation evoked unpleasant memories of Lakesh's abortive plan to turn Cerberus from a sanctuary to a colony. To that end, babies needed to be born, children with superior genetic traits.

Making a unilateral decision, Lakesh arranged for a woman named Beth-Li Rouch to be brought into the redoubt from one of the baronies to mate with Kane, thus insuring that his superior abilities were passed on to offspring.

Without access to the techniques of fetal development outside the womb that were practiced in the villes, the conventional means of procreation was the only option. And that meant sex and passion and the fury of a woman scorned.

Kane had refused to cooperate for a variety of reasons, primarily because he felt the plan was a continuation of the sinister elements that had brought about the nukecaust and the tyranny of the villes. His refusal had tragic consequences. Only a thirst for revenge and a conspiracy to murder had been birthed within the walls of the redoubt, not children.

And now Beth-Li was dead, killed by Domi and buried in a simple grave out on the hillside. Kane could only pray Quavell's involvement in the lives of the Cerberus residents did not have equally tragic consequences. The countdown to her delivery date had begun. As far as he knew, by the time he returned to Cerberus, a newborn *something* might be waiting for him. The prospect didn't warm his blood.

To distract himself from dwelling on the possibility, Kane tested the action of his Sin Eater, snugged in the power holster strapped to his right forearm. He raised his arm, bending it at the elbow. A tiny electric motor whined as he flexed his wrist tendons. Sensitive actuators activated flexible cables in the forearm holster and snapped the Sin Eater smoothly into his gloved hand. He repeated the maneuver several times until he was satisfied—and grew bored.

Folding his arms over his chest, he leaned as far back in the pilot's chair as he could and, after a bit of twisting and hitching around to find the most comfortable position, he managed to drift off.

The blazing glory of dawn flamed in the sky as the Manta's navigational computers brought it on a direct trajectory across the whitecapped waters of the South China Sea, then over Vietnam. Within minutes the craft crossed over the border in to Cambodia. Signaled by the GPS, the TAV automatically dropped its airspeed to five hundred miles per hour.

The change in speed roused Kane from a fitful slumber and he came to full alertness. Swiftly, he oriented himself then lowered the Manta's altitude to three hundred feet and reduced the airspeed even further.

As he did so, dawn became a fine sunny morning. The terrain below looked interesting and rich. The TAV cruised over a seemingly limitless panorama of forested hills and wooded valleys. He glimpsed the mirrored surface of Tonle Sap, dancing with multicolored highlights. Tinted by the early-morning sunshine, suffused by streamers of mist curling up from the tree line, the Cambodian jungle looked like an Eden. But he already knew the jungle held nasty surprises.

Remembering the half-glimpsed figures from the satellite transmission, he cut in the low-power gravity-modifier field, effectively silencing the engines. The rain forest fell away and he skimmed over rich grasslands. He saw a collection of bamboo houses and tilled fields, all laid out precisely as an estate garden. Although he didn't see anyone, he figured farmers would be rising very soon.

Touching the low-observability-camouflage switch on the control console, an electrical impulse fed through circuitry all over the hull of the Manta. Ambient waves shifted over the bronze colors of the exterior, coating it as if with a film of ink. Within seconds, the TAV was the hue of the early-morning sky, melting indistinguishably with it.

Below him stretched a vista of huge reservoirs, irrigation canals and a series of moats and other waterworks. At first glance, their engineering skill almost on the level of the architecture of the buildings rising from the plain.

Kane decided to move in very slowly and circle Angkor Thom. He initiated the telemetric sensor, hoping to detect a signal from the transponders carried by the three missing people. The instrument registered nothing.

He lifted the Manta to a thousand feet, cut the ramjet thrusters, coasted in on the gravity modifiers. Putting the TAV into a hover position, he looked down. Seeming to float in the air between his eyes and the visor, a column of numbers appeared, glowing red against the pale bronze. When he focused on a distant object, the visor magnified it and provided a readout as to distance and dimension.

The huge multitowered temple Lakesh had identified as Angkor Wat glistened with early-morning dew but there was no sign of movement anywhere. For a moment, Kane had the impression he was looking down upon a gargantuan, alien cemetery, as strange as the citadel of Enki he had seen on the Moon. According to Lakesh a number of the megalithic structures had served as tombs of the Khmer rulers so it was possible that Angkor Thom was nothing but a miles-long mausoleum.

He completed the first pass over the city and was just beginning the second when his point man's sense kicked in. He experienced an intense sensation of uneasiness, of apprehension. He looked down and saw the tapered tips of the Angkor Wat towers seeming to shine, becoming almost luminescent. At first he attributed the light to a dewy reflection of the early-morning sun.

Then the HUD thermometer icon began flashing. As he looked at it in amazement, the temperature climbed rapidly, first one by degree, then in multiple jumps. At the same time, several of the other icons winked out. Kane didn't hesitate—he kicked in the ramjets full throttle, not worrying about the noise. Acceleration slammed him hard against his chair.

The Manta shot away from Angkor Thom like a rock launched from a catapult, hurtling in the general direction of Tonle Sap. At the moment, he didn't care about the heading of the TAV as long as it was away from the city. The engine roar skipped and faltered. The ship shuddered.

Jockeying the port and starboard maneuvering jets, Kane sent the Manta skittering wildly, veering off on another course entirely. He jabbed a series of vent switches on the control panel, hoping that if he opened them the influx of air would cool down the cockpit. They were all locked in place. The heat inside the Manta climbed to 150 degrees. If not for the internal thermostat of the shadow suit he wore and the oxygen provided by the helmet, he would have lost consciousness.

He wasn't sure how many miles he put between him and the city when all the CGI icons on the inner curve of his helmet's visor faded away. The Manta began to lose altitude. Although he was loath to ditch, Kane reached for the ejector-seat lever beneath the pilot's chair. He could come down by glider chute and find the TAV later to remove the supplies and ordnance in the storage compartment. He adjusted his harness and wrenched at the lever.

Nothing happened.

Kane braced himself and pulled again but still nothing happened. He straightened, whispering softly, "Oh, shit."

The Manta dropped fast in a dead-stick dive. The ship's wing configuration provided a certain amount of air resistance, but Kane wasn't at all sure it was sufficient to slow the craft's descent and keep it intact—or for him to survive the impact.

The ship began to wobble, tipping up on its starboard wing, then on its port side as it plummeted down toward the jungle. Nausea churned in Kane's belly as he watched the horizon slide up and down.

Suddenly, a couple of the HUD icons flickered and flashed back to life. He felt a surge of desperate exultation. Whatever had knocked out the Manta's power system apparently had a limited range.

Not all of the ship's systems came back online, but Kane partly succeeded in stabilizing the Manta's attitude so it no longer wobbled. He could feel the vibrations of the powered-up stabilizers rattling through the deck at his feet. A queasy, liquid sensation began in his stomach, and the shuddering that racked the TAV from stem to stern didn't help it any. The green mass of foliage still rushed up far too fast.

With a sense of detachment that bemused even him, he wondered at his odds of survival. Two to one against, he concluded. Not too pessimistic since it left a margin of error. There was a possibility he would survive.

He braced himself against his chair and tried to go limp. He recalled Philboyd mentioning that the Annunaki had built the Mantas with at least three different kinds of shock absorbers. They had designed their ships to give the pilots the best chance of survival if the engines failed.

The Manta skimmed over three palm trees, shearing off the tops as if it were a scythe. Flat wide fronds slapped against the canopy and flattened themselves, effectively blocking Kane's line of sight, not that there would be much to see, he reminded himself sourly.

The TAV hit the ground on its belly, bounced several times like a flat stone skipping across the surface of a pond, crashed through a wall of foliage and bulldozed its way over fallen logs, snapping saplings like matchwood. The wing tips dragged along snarled tangles of brush. Branches were stripped of leaves and trees of bark as the armored hull whipped past them.

Kane's body strained against the recoil harness and then slammed back into the seat violently. All the air exploded from his lungs as he was engulfed in a thundering wave of shock, followed by pain. For an instant, he heard only his own strangulated gasps as he fought for air and struggled against the cloak of darkness settling over his mind.

The Manta sledded along the damp ground like a down-sliding boulder, leaving a wide, scoured path in its wake, turf rolling up before it like a strip of carpet. By the time the ship careened to a stop, Kane sagged unconscious in the straps.

Chapter 13

Kane floated back to consciousness like a waterlogged timber bobbing to the surface of a pond. The closer he came to awakening, the more aware he became of the pain and the tang of his own blood in his mouth. Dimly, Kane heard the squeak and creak of metal. He ignored the sound. The temptation to drift back into the dark was strong but he forced his eyes open. It took him a few seconds to focus and when he did, he almost closed his eyes again.

He looked up at a vision torn from the delirium of a lunatic. Double rows of needle-pointed teeth gleamed wetly from a saurian snout. Beady, snakelike eyes stared unblinkingly down at him. The scaled head was almost the size of that of a horse. Squeezing itself through the sprung-open cockpit canopy, its long wet forked tongue slithered in and out of its maw, between upper and lower rows of yellowed fangs.

Kane heard his own groan echoing within the confines of his helmet. He stared without comprehension at the reptilian head pushing its way into the cockpit, saliva dripping from its mottled tongue onto his faceplate. It took his stunned brain a moment to identify what his eyes were seeing, and his brain didn't like it one bit.

Although he was wondering wildly if he were uncon-

scious or asleep and just having a nightmare, he decided
not to take the chance that either was the case. He flexed
his right wrist tendons, and the Sin Eater slid into his
palm. He pointed the bore at the scaled head glaring
down at him. A sibilant hissing, like a faulty steam
valve, issued from its jaws amid droplets of saliva.

Kane tapped the trigger stud. Three 9 mm rounds
cored through the creature's underjaw, cleaving paths
through its cranium and pulping its brain. The reptile's
head jerked backward, the top of its skull bursting open
in a spray of blood, bone and viscera. As it slid out of
sight, Kane heard its claws scrabbling and squealing on
the hull like fingernails dragged over a blackboard.

The snapping reports of the shots brought Kane back
to more or less full awareness, and he slowly took stock
of his surroundings. The Manta had come to rest at
angle of about thirty degrees, and he was held in position only by his safety harness. The canopy was partially
open and he saw a patch of blue sky overhead, between
swaying palm fronds. Judging by the position of the sun,
he figured it was midmorning, so he had been unconscious more than an hour.

His chest and back hurt abominably but when he
shifted position, nothing felt broken. He tasted blood because his teeth had cut into the tender inner lining of his
lower lip. Reaching up, he touched the latch on the underside of the helmet to open the seal. With a hiss of air,
he felt the pressure relax around the base of his neck and
he pushed the helmet up and back from his head.

Teeth clenched on a groan, Kane's hand hit the harness release and he shrugged out of the straps. Slowly,
his thought processes returned to normal and he recov-

ered his equilibrium. He thumbed a few switches on the console. Power lights glowed, wavered, died, glowed again and then faded out completely. He swallowed a curse of frustration. Whatever kind of force exuded by the temple had acted like a bucket of water dashed onto a fire. A few embers still sputtered, but no flames could build until the fuel dried out.

Carefully, Kane heaved himself upright and pushed open the canopy all the way. He struggled out, but because the Manta was canted at an angle, he fell from the wing and landed amid a bed of ferns. He would have lain there, suffering, except for the corpse of the giant lizard lying on the ground only a few inches away.

Shoving himself to his feet, he staggered back and half fell against the hull of the ship, his heart pounding in sudden fear, Sin Eater aimed at the creature. Its maimed head lolled limply on the long scaled neck, which joined a barrel-bodied torso. Its four bowed legs looked almost too short for it, but the four-toed paws were tipped with hooked talons.

Its belly was whitish, but the rest of the body was coated by an interlocking pebbled pattern of gray-green scales, from the tip of the snout to the long muscular tail that stretched out of sight into the underbrush. He took a deep breath to calm himself, despite the pain in his chest. His stomach jumped in adrenaline-fueled spasms, even though he knew the monster was dead.

Although he had always prided himself on being free of phobias, with a surge of shame he realized he had developed a fear of things reptilian over the past couple of years. It wasn't an irrational fear, but one derived from terrifying firsthand experience.

First there was his encounter with Lord Strongbow and his mutagenically altered Imperial Dragoons, with their scale-ringed, snakish eyes. Then there was his terrifying battle with a gigantic constrictor atop a ziggurat in South America. One the natives had been decked out in a feathered headdress and christened Kukulkan, in homage to the ancient Mayan god.

That incident was followed only a short time later by walking a gauntlet of diamondbacks in California. His fear of things reptilian had reached its culmination a few months before, during his nightmarish bareback ride on Monstradamus through the jungle of Thunder Isle.

Within a few moments he had calmed sufficiently to eye the creature a bit more clinically. He realized it was a large version of a monitor lizard, a species that had been called Komodo dragons in predark days. He estimated this one to be at least twenty feet long and probably weighing in at a thousand pounds. The mutant animals spawned in the aftermath of the nukecaust that tended toward gigantism were rare, although he had encountered several oversize monsters since joining Cerberus, including a truck-sized snapping turtle.

Still and all, a monitor lizard afflicted with polyploidism, a doubling of the chromosome count, which accounted for its unusual size, was nowhere near as terrifying as the tyrannosaur he had christened Monstradamus.

Kane pushed himself away from the Manta and glanced around. In every direction, wherever he looked, he saw thick green foliage. Tangles of flowering creeper vines carpeted the jungle floor. The boles of huge trees stood like pillars all around, some of them showing fresh scars inflicted by the wings of the Manta. Dozens of flying insects swirled in the air, a swarm of beautifully colored butterflies among them.

The atmosphere was like that within a greenhouse—impregnated with the overwhelming odor of vegetation and heavy with humidity. The hot air lay on his face like the touch of soft, moist hands. His shadow suit kept him comfortable, as the internal thermostats adjusted to the high temperature.

He made a circuit of the Manta but found no major damage. Rather than wasting more time trying to start the ship, he decided to leave it where it was for the time being until he scouted out the surroundings. From a storage compartment in the undercarriage, he removed a backpack of emergency rations, a Copperhead subgun, extra magazines for the weapons and a small, handheld PDA. He attached his fourteen-inch combat knife to the scabbard outside his right boot.

From the backpack he removed a bottle of analgesic tablets and washed down two of them with a swig of water from a canteen. In the pack were various painkillers and stimulants. He sat down in the shadow of the portside wing and soon he began to feel better, the pain easing.

Reaching up behind his head, he touched the Commtact, making sure the contact was still tight: The tiny transceiver fit tightly against the mastoid bone behind his right ear.

Implanted steel pintels embedded in the bones slid through the flesh and into tiny input ports in the small curves of metal. The Commtacts had been found in Redoubt Yankee and were described as state-of-the-art multiple-channel communication devices.

Their sensor circuitry incorporated an analog-to-digital voice encoder that was embedded in the mastoid bone. The pintels connected to input ports in the comms themselves. Once they made contact, transmissions were picked up by the auditory canals and the dermal sensors transmitted the electronic signals directly through the cranial casing. Even if someone went deaf, as long as they wore a Commtact, they would still have a form of hearing.

The Commtacts were still being field-tested, since in order to make them operational, surgery was required and few people wanted to make that sacrifice. But the surgery to implant the sensors was very minor, with only a small incision behind the ear to slide them under the skin.

The Commtact's five-mile range was superior to that of the handheld transcomms. The range of the radiophones was generally limited to a mile, but in open country, in clear weather, contact could be established at two miles. Brigid and Philboyd had agreed to the surgery but Nora Pennick had not.

The Commtacts had other uses, as well. In conjunction with a sophisticated translation program within the PDA, the Commtact analyzed the pattern of a language and then provided a real-time translation. Some foreign phrases and words would not be exact translations, but the program recognized enough words to supply an English equivalent. Conversely, the program would supply him the appropriate responses in the language it heard.

Consulting the digital compass within the PDA, he looked up at the bright Asian sun and set off in what he hoped was the direction of Angkor Thom. High above him, a hundred feet or more, giant palm fronds met to make a bright green roof over much of the jungle, tinting everything with an emerald hue.

A profusion of huge butterflies, dozens of them, wheeled and glided overhead. Their fluttering wings were almost as broad as his hand and were painted with all the colors of nature's palette—scarlet, orange, yellow, white and bright blue. They dodged and darted through the alternating stripes of dark shadows and shafts of greenish sunlight. Under other circumstances, Kane would have been enchanted by their beauty. Near and far, tropical birds called in screeches, clacks and hoots.

Within a few minutes, Kane crossed a trail, a narrow road that cut through the forest. It was old and well-used, worn deep in the mulchy jungle floor and beaten down to a smooth channel. It came from the southeast and looped through the undergrowth.

He stood and stared at the path, glancing first in one direction and then the other, absently kneading his aching chest. The analgesics had dimmed the pain but hadn't completely smothered it. He heard a chittering above him, and he swung his head up. A sad-eyed monkey calmly watched him from a branch.

Kane smiled dourly and saluted. The monkey yawned and turned away. Glancing at the compass again, he chose to turn right onto the road. He walked less than a hundred yards when the road curved lazily to the right. From around the bend he heard a faint dry creaking sound and a metallic rattle.

His nostrils caught the whiff of an odor he had smelled many times in his life but never grown accustomed to. A prickling of dread began inching its way up

The Gold Eagle Reader Service™ — Here's how it works:

If offer card is missing write to: Gold Eagle Reader Service, 3010 Walden Ave., P.O. Box 1867, Buffalo, NY 14240-1867

NO POSTAGE
NECESSARY
IF MAILED
IN THE
UNITED STATES

BUSINESS REPLY MAIL

FIRST-CLASS MAIL   PERMIT NO. 717-003   BUFFALO, NY

POSTAGE WILL BE PAID BY ADDRESSEE

GOLD EAGLE READER SERVICE
3010 WALDEN AVE
PO BOX 1867
BUFFALO NY 14240-9952

GET FREE BOOKS and a FREE GIFT WHEN YOU PLAY THE...

Lucky 7

SLOT MACHINE GAME!

Just scratch off the silver box with a coin. Then check below to see the gifts you get!

YES! I have scratched off the silver box. Please send me the 2 free Gold Eagle® books and gift for which I qualify. I understand I am under no obligation to purchase any books, as explained on the back of this card.

366 ADL D36Z   **166 ADL D36Y**

FIRST NAME	LAST NAME

ADDRESS

APT.#	CITY

STATE/PROV.	ZIP/POSTAL CODE

7 7 7	**Worth TWO FREE BOOKS plus a BONUS Mystery Gift!**
🍒 🍒 🍒	**Worth TWO FREE BOOKS!**
♣ ♣ ♣	**Worth ONE FREE BOOK!**
🔔 🔔 🍒	**TRY AGAIN!**

(MB-05)

DETACH AND MAIL CARD TODAY!

his spine to settle in a cold knot at his nape. His scalp felt as if was pulling taut. Something was wrong. He could sense it the way a seasoned wolf sensed a trap.

Kane moved into the brush that flanked the path, working his way cautiously around the bend. On the far side of the road he saw the trunk of a huge fig tree. A dead man hung crucified from it.

Spread-eagled to a bamboo framework in the shape of an X, suspended by chains from a thick bough of the tree, the corpse was secured to the frame by spikes driven through his wrists and ankles. He had been hanging there for at least two days, perhaps longer.

Birds, insects and other carrion feeders had stripped his face almost of all flesh so it was impossible to gauge the corpse's age. Although his clothes hung in tatters, Kane realized he wore the remains of a drab green uniform. A placard hung from the man's neck. The swirling, curving letters were large and crudely wrought, and although he couldn't read the language, he guessed the legend was meant as a warning.

He began walking again, more alert for sounds and signs of habitation than before. Before long, he came across a few—footprints intersecting, brush trampled, stems of shrubbery broken. Bending to study the footprints, he estimated that at least three men had passed by, dragging a fourth whose toes dragged in the dirt, digging narrow gouges. He guessed they were the same people who had crucified the dead man.

Looking across the path, he saw an area where brush and tall ferns had been pushed aside to allow passage into the jungle. He didn't care to follow the trail so he turned back down the road. He walked steadily for half an hour, when the path skirted the banks of a pond. Frogs croaked from the tall rushes sprouting from the water's edge.

Kane eyed it, looking for indications that anyone had passed it by recently but he saw nothing except for what he took to be an animal trail to the water. Suddenly he received the sudden but no less distinct impression he was being watched. He glanced all around him but could see nothing but foliage. He started walking again, but now he felt claustrophobic beneath the green umbrella of the rain forest.

The croaking of frogs abruptly ceased. A rustling commenced in the line of reeds bordering the pond. Kane stopped, his Sin Eater springing into his hand, but the noise stopped almost instantly. He waited to hear it again. He began to sweat, despite the internal thermostat of the shadow suit.

When the sound was not repeated, he marched forward again, the sense of being observed persisting. At the very edges of audibility, he heard the swishing sound of plants being pushed aside. He stopped again and so did the noise.

Kane considered firing a 360-degree full auto burst, but decided it was not tactically or diplomatically sound. On impulse, he decided to try an experiment. He kicked himself into a flat-out sprint, running down the road as fast as he could. With the possible exception of Domi, he was the fleetest of foot of everyone in Cerberus.

He ran for the count of twenty, ignoring the pain the exertions brought back to his chest. He came to a halt and tried to soften the harshness of his breathing as he stood still and listened. He definitely heard the crash of undergrowth behind him, although it ceased within seconds of him stopping.

He stared into the brush, recovering his breath, waiting for the ache in his chest to subside. His imagination populated the undergrowth-screened jungle with all varieties of monster, far more fearsome than a giant monitor lizard.

But neither a lizard nor any other variety of monster showed itself so he opened his pack and took out the canteen. He tilted his head back as he drank, admiring the way shafts of sunlight pierced the canopy of the rain forest. He liked the contrast of pale yellow against the dark green. He was still aware of the sensation of being watched, but he wasn't too concerned anymore. Running himself ragged to outdistance an unseen observer fit his definition of the law of diminishing returns.

When Kane lowered the canteen, he caught only a glimpse of the shadowy figure standing on the edge of the road before he spat out the last mouthful of water in a spray. He clutched at his Copperhead, trying to bring it bear.

A raspy voice said, "If you seek a young woman, I can tell you where you might find her."

Chapter 14

A small bent man spoke to Kane from the brush line. He wore an olive-drab tunic laced with rawhide strings, homespun shorts and leather sandals. His black hair was long and unkempt, speckled with gray. Three of his lower front teeth were missing.

The man's wrinkle-netted face was impassive, having much the same color and texture as his sandals. Kane assumed his eyes were jet-black, but it was hard to tell since all he could see were slightly curved slits surrounded by baggy flesh. He looked to be about five and a half feet tall, but because he was bent in an apparently perpetual crouch, he looked smaller still.

The man's voice reverberated within Kane's head, first as a conglomeration of liquid syllables before the translation program from the PDA fed him the English equivalent through the Commtact.

"You are an outlander," the man observed in his harsh, hoarse voice. "As was the girl."

Kane, keeping his Copperhead trained on the man as he capped the canteen, looked behind him. He didn't see anyone else lurking in the brush. "You saw a girl?"

"Oh, yes," the small man replied. "Saw her as clear as I'm seeing you now. Very pretty girl, very spirited."

Kane's sudden surge of relief ebbed when the man

added, "Yes, a very pretty girl with wavy dark hair. Too pretty for these parts."

"Did you see anyone else with her?" Kane asked.

The man frowned. "What do you mean?"

"Was there a man and another woman with her…a woman whose hair was like sunset?" He surprised himself with his poetic turn of phrase. He hoped it translated accurately.

The little man shook his head. "No. I saw only the dark-haired pretty girl. Too pretty for her own good, she was."

"You keep saying that," Kane snapped. "What are you talking about?"

The small bent man uttered a wheezing laugh. "She caught the general's eye. He's always interested in pretty young girls."

"The general of what?"

"The general, warlord of these territories. Soon he will rule all of Angkor Thom." There was a touch of pride in the old man's tone that aroused Kane's suspicions.

"How long ago did the general take her?" he asked.

The man shrugged. "Four days, I think."

"How far to Angkor Thom?"

"Nearly fifty miles, but she is not there."

Kane stepped forward, jaw muscles bunched as he struggled to tamp down his rising temper. "Then where the hell is she?"

The man's rasping laugh was louder this time, almost scornful. "Like I said, the general has her. If you would go to him, I can show the best route to take. My name is Chou Chan, and I can serve you as a guide."

Kane scowled down at him. "That's very convenient.

Do you expect me to believe that you just hang around out here in the jungle, waiting for outlanders to pass by so you can guide them to places of interest?"

Chou's expression didn't change, but the timbre of his voice did when he answered, "No, outlander, I do not expect you to believe that. I was here to see the body of my son and pay my respects."

Kane believed him but he asked, "Why didn't you cut him down?"

"And end my own life by hanging from one of these trees?" He shook his head mournfully. "No, outlander. My life is hard, but I do not wish for the Cobra Guard to relieve me of it in the same fashion they did my son's."

Kane didn't like the implications of the Cobra Guard, but he didn't respond to it. "All right. I accept your offer."

"My usual fee is five quills a day."

Not having any idea what a quill might be in Cambodia, Kane replied, "I don't have any your local currency."

Eyeing the pack slung from the tall man's shoulder, Chou said silkily, "Perhaps you have some goods, some objects of value from your own land that can be traded. There's a trading post not far from here which you might exchange some items for quills."

"How far is it to this general of yours?" Kane demanded.

The bent little man gestured diffidently down the road. "If we start now, we can make the trading post in less than an hour. Once I have my quills, we will reach the general very quickly."

Kane studied the man's wrinkled face for a moment,

looking for signs of deception. He found none, but then he found nothing at all there but creases and seams. Chou Chan possessed a perfect poker face.

Kane sighed. "All right. Let's go get some quills."

DESPITE THE OCCASIONAL sour aspersions cast by Brigid Baptiste, Kane was not a fool, nor did he believe in co-incidence. He didn't trust Chou Chan any further than he could have carried Grant piggyback—which wasn't far.

The little man had not evinced much surprise at en-countering a foreign stranger in the jungle, much less one dressed as oddly as Kane. Although he didn't think Chou Chan had been deliberately lurking near the road waiting for his arrival, he definitely suspected he had been lying in wait for someone. More than likely the man was a spy or a scout for a party of brigands.

After several minutes of marching down the green shadowed tunnel formed by the intertwined boughs of trees overhanging the road, Kane heard the gurgling rush of water. "Is there a river up ahead?" he asked his guide.

Chou Chan nodded. "The Siemrap. It is one of the many waterways that feed the city of Angkor Thom."

"You've been there?"

The little man angled a shaggy eyebrow at him. "Of course."

"What do you know about it?"

"What everyone knows."

"Which is?" Kane prodded impatiently. He added sarcastically, "Pretend I really *am* the outlander that you've been calling me."

Chou Chan sighed wearily. "The ruler of Angkor Thom was originally a Naga princess called Ye-liu.

There was then a foreigner, called Kaundinya, who practiced the cult of spirits. He dreamed that a spirit gave him a bow, and then ordered him to board a trading vessel and take to sea.

"That evening, Kaundinya returned to the spirit temple, where he found a bow and then, following the merchants, embarked upon the seas. He arrived at the town of Funan. Ye-liu led her troops to resist him. Kaundinya raised his bow. Ye-liu took fright and submitted to him. Thereupon Kaundinya took her to wife and took her kingdom. Of course that was a very long time ago."

"Of course," Kane conceded dryly. "I was thinking of something a little more recent. What I want to know is who rules there now."

Blandly, Chou Chan replied, "Kumudvati, the Naga princess, direct descendant of the original Kumudvati who married Kusha, the son of great god Rama. It was part of a pact, you see, to end centuries of unremitting warfare. A human tribe known as Mauneya were fighting with the Naga in the subterranean regions, whose dominions they seized and whose treasures they plundered."

"That has a familiar ring," Kane commented.

The little man acted as if he hadn't heard. "The Naga chiefs appealed to Vishnu for relief, and he instructed them what to do. The Naga sent one of their princesses to the Mauneya's king, Pariksit. She cursed him to die within seven days as a result of a snakebite. The king decided to accept the curse as a will of providence and sat down at the bank of the Mekong to prepare for his death. At that time, the great young sage, Shuka, the son of Vyasa, arrived there, and the king asked him to explain the most important knowledge meant for a person about to die. Thus the sage started to narrate the great Purana. As a result the king attained self-realization before he died."

Kane stopped short of sighing wearily. He forced himself to listen as he and Chou Chan tramped on down the trail, hoping he would eventually hear something of use.

"But," the little man continued, "the king's son Janamejaya became angry at the serpents and to avenge his father's death he started a great sacrifice meant to destroy all the serpents and the Naga. But later he stopped it to please the sage Astika, their relative. You see, Astika's father was the sage Jaratkaru who married Kumudvati, the sister of the Naga king Vasuki, who married Rama, who blessed Angkor Thom."

Chou Chan fell silent and after an expectant moment, Kane demanded, "What the hell was the point of that story?"

"You'll find out soon," Chou Chan answered with a cryptic smile.

"Not if I can help it," Kane snapped irritably. "Can't I just follow the river to Angkor Thom?"

The little man flashed him a gap-toothed grin. "Do not fear, outlander. I will make sure you reach your destination, one way or another."

Kane narrowed his eyes at the peculiar choice of phrase but before he could demand clarification, Chou continued, "You are very lucky that I encountered you. The forest isn't kind to strangers."

"I kind of got that impression when I came across your son," Kane retorted darkly.

Chou Chan's grin vanished and he said nothing more

for the next few minutes. The road doglegged to parallel the muddy bank of the Siemrap River. Brown water swirled and foamed around the buttressing roots of colossal trees that rose from the shallows like pillars.

"Am I to understand this trading post of yours is on the river?" Kane asked.

Chou Chan nodded. "That makes it easier to reach for villagers who live downriver."

A sudden thrashing in the undergrowth ahead of them brought the little man to a halt. He gestured for Kane to do the same. After a few seconds of tense, alert listening, he whispered, "There is a dragon stalking us."

"How can you be sure?" Kane wanted to know in the same low voice, pitched low to disguise the tremor of fear in it.

The little man's splayed nostrils dilated. "I smell it."

Kane took a tentative sniff of the air and detected the faint, musky reek of reptiles. "I think you're right," he murmured. "Let's find a place to—"

The rest of his words were drowned out by a snapping and rending of bushes and saplings. Palm fronds and leaves scattered in an explosion as the scaled monstrosity came blundering onto the road, its long tail lashing, whipping up loose twigs. With lumbering steps of its four squat legs, the giant lizard crept forward to block their path.

Kane realized the dragon was smaller than the one he had killed earlier, but not by much. Its whitish belly nearly dragged on the ground, but the height of its head was almost the same as Chou Chan's.

Tamping down the panic that threatened to consume him, Kane unleathered his Sin Eater and raised the Copperhead. Chou Chan took several unsteady steps backward. Faintly, he said, "We can try to run, but I am not very fast."

Kane carefully stepped around him, putting his body between the little man's and that of the giant monitor lizard. "I don't feel much like running," he sidemouthed. "Feel free to go if you want."

The little man cast Kane a frightened look, then turned on his heel and began sprinting. As Kane hoped, the dragon lunged straight for the bent little man, its jaws gaping open and revealing needle-pointed fangs and a huge split tongue lolling in its mouth.

Kane fired both the Sin Eater and Copperhead simultaneously, the double reports sounding like a crazed jackhammer beneath the closed canopy of the rain forest. The 9 mm rounds spat by the Sin Eater pounded into dragon's barrel-shaped body, stitching the scales with a series of little blood-rimmed holes.

The 4.85 mm bullets fired by the Copperhead ripped crimson gouges through the creature's slab-muscled neck, tracking up to punch through the side of its skull. Emitting a hissing screech, it turned to snap at the wounds, as if it were being stung by insects.

The giant lizard went into thrashing convulsions, writhing and thrashing through brush, crashing headlong into a tree trunk, making great gurgling cries. Kane watched as its huge body spasmed wildly, its claws tearing up great clots of earth and its whiplashing tail shredding the undergrowth.

The monster reptile flipped and flopped and struggled crazily, as if its brain refused to admit that its body was dying. Rolling over and over, it crushed a bed of ferns, then fell into the river with a great splash. The heavy flailing tail sent spuming sheets of water cascading over the bank.

The dragon's violent death throes slowly ceased, although its tail continued to twitch with postmortem spasms. Crimson-tinged ripples spread out from its body.

Chou Chan gingerly returned to stand beside Kane. In a whispering voice made husky by awe, he said, "You have powerful weapons, outlander. You would be wise to conceal them if you travel to Angkor Thom. To be caught with such weapons by the Cobra Guard would mean certain death."

Kane gazed down at him and said coldly but with a great deal of meaning, "I wouldn't die alone."

The little man nodded in comprehension. "You needn't fear that I will betray you to them. I would not betray an enemy to those pigs, much less a man who just saved my life."

"Good," Kane said sarcastically. "Somebody else who claims they owe me big."

Chou Chan squinted up at him puzzledly. "I do not understand."

"I didn't expect you to," Kane replied. "But I do expect you to stop calling me 'outlander.' It has unpleasant associations for me. My name is Kane."

Chou Chan repeated the name several times until he had mastered its pronunciation. "Very well…Kane."

"Yes," Kane drawled sardonically. "Very well. Is there any other carnivorous wildlife I should know about before we go on?"

Chou Chan's brow furrowed as he pondered the question. "Tigers."

"Tigers?" Kane echoed uneasily. "Big ones?"

Chou Chan nodded. "Oh, yes. Very big tigers indeed. With very big appetites. So we should hurry before one of them smells the dragon's blood and comes to feast…and decides we might make a good dessert."

Kane very swiftly ejected the empty clip from the Copperhead and toggled a new one home. "Giant lizards, tigers and warlords," he murmured. "Oh, my."

Chapter 15

Brigid Baptiste had been taken prisoner too often over the past couple of years to delude herself into thinking that by lodging complaints with her captors she would receive better treatment. As it was, she had been dealt with much more humanely by the self-proclaimed Magickers than by most of her prior abductors.

With her back pressed against a damp stone wall, her wrists and ankles were bound to pitons driven deep into the floor and wall. Multiple strands of leather thongs were drawn through eyebolts in all three pitons and expertly twisted and knotted around her extremities.

Several yards across the dark gallery, a small fire burned in a bowl-shaped brazier, sending sooty smoke curling up to vanish in the dense gloom. Seated around the fire were three lean men wearing hooded, cassock-like robes and sandals. Despite their Asian features, they reminded her of pix she had seen of Franciscan monks, but after three days in their company, she knew they weren't holy men. The surreptitious glances they flicked up and down her figure, as tightly encased as it was in the black shadow suit, were anything but pious.

All were bald, with heads so closely shaved no stubble was evident on their scalps. Their skins were a pale saffron hue, their eyes dark and for the most part their faces were expressionless. The men all appeared to be identical at first, but after a couple of days Brigid discerned differences among them, primarily due to their ages.

Each bore upon his brow a symbol worked in metallic ink, that of a spiral surrounding a starburst. The spirals were of all the same cobalt blue, but the starbursts varied as to hue—red, yellow and white.

The Magickers acted as her warders, but she learned almost nothing of them except they employed the honorific "Brother" when they addressed one another in the Khmer dialect.

Despite her eidetic memory, Brigid retained very few solid recollections of how she came to be in their custody. All she could call forth in her mind were dazed and chaotic visions—the staccato hammering of autofire, voices shouting words in a strange tongue, fleeting glimpses of rushing figures, Nora Pennick's loud scream of terror, then a fragmented image of Brewster Philboyd falling down, blood streaming over his face.

A blow on the back of her head detonated a bomb of stars within her skull. She vaguely remembered a sensation of falling, but not of landing. She plunged into a sunless gulf of unconsciousness.

When Brigid awoke, she found herself securely bound, her thought processes moving like half-frozen mud, her stomach jumping with nausea. Her head ached with a blinding pain. Not too long ago, a blunt trauma to her skull had put her in a coma for several days and severely affected her short-term memory. Since then, she had harbored a fear of suffering a similar injury that would result in permanent mental impairment.

The dull realization she was physically sound finally

occurred to her. She accepted the miracle grimly because she had no idea of where she was being kept prisoner or even why.

At first Brigid could make out very little of her surroundings. All was gloomy and dim, with little more than monstrously elongated shadows shifting over roughly hewed rock walls. She heard only whispering echoes of a sibilant language. She smelled mildew and stagnant water. After a little while, objects, sounds and actions assumed proper proportions to reality.

She made out hooded figures moving to and fro within a stone gallery, firelight glistening from damp, mossy walls. The language the figures spoke was Khmer, a sample of which she had briefly listened to in Cerberus before embarking on the interphase transit. She assumed she was within a temple, perhaps one similar to that she, Nora and Philboyd had phased into.

Brigid had no difficulty recalling the few minutes preceding the attack and her abduction. Followed by Nora and Philboyd, she had carried the interphaser into the Cerberus mat-trans unit. The shape of the interphaser resembled a very squat, broad-based pyramid made of smooth, gleaming alloy. Only one foot in overall height, its width did not exceed ten inches. From the base protruded a small power unit and a keypad.

Philboyd had commented again, in his wry way, how closely the pyramidion reminded him of incense burners that could be purchased in "head shops" during the 1960s and '70s. Inasmuch as he had helped construct the latest version of the device, Brigid didn't take his slightly dismissive comments seriously.

Philboyd understood how the interphaser's pyramidal configuration was neither arbitrary nor aesthetic. The energy generated by the device progressed by four different routes, rejoining in a single point at the apex. The energy output flowed in a helix spiral pattern with opposite but equal frequencies of wavelength and radiation. The intensity on each side of the vortex at any given point triggered the quantum induction shift by vibrational resonance.

Still, Philboyd had expressed doubt many times about the interphaser's ability to function, despite the fact if it had not been for the second version of the device, he would have never been given the opportunity to help in the construction of a third.

A little over three months before, when the Parallax Points program was being decrypted, the Cerberus personnel involved in the process were nonplussed when one set of coordinates led to a location off the planet itself, on the Moon. All of them knew the stories about predark space settlements, even of secret bases on the Moon, one of the largest built in Manitius Crater region. That particular site was chosen because of its proximity to artifacts that some scientists speculated were the shattered remains of an incredibly ancient city, once protected by massive geodesic domes.

A remote probe had been dispatched first and it returned not just with evidence the Manitius Moon colony was still inhabited, but populated by a disaffected group of scientists, marauding packs of carnobots and both a flesh-and-blood devil and a machine known by the acronym of DEVIL.

Brewster Philboyd and Nora Pennick were two of the scientists living there who had agreed to relocate to

Earth. Brigid found something very appealing about the lanky, myopic astrophysicist. Whether it was his self-deprecating sense of humor or his intellect, she wasn't sure. He wasn't a man of action, but he wasn't a coward, either. Both of them had faced Enki, the last of the legendary dragon kings, in his lunar citadel. Philboyd's courage, although it had cracked, hadn't completely crumbled, and Brigid had been glad to have a solid bulwark at her side on that terrifying night.

The downside of that event was how Philboyd began looking to Brigid as something of an anchor in his new life in Cerberus. He had insisted on accompanying her and Nora on the new interphaser's inaugural transit, and Brigid figured the prospect of losing her due to the malfunction of a machine he had helped to build awakened an almost childlike insecurity within him.

Brigid didn't know Nora Pennick particularly well, since she was a quiet young woman with a reserve Brigid attributed to her calm and collected British upbringing. She and another Britisher, Cleve Randolph, had been part of the DEVIL scientific staff on the Moon. Cleve, however, had been killed when he helped Grant steal a transatmospheric Manta ship.

Unlike some of her colleagues, Nora didn't display a thinly veiled attitude of superiority toward her hosts. Many of the Moon base personnel seemed amused by the Cerberus exiles' ignorance of a number of twentieth-century events and items, but she wasn't one of them, and Brigid readily accepted her offer to accompany her on the test phase.

After a little argument, Brigid agreed that Philboyd could join her and Nora. The mission was not to launch an exploration, but simply intended to test the interphaser's capabilities, to make sure it could correctly process the Parallax Points data. They would make the phase transit, ascertain they had arrived where they were supposed to and then phase back to Cerberus. Brigid anticipated the entire journey would take only a few minutes. However, as a veteran of a number of past missions that went awry, she carried a pack containing MREs, bottled water, first-aid supplies and her TP-9 autopistol.

Brigid carried the interphaser into the gateway unit and placed it on the center of the floor. When making phase transits from the redoubt, they always used the mat-trans chamber because it could be hermetically sealed. Philboyd pulled the brown-tinted armaglass door closed on its counterbalanced hinges.

Brigid knelt and touched the interphaser's inset activation toggles on the keyboard. She slid it back into the base as a waxy, glowing funnel of light fanned up from the metal apex of the pyramidion. It looked like diffused veil of backlit fog, with tiny shimmering stars dancing within it.

Philboyd and Nora stared at the display in wonder. The light expanded into a gushing borealis several feet wide, spreading out within the chamber. A thready pulse of vibration tickled their skin, and shadows crawled over the armaglass walls, moving in fitful jerks and leaps. A faint hint of a breeze brushed their faces and ruffled their hair.

The veil of light produced from the apex of the pyramidion extended up and outward in wavering arc, giving the illusion of a Chinese hand fan opening up, with the interphaser acting as the handle. Both Nora and

Philboyd had been briefed on the phenomenon but they didn't move—until Brigid stepped toward the pyramid, strolled through the fan of light and vanished.

Unlike a mat-trans gateway jump, phasing along a hyperdimensional conduit was more akin to stepping from one room into another—if the rooms were thousands of miles apart. The phase jumper experienced a giddy second of acceleration, a half second of whirling vertigo as if hurled a vast distance at a blinding speed, then a strange cushioning sensation as if he or she had jumped into a wall of compressed air.

Upon arriving at the destination point, the period of disorientation was short, despite the fact that Philboyd stumbled and nearly fell. The lanky astrophysicist looked around dazedly, but he recovered quickly.

The three people from Cerberus stood within an enclosure of green-black walls, two of them crumbling due to the pressure exerted by enormous tree roots. They waited until the field effect generated by the interphaser collapsed before they cautiously moved out of the building, in order to take a sextant reading and ascertain they were where the Parallax Points coordinates indicated they would be.

Brigid estimated that was at least three days ago—three days of no word regarding the fates of Nora Pennick and Brewster Philboyd, no word of why she was being held prisoner or of what had happened to the interphaser and certainly no word of a rescue mounted by Kane or anyone else from Cerberus. The Commtact was still secured to her mastoid bone, hidden by the fall of her hair. She couldn't be certain that it hadn't been damaged and even now Kane was somewhere in Cambodia, trying to hail her on it. But then again, she couldn't be certain Kane, Grant and Domi weren't still engaged in the op to Minnesota.

Regardless, she felt that Kane was already somewhere nearby even though she had no way of knowing if her feeling stemmed from wishful thinking or a far deeper response. The head ruled the body, cerebration came before emotions, but Brigid always shied away from examining the bond between her and Kane. Logically, there was no explanation. They were bound by spiritual chains, linked to each other and the same destiny.

Resolutely, she pushed the conjectures away. What mattered most now was surviving until Kane and most likely Grant arrived. She knew they would, because entertaining any other alternative was intolerable.

It wasn't as if Brigid was frightened by the prospect of being held prisoner. Over the past two years, Brigid had come to accept risk as a part of her way of life, taking chances so that others might find the ground beneath their feet a little more secure. She didn't consider her attitude idealism but simple pragmatism. If she had learned anything from her association with Kane, Grant and Domi, it was to regard death as a part of the challenge of existence, a fact that every man and woman had to face eventually.

She would accept it without humiliating herself if it came as a result of her efforts to remove the yokes of the baronies from the collective necks of humanity. She never spoke of it, certainly not to the cynical Kane, but she had privately vowed to make the future a better, cleaner place than either the past or the present. Dourly, she reflected it was probably a good thing she had never mentioned her goals to Kane since he would have no doubt asked how she intended to achieve them by being captured and held in a stinking cell.

If nothing else, the so-called Magickers had not offered to harm her in any way although they were not the most attentive of warders or hosts. The food they supplied at irregular intervals was of poor quality, usually consisting of a fish stew mixed with a handful of unbleached rice and tasteless root vegetables. The water had a foul taste so she drank sparingly of it, fearful of contracting dysentery.

Several times she heard strange trumpeting calls outside the walls of her prison, the noise reminding her of a combination of bugle and roar. Although she couldn't be sure, she guessed elephants were the source of the sound. After she felt confident enough with the dialect, she asked what happened to the emergency ration kit she had carried. She received only a head shake. When she inquired about her pistol, she received no reaction whatsoever, which made her suspect the TP-9 was in the possession of the robed men.

Her hands were untied so she could eat, and three times a day she was escorted to a place where she could relieve herself, little more than a hole in the stone floor. Her escort considerately turned his back when she was so occupied, but he inserted a hand into the belled sleeve of his robe, a silent warning he kept a weapon there.

If the weapon was a knife, Brigid doubted the blade could penetrate her shadow suit, but she wasn't inclined to escape until she gathered more information. She learned the language quickly and overhead whispers of the imminent arrival of someone in authority named Brother Javalara.

She wondered if he was the reason she had not eaten all day. She tried to be stoic about it, but finally she leaned forward as far as the leather cords permitted and called to the men at the fire, "Gentlemen, I have an excellent time sense, and I think I haven't eaten in at least twelve hours."

Her pronunciation of a few of the words might have been less than perfect, but the Magickers seemed to understand her nevertheless. One of them, a young man called Brother Yasovar, walked over to where she sat trussed.

"I am sorry," he said in a soft, almost feminine voice. "You must be patient. These are difficult times. Many people in Phnom Kuleh go hungry. It is particularly difficult for us, the guild of Magickers."

"If you were any kind of decent sorcerers," Brigid answered wryly, "you'd conjure up something to eat."

"We're not those kind of magicians. You must wait until Brother Javalara arrives. He will see to all your needs."

Brigid stopped short of muttering, "That's what I'm afraid of," but she did inquire, "May I ask you something, Yasovar?"

"Does it have to do with food?"

She chuckled in spite of herself. "No, not this time."

The hooded head inclined in a nod. "Proceed."

"Why are you holding me prisoner in the first place? You scarcely seem able to look after yourselves."

"We believe you can do much to aid the Magickers' cause." The response was quick, almost by rote.

"What cause is that?"

"Brother Javalara will be here soon to explain. You

can dine with him, and he'll tell you what he deems suitable."

"I hope he brings something suitable to dine on," Brigid retorted. "Unless you consider what you've been feeding me a delicacy."

Yasovar stiffened as if offended by the remark. "We lived in Kumudvati's court before Colonel Puyang had us banished."

"And who would Kumudvati be again?"

Sounding slightly surprised that she had to ask, Yasovar answered, "The Devi-Naga, the serpent princess. She outlawed my guild."

Brigid's lips quirked in a smile. "Her administration didn't care for your brand of magic? I know I can see some areas of improvement."

Sadly, Yasovar stated, "We were not always sorcerers."

"But were you always Magickers?" Brigid pressed.

Before Yasovar could reply, a male voice cut in. "You must overlook the young brother's tendency to overdo the bitter-exile routine. It's been several years, and he's yet to come to terms with it."

The tone of voice was pleasant and conversational. A tall, gaunt man carrying a burlap bag strode toward her. He wore a thin leather skullcap on his hairless head, the forepart curving down toward the bridge of his nose like a widow's peak. It bore a golden starburst symbol but without the addition of the spiral. The ends of a down-sweeping mustache joined with a wispy goatee on his chin.

"I am Brother Javalara."

He gestured toward her wrists and said to Yasovar, "Release her."

The younger man bent over Brigid, withdrawing a slender knife from his sleeve. He began sawing at the bonds encircling her wrists.

"You know," Brigid suggested helpfully, "if you just untie me, you can use the thongs to tie up another woman."

To her surprise, Yasovar laughed apologetically. "I'm no good with knots. We'd be here all night."

"I hope you don't mind dining on rabbit," Javalara said.

"At this point," Brigid replied, "I eat most anything." She paused and added quickly, "Within reason, that is."

Yasovar finished slicing through the thongs binding her wrists and ankles. Javalara stepped forward, extending a hand. Brigid waved him away and stood, rubbing her wrists to restore the circulation. She realized she was almost as tall as Javalara.

"I am sorry we had to treat a woman of your obvious intellectual capacity in such a fashion," Javalara said. He sounded sincere. "What is your name?"

She tossed her tangled red-gold mane over her shoulders, noting sourly the dire need for a shampoo. "Baptiste."

He bowed his head respectfully. "I'm happy to have you among us, Baptiste."

"But not," she countered dourly, "happy enough to let me go so I can find my friends."

"I am afraid for the time being we must keep you with us."

Javalara handed the bag to Yasovar. "Prepare this, my brother."

As the young man walked toward the fire, Javalara said quietly, "There is a certain and ongoing problem we need to find a solution to and you appear to be qualified to help us. Tomorrow morning we will begin our journey to Angkor Thom."

Brushing off her shadow suit, Brigid asked, "What kind of problem are you talking about?"

Javalara hesitated a second before answering, "It has to do with the generation, balance and manipulation of energy."

Brigid stared at him, her mind racing. When he didn't elaborate, she said flatly, "That doesn't tell me much."

"I realize that, Baptiste. You will learn more, I assure you."

Another one of the Magickers approached, carrying a cloth-covered bundle in his arms. Coming to stand beside Javalara, he whispered into his ear for a few seconds. Javalara nodded gravely.

With an edge in her voice, Brigid asked, "Do you know anything about the two people who were with me when we were set upon?"

Javalara nodded dolefully. "The news is not encouraging. The man was captured by the Cobra Guard, the Devi-Naga's royal police. The woman, as best as I can adjudge, is in the custody of the general."

Brigid narrowed her eyes. "The general? I take it he has nothing to do with the Devi-Naga?"

Javalara snorted out a laugh. "No, indeed."

"Do you know if they're alive?" she demanded impatiently.

The man shook his head, lips creased in a frown. "I haven't heard anything one way or the other as to their final fates. I'm sorry."

A cold knot of angry frustration tightened in the pit of Brigid's belly. Between clenched teeth she said, "For

Magickers, you're about the most incompetent and poorly organized group of sorcerers I ever heard of."

Javalara drew himself up in an attitude of wounded dignity. Sadly, he replied, "I cannot debate you on that observation, Baptiste. But like Brother Yasovar said, we were not always sorcerers."

"Then what were you?" she snapped.

Quietly, but with a touch of pride, Javalara intoned, "Scientists."

He turned to the Magicker standing at his side and whisked away the cloth. The man held the interphaser, balanced carefully on the flats of both hands.

"As, apparently, are you."

Chapter 16

The trading post wasn't quite what Kane expected. Built of ornately carved and decorated wood, the structure reminded him more of one of the temples he had glimpsed in his flyover of the Angkor plain.

Upon a second, closer look he realized his assessment had been correct. The building had once been a temple. Pinnacled towers rose from the river like masts of submerged ships. Part of the structure had sunk and broken away, tilting into the river beneath the waterline. The sections made of wood were obviously added at a much later date.

A small settlement had grown up around the trading post. Thatch-and-reed huts were scattered along on the bank, and the smoke of cooking fires lay in planes across the water. Half-naked children, browned by the sun, played at the river's edge. People of both sexes and all ages moved among the huts, going about their daily business. Most of them were dressed in similar fashion to Chou Chan. A half-dozen wooden docks extended from the riverbank. Fishing boats, dugout canoes and skiffs were tied up at them or being paddled out into the brown water of the Siemrap.

Chou Chan cocked his head toward the partially submerged building. "We have arrived at the trading center safely."

Kane resisted the impulse to tell him his evaluation might be premature. A group of Asian men lounged in the shade of a tarp tacked to a bamboo arbor near the entrance of the trading post. They were a bit too obvious in their lack of interest in Kane and his guide.

All relatively young men, they were dressed much like the other people in the village but they didn't exude an indolent personality. They reminded Kane of watchdogs, tense and ready to raise an alarm. Their poses of studied indifference and sideways glances toward Kane bespoke sec men.

"Who did you say runs this trading post?" Kane asked uneasily.

"I didn't," Chou Chan responded brusquely.

"Right, and that's why I'm asking now."

Chou Chan hesitated a second before saying, "His name is Zhou Tzu."

"Zow Zoo?" Kane echoed.

The little man nodded. "He is very well respected in these parts and will not cheat you."

"I'm not worried about being cheated," Kane muttered as they walked passed the Asian youths.

Thunder boomed in the near distance, a rumbling roll. Kane glanced up at the gray clouds gathering in the sky.

"It rains several times a day this time of year," Chou Chan remarked.

Kane followed the little man up the stone steps leading to a beaded curtain that served as a door. The room they entered was large, with a high, beamed ceiling, and it resembled nothing so much as a storage warehouse that had exploded due to the pressure of shoving far too many objects into it.

Kane swept his gaze over the freestanding shelves, cases, racks and bins. He could make no sense of the order in which the items were displayed but he doubted there ever had been one. Shelves laden with ceramic jars, unidentifiable bits of rust-flaked metal, bins containing bolts and scraps of cloth and freestanding racks holding a variety of small statues occupied almost every inch of floor space.

Most of the figurines depicted a fat-bellied Buddha, but many others were worn by the weathering of the ages, so it was impossible to tell what they were meant to represent, animal, mineral, human or otherwise. None of the items Kane glimpsed looked like viable trade goods. They more closely resembled a sampling of objects dug out of a garbage pit.

The trading post apparently provided double service as a tavern or café. Two men wearing dark tunics and high-topped laced boots sat at a table near an open door that led out to a deck. One of them wore a scarlet headband with a strange spiral symbol embroidered on it. The other had a single loop of silver dangling from his left ear. Both looked to be in their early twenties.

A fat man wearing a leather vest that concealed only a portion of his flabby torso made a lazy effort to oil the blade of a short sword. Its edge showed numerous V-shaped nicks. He nodded toward Chou Chan sleepily.

Gesturing to Kane, the little man said, "My friend Kane has traveled a long way, from a far-off territory. He has valuable treasures from his land to trade for quills."

The fat man looked at Kane with a sudden, penetrating interest. His eyes darted to the pack strapped to his back and then to the Copperhead dangling from a lanyard stretched across his chest. "My name is Pheng-Ki. I review all the merchandise before any business is done."

"I thought a guy named Zhou Tzu ran this operation," Kane said nonchalantly.

Pheng-Ki's lips pursed disapprovingly. "Zhou Tzu is responsible for the disbursement of quills. He is far too busy to look at every piece of junk brought in by vagabonds."

Kane decided to ignore the implications of the remark but he asked, "Maybe you can tell me what quills are."

Pheng-Ki grunted and turned toward a small desk set against the wall. Kane saw a narrow curtained doorway to the left of the man. Flickering light glowed feebly on the other side of it.

The fat man opened a drawer, rummaged around inside it for a moment, then withdrew a long white feather, apparently one from the wing of a large waterfowl. He held it out toward Kane, who frowned in puzzlement. Then light glinted from a sprinkling of gold dust within the vanes.

"Now do you understand our currency, outlander?" Chou Chan asked. "You owe me five of those…or something of equal value."

The hard edge to his voice and the reversion to addressing him as "outlander" raised Kane's nape hairs. At the same instant he heard the scuff of leather against floorboards. Wheeling on the ball of his right foot, he drove the toe of his left between the thighs of the man wearing the red headband.

The man grunted, jackknifed at the waist, and Kane

hammered him face first to the floor with a blow from his Sin Eater-weighted forearm. He kicked him in the side of the head, rendering him unconscious.

The man with the silver earring reached for Kane's backpack, securing a grip on a strap. He tried to wrestle Kane into a corner. Both Pheng-Ki and Chou Chan began shouting instructions and screeching in outrage.

Kane turned in the direction of the pull, grabbed a handful of tunic and butted the man in the face with his forehead. His attacker's nose collapsed with a wet crunch of cartilage. Blood squirted from his nostrils as from a squashed tick. Staggering the width of the room, he stumbled out on the deck, where his heels snagged on a loose board and he collapsed heavily onto his back.

Bellowing in wordless fury Pheng-Ki swung at Kane with the notched knife. Kane shifted to the left, and the blade crashed into a shelf, causing small items to jump from it and thump to the floor. It took all of Kane's willpower to restrain himself from unleathering his Sin Eater and deflating the man's swag belly with a 9 mm triburst.

Pheng-Ki lunged at him, and lifted his arms, depending on the tough fabric of his shadow suit to turn the blade. As the nicked edge sawed uselessly against his sleeves, Kane drove a knee into the man's ballooning stomach.

Pheng-Ki uttered a noise between a belch and a squawk and stepped backward. He managed to stay on his feet and renew his attack with the knife. Kane ducked a vicious roundhouse from the blade. The force of his unconnected blow turned Pheng-Ki completely, and Kane dropped, sweeping the fat man's feet out from under him with his right leg. As Pheng-Ki sat heavily on the floor, Kane bounced erect and hooked the corner of a freestanding cabinet with the fingers of his right hand and heaved.

The case tottered, cabinet swayed and items fell from the shelves, clattering to the floor, pelting Pheng-Ki. The man raised an arm and his lips parted, but only a high-pitched keening wail issued from them as the heavy case crashed down atop him.

Teeth bared in a silent snarl, Kane whirled toward Chou Chan, who made a shambling run around him toward the curtained doorway. Kane clotheslined him in the throat with his left arm, lifting him up and dropping him hard on his back. Bending over and grabbing him by a handful of his greasy hair, Kane jerked the little man to his feet and swung him around. The man squealed in pain, reaching up to prise Kane's fingers open.

"You misunderstand, outlander—"

"That's *my* line, you sawed-off little turd," Kane snapped, the Sin Eater sliding into his hand. He jammed the bore against the side of the little man's head. "Why'd you bring me here? You've got about three seconds to talk or you won't tell anything to anybody ever again."

Despite the temptation, Kane had no intention of killing the man, but he knew such a bluff would work well with a sleazy con artist like Chou Chan.

"You said you sought a girl, Kane! I sought only to help you!" he bleated.

"It's 'Kane' again, now, is it?" He laughed scornfully. "Let's go back to outlander…and back to the girl."

"Kane!"

The female voice was sharp, strident and familiar.

His head swiveled so fast his neck tendons twinged in protest. Nora Pennick stood before the curtained doorway, her right arm supported by a sling. The left leg of her bodysuit was torn, showing a white, crimson-splotched bandage on the thigh beneath. Although her hair was in disarray and her eyes dark-ringed, she appeared to be in fairly good condition.

Kane shoved Chou Chan away from him. The bent little man stumbled backward, tripped over a fallen statue and fell heavily. Kane paid him no attention, as with two long strides he crossed the room to where Nora stood. "Are you all right?" he asked, looking her up and down.

She smiled wanly, touching her arm in its sling and shifting her left leg. "It's not quite as bad as it looks…dislocated arm, gash on my thigh." Her voice was soft, almost subdued. "I have been well cared for."

"By who?" Kane demanded.

"By me, Mr. Kane." The quiet male voice floating out of the doorway was fluid, his English free of any hint of an accent. It was as if the speaker had learned the language from a computer's speech program, because there was a certain sterility of tone, an almost machinelike lack of tonal inflections.

Kane snapped up his Sin Eater, pointing it at the shadowy figure standing just behind Nora. "Who the hell are you?"

"You may kill me, but that will do no good," the man said. "You will never find your other two friends."

"You didn't answer my question."

The man stepped forward into the light, thrusting aside the curtain. He was almost a head taller than Nora Pennick, his clean-shaved face impassive and hard, the soft-ness of youth long vanished from it. His eyes, narrowed by the Asian epicanthic fold, glittered with a cold deter-mination. Jet-black hair hung loose about his lean face in a tangle of witch locks. A long thin white scar crooked down from his hairline to bisect his right eyebrow.

He was a striking figure in his bright red Chinese robe, embroidered with heavy gold thread in dragon forms and tiny figures of Mandarin nobility from a past epoch of Asian history. The high collar and velvet-trimmed belled sleeves didn't detract from the charis-matic force he radiated. A tigerish force burned within him, the fire of a dangerous, professional warrior with a purpose. The gaze Nora directed toward him was one of complete adoration.

In the same quiet, cultured tone, the man said, "My name is Zhou Tzu. *General* Zhou Tzu."

Kane's finger hovered over the Sin Eater's trigger stud, his eyes slitting in an effort to conceal his confu-sion. At that second, the tramp of running feet filled the big room. Kane turned slightly as the young men he had seen lounging outside rushed into the trading post, en-closing him in a semicircle. They moved swiftly, with military precision. The manner in which they wielded small, wicked-looking subguns, aiming the bores only on him showed they had been exceptionally well trained in the use of small arms.

For a long, stretched-out moment of tension, the tab-leau held, everyone frozen in place. Then General Zhou Tzu stepped to one side, gesturing toward the doorway. "Some tea, Mr. Kane?"

Chapter 17

Colonel Puyang stood on the balcony of the high tower, gazing at the vast city spread out below the gray skies. His mood was equally gray as he tried not to think about the whereabouts of Zhou Tzu or two of the strangers.

The start of the rainy season always put him in a bad mood. Persistent downpours would turn the fields outside of the walls into quagmires. The foundation of some of the older buildings had sunk deep into the ground, and they suffered from intermittent flooding.

At least it was a clean, nourishing rain, which would feed the crops and the citizens of Angkor Thom and in turn, draw new citizens to repopulate the ancient city. He found the thought a very small, very cold comfort. It was best if the people remained hungry.

Angkor Thom was a city of towers and spires and empty legends, Puyang reflected. Ruled by a myth in the form of a child. But that would change, he thought. It *must* change.

He turned, straightening his uniform tunic, and walked to the round table upon which lay a square of rice paper. The table was huge and ornately carved after the fashion of imperial Khmer. A golden candelabrum, whose branches bore the likenesses of seven intertwined cobras, illuminated the red wax seal at the bottom edge of the paper.

"You have yet to sign the decree, Your Glory," he said gruffly.

A figure stirred upon the high-backed chair elevated atop a dais. "I have my doubts, colonel, about the efficacy of this decree. How will it help?" The feminine voice was soft, pitched very low.

Puyang answered, "We have given the people such a grand and gracious capital for our empire, yet the ingratitude, the rebellious attitudes are still on the rise. We cannot risk losing all we have built over the years."

He gestured dramatically, as if wishing to embrace the chamber. No expense had been spared to render the vaulted room a seat of luxury. Walls of damp, rough stone were hung with richly embroidered tapestries. The cold flagstone floor was covered by thick, soft carpets of many colors and complex designs.

A taboret of glided wood, decorated with sensuous groupings of meticulously detailed nude dancing girls, held silver platters of various viands and liquors.

Puyang tapped the paper meaningfully. "I fear there is nothing to do but increase the public executions."

"We are approaching the harvest season," the soft voice said, "and there is already a serious food shortage in some territories. My people—"

"*Our* people," Puyang broke in, trying not to sound too harsh. "Your Glory, what you do not yet understand is how our people are seriously lacking in basic intelligence. For the most part they are simple fisher-folk. Peasants, farmers, grubbers of the soil. We cannot rely on them to act logically, in the best interests of the empire.

"They must be coerced, and sometimes, unfortunately, instilling fear is the only way. Remember the inducement offered by your late, beloved mother? It offered several solutions to the alleged famine, yet they persisted in agitating and ignoring imperial wisdom."

He took two steps toward the chair, his heavy footfalls muffled by the carpets. "Surely Your Glory finds the situation as intolerable as I do."

After a long moment came a "Yes," little more than a breathy, sorrowful exhalation.

Puyang repressed a smile of triumph. He moved to the base of the dais and extended a hand. He found the scent of Kumudvati tantalizing. She smelled of fresh morning flowers. She smelled of his future, of power.

Kumudvati took his hand, his spatulate thumb nearly covering the entire area of her palm. She allowed herself to be led down from the dais, one dainty step at a time. She was tiny but her proportions were perfect on a minuscule scale.

Her skin was pale amber in a complexion which contrasted sharply with the multitude of gems scattered about her near naked body. Uncut rubies gleamed in both earlobes, and alternating strings of white and black pearls hung in multiple loops from her slender neck, concealing her small breasts.

Bracelets of pure gold jingled on her arms and wrists. Her only garment consisted of a red silken clout hanging from a delicate gold chain about her hips. It flowed down between her thighs, almost to her knees. On her tiny feet were soft leather sandals with long thongs cross-tied around her calves.

Kumudvati's glossy black hair was carefully brushed

back, and it streamed down her back like a cloak. A jeweled coif drew it away from her face so her hair would not obscure the glittering gold scale design painted on and around her eyelids. Surrounded by sweeping lashes, her eyes were a soft, luminous brown, as limpid as a doe's.

"If they ignore our sound wisdom," Colonel Puyang continued, "then they must suffer the consequences. We shall have four additional public executions in the next week—one from each of the most rebellious villages. All you need do is sign the order."

Kumudvati glanced down at the paper and nibbled her underlip nervously. "The people to be executed…are they here in the city?"

"Yes, we have them in custody, Your Glory."

The girl took a deep breath as if steeling herself to perform an unpleasant task. In a rush she said, "Colonel, I have been told there is no actual famine, no real food shortage. I have heard that farms have been razed, paddies destroyed, storage bins fired—"

"Your Glory," Puyang bit out sharply. "I made two vows to your mother before she died—to guide you with my counsel and to revive the might of the Khmer empire by any means possible. One vow cannot be fulfilled without the other. Do you understand that?"

Kumudvati ducked her head, veiling her eyes with her long lashes. Her "Yes, colonel" was a barely audible whisper.

He pushed a quill pen into her hand. "Then sign the order, Your Glory, and permit me to continue honoring your mother's last wishes."

Kumudvati stared at the paper, then at the pen, and

swiftly scribbled a string of flowing characters above the wax seal.

"Very good, Your Glory," Puyang said approvingly. He reached for the quill but she spun away, letting it fall to the floor.

As Colonel Puyang lifted the decree and carefully blew on the signature to dry the ink, Kumudvati asked, "What about the three strangers apparently from some alien land that were taken prisoner?"

Puyang paused, his lips pursed, and cast the girl a glare meant to silence her, but she stood with her back to him. He grunted. "*Apparently* is the key word, Your Glory."

"But there were three strangers captured?"

He hesitated before replying, "We captured only one. I have men scouring all the outlying villages for any sign of the other two."

"And if they are from alien land?" Kumudvati pressed. "Why do we assume they are enemies?"

"I don't assume that," Puyang replied. "But they may have knowledge useful to us and to the empire."

"What kind of knowledge? Magic or science?"

Puyang frowned. "Perhaps both. And both are dangerous in the wrong hands."

Kumudvati fell silent for a thoughtful moment. Then she asked, "And what of Zhou Tzu? What of the general?"

The colonel's hand went reflexively to finger the mass of scar tissue on the right side of his face. "What of him?"

"Your report claimed he and his followers ambushed your patrol. How do you know he does not have the other strangers in hand and is already tapping that useful knowledge?"

Colonel Puyang wasn't sure, but he thought he detected an undercurrent of sarcasm in the girl's question. He struggled to keep his temper in check. The suspicion he was involved in the death of Kumudvati's mother was restricted to very few in the court, but no one dared to lodge a formal accusation as long as he stayed in the daughter's favor. If word of the Devi-Naga's death leaked out to the commoners, a revolt was a very real possibility. At best, people would desert Angkor Thom, fleeing back to their villages in the jungle. There could be no empire without subjects.

However, if the girl should die mysteriously, he could not rely on the Cobra Guard to protect him from reprisals from the nobles in on the gambit to pass off Kumudvati's daughter as the original Devi-Naga. Far too many junior officers coveted his rank and position.

Living as the consort of a princess, of a demi-goddess, was an exciting prospect for many men, but Puyang knew if he were to play that role, he would have to force the girl to accept him in it over a period of time. At the moment, she was still mourning the loss of her mother and looked to him as a counselor, not a potential suitor.

Stiffly, he said, "We should not be concerned with Zhou Tzu. Many of his men are dead, and he poses no immediate threat to us."

"And the Magickers?" she inquired. "Were they not also involved in the event you reported?"

Puyang's lips twisted in a sneer of derision. "The Magickers are fools, they are thieves, they live like fugitives.

Your mother was right to banish them when they failed to harness the gift of the Naga left for us beneath our palace."

Kumudvati nodded as if she expected the response and she stepped toward the double doors at the far end of the chamber. "And is that why you have imprisoned one of the strangers—you hope he will have the means to harness the gift?"

Puyang's back stiffened in reaction to the question. "Who told you that?"

The girl cast a glance over one bare shoulder, and Puyang felt a quiver of unease in the pit of his stomach. For an instant the iron will of her mother could be glimpsed glittering in her dark eyes. "*You* just did, colonel."

With a tinkle of baubles, Kumudvati swept out of the chamber. Puyang stared after her, clenching his fists and his teeth. The Devi-Naga had just revealed a hint of her mother's strength beneath the callow covering of a child.

The flickering trace of her mother's resolve didn't frighten him. But for a microsecond, Kumudvati's face had rippled away, like water sluicing over a pane of dusty glass. Then he saw Zhou Tzu's dark eyes piercing him to his very soul.

Icy fingers of terror closed around his heart when he realized Kumudvati was not just her mother's daughter, but her father's, as well.

BREWSTER PHILBOYD'S CELL was a miserable affair, the stone walls blackened by years of water incursion and dead lichens. The floor wasn't exactly mud, but it wasn't dry, either. A scatter of moldy straw served as an unsatisfactory substitute for a carpet. A circular hole high in the left-hand wall provided the only source of light and ventilation. In a far corner, water continually dripped.

There were no furnishings, so Philboyd sat on the floor, hugging his knees, and tried to dwell on anything but his pain and his predicament. Neither was possible. Recollecting his impassioned plea to Brigid to be allowed to be part of the mission, he mimicked himself: "'Ah, come on! What's the worst that can happen? I might be able to help if anything goes wrong.'"

Snorting out a laugh of self-disdain, he said, "Yeah, I can get shot in the head and captured and thrown into a stinking cell by a bunch of Asian maniacs wearing snake heads. But hey…I might be able to help if anything goes wrong."

He shook his head, disgusted with himself and his situation. Then a hammer blow fell within his skull and he bit back a cry of pain. He gingerly probed the edge of the blood-crusted bandage wound around his head. He still wasn't sure of the entire sequence of events that had followed the interphaser transit.

Philboyd recalled hearing the staccato drumming of autofire, the gloom lighting up with strobing spears of flame. Shouts, yells and a cry of alarm from Brigid filled his ears—then something hot and hard smashed across his forehead and set him flailing backward. He felt himself falling, suddenly blinded by a fiery wetness. Then it was as if he were drowning in an incredibly thick fog.

His next recollection was of pain and sunlight pouring down through the round hole in the cell wall. Although his head wound had been treated by wrapping it with an unguent-soaked bandage, it throbbed in cadence with his pulse. His vision was blurred, and by touching his face he realized his glasses were missing.

Although it was difficult to move at first, Philboyd tottered to his feet, stumbled over to the wooden door and peered through the barred window. He saw nothing but flickering torchlight and twisting stone corridors. He called out a number of times but received no response.

Dizzy, weak and slightly nauseous, Philboyd figured he had no option but to sit on the floor and wait for something to happen. By carefully examining the wound on his forehead by touch, he concluded he had been struck a glancing blow by a ricocheting bullet. The front of his bodysuit was caked and sticky with blood, although his face had been cleansed of it.

He dozed for a time, but a scuffling of feet awakened him. Through the window in the door he glimpsed the flickering blossom of torchlight. Philboyd rose on unsteady legs and made his way to the door, peering through the aperture.

Two Asian men wearing bizarre metal helmets resembling the heads of cobras appeared, moving sideways with handguns aimed at a line of chained, shuffling men. There were four of them, shackled at wrist and ankle. They wore only tatters of clothes, and all of them were covered in bruises and bloody abrasions, as if they had been severely beaten. Behind them marched another armed man, holding aloft a guttering torch that stank abominably of fish oil.

One of the snake-helmeted men noticed Philboyd watching from the door and shouted unintelligible words, waving his pistol toward him. Despite the languagc barrier, Philboyd understood perfectly and re-treated out of sight.

He heard the jingle of keys, the clank of the chains, the thump of doors closing and finally the tramp of marching feet. After that, utter silence draped the cata-combs for what seemed like a very long time. Hunger and thirst assailed him.

Lice abounded in the cell and were attracted to his blood-caked clothing. At first, Philboyd just scratched and cursed, but after a while, he passed the time by plucking them from his body and crushing them be-tween the nails of his thumb and forefinger.

He was so engrossed he almost didn't hear the key turning the lock. He glanced up as the door was pulled outward. A young Asian man, barely into his teens, stepped in cautiously, carrying a wooden trencher con-taining a stew that exuded a strong fish smell. He car-ried a clay jug of water in the other hand.

Looking past him out the doorway, Philboyd saw a snake-helmeted guard standing in the corridor holding a small submachine gun. The youth placed the food and water on the floor and backed away, never making eye contact, not even when Philboyd thanked him.

By the time the door was closed and relocked, Phil-boyd was downing the container of stew. The taste was midrange revolting, but the food was filling and he saw no reason to offer a critique. Within a few minutes, the door opened again and the young man returned to re-move the containers.

Shortly after that, light faded from the window and Philboyd spent his first full miserable night in the damp, dank cell. Fortunately, the air, though clammy, wasn't cold and he didn't share his quarters with any vermin other than the lice. They were quite sufficient.

Although he dreaded the dawn and what the new day might bring, he was accustomed to living in degree of fear. His many years on the Moon base had been little more than a series of terrifying pursuits, of ambushes, of his friends and colleagues dying one by one. Compared to the fear evoked by carnobots and the faceless furies, little Cambodian men wearing snake regalia didn't even rate.

When sunrise arrived, nothing happened except that his cell became almost unbearably humid. He shouted through the barred window of the door for water, but only once did he receive a reply, a stream of angry-sounding gibberish yelled from a place outside of his range of vision. The language barrier seemed insurmountable.

The only way Philboyd measured the passage of time was by the intensity of sunlight shafting through the cell window and the arrival at midday of his daily ration of fish swill and water.

When he calculated his third full day of imprisonment was drawing to a close, with cool shadows crawling across the damp floor, he suddenly detected an odor that wasn't the fishy stink of the torches or of his stew. He heard the jingling clank of a key in the lock and the door swung open. Philboyd expected to see either his serving boy or a snake-helmeted guard standing there.

Instead, a heavily muffled figure stood watching him from the doorway. A cloak of loosely woven silk fell almost to the floor, completely concealing the person's body. A white veil secured to a coif above each ear masked the face.

But Brewster Philboyd knew the cloaked figure was that of a woman, if not by the rich scent of perfume then by the heavily mascaraed eyelids with the delicate gold-scale pattern painted around them. He also received the impression she was a woman of some importance, despite her height of less than five feet. Slowly, he pushed himself to his feet, knee joints cracking.

Behind her, Philboyd saw an armed guard standing watchfully against the wall, a subgun held across his chest. The woman spoke first, very softly in the fluid language he didn't comprehend. Shaking his head, he said bleakly, "I'm sorry. I don't speak your tongue or understand it."

The dark eyes above the edge of the veil widened in surprise, then flicked up and down his body. She spoke again, very slowly. "English. You speak English. So you *are* from an alien land. What is your name?"

"Brewster."

A line of consternation appeared at the bridge of her nose. "Boo-star?"

He started to correct her then decided her pronunciation didn't matter as long as she understood him. "Close enough."

"How did you arrive here, Boo-star? Did you come by flying machine?"

Philboyd was surprised into speechlessness for a long moment. The woman's diction was perfect, almost machinelike in its precision, with no emphasis on any one word or syllable. Finally, he husked out, "It's not easy to explain."

"Science or magic?"

He blinked at her. "Pardon?"

With a touch of impatience underscoring her tone, the veiled woman said, "Did you use science or magic to come here?"

"Science," he replied, then regretted committing himself. If she requested an explanation of the interphaser, then his description would no doubt sound like magic to her.

She nodded as if satisfied by his answer. "That is good. I have a need of a man of science. Are you such?"

Philboyd could only nod numbly. The woman started to step farther into the cell but she turned at the sound of running, scuffling feet in the corridor. She cried out sharply as one of the ugliest men Philboyd had ever seen grabbed her by a handful of her cloak and hauled her roughly into the hallway, literally hurling her into the arms of the frightened guard.

"Hey!" Philboyd shouted, indignant at the handling of the girl, for he realized that was what she was. He took several steps forward.

The scarred man spun to face him, shouting incomprehensibly. Philboyd didn't understand the words but he perfectly grasped the tone. The man was both frightened and angry. The man feared him, and what he might have said to the veiled girl.

Chapter 18

Zhou Tzu extended a small cup and saucer toward Kane. "It is a special blend, grown only here, Mr. Kane...and one of the few civilized customs in which I still indulge. Teatime."

"No, thank you."

His eyebrows lifted like dark wings over amused almond eyes. "It is not poisoned, Mr. Kane. Or drugged. You are far too valuable for me to waste you in such a fashion."

As Zhou Tzu's eyebrows rose, Kane's drew down. He cast a sideways glance at Nora Pennick, who said quietly, "I have learned the general's word is sufficient in all things. You may trust him."

The room was dimly lit. Silk tapestries depicting scenes from myths covered the windowless walls, acrawl with tigers, dragons, archers and marching warriors armed with swords. Zhou Tzu and Nora sat side by side on thick pillows before a long, low table. A tendril of gray smoke curled from the single tea candle floating in a clay bowl of water.

Kane stood scowling down at the two people and the proffered cup of tea. Then he flexed his wrist tendons, holstering the Sin Eater with a rasp of metal against leather and plastic. He performed the motion with a little flourish, as demonstration of how much control he exerted over his weapon and how quickly it could return to his hand if he perceived the need for it.

Kane sank down on a pillow directly across from General Zhou Tzu and took the cup of tea. The man said, "As I understand it, Mr. Kane, you hold no military rank in your own country although you perform military duties and live in a military base."

Kane took a tentative sip of the tea and found the flavor rich with just a hint of a bittersweet aftertaste. "And you?" he countered. "You call yourself a general. A general of what?"

A faint smile ghosted over the man's lips. "I am what was once known as a warlord, Mr. Kane. A relic of a very old, very obsolete resistance movement against imperial tyranny. I am the last of the line."

"Line of what, exactly?"

"A line of men who act as yang to yin, as black to white, as north to south, as winter to summer. The movement I lead provides the necessary balance in our microcosm here."

"Balance?"

"Our doctrine, our laws, Mr. Kane. The Laws of Manu which deal with the ancient Vedic doctrine of world ages—the yugas. Manu indicates that a period of twenty-four thousand years consists of a series of four yugas, or ages, each shorter and spiritually darker than the last. In the mythology of our land, a fabled dawn time existed in the distant past, when human beings had direct contact with the divine intelligence emanating from Brahma—the seat of creative power and intelligence in the cosmos. As the teachings tell, Kali, the creator destroyer goddess, will appear at the end of the Kali Yuga to sweep away the wasted detritus of a spirit-dead humanity, making way for a new cycle of light and peace."

Choosing his words carefully, Kane said, "There are some feel that already happened, two centuries ago."

"As do I," Zhou Tzu stated. "As I thought Kumudvati did. Apparently she has decided to oppose the cycle, the turning of the wheel."

Kane glanced over at Nora. She looked pale and wan, but she seemed perfectly at ease at the side of the strange man. "General," he said quietly, "Nora apparently told you something about where we came from and what we do."

Nora nodded. "I did. I saw no reason to withhold anything from the man who saved my life."

Kane shifted his gaze back to Zhou Tzu. "Then maybe you'd better tell the man who saved your life how I hate people talking to me in esoterica."

The general's lips tightened. "As you wish, Mr. Kane. Let us be more direct. You have not asked about your other friends." His tone held a sharp edge.

"I expect you'll tell me about them when you please," Kane shot back. "I'm not as easy to impress as Nora, and I won't play guessing games with you."

"You do not wonder if they are still alive?"

In a tone exceeding that of Zhou Tzu's for sharpness, Kane bit out, "They had better be."

"You threaten me?" The man's face didn't change expression. "Miss Pennick told me you were brave and intelligent but prone toward reckless behavior. I can see she was right."

Kane opened his mouth to voice a profane retort but Zhou Tzu raised an imperious hand. "We are both soldiers in a cause, Mr. Kane. One does what is needed to fulfill a duty or to discharge an obligation or one is no more important to the cycle of life than a grain of sand in the Gobi. As soldiers you and I can make common cause and perhaps fulfill our respective duties."

To cover his growing confusion, Kane took another sip of the tea. He glanced over at Nora. "How did the general save your life?"

In a subdued voice, she said, "Troopers of the Devi-Naga attacked us shortly after we made the phase transit. Another faction was involved, as well, called the Magickers. They were dragging me off when providence sent the general to intervene. He rescued me."

"Who was dragging you off?" Kane asked. "The Magickers or the troopers?"

"The Cobra Guard had her," Zhou Tzu said. "And her male companion."

Nora nodded in agreement. "They managed to get Brewster to Angkor Thom, from what we have heard."

"And Brigid?"

"We have heard nothing of her from the city," the general answered. "It is reasonable to assume the Magickers have her and your interphaser."

Kane struggled to stay on top of the anger rising within him. "So you told him about the interphaser?"

Her response was simple but not contrite. "I did."

"It sounds like a singularly extraordinary device," Zhou Tzu interjected.

Kane ignored his comment. "Why were you, the Cobra Guard and the Magickers all in the same place at the same time?" He didn't try to conceal the suspicious note in his voice.

The man's shoulders lifted beneath his red robe in a negligent shrug. "Who can say? Serendipity, the will of the gods, karma… Speaking for myself, I just survived an assassination attempt by Colonel Puyang, commander of the Cobra Guard. A number of my most devoted soldiers were killed. They had violated the borders, and so I trailed the murderers responsible."

Addressing Nora, Kane demanded, "Maybe you can explain to me why you think you're better off in the hands of a warlord than those of the Magickers or this Devi-Naga. Why are you so sure he doesn't deserve to be assassinated?"

"I am right here, Mr. Kane." Zhou Tzu's voice was gently chiding. "You might ask me."

Kane fixed his gaze on the man's face. "Fine. Answer the question, then."

"The fact that you and Miss Pennick are still alive and unharmed should be a satisfactory answer."

"You already said I was valuable to you. As what?"

Zhou Tzu sighed. "Miss Pennick told me about her friends, about you and her conviction that you and quite possibly others would come looking for them. I gambled that I would find the party from Cerberus before the other players in the game. That is how you came to meet Chou Chan."

"I figured as much. What game are you talking about?"

The general leaned back, closing his eyes for a moment as if he were viewing the past. "Perhaps I chose the wrong term. It has only been since Miss Pennick's arrival that I have had the opportunity to speak English since I learned it, many years ago."

"Learned it from whom?" Kane asked.

"Not a who, but a what. As child of noble birth I was sent to a monastery far from here to learn all that the monks could teach me. They had a machine—you would call it a PC—which taught me several different languages, English among them. The PC also taught me how to play a game known as chess."

Kane nodded in understanding. "As far as you're concerned, we're engaged in a chess match with this Devi-Naga of yours and the Magickers."

Zhou Tzu opened his eyes. "Precisely. The Devi-Naga is apparently making a gambit to centralize control of Cambodia and so create a ruling hegemony—in blatant violation of our traditional roles in obeying the laws of yuga. Therefore, I have no choice but to embark on a gambit of my own to restore the balance."

Kane shook his head in frustration. "I don't understand."

"What do you know of my country, Mr. Kane?"

"Almost nothing," he replied frankly.

Zhou Tzu took a deep breath and declared, "My people were a noble race who honored their place under the stars, and built the world's most profound temple city, that of Angkor Thom. What is even more profound, it seems, is the complete disappearance of the very civilization that built these temples, with no trace of where they went, and no trace of their continuing their culture anywhere else."

"Where did they come from?" Kane asked, interested in spite of himself. "Maybe that will tell you where they went."

Zhou Tzu smiled a small, sad smile. "That is almost as deep a mystery. According to an account written in 916 CE by the Arab trader Abu Zaid, the maharaja of Java once sailed his fleet up the Mekong River to the Khmer capital for the express purpose of capturing and decapitating the Cambodian ruler. Historians have ascribed the construction of several of central Java's Buddhist temples to the Sailendra dynasty of kings that ruled during the late eighth and early ninth centuries. So, perhaps the Javanese originally settled this country.

"But in 802 A.D., Jayavarman, the founding king of Cambodia's Angkor civilization, appeared. He participated in a ceremony that involved the installation of a linga—the phallic emblem of the Hindu deity Shiva—on top of Mount Kulen north of Angkor. This act launched the Khmer empire and royal dynasty that flourished for more than six hundred years."

"Is this Jayavarman who you claim descent from?" Kane asked.

"Not exactly," Zhou Tzu answered smoothly, so smoothly Kane suspected he was sidestepping the question. "The inauguration of King Jayavarman established the exalted position of deva-raja, literally 'god-king.' According to Miss Pennick, that is a concept that has been revived with some success in your own country."

Grimly, Kane retorted, "The barons aren't kings, much less gods."

Zhou Tzu acknowledged his remark with a nod. "Each succeeding Khmer ruler during the Angkor period of Cambodian history followed Jayavarman's example by building a sanctuary for the cult of the deva-raja in the form of a pyramid-mountain, either natural or artificial, that was located at the very center of the Khmer ruler's realm."

"Why?" Kane asked.

"Have you ever heard of geomancy?" the general asked.

Kane sighed wearily. "Yes. I can't say I understand it."

"The goal of the ancient Khmer architect was to harmonize the microcosmic forces that govern life in the human world with the macrocosmic forces that rule over the realm of the gods. According to this point of view, the extent to which any building fails to conform with an architectural plan designed to mirror the perfection of the cosmos can make the difference between a living structure that will allow benevolent spiritual forces to enter and take up residence and a structure that is considered to be blocked, closed off or dead."

"What spiritual forces are you talking about?" Kane asked, even though he half expected the answer.

"The Naga," Zhou Tzu said calmly. "The forebears of the Khmers."

"I was afraid you'd say that. I was briefed about them before I embarked. These Naga of yours sound very much like the Annunaki." He inclined his head toward Nora. "She could tell you a few things about them...or at least some of the technology they left behind on the Moon."

"I already told him," Nora stated. "And from what the general told me, it sounds as if the Naga left some of their own technology behind—or beneath—Angkor Wat."

"What makes you say that?" Kane asked.

Zhou Tzu said, "Naga is a term used to describe unseen beings associated with water and fluid energy, and also with persons having powerful animal-like qualities, or an impressive animal with human qualities, deities of the primal ocean and of mountain springs; also spirits of Earth and the realm beneath it. In the mythology of my land, Naga are primarily serpent beings living near flowing water...fluid energy."

"The entire city of Angkor Thom was built near rivers, over underground springs and reservoirs," Nora put in. "The city was dedicated to the worship of Naga. Where there is flowing water, there is energy. The art of geomancy is based on Earth's life energy flowing the path of water. Where water flows, life goes. The Naga apparently taught the Khmer people this...and how to channel it."

Kane arched an eyebrow. "How so?"

"I'm only speculating," Nora replied. "Based on what the general has told me. But what lies beneath Angkor Wat is a kind of channeling mechanism for the electromagnetic field concentrated in the city."

"For every type of energy," Zhou Tzu said quietly, "there are positive and negative charges. The ideal situation is one where a balance between the two is established and maintained."

"Yin and yang," Kane murmured. He eyed the general keenly. "And you represented the balance?"

"With the cooperation of the Devi-Naga, of course."

"And of course," Kane replied sarcastically, "the balance has now tipped into the negative."

"I'm glad you understand."

"I think I do," Kane said flatly. "You said it was a chess game, right?"

Zhou Tzu nodded.

"And you expect us to join the game?"

"I see no other option." The man sounded genuinely regretful. "Not if you wish to be reunited with your friends."

"What pieces do Nora and I represent in the warlord's gambit?" Kane snapped. "Knights or pawns?"

General Zhou Tzu smiled faintly, a slightly amused, almost pitying smile. "Miss Pennick has been removed from the board, Mr. Kane. As for what chessman you will play…I expect you will prove that to me once we begin our journey downriver. But you may take some solace in the fact I do not intend to sacrifice you needlessly."

Chapter 19

The road cutting through the fields was muddy from the rainstorm the night before. The heavy footfalls of the two elephants made an incessant squishing that Brigid found to be more than a little nerve-racking after a few hours.

She was also slightly queasy due to the swaying gait of the creature upon whose back she was perched. She attributed at least eighty percent of her nausea to the dried fish and fruit that had served as her predawn breakfast. The saddle pad beneath her provided an unsatisfactory protective layer between human skin and bristle-brush pachyderm hair sprouting from its gray wrinkled hide. The thick musky odor the creature exuded didn't help much either.

Brigid had seen pix of elephants of course, but the photographic representations of the animals didn't do justice to the massive, smelly reality of the Asian elephant, the *elephas maximus*. The elephant she shared with Brother Javalara was named Maya. A female and only three years old, she had not attained her full height and like most Asian elephants her ears were far smaller than her African counterparts. Her face bore a large unpigmented patch between her wise eyes, a pale pink against the gray.

Brigid reached up under the edge of her turban and

wiped her perspiration slick brow. The air was already hot and humid for such an early hour and with no shade available, the heat was quickly growing unbearable.

She wore a draping garment similar to a sari, but it left her arms bare and she feared they would soon burn in the intense sunlight. Her rolled-up shadow suit was in a saddlebag lying between her and Javalara. He had insisted she shed the skintight black garment because it would draw far more attention from passersby than the simple robe and breeches favored by loggers.

Farmers and peasants wouldn't spread the word of three loggers riding on elephants through their territory, but they would certainly gossip about spying a flame-haired woman in basic black. That gossip would spread to the ears of informers in the pay of the Cobra Guard.

Although a little suspicious, Brigid did as the chief Magicker bade her to do. She didn't perceive that she had many options available to her. The interphaser rested inside a crate on the elephant ridden by Yasovar, therefore the Magickers were the only hope she had of secretly entering Angkor Thom. Both Yasovar and Javalara had made cryptic references to acquiring a much faster method of transportation than elephants but they had refused to elaborate.

In the field to her left, Brigid watched a flock of birds pecking at what she first assumed was a pitifully ineffective scarecrow. Then when she realized the tattered figure hanging from the T framework was the body of a man, her nausea redoubled.

Javalara followed her gaze and said quietly, "Executed at Colonel Puyang's orders."

"For what reason?" Brigid asked, pitching her voice low to disguise the tremor in it.

Javalara shrugged. "His crops failed as did many others in this vicinity."

"Crucifixion seems a rather harsh penalty for bad luck."

"Puyang didn't believe it was bad luck," Yasovar declared flatly. "He thought the farmers here were deliberately destroying their crops, harvesting just enough to keep themselves fed so they could starve out the people in Angkor Thom. He forced the farmers to turn over their entire harvest, and then burned their fields so they would be solely dependent on their own food distributed from the city."

"Will no one cut down the man and give him a burial?" Brigid asked.

"That would mean crucifixion for whoever did it," Javalara answered. "If the Cobra Guard is unable to find the people who actually did the deed, they would pick someone at random from one of the farms and execute him."

Shifting her weight on the saddle pad, Brigid murmured, "This Colonel Puyang and the Cobra Guard sound as though they would be right at home in my country."

Javalara looked over his shoulder at her. "Perhaps now you understand why we so desperately need your help."

"I wouldn't mind seeing this colonel of yours put out of business," Brigid admitted.

"Such is our main objective," Javalara declared sternly.

"But it's not mine."

He nodded. "Your goal is to find your friends and return home. But you cannot achieve your objective without our help and we cannot achieve ours without yours."

"Convenient how it works out that way," Brigid

snapped. "Some might see it as nice and neat bit of manipulation. I'd call it blatant opportunism. Or blackmail."

Javalara opened his mouth to reply, then closed it with a snap. Craning his neck, he scanned the sky. His entire body tensed. Maya's plodding gait slowed a trifle and she curled her trunk, trumpeting briefly.

"What is it?" Brigid demanded.

"Keep her your head down," Javalara said, his tone quavering with barely suppressed apprehension. "A *vimana* is coming."

"A *vimana?*" she echoed incredulously. Brigid stared at him, nonplussed. Then, despite what the man said, she looked up, her gaze sweeping across the sky. At the same time she heard a faint melodic hum. Slightly to the east of their path she saw a shape gleaming silver against the blue sky. It hovered above a tree line a quarter of a mile or so distant.

"A flying craft from Angkor Thom," Yasovar called from the back of his elephant. "A very old design, dating back to the days of the Rama, as chariots of the gods. What the *vimanas* are used for here isn't quite as grand."

Brigid knew what *vimanas* were reputed to be, at least in legend. The ship hove closer, and she saw its configurations resembled nothing so much as a bewinged throwing dart. The hull gleamed like mercury in the sunlight. The craft looked graceful, almost beautiful, like a chrome-plated dragonfly, its wings glistening with the morning dew.

The faint hum changed in timbre, lowering to a deep, rhythmic throb. Two streaks of fire lanced downward from the *vimana*'s underbelly. Clumps of jungle erupted into smoke and flame. The boom of the double explosions sounded like a fist beating on a muffled kettle drum.

"What the hell!" Brigid exclaimed.

"They must have located a paddy," Javalara said grimly. "They fired missiles with incendiary warheads to destroy the crop."

"This is no way to run a country," Brigid said under her breath in English.

The pointed prow of the *vimana* swung about, giving the impression the craft was questing for a target. Then it lanced across the sky, skimming over the fields directly toward them.

"We've been spotted," Yasovar said, his voice tight and breathless with anxiety.

"What do we do?" Brigid asked. "Just carry on like nothing is wrong?"

"No," Javalara said. "They would wonder why we weren't frightened. Crouch low, as if you're supplicating yourself to the *vimana*."

He spoke sharply to Maya and tugged on her right ear. The elephant lurched to a halt as did Yasovar's. The two animals shifted from foot to foot in nervous agitation. They didn't like the sight of the airship soaring toward them.

Neither did Brigid but when the craft drew closer she saw it was a poor thing in comparison to the Manta ships. It seemed to struggle across the sky rather than glide, despite the ribbed wings stretched out on either side of it.

The *vimana* was less than twenty feet long, the wingspan perhaps double that. The fuselage was a patchwork of metal plates and lacquered wood. An open port in the center of its undercarriage gaped open, and she glimpsed the hollow muzzle of a handheld rocket launcher. The engine droned as the craft dropped in altitude.

Javalara bent over Maya's broad skull, hands clasped at the back of his head. Brigid followed suit, leaning against him. The sound of the *vimana*'s engine suddenly increased in volume and rose in pitch. For a second, a shadow blotted out the sunlight. The craft roared over the elephants, probably at the highest rate of speed of which it was capable.

The downdraft buffeted them, and Brigid nearly tumbled from Maya's back. She clutched Javalara by the waist in order keep seated. Yasovar's elephant lifted its trunk and bleated indignantly as dust and plant scraps swirled around them.

"Are they coming back?" Brigid husked out.

After a moment, Javalara said, "No. They're resuming their search pattern. They had their little joke. Those missiles are hard to come by, and they won't waste them on us."

"Ha-ha." Brigid straightened, watching the *vimana* swoop upward. "I had no idea the level of technology was so high here."

Yasovar snorted disdainfully. "There are only two such craft in existence, at least in operation. The Cobra Guard uses one."

"What about the other?"

Yasovar didn't answer immediately. After a moment of hesitation, he cut his eyes over to Javalara, who said quietly, "The other is in our possession. That is one reason we are so hunted by the Cobra Guard."

Angrily, Brigid demanded, "Why didn't you tell me that in the first place?"

"It's a question of security, Baptiste," Javalara stated matter-of-factly. "If you were captured by the Cobra Guard before we reached the *vimana*, you might have told them about it. We still have several miles to travel before we reach it. Then it will carry us the rest of the way to Angkor Thom."

Brigid glared at the back of the man's turbaned head for a long moment, then she uttered a resigned sigh. Javalara was right. At sharply spoken commands from the men, the elephants began trudging down the road again.

As the animals rounded a bend, they shied momentarily from two nearly naked boys who crept from the brush line. The taller of the pair, who looked to be about ten years old, wore a dirty strip of cloth over his right eye. He held the smaller boy by the right hand—or rather the stump where his hand had once been. Both of them were scratched and very brown, their limbs stick thin and bellies swollen from malnutrition. Brigid guessed they were brothers.

The taller boy held out a wooden bowl and chanted, "Food, quills, food."

Brother Yasovar called down, "We are a family of poor woodsmen who cannot spare quills and you are a long way from any place where you might find charity."

"We do not wish to venture too close to the city today," said the boy with the makeshift eye patch.

"Why is that?" Javalara asked, tossing down two sealed packets of cheese, fruit and dried fish.

"Five men are to be hanged today," the smaller boy answered, eyes fixed on the package of food his brother tore open.

"For what crime?" Brigid asked.

If they found Brigid's voice strange, the boys gave no sign of it. Mumbling around a mouthful of banana, the tallest of the pair said, "Not for any crime. As an example. One of them is said to be an outlander who defiled the person of the Devi-Naga."

Brigid stiffened but Javalara turned toward her, a warning finger to his lips. "Do not draw attention to yourself," he whispered.

"Where are you parents?" Yasovar asked.

"Dead," the smaller boy replied dispassionately. "An example was made of them and our farm."

The elephants plodded onward and Javalara muttered grimly, "We have all seen more than our share of examples. Long past time they came to a stop."

Brigid glanced back twice at the two naked boys stuffing their mouths with the simple food as if it were ambrosia. Narrowing her eyes against the sting of tears in them, she asked, "Are these public executions held often?"

"Too often," Yasovar replied. "They're intended to keep the people fearful and docile."

Brigid nodded. "In my experience, it frequently has the opposite effect."

Javalara blew out a disgusted breath. "Not frequently enough, I fear. We had hoped the warlord, General Zhou Tzu, would become aware of these depredations and intervene but so far he has done nothing."

"Is he the enemy of the Cobra Guard?"

"Only if they cross the borders into his country. They have apparently done so, yet he has not retaliated. It is a frustration and a mystery."

"He doesn't sound like much of a warlord," Brigid commented dourly.

Yasovar smiled slightly. "It is a hereditary title, as his hostility to the Devi-Naga. But he does not fight her because it would upset the balance. He safeguards the borders from incursions by Vietnamese and Laotian bandits."

Brigid found the situation puzzling, but rather than request clarification she asked, "Will we arrive in Angkor Thom in time for the executions?"

Brother Javalara studied the angle of the sun in the sky. "Perhaps."

"Will we be able to enter the city dressed as loggers?"

Yasovar took it upon himself to answer. "In this guise we are free to move freely through the land, since we perform a valuable service. Although if the Cobra Guard learns our real identities, they would be swift to act against us. We would join the ranks of the condemned and be three more examples."

"Doesn't anybody ever try to stop these executions?" Brigid asked irritably.

Javalara shrugged. "It would mean instant death for any who tried."

"Not necessarily."

"What do you mean?"

Not answering, Brigid reached into the saddlebag and withdrew her TP-9 autopistol. Brother Javalara, putting her on her honor she would accompany them to Angkor Thom, had returned the weapon before they began their journey. Brigid detested guns in principle, but she wasn't so blinkered by dislike that she was ignorant of circumstances when they had their uses.

Swiftly she examined it, popping up out the magazine and testing the slide mechanism. It worked smoothly and she reinserted the ammo clip.

At the metallic, mechanical sounds, Javalara hitched around the elephant's back and regarded her with quizzical eyes. "You apparently didn't hear or understand what I said. It would be death for any who tried to interfere in the executions."

Brigid smiled at him, a cold, stitched-on kind of smile she had seen on Kane's lips more than once. "And you apparently didn't hear or understand what I said, so I'll repeat it. Not necessarily."

Chapter 20

The early-morning sunlight shone down upon the deck of the wooden barge in an intricately dappled pattern, filtered as it was through the leafy boughs intertwined over the river.

Kane stood at the starboard rail, studying the terrain on either bank. It was all thick foliage, growing right down to the water's edge. The prow of the flat-bottomed boat cleaved through the rippling water with barely a sound. At the stern, the steersman lay drowsily over the sweep. He was a round-shouldered man with a scarlet kerchief tied around his head, which lent him a piratical air.

General Zhou Tzu and the other six members of the little river barge's crew stood forward, at their morning meal. Once or twice, Kane heard half-whispered words as they conferred and furtive glances were cast his way.

The heat was cloyingly oppressive. Sweat gathered on Kane's face. His shirt clung to his back. The air was thick with moisture. He silently swore at himself for allowing Zhou Tzu to persuade him to adopt less conspicuous clothing than a black shadow suit. He wore a white sleeveless cotton shirt, baggy trousers, sandals and a broad-brimmed hat made of woven straw. He knew he looked ridiculous, but without a mirror he could only guess at just how ridiculous. However, he had refused to part with the pack, which contained the items taken from the Manta. It, as well as his Sin Eater and Copperhead, lay on the deck at his feet.

The barge had been floating slowly downriver since before the sky had turned golden with dawn. So far, it had passed little more than jungle although Kane had glimpsed the tawny striped form of a tiger drinking at the water's edge. The huge cat had not raised its muzzle from the water, but watched the craft's passage with pensive, yellow-green eyes. Kane remembered the brave tiger he had been forced to kill in India a short time before and turned away.

Kane was full of impatience, irritation and a gathering premonition of danger. He had slept poorly due to the heat. His mind continually flashed with visions of the snowcapped mountains of Montana. Even the barren ice-fields of Antarctica seemed attractive. He wasn't certain why he had accepted General Zhou Tzu's hospitality other than he really had no choice.

The men Kane had incapacitated in the trading post apparently did not hold grudges, but neither did they seem anxious to treat him as an equal. He noticed they showed a great deal more deference to Nora Pennick, as if she were more than Zhou Tzu's guest.

The warlord had promised they would arrive in the vicinity of Angkor Thom by noon and it was there he hoped to find Brewster Philboyd, and maybe a clue to Brigid's whereabouts.

He tried not to worry about her, but that was impossible. He cursed quietly, damning the gestalt of their relationship that had them depending on each other one minute, then at each other's throat the next.

The memory of the kiss he'd given her when they'd taken the jump back in time to the eve of the nukecaust ghosted across his mind. It was no surprise that he remembered the kiss, but the intensity of the emotions associated with that memory disturbed him.

At the sound of a footfall on the deck planks behind him, Kane whirled, teeth bared, wrist tendons tightening, hand opening to receive the Sin Eater no longer fastened to his forearm.

Nora looked at him wide-eyed, startled by his reaction. She was dressed in a flowing skirt slit up one side nearly to her right hip. A black halter top left most of her midriff bare. Her hair, bound by a green scarf, was tucked up under a straw hat. The brim shadowed the distinctly occidental cast of her eyes and features. Her right arm was still crooked in the sling.

"My God, Kane," she said reprovingly. "You're as jumpy as the proverbial cat on the hot tin roof."

"I know," he retorted flatly. "And for the life of me, I can't imagine why. Can you?"

Nora refused to respond to his sarcastic rejoinder. A smile touched her lips, and she gazed up at the sunlight piercing the overhead tangle of branches, liana vines and leaves. Golden brown monkeys scampered among the high pathways. "Green Mansions," she murmured.

He cocked his head at her. "What?"

"The title of a very old book I read as a child in England. The heroine, Rima, was a girl raised in the rain forests of Amazonia. I feel a little like her now."

Kane frowned. "I'd say you're more like a hostage."

Nora's back stiffened and she stared at him unblinkingly. "How can you possibly say that? The general rescued me."

"Or captured you," he shot back. "Why is it that Brigid and Brewster just happened to be captured, but you were rescued?"

She pondered the question for a few seconds then said quietly, "I suppose it's all a matter of perspective, isn't it? I don't feel like a hostage or a prisoner."

"What do you feel like?"

She nibbled her lower lip then said, "A recruit in a cause."

"A revolution?"

"Perhaps."

"I thought that was your work at Cerberus."

Nora shook her head. "It is *your* work, Kane. I was only a houseguest, an émigré, an expatriate. Here I am helping a dedicated man to restore a modicum of freedom to a subjected people."

"Really?" Kane angled a sardonic eyebrow. "Once again, I thought that was what we were trying to do in Cerberus."

"There are many different kinds of revolution, Kane."

"As far as I know, every kind of revolution needs the same things...not the least of which are weapons."

Haughtily, Nora stated, "I'm not an idiot."

Kane wiped at the perspiration trickling into his eyes. He sighed wearily. "Frankly, I don't know *what* you are, sweetheart."

She fixed her eyes on him. "You never did, Kane. I'm just one of many people you evacuated from the Moon base. Cerberus isn't my home. But I've learned some important things about it."

"Like what?"

"Like there are more weapons there than can possibly be used by the personnel."

Kane gazed at her, eyes widening, then narrowing to slits. He showed his teeth in a hard, humorless grin. "I think I'm starting to get it now. You told your general about the armory, didn't you?"

"Yes."

The Cerberus armory was quite likely the best stocked and thoroughly outfitted weapons stockpile in postnuke America. Stacked wooden crates and boxes filled with ammunition lined the walls. Glass-fronted cases held racks of automatic assault rifles. There were many makes and models of subguns, as well as dozens of semiautomatic pistols, complete with holsters and belts.

There was also heavy assault weaponry, like bazookas, tripod mounted 20 mm cannons, mortars and rocket launchers. All the ordnance had been laid down in hermetically sealed Continuity of Government installations before the nukecaust. Protected from the ravages of the outraged environment, nearly every piece of munitions and hardware was as pristine as the day it was first manufactured.

Lakesh himself put the arsenal together over several decades, envisioning it as the major supply depot for a rebel army. The army never materialized—at least, not in the fashion Lakesh hoped it would. Therefore, Cerberus was blessed with a surplus of death-dealing equipment that would have turned the most militaristic baron green with envy, or given the most pacifistic of them heart failure—if they indeed possessed hearts.

"What else did you tell him about Cerberus?" Kane demanded.

"Anything and everything he wanted to know," Nora answered with a cool detachment. "I owe him that much."

"And what about the people back in Cerberus?" Kane asked angrily. "What do you owe them?"

"The general couldn't harm them even if he wanted."

"He could harm them by harming us. Just a couple of days ago I was used as a pawn in someone else's game. I don't think I feel like cooperating with another."

Nora's lips tightened. "It's not a game."

"A *game*, the warlord's gambit. His own words, Nora. He's dragging us into a revolution against, as far as we know, the lawful governing body of this country."

"General Zhou Tzu is the rightful ruler of this part of Cambodia," Nora declared. "It's by right of descent. His father and his father's father held the title. But now people from the Devi-Naga's territory have been slipping away to join him because they find they cannot live under her dictatorship and that of Colonel Puyang."

Kane swatted a fly off his forearm. "What makes you think General Zhou Tzu doesn't want to be a dictator himself?"

"He believes in a fairly democratic form of government. I have seen it at work. He commands justly and well."

Kane barely kept himself from snorting. "You sound like a convert to a religion, Nora. Or a woman in love."

He waited for a heated denial. When one was not forthcoming he stared into her expressionless face and groaned. "Oh, for the love of—" He turned away, staring into the foaming brown water of the Siemrap. "You're infatuated with the man but you don't know him."

"Neither do you," Nora retorted.

"I know men like him…outlaws, hunted men without scruple, doing whatever they think is necessary to survive."

"Are you describing the general," Nora asked dispassionately, "or yourself?"

Kane ignored the gibe. "You don't understand the back story of the struggle, of the political situation here."

"Politics is politics," she snapped. "Throughout the world."

"You met him less than a week ago, and you've already promised that Cerberus would help him overthrow this Devi-Naga?"

"She promised me nothing, Mr. Kane."

Glancing over his shoulder, he saw Zhou Tzu standing beside Nora. His long black hair was tucked back under his straw hat. He was dressed very much like Kane.

"It sounds to me like you gave her a hell of a sales pitch," Kane said darkly. "Or was it easier than that? Did you just take advantage of the fact she was vulnerable and grateful to a man who she thought saved her life?"

Zhou Tzu's face remained as immobile as if it were carved from amber. "I told Miss Pennick the truth. That is all."

"Which I sure as hell don't understand," Kane retorted, his tone and his patience ragged. "So how could she? How can you maintain a military hereditary rank and a state of war while observing a hereditary truce with your enemy? What kind of war can you wage that way…*General?*"

Zhou Tzu's lips moved in a cryptic smile at Kane's sarcastic emphasis on his rank. "You would be surprised, Mr. Kane, at the number of foes I war with here. Laotian and Thai bandits, tribes of Bottom Feeders. It is my duty, my role, my purpose in life to guard the borders of this land. The Devi-Naga's traditional role is to preside over the holy city of Angkor Thom and safeguard the gift of the Naga."

Kane scowled, repressing the urge to ask about the tribes of Bottom Feeders. "What's the gift of the Naga?"

"It's part of the mythology, the religious lore here," Nora interposed. "The temple-tomb complex of Angkor Wat was built over a site that contains the Naga's essence, kept in a harmonic balance. It was never to be trifled with or put out balance, else all of humankind would suffer."

"Yes," Zhou Tzu said. "A corollary myth would be that of Pandora."

Kane blinked in momentary puzzlement. "Are you trying to tell me there's a magic *box* under the city?"

"Actually," Zhou Tzu replied smoothly, "in the original Greek myth, it was a beautiful golden urn, given to Pandora by the gods as a wedding gift. Her husband, Epimetheus, warned her never to open it, but eventually human curiosity got the better of her.

"She prised up the lid of the urn and released lust, greed, hatred and all the other sins upon humankind. She closed the lid in time to keep hope at the bottom, to compensate us for the evil that men do." He lifted his hands, holding them palms up at the same level. "Thus, the balance between yin and yang to which I referred yesterday is achieved."

Kane shook his head ruefully. "Too damn bad you didn't rescue Brigid, too. She'd be right at home listening to this lecture."

"I mentioned I was an educated man," Zhou Tzu said quietly.

Nora gazed at him raptly. "You are far more than that, my general."

Kane's stomach slipped sideways at the tone of worship in Nora's voice, but Zhou Tzu didn't react to her comment. His expression inscrutable, he stated, "It is the balance I seek to restore or my land will be plunged into bloodshed and civil war…easy prey for our other enemies once they learn of our internal discord."

"What are you talking about with the essence of the Naga?" Kane asked. "The earth energies you told me about?"

Zhou Tzu nodded. "The ancient Khmer lived in Angkor Thom with the ability to manipulate them, maintaining them in harmonized balance. Most of that knowledge was lost over the centuries and I speculate that was the main reason the Khmer Empire disappeared. I think their fortunes took a turn for the worse when the essences of the Naga slipped out of balance."

Kane leaned against the rail, crossing his arms over his chest. His irritation was slowly being subsumed by interest. "I don't know how much I believe about geomancy, but could there be a machine under the place? Or is it strictly a natural phenomenon?"

"I surmise a bit of both," Nora said.

Zhou Tzu nodded. "It's possible a machine of sorts was constructed to channel the earth energies and to keep them in balance, in sync. My role as warlord and Kumudvati's as the Devi-Naga are expressions, physical manifestations of that balance…the effulgence of the Sudarshana chakra or the supreme personality of godhead."

He shrugged. "I admit the roles are largely theater, to keep an ancient tradition alive. Even though my line of descent is traced to the offspring of the first queen and king of Cambodia, legends of men who mated with serpent princesses and founded royal houses are widespread throughout Asia. Kumudvati and I are hardly unique, folklorically speaking.

"However, a very prominent man of my line, Jayavarman the Seventh, was the Khmer ruler most concerned with his subjects' welfare. He saw to the construction of roads, hospitals and even healing shrines built over intersection points of the Naga essence."

"He sounds like quite the benefactor," Kane commented dryly.

Zhou Tzu scoffed. "Jayavarman the Seventh was also the Khmer ruler most obsessed with celebrating his own divinity. All of the construction was performed by forced labor…free people pressed into slavery. He enslaved and impoverished the country.

"Thousands died due to his Olympian ego. Finally outlying territories revolted and after a long, bloody struggle he was deposed. As karmic restitution, male members of his line were charged with the task of opposing the rulers of Angkor Thom, if in principle rather than by actual deed. I am the latest in a long line, perhaps the last."

"And Kumudvati?" Kane ventured. "The Serpent Princess. Is she the last in the line, too?"

Zhou Tzu hesitated before replying, "I cannot tell you that because I don't know. It is forbidden that we ever meet, since we symbolize opposite poles. Yin and yang. However…" He trailed off, the corners of his mouth drawing down in a thoughtful frown.

"However what?" Kane asked.

Before the man could answer, Nora uttered a high-pitched shriek and took two stumbling back steps, her eyes fixed on the rail upon which Kane leaned. Swiveling his head in the direction of her wild stare, he saw a brown paw, glistening with river water and clotted with mud, rise up and slap around the side. The long square nails of the webbed fingers were caked with muck and beveled at the edges.

General Zhou Tzu stepped swiftly toward Nora, arms sliding protectively around her shoulders. At the same time, he shouted sharply, "To arms! Bottom Feeders!"

Chapter 21

Noon brought yet another heavy rain shower to the jungle. The downpour was so intense the branches of the trees couldn't keep the rain from soaking Brigid through to the skin.

Only a few minutes before she had been grateful that she, Javalara, Yasovar and the two elephants had left the open farmlands and entered the cool shade of the jungle. Now she huddled down on Maya's back as the tropical rain pounded her, virtually blinding her and making it difficult to breathe without inhaling water.

The elephants, on the other hand, were overjoyed by the cooling storm, lifting their trunks and bleating in pleasure. At the very least the downpour reduced the high level of Maya's stink to the tolerable point.

"We'll reach our *vimana* very soon," Javalara said reassuringly to Brigid. He had to half shout in order to be heard over the drumming of the rainfall on the foliage.

The downpour abated as abruptly as it had come, and almost as abruptly, tendrils of mist closed in, as if spewed from the undergrowth. Straightening, Brigid massaged the base of her spine. A dull ache had settled into her lower back and hip joints, making her wonder if she were getting, as Grant often grunted, "too old for this shit."

She swallowed a sigh of resignation. Riding on an elephant through a rain-soaked Asian jungle was just the latest in a long series of travails she had endured, from the time she'd first met Kane. She'd been an archivist for the baron then, and her eidetic memory had been a hidden blessing as she searched through all the files kept in Cobaltville's Historical Division. If she saw it, she remembered it.

As a trained archivist, though, she knew misinformation often began with half truths, then grew into speculative transitions as someone worked to record the event. No information was sometimes better than half information. The primary duty of archivists was not to record predark history, but to revise, rewrite and often times completely disguise it.

The political causes leading to the nukecaust were well-known. They were major parts of the dogma, the doctrine, the articles of faith, and they had to be accurately recorded for posterity. The Cerberus database contained unedited and unexpurgated data, and having access to it was one of the few perks Brigid found in her life as an exile.

Life in Cobaltville had been predictable and she sometimes missed the monotony of routine. She knew Grant and Kane often longed for it, as well. Their whole lives, from conception to death, were ordered for them, both at work and at home. Ville dogma, ville upbringing, convinced them how lucky they were to live on the bounty of the baron and not to have to scratch out a starvation existence in the Outlands. As long as they obeyed the maddening and contradictory volume of rules, they had security, medical and even retirement benefits.

It was the life Brigid had led, Kane and Grant had led, the only life they had known. Now they were forced to live with prices on their heads, which any so-called citizen could collect just by giving information about them and it was all because they had sinned by trying to learn a truth and develop a concept of a larger destiny. But during her time with Cerberus and her travels and travails, she had learned many people shared her hunger for truth. She counted the Magickers among them.

Brigid took a deep breath of the steamy, moisture saturated air and realized the thin fabric of her garb was plastered tight against her body. At the moment, she didn't care, because breathing in the wake of the storm was like trying to hyperventilate in a sauna on full boil.

The path the elephants followed twisted snakelike upon itself through a jumble of trees and vines. More than once the humans upon their backs were forced to lie almost completely flat to keep from being scraped off by branches. Brigid couldn't help but curse in pain when a thorny vine snagged her shoulder, inflicting scratches.

Yasovar called out, "Be of good cheer, Baptiste. We're almost at the end."

She resisted the urge to snap back, "For your sake, we'd better be."

Maya lumbered around a turn and entered a clearing. Huts of wattle, mud and thatch took shape out of the mist. No one seemed to be around. Javalara and Yasovar halted the elephants and had the big animals bend their forelegs so they could dismount easily.

Brigid silently endured the burning pain in her back and pelvis as she slid from Maya's back and dropped to the ground. She felt as if both hip sockets had been re-placed by rusty hinges but she made no complaint. She did, however, favor Brother Yasovar with an icy glare when she caught him eyeing her sari and how the wet cloth clung to her full breasts. He averted his eyes but didn't seem particularly embarrassed. While his ele-phant knelt, he took down the crate containing the in-terphaser and placed it safely to one side.

Javalara marched toward the huts, saying, "Follow me, Baptiste."

While Yasovar attended to the elephants, Brigid did as the man requested, carrying the saddlebag slung over her shoulders. She followed Javalara into the largest of the huts. Not surprisingly, the interior was completely bare of furnishings, despite its size. Only a scattering of straw and grasses lay on the hard-packed dirt floor. The sunlight peeping through the cracks in the walls glinted on a circlet of dull metal on the floor.

Grasping the ring with both hands, Javalara heaved up onto it, a grunt of exertion escaping from between clenched teeth. Brigid stepped forward to help the man, but a metallic clank resounded within the hut and the Magicker released the ring and rocked back on his heels. He panted, "Stand back, Baptiste."

Mystified, Brigid retreated back to the threshold, al-though as far as she could see his tugging on the metal circlet had accomplished nothing. Then, with a clank-ing rumble and a grinding of gears, the entire floor of the hut tipped upward. Javalara stepped quickly to her side as the floor continued to tilt, slowly rotating on hid-den, squeaking pivots.

The floor turned completely over. As it did, a small

teardrop-shaped craft hove into view, clamped securely to the underside by an arrangement of clamps and vises. As the floor completed its rotation, Javalara gestured grandly and announced, "The *vimana* of the Magickers."

Brigid wasn't impressed. The length and beam of the air cruiser appeared half that of the one that had buzzed them only a couple of hours earlier. She didn't see wings or any apparatus that allowed it to become airborne. The purple-tinted hull was smooth, almost seamless. Peering through the bubble-enclosed cockpit, Brigid saw nothing resembling a conventional control panel, either.

Javalara said apologetically, "I know it doesn't look like much—"

"That's an understatement and a half," Brigid cut in curtly, walking around the cruiser, eyeing it critically. "It doesn't look like it can seat more than two."

"Three," Yasovar spoke up from the doorway. "Providing the third person is fairly small, light of weight and doesn't mind being cramped."

Brigid cast him an annoyed glance. "I mind."

Javalara stepped up to the starboard side of the craft, knelt and ran his hands over the underside of the fuselage. "Do you know how the ancients built their *vimanas,* Baptiste?"

Swiftly she flipped through her mental index card file of data and at length admitted, "No, not really. Only that they operated on principles that combined the spiritual and with the mechanical."

"That's very astute," Javalara said. "Among the more famous ancient texts that mention *vimanas* are the Ramayana and Mahabharata. Other lesser known texts include the Samarangana Sutradhara, the Yuktikalpataru of Bhoja, dating back to the twelfth century A.D."

"There's the Rig Veda, too," Brigid interjected. "Many scholars feel the tales of the *vimanas* are the same as the legends of flying carpets."

Javalara nodded. "Possibly. The Samarangana Sutradhara says that they were made of light material, with a strong, well-shaped body—ah, here we are."

He pulled on a small lever and from either side of the *vimana* popped ribbed wings made of material that reminded Brigid of a polymer like Dacron or Mylar. They were folded tight against the fuselage like those of a bat at rest, and like bat wings, they were scalloped on the edges.

"According to the texts," Javalara continued, "iron, copper, mercury and lead were used in their construction. They could fly great distances and were propelled through air by motors. The Samarangana Sutradhara devotes 230 stanzas to the building of these machines, and their uses in peace and war."

Clearing his throat, he quoted in a singsong cadence, "'Strong and durable must the body be made, like a great flying bird, of light material. Inside it one must place the Mercury-engine with its iron heating apparatus beneath. By means of the power latent in the mercury that sets the driving whirlwind in motion, a man sitting inside may travel a great distance in the sky in a most marvelous manner.'"

Brigid smiled wryly and pulled off her turban, shaking her hair free. "That doesn't sound like any kind of theory of avionics I'm familiar with."

Javalara chuckled and straightened. "Me, either. But

the texts say that by using the prescribed processes it was possible to build a *vimana* as large as a temple. The Ramayana describes a *vimana* as a double-deck, circular aircraft with portholes and a dome. It flew with the speed of the wind and gave forth a melodious sound."

"Hmm," Brigid muttered. "Sounds like a classic description of the flying saucer or disk. I wonder which came first, the *vimana* or the flying saucer? The operation of either fits into accepted scientific theory."

"Who can say?" Javalara replied. "There is much about our land, its legend and lore that does not fit with modern scientific theory."

"Like the ongoing problem you want my help to solve?" Brigid challenged. "The one that deals with— and I quote—the 'generation, balance and manipulation of energy'?"

Yasovar said sadly, "Yes. In our attempt to solve it, we tried to force it into our perceptions of scientific law. We failed and were banished. But our attempts still resulted in an unfortunate result."

Brigid ran her fingers through the tangles in her heavy mane, trying to work them out. "Explain."

While he inspected the *vimana*, Javalara said matter-of-factly, "Angkor Thom is built upon a convergence of earth energy lines. Angkor Wat, the palace of the Devi-Naga, was deliberately constructed over a vortex of geomantic energy. Are you familiar with the term?"

"Somewhat," Brigid answered carefully. "The literal meaning of the word geomancy is to 'divine the Earth.' Generally, geomancers believe that the energy of the planet is the very force from which humanity draws its life."

Yasovar put in, "It's also a science, mapping out

places where strands of earth energy join together, forming a power point or a vortex. That's the function of your machine, isn't it?"

Despite her many years of working to perfect a poker face, Brigid couldn't completely conceal an expression of astonishment. "How do you know that?"

Javalara chuckled patronizingly. "We may wear robes, eat bad food and use elephants to get around, but we're not completely primitive. There are some among us who have experience with computers...me among them. I took your machine, your interphaser and downloaded some of its data into a PC we have hidden in a monastery. The information was very illuminating. It confirmed an aspect of the Angkor Wat vortex I had long suspected."

"Which is?" Brigid inquired.

"The energy web of the planet is multidimensional. Strands of it travel through space, connecting all things in the universe to one another. The so-called essence of the Naga is a point where the very fabric of dimensional space is distorted, but the distortion was maintained in harmony and balance for many centuries."

Brigid felt her heart speed up in sudden comprehension. "And you disturbed the balance?"

Yasovar nodded miserably. "On the orders of the Devi-Naga...or at least, Colonel Puyang claimed the orders came from her. We set into motion a process that allowed the geomantic energy to leak through and accumulate in a vessel, like a giant storage battery. When enough of a charge builds up, the towers vent it."

"Vent it?" Brigid echoed. "As a wave or a ray or what?"

"As a field," Javalara stated. "And as the earth energy

is generated, it is carried by the water and wind. Angkor Thom is built around natural and artificial waterways. Our blood interacts with the electromagnetic field, generating the life force within our bodies on a cellular level."

"I think I understand your concerns," Brigid said slowly. "When the vortex was in balance, any effect on people in the area was negligible. Now that it's out of true, you're afraid it will negatively impact their health, perhaps their minds."

"Negative effects have already manifested themselves," Yasovar stated grimly. "Else we would not have been exiled. The essence of the Naga, the Sudarshana chakra has both positive and negative aspects."

"Why do you call the vortex the essence of the Naga?"

"Are you familiar of the Naga, the serpent folk?"

She nodded. "To some extent."

Brigid didn't elaborate on the countless hours of research she had undertaken to learn all she could about the reptilian entities who played pivotal roles in the development of almost all human cultures.

For as long as humanity had kept records, there were legends of a mysterious serpent folk descending from the heavens to participate in the creation of humankind. Cultures in places as widespread as of Sumer, Babylonia, China, Japan and even Central America had myth cycles about these reptilian entities.

Serpents or dragons signified divine heritage in many Asian countries. The Sumerians called them the Annunaki, the Hebrews the Agathadaemon and the Celts the Na Fferyllt. Brigid was convinced they were the same race who interacted with different civilizations at different stages in human history.

"The Naga," Javalara declared, "just like humans, have good and bad among them. A group of evil Naga called Panis, Nivata-kavacas, Kaleyas and Hiranya were enemies of humanity. They lived in underground holes, like snakes. From birth they were extremely powerful and cruel, and although they were proud of their strength, they were always defeated by the Sudarshana chakra. They could not disrupt the supreme personality of godhead."

"That made them very angry," Yasovar said, picking up the thread of the tale. "So they created many demonic serpents called the Nagaloka. They were all extremely vicious but vain. Their hoods were bedecked with valuable gems, and the light emanating from the gems illuminated their underground abode, but they needed more light…and they sought it from the essence of the Naga."

"I see," Brigid said with a smile. "The vortex symbolizes the positive energy of the Naga and negative energy of the Nagaloka. Both emit light, but the effect is different."

"That is substantially it, yes," Javalara confirmed.

"Then why were you ordered to alter the balance of the vortex?"

Yasovar answered in an angry tone, "Colonel Puyang claimed it was the will of the Devi-Naga. She wanted to manipulate the energies beneficially, to use them to reshape and remold our country, to revive the glories of the Khmer empire. I believe it was his ambition, not hers."

"I suspect the same thing," Javalara put in. "Just as I suspect that when we tipped the balance, the change in the radiation tipped Colonel Puyang's mind in the same direction. He was never a good man—bitter, ambitious, petty—but he obeyed our ancient laws. Shortly after our interference with the vortex, his most negative, most rapacious traits came to the fore. When we expressed our intent to return to the vortex and try to rectify our error, he had us exiled."

Brigid pursed her lips thoughtfully. "You were never able to appeal to the Devi-Naga directly?"

Instead of answering, Javalara dropped to his hands and knees and crawled underneath the *vimana*. Brigid bent and saw him wriggle through a hatch in the craft's belly. A few seconds later he popped up under the cockpit bubble, appearing to be absorbed by something out of Brigid's range of vision. His eyes closed and his lips moved slightly as if he were whispering to himself.

"What is he doing?" Brigid asked, bewildered.

"Hush," Yasovar whispered, putting a finger to his lips.

Suddenly, so suddenly Brigid jumped in surprise, the *vimana* exuded a faint, strange hum that was a synthesis of a motor and a musical instrument. The clamps released the craft with loud clacks and the *vimana* floated free above the cradle, listing slightly from side to side.

"It works," Brigid husked out in awe.

"Of course," Yasovar said with a slight note of superiority in his voice. "We know what we're doing." He paused and added with an abashed smile, "Well, most of the time. Some of the time."

"Now what?" she asked, eyes fastened on the hovering cruiser.

"Now we wait until nightfall and fly into the city. Then we will make our way to the palace and—"

"I don't think so," Brigid broke in.

Yasovar stared at her, goggle-eyed and disconcerted. "You promised to help us restore the balance to the essence!"

"I'm still going to help," she replied calmly, "but we're not waiting until nightfall. We're leaving now."

"Now?" The tone of Yasovar's voice and stricken look on his face told Brigid the man feared she had lost her senses.

"Now?" Javalara's echo, somewhat muffled by the cockpit canopy, quivered with the same high note of outraged incredulity. "The city will be swarming with people attending the executions—"

He broke off when he saw the cold smile lift the corners of Brigid's lips. She said, "You're absolutely right. And we're going to crash the party—and save my friend. Or we're not going to do anything at all."

"But," Yasovar sputtered, almost too shocked to enunciate, "it's mad. All the Cobra Guard will be there. It's too risky. It's suicide!"

Brigid inserted her hand into the saddlebag and smoothly withdrew her autopistol. She did not aim it at either of the two men, but her intent was unmistakable, particularly after she intoned, in a voice steely with conviction, "I say again—or we're not going to do anything at all."

Chapter 22

The face leering up at Kane with a maniacal glee was human enough, but the contours of the hairless skull were misshapen, sloping back from the prominent brow so severely there didn't seem to be sufficient capacity for more than a spoonful of brains.

The texture and color of the skin looked like wet burlap. The man's mouth was open in a silent laugh, revealing sharp, narrow teeth. As he heaved himself up by his right hand, he menaced Kane with a long dagger in his left.

Not thinking, only reacting, Kane kicked him squarely in his open mouth. He felt teeth collapse under his sandaled foot. The man fell back into the river with barely a splash.

Almost in the same split second, an agonized scream came from the foredeck, a scream which quickly became a gurgle. Kane turned to see a crewman being yanked up from the barge by a rope and noose that had been dropped from the intertwining boughs above. The man shot straight up, clawing at the noose around his throat, disappearing with a crash among the limbs and branches.

A naked brown-skinned man, acting as counterweight, came down on the length of the rope as the crew member went up. With a snarling, slobbering laugh, he swept a flat blade in an arc to keep the shocked crewmen back. He was a corpulent, toadlike chunk of man, reeking of the swamp. The creature's nape was a thick roll of fat that thrust his head forward aggressively. His eyes gleamed like a pair of wet black pearls swimming in mud. Ornaments fashioned from bones were his only concession to clothing.

Kane used to his foot as a lever to flip the Copperhead up into his hands. His thumb dislodged the safety switch and he pressed the trigger, sending a full-auto burst smashing into the toad-man, knocking him backward over the prow.

As if the gunfire was a signal, the crew ran to and fro across the deck, opening up boxes and crates stacked against the deck housing amidships. Responding to General Zhou Tzu's shouted commands, they handed out weapons, most of them small subguns.

"What the hell are Bottom Feeders?" Kane demanded, picking up his Sin Eater and trying to strap it one-handed to his forearm. Zhou Tzu obligingly took the Copperhead from him.

"A tribe of inbred wretches who inhabit the swamps," the general replied curtly, eyes scanning the riverbanks. "Pirates and scavengers, they ofttimes raid barges like this seeking both plunder and sport."

He turned toward Nora. Gesturing to the housing, he commanded, "Get below."

She frowned. "But—"

"That is an *order*." Zhou Tzu's voice snapped as sharply as a whip crack.

Without another word, she turned on her heel and entered the small cabin. Kane stared after her for a stunned second, then completed securing the Sin Eater's power holster to his forearm. "Are the Bottom Feeders muties?"

Zhou Tzu cast him a swift, puzzled look. "They are adapted to life in and around the river and the swamps. They can hold their breath for a long time underwater. I've encountered them many times. I doubt they would have attacked us except they saw a woman aboard."

Just the concept of a woman like Nora in the hands of the Bottom Feeders was enough to evoke a surge of nausea in Kane's belly. They reminded him strongly of swampies, the mutants who haunted the southern bayous. He tensed his wrist tendons, and the Sin Eater slapped solidly into his palm. "Will they be back?"

The general nodded grimly. "I fear so. They just made a sortie, to feel out our defenses and unnerve us. They rely a great deal on their reputations to get what they want."

Within a second of Zhou Tzu's announcement, a concerted attack came from all sides. A horde of Bottom Feeders converged on the barge in a rush of naked bodies streaming with foul-smelling water. At least three more dropped from the tree limbs above.

A Bottom Feeder slid down a length of rope made of interbraided grass, a knife gripped between his jaws. His flat feet slammed to the deck where Kane had stood an instant before. The Sin Eater cracked once, and a 248-grain round slammed into the center of the man's chest at 335 pounds of pressure per square inch. The hammer blow to the Bottom Feeder's sternum emptied his lungs of oxygen and the hydrostatic shock stopped his heart. He toppled overboard, sliding beneath the surface of the Siemrap.

Three crewmen opened fire with their subguns, full-auto fusillades that smashed into a pair of Bottom Feeders, knocking them backward over the starboard side. The brown men continued to pull themselves aboard, their flat feet slapping wetly against the deck planks. A screaming sailor went down beneath the bulk of two toadlike bodies, gutted by knives.

The Copperhead in Zhou Tzu's hands chattered in a short burst. A Bottom Feeder spun on his toes, the top of his distorted skull floating away in a red mist. He glimpsed another of his crew, a youth who appeared to be no more than twelve, vainly trying to keep a knife from slitting his throat.

Zhou Tzu leaped, knocking the knife from the slimy hand with the frame of the Copperhead, then driving the butt full into the Bottom Feeder's squat throat, bowling him over the port rail. Another toadlike man dived at the general's back, long dagger in hand.

Kane opened up with the Sin Eater, the 9 mm rounds driving through the side of the Bottom Feeder's head, opening up his cranium like a ripe melon struck with a hammer. The creature flopped down onto the deck, feet kicking spasmodically.

The deck of the barge erupted with gunfire, screams and shouts. Steel-jacketed bullets tore ragged holes in naked brown flesh. More than once a slug struck splinters uncomfortably close to Kane. He was forced to dodge and duck instead of finding targets. The battle swirled around the housing of the cabin.

Zhou Tzu was careful how he handled the Copperhead, not hosing the ammo around indiscriminately. All of the rounds he fired found targets, the well-timed and

-placed bullets knocking another knife-wielding Bottom Feeder's legs out from under him. He squalled as he fell, toppling overboard with a great splash.

Back and forth the struggle swayed, gunfire crashing, all the combatants howling. The wooden planking underfoot streamed with blood. The barge's crew backed up to the foredeck. The cramped kill zone was packed and jammed with adversaries crushed together breast to breast.

The accuracy of the shots fired by Kane and Zhou Tzu finally split the Bottom Feeder ranks. The surge of toad men reluctantly ebbed back toward the rails in a chaotic, confused swirl of rear-guard combat. They retreated stubbornly.

A heavy, solid weight bowled Kane off his feet, cannonading him headlong into the port side, knocking almost all the wind from him. Only a last-second, frantic grab of the rail kept him from pitching overboard. As it was, his straw hat splashed down into the Siemrap but he was too dazed to care much about rescuing his disguise.

Trying to drag air into his lungs, Kane pushed himself up and around. A stinking webbed hand stretched out to clamp around his throat. Kane tried to bat it aside and bring his Sin Eater up, but the Bottom Feeder's other hand gripped his right wrist.

He drove a knee into Kane's groin. Although the blow didn't land squarely, pain flared through his testicles and bile leaped up his throat. Only the hand tightly squeezing his neck kept him from vomiting.

He heard a splitting sound as of a rock being dropped in muck. The Bottom Feeder's body jerked violently, and the grip on his hand and wrist loosened. Kane fought free, falling to the deck, dragging in a shuddery lungful of air.

A spur of red-stained metal protruded from the man's flabby left pectoral. He touched it wonderingly, then his lips peeled back in a vicious grimace. He tried to lock his hands around Kane's throat again, as though the Bottom Feeder's last conscious wish was to deal death even as he died.

Kane brought up the bore of his Sin Eater and depressed the trigger stud. The round entered the Bottom Feeder's receding chin and exploded through the top of his head, as if a grenade had detonated within it.

As the brown man fell over sideways, Kane saw Nora standing on the deck, her left hand still tight around the wooden haft of a pike, her face pinched tight with anxiety.

Struggling erect, he said hoarsely, "Thanks…but didn't the general tell you to stay below?"

In an eerily calm voice, she said, "They're chopping their way up through the keel. I thought somebody should know."

Kane felt the jarring impacts vibrate the deck beneath his feet and he swept his gaze over the struggling figures driving the last of the Bottom Feeders overboard. He glimpsed Zhou Tzu stroking short bursts from his Copperhead.

"General!" he shouted. "Those bastards are cutting holes in the bottom!"

Zhou Tzu didn't react, his ears filled with gunfire and screams. Kane yelled again and only then did the general whirl, his face a mask of implacable ferocity. At that moment, a Bottom Feeder lunged around the corner of the deckhouse, sweeping up Nora in his arms and bearing her forward.

She cried out in wordless alarm and pain. Kane bit back a curse, tracking the warty man with the bore of his pistol. He shifted position, trying to bring the creature into target acquisition without endangering Nora Pennick.

The Bottom Feeder was cunning—he knew exactly how to hold Nora to shield his vitals. He reached the rail and paused, one foot propped on it, arms tight around Nora, glaring at Kane in a silent dare. He put a hand around the slender column of her throat and she grimaced, either in pain or disgust.

Slowly Kane lowered the Sin Eater and a grin of malicious triumph crossed the man's face. The Bottom Feeder poised himself to leap overboard—then the figure of Zhou Tzu appeared on the barge rail, blocking the man's path to the river. Without hesitation, he kicked the brown man in the throat.

Gagging, the Bottom Feeder staggered back, his grip on Nora loosening. Bending her knees, she slid down through his arms and rolled frantically away from the man. Zhou Tzu's focus was on the creature that had attacked her. The Bottom Feeder screamed, hitting a high plaintive tone that Kane guessed was a plea for mercy. He raised his hands in supplication.

The general fired the Copperhead dry, perforating the toadlike man's belly. Fountains of blood arced from the wounds, painting the deck with crimson streaks. Zhou Tzu dropped the subgun and advanced on the squealing raider, doubled up around his belly wounds.

One of his crewmen handed him a knife a Bottom

Feeder had brandished. Zhou Tzu thrust the blade into the Bottom Feeder's back, stabbing him three times. Leaving the knife planted in his spine, he jerked the brown man erect, clutching him by the throat. He forced him backward, all the way to the stern. He twirled him around and with a contemptuous kick to the rear, the general dumped him headfirst into the Siemrap. Even Kane felt a quiver of unease at the controlled savagery of the man's actions.

When Zhou Tzu turned, the expression on his face was one of pure homicidal fury. He marched over to Nora, who Kane was helping to her feet. She winced, cradling her injured arm with her left hand. Grabbing her by the shoulders, the general shook her.

"I told you stay below!" His voice was a strident crash of fury.

Nora ducked her head, unable to meet the enraged eyes of Zhou Tzu. Kane tensed to insinuate himself to the two people. He half expected to witness a replay of the reunion of Ayn and Alf Thoraldson. Instead, the general hugged her to him in a tight embrace, wrapping his arms around her as if he feared to release her again.

Kane felt a sense of shock and even a little shame. Nora Pennick might indeed have been a woman in love, but there was no question she was loved in return.

One of the crewmen peered into the deck housing and shouted angry, frightened words in Khmer. Zhou Tzu reluctantly released Nora, exchanging a rapid-fire flurry of words with his men. Only two remained on their feet.

Bleakly, the general said to Kane, "We are taking on water. The bastards managed to chop completely through the hull. We have no choice but to abandon ship."

Kane gave the boat a swift visual inspection. Starboard astern was definitely tipping very close to the river's surface. "No chance of repairs?"

Zhou Tzu shook his head, lips a tight white line of worry. "Not without a dry dock. We must go the rest of the way on foot, and it will not be an easy or a safe journey."

Kane chuckled mirthlessly, glancing around for his pack. "As if it's been a pleasure cruise so far."

The water, though not cold, was at least a few degrees cooler than the hot humid air above the Siemrap. The swim was not a long one, but by the time Kane, Nora, the general and his three men reached the bank, the barge had filled with water and sunk to the bottom. The bodies of the crewmen and Bottom Feeders alike bobbed on the surface, carried away by the current.

They struggled up the slippery bank, using tree roots to haul themselves out of the river. The six people sat in the shade of palms, among a thick growth of ferns to rest. The smell of decaying vegetation blended with that of exotic flowers, which bloomed in crimson, gold and white against the dark green walls of foliage.

"How far do we have to travel?" Kane asked after he had regained his breath. He swiftly checked the contents of his pack to make sure the watertight seals had held.

Zhou Tzu consulted briefly with one of his men and announced, "A half day's march southeast should bring us within sight of the city."

Kane looked up, gauging the position of the sun. "Hell, it's not even noon."

"I doubt it's even eleven," Nora panted. "We can only pray the rest of the day is not as eventful as the morning has been."

"I hear that." Kane got to his feet and after a moment his companions did the same. "Let's get moving before more Bottom Feeders or tigers or dragons show up."

Zhou Tzu permitted himself a small smile. He said quietly, "You fought well, Mr. Kane. All of us would surely have been killed if not for your marksmanship. Thank you."

Kane nodded in acknowledgment of the gratitude, but he said slowly, "So far, your gambit hasn't been very successful. And Nora was most definitely on the game board."

"I realize that," the general said stiffly. "She acted rashly."

"But she saved my life."

It was Zhou Tzu's turn to nod. "Just so. But she acted rashly, nevertheless."

"I'd like to know what you have in mind once we reach the city."

Zhou Tzu didn't answer for a few seconds, then said slowly, "During my education, I learned some of your country's vernacular. One of the phrases that remained with me all these years was… 'need-to-know basis.' I'm afraid that information is on a need-to-know basis."

"If you want my help," Kane replied with a grave sincerity, "then you had better put it on your need to know list."

"By the same token," Zhou Tzu said with the same somber earnestness, "if you want my help so you can survive the trek through this jungle, then it would be best if you followed my orders. I am in command here, Mr. Kane. Not you."

"I won't be your pawn, general." Kane gestured toward Nora. "Neither will she."

In a remarkably gentle voice, but underscored by a silky soft thread of menace, Zhou Tzu stated, "She is not your concern."

Kane locked unblinking eyes with the general then decided it would be diplomatic to drop the subject.

For a time, the general's men hacked a path through the dense, tropical undergrowth with machetes they had salvaged from the sinking barge. No one spoke for a long time. There were only the grunts and wheezes of laboring men, the chopping of blades as they sheared through vines and saplings and the rustle of undergrowth as the small party pushed its way through the jungle.

The air was as hot and as steamy as if they were in a hothouse. Sweat glistened on everyone's faces and limbs. Almost no breeze disturbed the sweltering atmosphere. The close-growing palm trees draped with loops and braids of flowering lianas proved to be a more than adequate windbreak. The humidity kept their clothes from completely drying, making Kane feel as if he wore a bog.

Flying insects hummed above their heads in muggy air. Scarlet beaked birds cawed at them from the branches of banyan trees. Once Kane sighted a huge python slithering lethargically into the brush and the back of his neck flushed cold, but the rest of his body stayed hot and sweaty.

Suddenly, Zhou Tzu shot out a restraining hand to halt his companions. He tilted his head back, sniffing the still air.

"What is it?" Nora whispered, her hair soaked through with sweat.

"An odd thing," the general murmured. He pointed to the left. "A fire."

Kane inhaled through his nostrils and detected the odor of burning. He followed Zhou Tzu through a thicket of tall, clattering bamboo. They forged ahead through the labyrinthine tangle of vine and creeper. The ground was very damp underfoot, and Kane wondered what could have possibly caught fire in the swampy jungle.

General Zhou Tzu came to a sudden halt, so suddenly Kane nearly trod on his heels. About fifty yards ahead lay a long torpedo-shaped object, burnished silver in color. Wings were crumpled against the ground like abstract aluminum-foil sculptures.

"A *vimana*," Zhou Tzu said softly.

"A what?" demanded Kane.

"A flying ship," Nora said.

The craft had crashed into the jungle and flammables within it had caught fire, but had not burned for very long. The nose of the ruined ship was turned in on itself, charred black, exposing a skeletal framework of metal. Kane estimated the *vimana* was no more than twenty feet long. It didn't look very sturdy.

Zhou Tzu grunted in disappointment. "No chance of patching it up for our own use."

He stepped closer, then stopped again. "Do you see that insignia?" His voice was scarcely above a whisper.

Kane eyed the fuselage and made out a symbol that reminded him of a caduceus, only this one depicted a cobra with seven heads coiled around a pointed column. "Yes. So?"

"That is the royal seal of the Devi-Naga herself. This ship came from the palace." Zhou Tzu's tone of voice was perplexed, almost bewildered.

Kane moved toward the *vimana*. "We'd better check to make sure there's no one inside."

He had walked only a few feet when, far off in the jungle, a girl screamed.

Chapter 23

Zhou Tzu slashed apart vines and brush with the machete. "This way."

"Easy," Kane cautioned as he, Nora and the three soldiers followed in the general's wake. "This could be some kind of a trap."

"I agree," Nora said breathlessly. "From what you've told me of your enemies, you can't afford to take chances this close to the city."

"I think not," Zhou Tzu replied diffidently. "I've heard a good many genuine screams of fear in my life, and I can tell the false from the genuine."

He started to say more, then came to a halt, lifting the machete first to bring the people behind him to a stop and then to point. Kane looked in the direction Zhou Tzu indicated. Clinging to the low branch of a gnarled tree by her hands and feet was a small raven-haired girl. Her legs were muddied and her naked limbs, the color of polished opals, bore angry red lines where thorns had inflicted scratches. Her only clothing was a long silken loincloth. She appeared to be dressed more for bed than the jungle.

A giant monitor lizard squatted at the base of the tree and watched the girl unblinkingly. This lizard was larger than the creature Kane had killed on the way to the trading post, its hide the color of molten lead mixed in with patches of milky green. Its long yellow tongue flickered out from between its jaws, darting up toward the treed girl.

Apparently the dragon hadn't tried to heave itself up on its hind legs, else it would easily have seized the girl and yanked her from her perch. As it was the creature didn't seem overly eager in making the girl a meal, evincing more curiosity than hunger.

"I'd hate to waste ammo on another one of those things. Maybe we can chase it off," Kane said quietly.

Zhou Tzu shook his head. "Not a good idea. Even a nip from a dragon can be fatal. They have disease-ridden bacteria in their mouths. After it bites its prey, the victim will sicken and die from blood poisoning within a day or two. Then the dragon will scent out the body and eat it."

Nora made a faint retching sound, covering her mouth with her hands.

"Lovable," Kane muttered dryly. "All right, let's do it."

Sin Eater in hand, he and Zhou Tzu approached the huge lizard. The general held the Copperhead. The dragon uttered a sibilant fluttering noise, the loose flesh at its throat undulating, its eyes still fixed on the girl. Muscles rippled along its hindquarters. Kane guessed the creature was readying itself to rear up and he shouted, "Hey!"

Both the girl and the dragon swung their heads toward him. She cried out in surprise when she caught sight of the men, but the dragon inspected them silently. Zhou had taken up position near the animal's right flank. The laser autotargeter played the red kill dot along its barrel-shaped body.

Zhou Tzu shouted to the girl in Khmer. Without the PDA, Kane didn't understand his words, but the girl's response sounded relieved. Her voice was high and quavery, like that of a terrified child.

"I shall try for its heart," the general declared calmly. "Mr. Kane, you should concentrate your fire on the beast's brain."

Kane framed the creature's skull within the rear sights of the Sin Eater, cupping his right hand in his left. With the girl so close, the result of a missed shot might prove to be a cure worse than the disease of the carnivorous dragon. "On three," he said. "One…two… *three*."

Both men opened up with full-auto barrages. The dragon screeched in pain, snapped at the penetration points on its body. Round after round after round penetrated the scales and flesh and muscle. Refusing to give way, the dragon thrashed and screamed, its long tail lashing back and forth, slamming repeatedly into the trunk of the tree to which the girl clung.

Kane kept the Sin Eater's trigger stud depressed, bright brass flying up and out from the smoking ejector port. The 9 mm blockbusters pounded into the dragon's upper body, punching deep holes through flesh and muscle amid sprays of dark blood. The monster's sibilant snarling took on a high-pitched, keening note. Its jaws gaped open like those of a snake, and Kane squeezed off one more shot, the round drilling through the roof of the creature's mouth and into its brain.

Then the dragon swayed on its bowed legs and tumbled over sideways, wallowing like a dog trying to rid itself of a persistent itch. It opened and closed its jaws repeatedly, blood spouting from its nostrils. Its tail, whipping wildly in postmortem spasms, smashed into the tree, shaking loose a shower of leaves and shearing away a basketful of bark. The girl screamed and lost her grip.

Zhou Tzu dropped the Copperhead and bounded forward, managing to catch the girl in his arms before she hit the ground. He swiftly sprinted out range of the giant reptile's lashing tail.

As the monster's convulsing death throes became tremblings, Zhou Tzu carried to the girl over to Nora and set her upright gently. He spoke to her quietly in Khmer. The girl brushed back her waist-length hair, staring up at him in wonder and replied in a voice so faint Kane couldn't hear her.

"What'd she say?" he demanded, picking up the subgun from where the general so carelessly dropped it.

The girl's head swiveled toward him, eyes widening in surprise. She said softly, "English. You speak English like Boo-star."

"Boo-star?" Nora echoed. "Do you mean Brewster?"

The girl turned her head toward her. As she did so, the jungle-filtered sunlight glinted on the delicate gold-scale design painted on her eyes. "Another English," she breathed.

Zhou Tzu touched the design on her face carefully, the expression on his face studiedly neutral. "What is your name, child?"

The black-haired girl bit her lower lip before replying, "I am Kumudvati."

The general's face finally registered emotion, as did Nora's. Their astounded expressions mirrored each other's. "Ridiculous," Zhou Tzu said, although there was no real heat in his voice. "You are far too young to be the Devi-Naga."

The girl gazed up at him with searching eyes. "How would you know?"

Zhou Tzu sidestepped the question by asking one of his own. "What are you doing out here?"

Kumudvati lifted a bare shoulder in a negligent shrug. "I became very restless in the palace, cooped up in my rooms. This morning I took the *vimana*."

"You were allowed to fly it alone?" the general asked skeptically. "Without a pilot?"

She stated matter-of-factly, "It is the royal *vimana* and I am the Devi-Naga. No one allows me to do anything. I just do it."

Kane could tell by the tone and cadence of her voice the girl was lying. Intentionally sounding harsh, Kane said, "I don't believe you."

The girl drew herself up haughtily, attempting an air of regal indignation. "How dare you challenge the word of the serpent princess?"

"It's easy," Kane countered. "You're not my serpent or my princess. The one you called Boo-star is a lost friend of mine. I seek another friend, too. And I know a spoiled kid like you didn't fly out here from your safe palace because you were bored with having your face painted."

Kumudvati's sweeping eyelashes fluttered over dark eyes suddenly brimming with tears. She buried her face in her hands and began sobbing, her shoulders quaking. Kane exchanged a helpless glance with Zhou Tzu, who then looked pleadingly toward Nora.

She put an arm around the weeping girl and led her away from the two men. "It's all right, lass," she murmured, stroking her hair. "No need to cry. You're among friends here."

The girl clung tightly to Nora and continued to cry, speaking in Khmer, her voice blurred by sobs. Kane caught Zhou Tzu's jaw muscles bunch in reaction to her words. "What's she saying?"

Quietly, the general answered, "She wants her mother. She misses her mother. Apparently she died some time ago."

Kane shifted his feet impatiently. "I don't want to sound any more cold-blooded than I already have, but we've got no time for this. If she knows the whereabouts of Philboyd, she might know where Baptiste is, too."

Zhou Tzu nodded. He drew the girl away from Nora and gently lifted her tear-streaked face by a finger under her chin, a gesture sharply reminiscent of Ayn and Alf Thoraldson. He spoke in a calm, soothing voice, in English for Kane and Nora's benefit. "What are you really doing out here, child?"

Kumudvati brushed the tears away from her cheeks. "I seek the warlord, General Zhou Tzu."

"Why?"

"My mother…" She broke off, her lips trembling. Then she said in a whispering rush, "My mother told me that if anything happened to her, to the holy city, then I could rely on the help of only one man…my father."

THE REACTION of Zhou Tzu surprised Kane. His face remained completely immobile and inscrutable, with not so much as the lifting of an eyebrow. Nora's eyes darted from his face to Kumudvati's and she husked out, "Of course. It makes sense now."

Kane, standing to one side of the girl and the man, studied their profiles and was struck by the strong resemblance, particularly around the chin and mouth. But he had no inclination to stand around idly waiting for Zhou Tzu to process the information. Peremptorily he announced, "I need to know about Brewster."

Slowly, reluctantly, Kumudvati removed her gaze from Zhou Tzu's face and fixed it upon Kane. "He is a prisoner in Angkor Thom. I heard about him coming from a foreign land and that he might have scientific knowledge. I spoke with him yesterday. Colonel Puyang followed me to his cell and became angry, fearful of what he might have told me.

"Even though I explained that Boo-star told me nothing, the colonel did not believe me because he does not speak the English. Against my wishes, he will execute Boo-star today. I realized that the colonel is mad, so I took the *vimana* to find General Zhou Tzu and plead for his help, as my mother instructed. I saw the *vimana* of the Cobra Guard and I tried to hide from them but instead I caused the vehicle to crash."

"You weren't injured?" Nora asked.

The girl shook her head. "No, I managed to jump clear before it caught on fire. And then came the dragon—" She broke off, shuddering.

Kane inquired sharply, "There was no else with Boo—I mean, Brewster? A tall woman with red hair and green eyes?"

"No, only him."

Kumudvati returned her penetrating gaze to Zhou Tzu's face. "You are him, aren't you? The general?"

Zhou Tzu inhaled a deep breath and took one step back from the girl. "I am he, princess."

The girl ducked her head almost reverently, crossing her forearms over her jewel-laden bosom. "I put myself and the empire into your hands. I am the issue of the mingled essence of the Devi-Naga and her enemy, the warlord of Phnom Kuleh. I am the living expression of the Sudarshana chakra. And I need your guidance...Father."

Chapter 24

The *vimana* dropped gently down through the labyrinth of trees. Branches of incredible breadth crossed and twined, forming pathways of wood, leaf and vine. The *vimana* cruised among them, like a feather floating down a stream.

Brigid Baptiste peered through the bubble canopy, amazed at how skillfully and gracefully Brother Javalara piloted the ship through the thickets. Clouds of tiny gnats and midges swirled in the shafts of sunlight slanting down through the roof formed by the great trees. Here and there fell blankets of cool leaf-edged shadow.

In the shaded places monkeys and gibbons dozed, then shrieked and fled at the sight of the craft invading their arboreal refuge. A huge reticulated python, looking almost big enough to crush the *vimana*, coiled its body around a tree limb as the vessel eased past.

"This is about the best way to sneak into enemy territory I ever heard of," Brigid remarked.

Javalara grunted absently. "I still have grave misgivings, Baptiste."

"You can always drop me off and let me fend for myself."

The Magicker shook his head. "No, when you outlined your idea I told you I would help you…because the friend you want to rescue is also a great scientist."

"I never claimed to be a scientist," Brigid said reprovingly. "Great or otherwise. Brewster Philboyd most definitely is."

"I'm beginning to regret that I agreed to this. But you are a very persuasive woman. I just hate putting such a brain as yours at risk in a chancy undertaking like this one."

Brigid smiled wryly. "I guarantee you that I'll safeguard my brain so the Devi-Naga and Colonel Puyang won't be getting their hands on it before you do."

Javalara threw her a sour smile over his shoulder. "That comforts me, Baptiste."

The flight from the hiding place of the *vimana* to the outskirts of Angkor Thom had been surprisingly short, less than an hour. Once Javalara agreed to the rescue attempt, Yasovar elected to remain behind. He put the interphaser aboard and operated the mechanism which opened a hatch in the roof of the hut. The *vimana* had risen vertically into the sky as smoothly as if pulled by a celestial magnet.

Javalara extended the craft's wings, and the little cruiser shot over the vast vista of the jungle like an arrow loosed from a bow. Brigid didn't understand the system of aerodynamics at work. Although she heard the drone of some type of motor within a rear compartment, Javalara also claimed he controlled the *vimana* through a mental interaction with its mechanical motive power. He made a cryptic comment about utilizing a gravity-negative or gravity-repellent pressure.

Brigid knew of Einstein's studies in the field of electromagnetism and gravity, referring to them as the cosmological constant. The theory dealt with a form of antigravity, what he called a quintessence.

To Brigid's frustration, Javalara's concentration was such that he could not afford to be distracted to address technical questions. She speculated that the pilot of the *vimana*, in tandem with the motor, could alter the gravitation constant of the craft sufficiently to keep it airborne. She had witnessed feats of psychokinesis before so she guessed a variation of that ability was at work with the *vimana*.

When the aircraft entered the jungle, Javalara retracted the wings and the ship nosed its way carefully among the trees until he brought it to rest within the fork of a huge fig tree. Through the screen of leaves Brigid glimpsed pinnacled towers.

Releasing his pent-up breath, Javalara massaged his temples. "It's been some time since I've flown. It can be a strain."

"We were a long time in the air," Brigid said sympathetically.

"Not long enough. The longer one is airborne in a *vimana*, the easier the piloting becomes. The more the part of the mind that controls the *vimana* is exercised, the easier the process becomes…like strengthening a muscle."

He turned and undogged the circular hatch in the deck. "Let's see what we can see."

Javalara gestured for Brigid to precede him, and she squirmed down into the crotch of the great tree. Cautiously she walked out onto a bough three times the thickness of her body. She and Javalara walked to a point on the gigantic limb where they both had a fairly unobstructed view of Angkor Thom.

"Behold the holy city of the Khmer Empire," he said, his voice heavy with irony.

The towers and spires looked about close enough to touch. The architecture was more than impressive; it was magnificent, but Brigid had matters of greater weight on her mind than the construction techniques of an ancient civilization. She spied some small, well-tended fields on the northern outskirts of the city.

The early-afternoon sun shone bright and hot but the streets were crowded with people. They moved toward a circular courtyard, ringed by tall smooth stones engraved with smiling Buddha faces. From the center rose a high gallows. She counted five nooses dangling from the cross timber.

The people marching toward the scaffold looked thin and weary. The little clothes they wore were threadbare. They didn't speak among themselves. Brigid received the distinct impression they didn't feel attending a mass execution was an enjoyable way to break up their day.

Here and there she saw men in gray-green uniforms and polished helmets fashioned to resemble the heads of cobras. With gun barrels they nudged the procession of people toward the courtyard.

"How long do we have?" she asked anxiously.

Javalara inched closer, frowning down at the spectacle. "No more than an hour. They've got the prisoners locked up in that building. See it?"

Brigid followed his finger to a stone structure rising from the far side of the courtyard like a gray wart. Shading her eyes, she saw five of the serpent-helmeted men standing sentry around it.

"Three in front, two in back," she said thoughtfully. "If we hit the rear of the place first, we've only got two to worry about right off the bat."

Javalara swallowed hard. "You seem very sure of yourself, Baptiste. Have you done something like this before?"

Brigid repressed a wry grin as she recalled all the hairbreadth escapes and rescues she had been involved in over the past couple of years. "You might say I have a little experience at this sort of thing."

Javalara's frown deepened. "You might be…but I am quite the novice in matters of violence, especially against trained soldiers. Just our attempt to free the prisoners, regardless of its success, will alert every Cobra guard in the city, on and off duty. We won't be able to enter the palace unseen."

Brigid nodded, understanding the man's fears, but she said, "I seriously doubt the Cobra Guard will expect us to dash into the palace. More than likely they'll cordon off all the ways out of the city."

Javalara nodded in reluctant agreement. "That is true. But still—"

"You know your way around Angkor Thom, right?" Brigid broke in, deliberately trying to distract the man from dwelling on the gloomiest outcome. "It's your home, isn't it?"

"Of course. I've lived there for over twenty years, back when most of the buildings hadn't been restored."

"In that case, your knowledge of the city is our most valuable asset. Not only so you can tell us the best places to hide once we spring the prisoners but of how to get into Angkor Wat undetected."

Nervously, Javalara stroked his goatee. "How do I know that once you have freed your friend, you won't just use your interphaser to return to this Cerberus of yours?"

Brigid regarded him with a hard jade stare. "First of all, I've given you my word I'll help you. Secondarily, even after I free Dr. Philboyd, I still won't have retrieved Dr. Pennick. If she's been captured by the warlord Zhou Tzu, then I'll need your help to free her. Also, I'm very interested in seeing the 'essence of the Naga' phenomena for myself."

Javalara forced a bleak smile. "So we may die trying to free your friend, but at least I can expire knowing you intended to keep your word."

She returned his smile. "It's better than nothing, isn't it?"

He sighed. "That's debatable. However—"

He and Brigid returned to the *vimana*. She waited below in the fork of the tree while he crawled back aboard and handed her down the saddlebag. Swiftly, she stripped out of her still damp sari and began pulling on the shadow suit by opening a magnetic seal on its right side. The garment had no zippers or buttons, and she put it on in one continuous piece from the hard-soled boots to the gloves.

The fabric molded itself to her body, adhering like another layer of epidermis. She smoothed out the wrinkles and folds by running her hands over arms and legs. She didn't care if Javalara peeked at her or not. She had learned the hard way that modesty was a variable, an artifice.

Pulling herself back up into the *vimana*, she realized she felt about ten times better, particularly after the suit's internal thermostats cooled her. "Get us as close to the gallows and the hoosegow as you can," she instructed Javalara.

The man's eyes narrowed in confusion. "The what?"

"Where the prisoners are being held. I'd prefer a rooftop."

Javalara nodded, compressing his lips. "I'll do my best, Baptiste. I just hope it's enough."

The *vimana* slid through the forest canopy, collecting a camouflaging mat of vines and branches in the process. The ship stayed close to the shadowing trees as it circled Angkor Thom, coming around from the north end, which was essentially farmland and unrestored ruins.

The cruiser skimmed the surface of a reservoir, almost skating along like a water beetle. The edges were clogged and overgrown with vegetation. The vine-draped *vimana* looked like one more clump of foliage to the casual glance, or at least Brigid and Javalara hoped that was the case.

The Magicker brought the *vimana* to rest in an overgrown irrigation canal. He and Brigid disembarked, although they got wet in the process. Autopistol in hand, she followed Javalara on a circuitous route along alleys, side streets, over tumble-down blocks of stone and through empty temple galleries. She resisted the impulse to examine the elaborate carvings and statues. They turned down a cross street flanked by stone town houses on whose flat roofs blossomed gardens. Narrow lanes cut between them. Beyond and above, higher structures, those that surrounded the temple complex of Angkor Wat, rose massive.

Javalara and Brigid reached the rear of a three-story, flat-roofed building very near the courtyard but an old man sat outside it on a stool. Stripped to the waist, his skin was the texture and color of cured leather. He industriously cleaned fish with a small knife. A heap of guts drew flies on his right.

Brigid and Javalara drew back into the shadows cast by an overhang, crouching behind a crumbling wall. "Maybe he'll go inside if it gets too hot," Brigid suggested in a whisper.

Javalara shook his head. "He should be attending the executions."

As if on cue, a thickset member of the Cobra Guard marched around the corner and barked, "Execution day, grandfather. Your wrinkled ass is required in the square."

"I know," the old man said blandly. "But today I was lucky with my nets. Today I and my family will eat…unlike the last three days."

"Are you criticizing the benevolence of the Devi-Naga?" the soldier snapped.

The old man shook his head. "I am saying my family will eat today. I did not bring Her Glory into the discussion at all."

"You might eat," the guardsman said, "but only after you witness the executions of enemies of Her Glory."

"I have already witnessed a number of executions of her enemies. My belly is not interested in seeing more."

The snake-helmeted man strode over to the old man and slapped him across the face. "You don't seem to understand, grandfather. The Devi-Naga insists you at-

tend so that all may see what happens to enemies of the
Khmer Empire."

The old man probed the inside of his cheek with his
tongue. He looked down at the knife in his hand, then
eyed the Cobra guardsman. Brigid could tell he seriously contemplated driving the knife into the man's
chest.

The soldier knew it, too, and smirked at him contemptuously, silently daring him to make an attempt to
stab him. He hefted his subgun suggestively. At length,
the old man turned his head, spat a jet of blood toward
the heap of fish entrails and stood, jamming the knife
into the wooden stool. "Let us go. I do not wish to dis-
appoint Her Glory."

"Or die, grandfather," the guardsman said mockingly.
"Do not forget that part of it."

Grabbing the man by the back of the neck, the smirking soldier shoved him around the corner of the building,
delivering a kick to his rear to speed him along. Brigid's
finger crooked reflexively around the trigger of the
TP-9 and her thumb touched the safety switch. She
clenched her teeth while she struggled to contain her
anger.

Javalara touched her arm and shook his head. She
nodded impatiently, acknowledging her companion's
rebuke, realizing that even a single gunshot would be
heard by the Cobra Guard attending the execution.

When the old man and the soldier were completely
out of sight, she and Javalara crept out of the shadows
and scaled the building. The many bas-relief carvings
provided adequate hand- and footholds. They climbed
quickly to the roof, crawling to the edge, looking at the

rear of the scaffold and the round stone hut. Brigid estimated that twenty or so yards of open ground lay between them.

The two guards leaned against the building, conversing idly, their subguns dangling carelessly from shoulder straps. But even as torpid as they appeared in the afternoon heat, Brigid knew they would easily see her approach.

"What now?" Javalara whispered.

Brigid scrutinized the buildings around the courtyard, noting how it was filling up fast with people. "We need some kind of distraction."

Javalara looked apprehensively at the towers looming above them. "Someone could look out a window, perhaps the Devi-Naga herself, see us and raise an alarm. That might work."

"You're not only a scientist but a comedian," Brigid intoned flatly. "You're not being very helpful."

"You were the one who claimed you had experience at this sort of thing," the man pointed out waspishly.

Brigid fought down a swell of hopelessness, as well as a surge of self-directed anger. She knew if Kane and Grant had been present they would have concocted half a dozen scenarios by now. Almost all the possible courses of action flitting through her mind ended the same way—with Brewster Philboyd hanging from a rope with a broken neck and she and Javalara shot dead.

She glared at the scaffold and the stone holding cell. The sun drove a nail of pain into the back of her head, and she slitted her eyes against the shimmer of heat waves rising from the paving stones.

Javalara suddenly uttered a groan of terror. She glanced over at him. "What?"

He didn't answer in words, but pointed skyward. Looking up, shielding her eyes with a hand, she scanned the limitless blue. Movement caught her attention, sunlight flashing on metal. Her belly flip-flopped when she spied the silver *vimana* cruising over the treetops. She recognized the craft as the same one that had buzzed them earlier that day.

"The *vimana* of the Cobra Guard," Javalara moaned between clenched teeth. "They will see us. There is no way they cannot."

Brigid silently agreed with the man's assessment. With her black shadow suit she was as conspicuous as an ink stain on a tablecloth. "Get off the roof, blend in with the crowd," she snapped. "I'll draw their attention."

Javalara began to comply, backing away from the edge, then he gusted out a sigh. "No. Even if I managed to get away, the main problem will remain. The essence of the Naga will still be in imbalance. Nothing will change."

Brigid kept her gaze fixed on the *vimana*. "Not very pragmatic, but thank you."

The nose of the winged craft turned in their direction, and she announced, "We're spotted. What do you want to do? Surrender or make a fight of it?"

Javalara's response, if he had one, was smothered by the crash of static filling her head. She winced, biting back a cry of surprise. A voice transmitted through the Commtact asked, "What kind of party are you dressed up for, Baptiste? And why wasn't I invited?"

Brigid stared in mute astonishment at the *vimana* and then she laughed, relief washing over her in such a wave she grew weak. She laid her head down on her crossed forearms.

Javalara, bewildered and frightened, cried, "We can't stay here! The *vimana* is—"

"Carrying the distraction we need," Brigid broke in calmly. "His name is Kane, and it's about time he got here."

Chapter 25

"My," Kane said inanely after clearing his throat. "Is everybody as thunderstruck as I am?"

Nora Pennick threw him a frosty glare meant to silence him. Kane ignored her. What passed for a cold look from the Englishwoman was lukewarm compared to the subzero iciness generated by the eyes of an annoyed Brigid Baptiste.

Addressing Zhou Tzu, Kane said, "General, I know this is all very emotional for you, but we need to find a way to get to Angkor Thom before 'Boo-star' has the kinks worked out of his neck permanently."

Kumudvati lifted her head and stared directly into Zhou Tzu's eyes. He inhaled deeply and exhaled slowly. "My...daughter has herself provided the way. I'm sure the Cobra Guard's *vimana* is still searching for her. Our most sound tactic would be to find a clearing, light a signal fire and wait."

"Wait for what?" Kane demanded. "Aren't you wanted by Puyang and his Cobra Guard—?" He broke off when he saw the general's lips purse in disapproval. "I get it. They'll land to pick up the snake princess here and we hijack the ship, sailing back to the city in style."

"Precisely. Let's put this strategy into effect immediately. I doubt the Guard is too far away."

Hand-in-hand with Kumudvati, Zhou Tzu marched into the jungle. Nora, Kane and the three soldiers followed closely on their heels. As they walked down a forest corridor formed by giant tree boles, Kumudvati spoke softly but quickly in English.

"My mother began to sicken nearly three years ago," she said. "She had no choice but turn over more and more administrative duties to Colonel Puyang. I was then but twelve and too distraught by Mother's illness to pay attention to understand that he soon ruled Angkor Thom in all but name. His ambitions and influence expanded as my mother's strength diminished."

"I know of the colonel's ambition," Zhou Tzu stated matter-of-factly. "Ten years ago he served as an officer in my army, my liaison with your mother's Cobra Guard. He coveted my position and my rank. He sought to gain both by killing me in a trial by combat. He failed."

Kumudvati nodded. "He blamed you for mutilating him. He never forgave you."

"I put my mark on him, true enough," the general replied stolidly. "As was my right as the victor. But he could not live with the shame of it on his face and so he peeled off the offending piece of flesh himself. That was his choice. I am not a butcher."

The girl stated, "My mother said you were an honorable man, although she met you but the once. You abided by the truce and obeyed the Laws of Manu and accepted your karma...to act as the masculine yang chakra to my mother's feminine yin. You maintained the balance."

Kane couldn't stop himself from asking, "What does all that mean?"

"The traditional four-chakra system is considered yang," Zhou Tzu offhandedly answered. "That is, masculine in nature. The configuration of the system proceeds in a straight line. The line begins at the first chakra, at the base of the pubic bone, and ascends through each chakra until it reaches the seventh chakra, at the crown of the head. The fourth chakra is the heart chakra, and it represents the transition between the upper and lower chakras. It integrates the masculine and feminine energies."

"Oh," Kane said, mystified.

"Conversely," the general continued, "the Yin chakras are feminine in nature. The yin moves you toward the harmonic balance and resonates with its opposite partner. Together the yin and yang chakras produce the Sudarshana chakra…sometimes known as the Divine Child."

"And that," Kane stated, "is what the junior miss Devi-Naga is here?"

Zhou Tzu hesitated before saying, "Essentially."

"It all sounds very damn complicated."

"That's because it *is* very damn complicated."

Turning toward Kumudvati, Zhou Tzu said, "When your mother and I were only a few years older than you, we participated in the mingling ceremony the essence of the Naga. I recall very little about it, even today. It seems like a dream. However, the fact you are here proves it was not a dream."

Kane cast a sideways glance at Nora, but it was impossible to gauge her reaction because of her calm, unperturbed expression.

Kumudvati replied, "My mother told me it was like

a dream for her, as well. But when she grew heavy with me, she knew the truth. I had been conceived while bathed in the glory of the essence of the Naga. She called me the Divine Child, symbolizing our people's return to harmony and union." She paused and shook her head sadly. "My destiny can never be achieved now."

"Why do you say that?" Zhou Tzu asked sharply.

"For years Colonel Puyang has been fascinated by the power generated by the essence. He thought it could be channeled into use as a weapon, a way to force his beliefs into the minds of our people so they would obey him unquestioningly. He commanded the Magickers to alter the harmonics of the essence. They thought they were obeying an edict from my mother.

"When their efforts failed to meet the colonel's expectations, he banished them in the name of the Devi-Naga. Shortly after that, my mother died. I cannot prove it but I'm sure she was slowly and systemically poisoned by Colonel Puyang. I don't think he expected her to die, but when the balance of the essence shifted, her already weak life force could not maintain itself."

Zhou Tzu's jaw muscles knotted but he didn't otherwise react to the pronouncement.

"But before she died," Kumudvati went on, "she revealed to me all the secrets she knew of you, of our people and the Naga. Much of the ancient knowledge has been lost, but enough remains that can be corrupted. The colonel has kept me a virtual prisoner since my mother's death, hiding that fact from the people. As far as they are concerned, the Devi-Naga still lives."

"He has done a very good job," the general replied

grimly. "I knew nothing of her death, feared she had gone mad. Now I wish that was the reality instead."

"Only Colonel Puyang's inner circle are his confidants," the girl said. "Some of them have expressed doubts to me about the colonel's sanity. He has turned the holy city into the seat of a tyranny not seen since the reign of Jayavarman the Seventh."

Zhou Tzu's shoulders jerked slightly at her words.

"He breaks the Laws of Manu," Kumudvati continued. "He violates tradition and ignores our place in the cycle of karma. But I can do nothing to stop him. Only when I heard about the three strangers and the one the Cobra Guard had captured did I dare hope I could do anything to stop the colonel's depredations and restore the balance of the essence."

"It will be done," Zhou Tzu declared quietly. "It is the legacy of a thousand years of karma. It is now to be discharged. I understand it all now."

Kumudvati leaned her head briefly against his arm. "As do I."

Kane felt his eyebrows crawling toward his sweaty hairline. He understood very little of what had passed between the girl and the man. He looked over at Nora but she wore the same expression of serene detachment as before. He was a little discomfited by the elemental power the so-called essence of the Naga exerted over the Khmer people. It filled their whole lives, a guiding force that directed them to walk a never-ending path through the myth and mystery wrought by their ancient forebears.

But, he reflected, they were not all that different from the way he and his friends at Cerberus lived their own lives, since the shadow of the hidden origin of human-

ity lay heavily over all their actions. He, Grant, Brigid
and especially Lakesh seemed to exist only to expose a
conspiracy that had lasted for many thousands of years.
It was axiomatic of conspiracies that someone or something else always pulled the strings of willing or ignorant puppets.

Lakesh had expended many years tracing those fila-
ments back through convoluted and manufactured his-
tories to the puppet masters themselves. He attempted to
solve the mystery of the so-called Archon Directorate
and its agenda by delving into the dark corners of human
history, sifting through the morass of complex and often
contradictory legends. The little he had learned, the intelligence Kane, Grant and Brigid had gathered, was
still the most shallow, imperceptible scratch on the surface of a vast tapestry of lies and secrets.

It seemed that as far as the new Khmer people of
Angkor Thom were concerned, they accepted their destiny of reliving over and over the ancient myths of serpent princesses and royal heroes and achieving a
balance with the very forces of creation. There would
be no ultimate end to the quest, only a new cycle, with
new faces playing out the same drama. Kane only hoped
that was not the fate awaiting him in his war to end baronial tyranny.

The party of people splashed through a tiny creek that
was solidly slimed, and Zhou Tzu swept Kumudvati up
in his arms when crawling things wriggled in the wet
green mass. Perspiration ran in streams from each face.
The general set the girl down and pushed through a par-
tition of shrubbery.

He looked around cautiously, then entered a glade

carpeted by ankle-high grass but not overhung by trees. He spoke in Khmer to his soldiers, and they began gathering up armfuls of vegetation that appeared fairly dry. They piled it in the center of the clearing, and Kane used one of the flares in his pack to set the heap afire. Plumes of gray smoke sluggishly climbed into the sky. Zhou Tzu ordered everyone into the cool shade offered by the trees edging the glade. "When the *vimana* appears," he said, "I want them to see only Kumudvati."

"What's the crew complement of the *vimanas?*" Kane asked.

"It depends," the general replied, "on their mission. Probably no more than four."

"Do you have a plan for dealing with them?"

"Once the ship lands, we will show ourselves. If they surrender, then we will let them live. We will leave them here to find their own way back. If they decide to resist…" He shrugged and turned away.

He walked over to Nora and, taking her by the elbow, he led her to a spot between the trunks of two silk cotton trees. Kane couldn't hear what they were saying, but Zhou Tzu spoke to her earnestly. She nodded as he spoke. He busied himself reloading his Sin Eater and Copperhead.

"You are English?"

Kane jumped and cursed, startled by how stealthily Kumudvati had walked through the brush to come up behind him. She regarded him intently, gazing up at him from somewhere near his clavicle.

"No, actually," he replied. "I only speak it, after a fashion. I'm an American."

"You are a friend of Boo-star?"

For a moment Kane silently contemplated how he actually felt about the supercilious astrophysicist. Although annoyed that Brigid seemed to prefer the company of the lanky, myopic scientist to his as of late, Kane didn't really dislike him. He just didn't understand what Brigid found so appealing about him, even if Philboyd's intellect was a little more equal to her own.

"I suppose you might say that," he admitted. "But don't tell him I said he was."

Her expression did not change. "As you wish. Are you a friend of my father's?"

Kane glanced over to where Zhou Tzu stood with Nora. The general caught him looking in their direction and led Nora behind the tree. "I only met him yesterday," he replied. "But apparently Nora is a good friend of his."

"The American woman?"

"No, she's English."

"But you said—"

"I'm American, she's English." When he saw the lines of consternation crease her brow he said, "It's complicated…but not as complicated as the story of you, your mother, the warlord and the essence of the snake people."

The lines of consternation became creases of anger through the golden scales painted around her eyes. "You are very impudent."

"And you are a very self-possessed young woman. But I suppose that's to be expected of a Divine Child, isn't it?"

"You mock our beliefs?" A hint of imperious anger was evident in her voice.

Kane bit back the profane retort that jumped to his tongue. Shaking his head, he said apologetically, "I don't understand them and I suppose that gets on my nerves. I'm worried about my friends. I came to your country only to save them."

"They were drawn here by the wheel of karma." The girl spoke flatly, as if she were delivering a speech on scientific principles. "As were you. All of our fates are intertwined now…the general's most of all. His soul's thousand-year journey on the road of reparation draws to a close."

Kane scowled down at her. "Reparation? What are you—?"

A shout echoed from the underbrush. Kane turned as one of Zhou Tzu's soldiers stabbed a finger at the sky, speaking in rapid-fire Khmer. Kane looked up and saw sunlight gleaming from a sleek winged object. It seemed to crawl across the sky, not soar.

The general reappeared with Nora in tow. He snapped out orders to his men, then said to Kane, "You will follow my lead, Mr. Kane. Take no action until I initiate it. That is an order. Understood?"

Before Kane could stop himself, he answered, "Yes, sir." He tossed him the Copperhead.

Taking up position within a thinning fringe of undergrowth, Kane sank down beneath the flat fronds of a banana tree and peered up at the sky. The aircraft called the *vimana* appeared unreal to Kane, more like a kite rather than an actual vehicle. Its extended wings put him in mind of a dragonfly's, veined as they were with a network of flexible braces. As it drew closer to the smoke-belching fire in the glade, he estimated its length at twenty-five feet and its beam at a little under half that.

Kumudvati walked into the clearing, lifting an arm in a very casual greeting, as if being stranded in a rain forest had distressed her no more than being late for dinner. Kane glimpsed Zhou Tzu's three men huddled beneath a leafy canopy formed by the boughs of a fig tree, their subguns at their shoulders. He didn't see Zhou Tzu or Nora Pennick.

As the *vimana* slowly descended, Kane's ears detected the low drone of an engine. Through a curved view port on the craft's upper hull he glimpsed the outlines of two helmeted heads. The ship landed on the floor of the clearing as gently as a wasp on a flat stone. The throb of the engine lowered in pitch, and a dull silver hatch on the side of the vessel slid open and two men stepped out.

Both of them were short but one was far stockier. They wore identical uniforms consisting of greenish gray tunics, baggy black trousers and rather ungainly brass helmets meant to suggest cobra heads. They carried submachine guns similar to the ones wielded by the general's men.

Kumudvati stood near the smoldering fire, hands on her hips. She spoke sharply, autocratically to the Cobra Guard. The two men trotted quickly toward her, one of them holding his wobbling helmet on his head. As they approached, Kumudvati stepped behind the fire, putting it between her and the soldiers. They fanned the smoke away from their faces as they circled it.

An errant breeze cloaked the girl's figure in vapor for a moment. When it thinned, much to Kane's surprise and the dismay of the Cobra Guard, Zhou Tzu stood beside the Devi-Naga.

At the sight of the man and the gun trained on them, the pair of soldiers stumbled to unsteady halts. They clumsily began to unlimber their subguns, but Kumudvati snapped out a stream of hard-edged Khmer invective and they subsided immediately. The two men dropped their weapons to the ground and stepped away, hands atop their helmets. Zhou Tzu lifted his voice in a barking command and his men slid out of the brush, swiftly approaching the grounded *vimana*. Kane stayed where he was, watching and waiting.

A snake-helmeted man appeared in the hatch of the ship, and without hesitation, preamble or even careful aim, began firing his subgun. One of Zhou Tzu's warriors clutched at his chest and went down in the grass. The other two dropped flat. The machine gun in the hands of the Cobra guardsman continued to chatter.

Kane ducked as the banana fronds drooping over his head were torn to tatters as a half-dozen rounds ripped through them. Flying pieces of pulp stung his face and upper arms. He caught a brief glimpse of Zhou Tzu pulling down Kumudvati. The two disarmed soldiers dashed madly for the underbrush.

Heaving himself to his feet, holding his Sin Eater in a two-fisted grip, Kane sighted down its length and squeezed off a three-round burst. Two of the three rounds caught the trooper in the chest.

The third struck him on the left shoulder. Scraps of tunic exploded in a clot of blood. He screamed something incoherent and stumbled backward, arms windmilling. The man fell against the bulkhead at his back and slid down it. By the time his body settled to the deck, Kane was sprinting across the glade as the sound of the *vimana*'s idling motor rose in pitch and volume.

As it began to rise from the ground, Kane bounded through the hatch, leaped over the Cobra guardsman's body and raced up a short aisle formed by a double row of chairs. When Kane bulled his way into the cockpit, the man he guessed to be the pilot half rose from his seat, jabbering in wild-eyed fear.

Kane used the Sin Eater as a bludgeon, slamming the barrel against the trooper's helmeted head. A shivery gonglike note echoed and the man sagged down in the chair, a deep dent bisecting a molded eyeball atop the helmet. The *vimana* settled back down in the clearing with a lurch that sent Kane falling into the copilot's chair.

Footfalls thudded out in the gangway and Zhou Tzu appeared, breathing hard, Copperhead held so the barrel pointed at the ceiling. Glancing at the unconscious pilot he asked, "Is he dead?"

Kane pushed himself erect. "I don't think I hit him that hard. I figured we might need him to fly us out of here."

Zhou Tzu nodded. "Very astute, Mr. Kane. My training in the operation of *vimanas* was long ago, and my daughter is still a novice. You acted very quickly in securing this ship and neutralizing the threat."

"You might say I have a little experience at this sort of thing," Kane said dryly, pushing past him.

A section of the deck plates rang hollowly under his feet. After a bit of scrutiny, he located an inset handle and upon pulling it, lifted away a rectangular piece of flooring. It concealed a fairly spacious crawl space that terminated in a round port near the bow. Bolted to the inner wall he saw the long column of a collapsible rocket launcher.

After resealing the crawl space, Kane left the *vimana* to retrieve his pack. He paused to check on the warrior who had been shot and learned he was dead, due to one of the bullets fired by the Cobra guards, puncturing his heart. His companions attended to him.

Screened by foliage, Kane gratefully removed the still damp native clothing and tugged on his shadow suit. Not only was it dry, but also its temperature controls cooled him within a minute of donning it. The rounds fired at him by the soldier had come uncomfortably close and even though the fabric of the suit would not have deflected them, he wanted every advantage he could acquire before they arrived in Angkor Thom. He strongly suspected he would encounter gunplay aplenty in the holy city of the Khmers.

When he crossed the clearing again, returning to the *vimana,* he saw Nora and Kumudvati standing near the fire, speaking to each another urgently. The girl glimpsed Kane, glanced away and then did a double take, eyes widening in surprise.

"If you think this is something," he called to her, "you ought to see what I wear when I'm at home."

She didn't laugh, nor did Kane expect her to. Nora affected to have not heard the remark at all.

General Zhou Tzu didn't take the time to bury his dead warrior, for which Kane was grateful. His two comrades carried him into the *vimana* and wrapped his body in a shroud of muslin taken from a storage locker in the bulkhead.

By the time that task was accomplished, Zhou Tzu

had revived the pilot by the simple expedient of exposing his nostrils to an ammonia capsule taken from Kane's medical kit. He was glassy-eyed and in pain, but he obeyed the commands of Kumudvati after he swallowed a couple of analgesic tablets provided by Kane.

Within minutes, the *vimana* was airborne again, rising smoothly from the jungle glade with almost no sensation of lifting. Kane was both perplexed and enthralled by the operation of the air cruiser. He had flown in several advanced craft, from giant cargo planes to the Aurora stealth ship to the Manta TAVs, but the *vimanas* were unique. Kumudvati couldn't accurately verbalize the operational principles of the craft, and Zhou Tzu claimed they were too complicated to be explained in a way Kane could comprehend.

Sitting beside Nora in the passenger compartment, Kane looked out through the view port and saw a collection of towers and spires rising above the treetops a couple of miles distant. "We weren't that far away after all," he commented.

"I suppose not, as the crow flies," she replied, voice and demeanor very subdued.

Kane eyed her masklike face. Her expression was composed but her lips were white, as if she were struggling to bottle up an extreme emotional reaction. Leaning toward her, speaking quietly so Zhou Tzu and Kumudvati, who sat in the cockpit, wouldn't hear, he asked, "What's going on?"

She swallowed hard. "That's a rather broad question under the circumstances, would you not agree?"

"I'll be more specific, then. What were you and the general talking about? And you and the Devi-Naga?"

Her eyes flashed with anger. "Personal matters and therefore none of your concern."

Slipping a hard edge into his voice, he intoned, "If your personal matters affect me and the chances of rescuing Baptiste and Philboyd, I'll make it my concern. I've gone along with your warlord so far because he was my only option but that doesn't mean I trust him. I'll tell you this—if he or you interferes with what I came to this country to do, you'll be wishing you had a dragon sitting here instead of me."

If Nora Pennick felt disquiet at Kane's words she showed no sign. Whatever occupied her mind held far great and grimmer weight than his threats. Demurely she said, "What the general will do—what he explained to me he *must* do—will bring no harm to Brigid or Brewster unless it is destined to be so."

"I don't believe in destiny," Kane said flatly.

Nora brushed a lock of blue-black hair away from her forehead and her lips curved in a sad smile. "No," she said softly. "Up until six days ago, neither did I."

Before Kane could draft a response, Zhou Tzu leaned out of the cockpit. "We've reached our destination at last, Mr. Kane. Come forward and have a look if you've a mind to."

Kane rose and joined the general in the cockpit, gazing out at the city spread below, at the sculpted towers, artificial waterways and many-pillared temple complexes. Zhou Tzu handed him a set of battered binoculars, saying, "If you look to your right at four o' clock, you'll see where your friend Philboyd will shortly make his appearance…hopefully not his last."

Squinting through the eyepieces, Kane adjusted the

focus and peered down at a courtyard filled with people surrounding a wide wooden scaffold. Looped ropes were wrapped around a cross beam. The floor of the scaffold was open with a flat plank stretched across the gap. Once the nooses were secured around the necks of the condemned, the plank would be kicked away. The victims would strangle to death, not perish quickly from broken necks.

Kane gritted his teeth in revulsion and swept the binoculars around, trying to count the number of brass-helmeted soldiers in attendance. For an instant he glimpsed a black figure lying flat on a rooftop, but the pilot directed the *vimana* away before he focused fully.

"Turn back," he snapped.

The pilot blinked up at him, and Kane pointed to the left. "That way."

Kumudvati conveyed Kane's wishes and the man adjusted the rudder. The nose of the cruiser swung back around. For a couple of frustrating seconds, Kane couldn't locate the rooftop again. Then he saw the black, prone figure and noted how the bright blast of sunshine struck flame-colored highlights from a thick mane of hair.

Relief so profoundly overwhelming rushed through Kane. His throat constricted and his breath seized in his lungs so for a long moment he could not neither breathe nor speak. He used that moment to examine the person lying beside Brigid Baptiste. At first glance he thought it was a woman because of the skirtlike garment, then realized it was a man.

Keeping the binoculars pressed to his eyes with his left hand, Kane touched the tiny transmit stud on the Commtact behind his right ear. He waited through the hiss of static, heard the beep of the frequency lock and said cheerfully, "What kind of party are you dressed up for, Baptiste? And why wasn't I invited?"

Chapter 26

"Who's your date, Baptiste?" Kane asked.

Brigid glanced over at a wide-eyed Javalara and grinned. "A Magicker by the name of Javalara. But the name is a misnomer...he's really a scientist."

Hiking around on the roof, she gazed up at the hovering *vimana* from beneath shaded eyes. "How did you get aboard that thing, much less commandeer it?"

"It's a pretty long story, and unless we want a tragic end to it, we'd better agree on how we're going to save Philboyd."

Startled, Brigid asked, "How do you know about that?"

"How do I know about what?" Javalara asked in confusion.

"Not you," Brigid retorted, pointing toward the *vimana*. "Him."

"I have my sources," Kane replied.

"Who's with you? Grant? Domi?"

"What?" Javalara's face was deeply creased in puzzlement.

"It was a one-rescuer trip. But I have Nora up here—"

"Thank God," Brigid broke in. "Is she all right?"

"She's a little banged up but nothing serious. I'm also traveling in the company of a young lady named Kumudvati—also known as the Devi-Naga—and her father, the warlord General Zhou Tzu."

Brigid gaped up at the ship, glimmering in the sunlight. "How in the hell did you manage all of that?"

Kane chuckled. "Like I said, it's a long story."

"Right." She pointed toward the scaffold. "Can you see where I'm pointing? Look on the far side of the gallows."

After a couple of seconds, Kane said, "I see a little stone building. Kumudvati just told me that's where the prisoners are held prior to execution. Philboyd's in there?"

"I hope so."

"Do you have a plan to break him out?"

"I didn't," Brigid answered, "but now I do. Earlier today I saw that self-same *vimana* you're flying around in shoot a couple of rockets at a paddy."

"Yeah, I found the launcher. Didn't find the rounds yet, though. Assuming I do, blasting open the holding cell might qualify as a cure being worse than the disease."

"I realize that," Brigid said, inspecting members of the Cobra Guard monitoring the crowd packed into the plaza. "But there's not much I can do from here. I'm outnumbered, way outgunned and a little too conspicuous to sneak over there."

The Commtact accurately transmitted Kane's appreciative chuckle. "I agree, but I have the distinct impression that those guys wearing the snake pots on their heads aren't accustomed to handling surprises. If I can find the rockets, I'll fire near the gallows and the cell and try to start a panic.

"While that's going on, you might be able to make your way over and free Philboyd. After that's done, we'll land as close as possible. You jump aboard and we'll float on out of here."

"As much as I'd like that," Brigid stated dourly, "I promised my Magicker friend we'd help him out with a scientific problem here in the city."

Kane grunted. "Let me guess. It has something to do with the essence of the Naga. It's all I've heard about since I've been here."

Brigid was surprised into laughing. "I'll say one thing, Kane...you never fail to amaze me."

"Funny," he countered, "I was about to say the same thing about you. Standby."

Beneath a shading hand, she watched as the *vimana* turned slowly, its blunt nose moving in the direction of the courtyard. Its movements put her somewhat in mind of vids she had seen of dirigible flights. She averted her face when sunlight flashed dazzlingly from its silver hull.

"What is happening?" Javalara demanded impatiently. "Who were you talking to?"

"I have a means to communicate long range," Brigid told him, pulling her hair back and showing him the Commtact behind her ear. "My friend is in the *vimana,* and the prison break is about to commence. Keep watching the skies."

The air cruiser dropped in altitude and sailed toward in the gallows. The murmuring crowd in the plaza fell silent when the shadow passed over them.

Javalara suddenly tensed up and blurted, "Puyang!"

Glancing over at Javalara, she followed his frightened gaze and saw a heavyset man in uniform standing on the edge of the scaffold. His deeply scarred face was tilted up toward the *vimana* overhead. A scarlet plume attached to the crown of his helmet stretched down between his shoulder blades. His mouth worked as if he were shouting to someone.

The crowd assembled in the plaza shifted, jostling one another in sudden apprehension as the *vimana* cruised over them at a height of no more than one hundred feet. The Cobra Guard in the courtyard began pushing the people back, keeping them from bolting.

Kane's voice, sounding slightly strained, whispered through her auditory canal, "I'm set, primed and loaded. The warheads are high-ex, about 94 mm. I don't how stable they are so make ready."

"Acknowledged."

On the underbelly of the *vimana,* a small round port opened and a hollow tube protruded. With a sound as of wet canvas tearing, it belched a puff of smoke and a streak of fire lanced down. A section of the ground behind the scaffold erupted in a billowing ball of flame-shot black smoke. The air shivered with the concussion of the detonating warhead. Chunks of paving stone rained down in the courtyard. The crowd screamed as they were pelted, covering their heads with their arms, surging back and forth. Colonel Puyang dropped flat onto the scaffold, hands clasped over the top of his helmet.

A second projectile came arrowing down, propelled by a wavering ribbon of fiery vapor. It impacted much closer to the gallows. A mushroom of flame boiled up from underneath it, lapping at the cross braces. The explosion sent a Cobra guard flailing madly through the air.

The citizens of Angkor Thom, jammed belly to back, shoulder to shoulder in the plaza, became a wild, howling, stampeding mob. They spilled out of the plaza, sweeping over the Cobra Guard like a tsunami of flesh and blood. Two of the uniformed men stroked short bursts from their subguns, but the bullets did nothing to slow the mad rush. Almost the entire population of Angkor Thom washed over the soldiers like a vengeful sea.

Brigid couldn't help but smile in grim satisfaction. She hadn't extrapolated that the rocket attack would trigger an insurrection, but as the crowd flooded the streets, she wasn't unhappy about it. She and Javalara stood on the roof of the building as the Cambodians swirled around it.

Once their initial fright passed, the people turned on the serpent-helmeted soldiers, burying them under pounding fists and stamping feet and clubbing them with makeshift bludgeons. Brigid looked toward the scaffold to see what had become of Colonel Puyang but he was nowhere in sight. A number of the citizens were already clambering atop the gallows, intent on tearing it down with their bare hands. She recognized one of them as the old man who had been dragged away from his peaceful pastime of fish cleaning.

Javalara, in a voice made hoarse by awe, said, "May the Naga and the Buddha have mercy. This I did not expect."

"You wanted the balance restored," Brigid declared. "Maybe this is the first step."

"Looks like we really started something, Baptiste," Kane's voice said.

"Finished it is more like it," she replied. "I'll wait until the crowd calms down before checking out the hoosegow. I don't want to be mistaken for one of the bad guys."

"Little chance of that. We'll set down and join you as soon as we can. Watch yourself...there may still be some adders around."

Brigid walked to the edge of the roof and swung her body over, planting her feet firmly on the sculptured walls. Javalara asked worriedly, "Where are you going?"

"To free my friend. You can stay here."

The Magicker cast a nervous glance toward the crowd swarming around the scaffold and shook his head. "I think I should go with you. I'm known here and I might be able to protect you."

The two of them climbed down and circled the edge of the courtyard. Javalara acted as the prow of a ship, pushing his way through the sea of rejoicing humanity. At the sound of a splintering crash, Brigid turned, seeing the scaffold with the nooses collapsing in on itself. A wild, triumphant cry exploded out of the Khmer people, a victorious shout of the inadvertent revolutionaries. She guessed the fact an attempt to flee had turned into a coup that overturned tyranny would become the source of an entire cycle of songs and stories.

Pairs of dark eyes fixed on the sunset-haired woman who towered half a head over the tallest of them. A few of the Cambodians, still in the process of dismantling the scaffold, froze, gawking. Brigid saw fresh blood glistening on the hands of a number of people. Some of them wore the brass cobra headpieces.

However, the sight of Javalara leading her across the plaza softened the hard edge of fear and suspicion on their faces. They shouted jubilant questions at him, but he only smiled, clapping a shoulder here and clasping a hand there. Brigid looked up to see the *vimana* sinking down near the east tower of Angkor Wat.

At the stone hut, plaintive voices cried out from behind a metal-reinforced wood-plank door. Fists pounded from the interior. A smoking crater had been punched deep into the ground less than five yards away. Three women of various ages and sizes stood at the door, responding to the shouts from within. Tears flowed down their faces. One of them fumbled futilely with the heavy padlock.

"Sons and husbands locked up in there," Javalara told her. "They're desperate to get them out. A couple of them need medical attention."

Brigid gently pushed the woman away from the door. After taking a long look at her, she was in no hurry to linger. "Brewster!" she called. "Brewster Philboyd! Are you in there?"

For a long, tense moment, no response was forthcoming. Brigid was on the verge of calling out again when a man's thoroughly astounded voice reached her. "Brigid? Holy God, *Brigid!* Is that you?"

"Last I looked," she called back, fisting her TP-9. "Get everybody away from the door. I'm going to shoot off the lock, and some stray rounds might come through the wood."

After a few seconds, Philboyd shouted, "All clear!"

Javalara motioned everyone else out of the immediate area as Brigid sighted down the length of the pistol. She squeezed the trigger three times, the reports sounding like sharp hand claps. The lock jumped in the hasp and flew apart. Using the butt of the TP-9 to knock loose a few pieces of metal, she shouldered open the door.

It swung inward, pulled by a half-naked Cambodian man who plunged past her, blinded by the sunlight. Brigid stood aside, wrinkling her nose at the stench of commingled human sweat and waste. Three other men stumbled out, into the arms of the women.

Peering into the gloom of the cell, Brigid asked, "What are you waiting for?"

Philboyd shuffled out and Brigid winced at the sight of him. His entire face was a mottled blue-and-purple bruise. Dried blood encrusted the crude bandage tied around his head. Biting back an exclamation of horror, Brigid helped him hobble out of the stone hut, supporting him by the left arm.

Squinting at her, mumbling through swollen, split lips, he said, "I know I must look a sight, but you're certainly the most gorgeous thing I've ever seen in my entire life."

Rather than address his comment, she asked, "Did this happen to you when you were captured?"

He shook his head. "No, yesterday. I apparently said the wrong thing to the wrong girl. She was asking me questions, and a scar-faced psycho didn't like the fact I answered them."

"Colonel Puyang?" Brigid inquired.

"I think that's what the kid called him when she tried to stop him—"

Philboyd broke off, eyeing the still smoking crater made by the rocket. "I heard the explosions. What the hell was going on?"

"Kane," Brigid said simply as if the one word explained everything.

"Oh," Philboyd replied as if he needed no further explanation. He glanced over at Javalara curiously. "Who is that?"

The man bowed his head. "My name is Javalara, chief of the guild of Magickers."

"That's what they call scientists in these parts," Brigid offered. "I ended up with him and his bunch. We came to an understanding."

Almost shyly, Javalara said, "Baptiste says you are a great scientist."

Philboyd tried to grin. "I suppose I'm a better scientist than I am a fighter. But I make an even better prisoner." He chuckled, then his face twisted in pain and he clutched at his stomach.

"Are you badly hurt?" Brigid asked.

"I don't think any bones are broken," he replied. "But I *do* hurt…badly."

"We'll see what we can do about that."

"Perhaps we can find a physician to treat you before you study my problem," Javalara said solicitously.

"Problem?" Philboyd echoed.

"I promised we'd help him work out a matter of balancing energy," Brigid stated.

"We have our own problems," Philboyd grunted. "The least of which is trying to find Nora in this shit hole of a country."

"That problem is solved," Brigid said with a smile, turning Philboyd to the right.

He squinted toward a cluster of people approaching from the shadows of the Angkor Wat complex. When they drew nearer, he discerned Nora Pennick, dressed much like the Khmer women in the city, flanked by the black-clad Kane and an unusually tall Asian man. Three people walked behind them.

"Thank God for that," Philboyd murmured fervently. "How did Kane ever find her?"

"It's a long story," Brigid answered wryly.

"However he did it, he can insult me all he wants for the next month."

"He'd do that anyway," Brigid retorted as she, Javalara and Philboyd walked toward the group.

They had not walked far when Brigid noticed a peculiar reaction among the citizenry that the group of people passed. They fell to their knees, fingers steepled at their chins, chanting, "Devi-Naga, Devi-Naga!"

A slight figure suddenly shouldered between Kane and Nora, taking the lead position. A teenaged girl strode with a dignified purpose, head held high, despite the mud on her limbs and a generally disheveled appearance. Long raven-dark hair hung loose. A delicate scale design glittered in gold around her eyes. Javalara uttered a cry of shock, quickly smothered by putting his hands to his mouth.

"That's the kid!" Philboyd exclaimed. "The one who asked me questions!"

Brigid briefly studied the girl, noting her resemblance to the man walking beside Nora. She suddenly received the strange feeling she was in the presence of a royal family—a princess, a king and a queen.

"At this point," Brigid said quietly, "it's our turn to ask the questions. I don't know about you, but I have a *whole* lot of them."

Chapter 27

Within Angkor Wat, all was dark, cool stone and long galleries echoing with silence. Late-afternoon sunlight slanted in at regular intervals, but didn't illuminate much beyond where the shafts fell.

Kumudvati led them down a long, broad hall lined by monolithic columns carved with images of kings, princes, queens, devils, monkeys and snakes. Every place the eye rested held serpent imagery. The stones of the floor bore colored tiles that formed the immense mosaic of a seven-headed cobra.

In a ghostly, reverent whisper, Kumudvati said, "The Naga left their souls in the stones of this hall."

Kane leaned toward Brigid and murmured in her ear, "And all this time I thought they stored them in the basement."

Annoyance flickered briefly in Brigid's jade eyes, but it faded when he smiled in a slightly abashed fashion to let her know he was trying to lighten the mood and meant no offense.

For a long time at the beginning of their relationship, it was very difficult for Kane and Brigid not to give offense to each other. Both people had their gifts. Most of what was important to people in the twenty-first century came easily to Kane—survival skills, prevailing in the face of adversity and cunning against enemies. But he could also be reckless, high-strung to the point of instability and given to fits of rage.

Brigid, on the other hand was compulsively tidy and ordered, with a brilliant analytical mind. However, her clinical nature, the cool scientific detachment upon which she prided herself sometimes blocked an understanding of the obvious human factor in any given situation.

Regardless of their contrasting personalities, Kane and Brigid worked very well as a team, playing on each other's strengths rather than contributing to their individual weaknesses.

Kane and Brigid trailed behind Kumudvati, Zhou Tzu, Javalara and Philboyd but not too far since they could easily become lost in the cavernous building. The gallery they walked through was so long its vista grew indistinct in the distance.

Although built nearly a thousand years before as a temple and a tomb for the Khmer rulers, Angkor Wat had become the royal palace, the centerpiece of the new empire, housing all the administrators, the household staff and the barracks for the troops. But its size was so gargantuan only portions of the sprawling structure were occupied. So far, the visitors had seen very little of it.

After all the outlanders were reunited, Kumudvati escorted them to her private quarters high in a tower of the immense building. Once there, stories of experiences and hardships were exchanged, reports received from advisers and injuries treated by a clucking physician. Both Zhou Tzu and Nora were given a change of clothes. He attired himself in an officer's uniform of the Cobra Guard, Nora in a sari not much different than the one Brigid had worn.

Philboyd, although stiff and sore, was not seriously hurt. Once his wounds were bathed, cleaned and dressed and his pain relieved by medication supplied by Kane, his attention focused on the essence of the Naga.

As a freshly bathed and clothed Kumudvati told him what she knew, Nora Pennick and Zhou Tzu presented a quiet, almost private demeanor to everyone.

As she concluded telling Philboyd the myths of the essence, she said, "I am truly sorry for what I caused to happen to you. But I was so desperate to rid the kingdom of Colonel Puyang I snatched at any straw of hope."

"It looks like the kingdom *is* rid of him," Brigid commented.

Zhou Tzu spoke for the first time since they had been introduced. "That might be a rather premature judgment. He has not surrendered like the other survivors of the Cobra Guard nor has his body been found. He will not give up what he has enjoyed because of a peasant revolt."

"Just what *has* he enjoyed?" Kane asked. "Other than beating up on skinny scientists?"

Kumudvati beckoned her outlander guests to join her at one of the tall, narrow tower windows. From it they could see the broad avenues of Angkor Thom, the cultivated fields, the waterways and ornate buildings. "Life is pleasant here," she said. "At least it is so for those who rule it. We are not as backward a people as you may think we are. I was educated in monastery, taught several different languages and learned the history of the world. I know it has changed since the skies grew dark and the long winter fell. We know there is life outside this sheltered place, across the seas. But few of us desire to leave our land or to see it invaded by others."

She gestured toward Zhou Tzu. "Safeguarding us against invasion has been my father's duty and his father's…and all the fathers before his. But neither I nor my mother ever suspected we would have to safeguard our land from our own people…or at least safeguard it from those who feared our people would leave our country and the new empire for a different world beyond our jungle borders. But we would not make prisoners of our citizens—that would be a violation of the Laws of Manu. So Colonel Puyang sought to control our people by altering the texture of the essence of the Naga. Since that happened, our lives here have been full of sadness."

The girl turned to sweep her dark gaze over her guests, resting it finally on Javalara, who ducked his head contritely. "I live only to rectify my error, Your Glory."

"You shall have your chance, Magicker," Zhou Tzu declared. He extended a hand toward Kumudvati, who took it. "Take us to the essence, Devi-Naga."

And the Devi-Naga did so, leading the six people through one green-shadowed corridor and cavernous gallery after another. The passageway they traversed ended at the threshold of a square doorway, at least twelve feet wide. A frieze of coiling serpents and barebreasted women surrounded the frame.

The steps beyond were steep and wide, almost like separate levels, four feet across and two feet deep. They disappeared into a yawning black abyss. Kumudvati paused, taking a deep breath. She extended her hands to Zhou Tzu and Nora. The man and woman tightly clasped the hands of the girl and together they stepped over the threshold.

Kane and Brigid exchanged puzzled glances, then followed, walking into a vestibule lighted by wall crescents burning with clear white flames. The walls bore carved scenes of procession, of ritual, of ceremony. Brigid noted that a spiral design, much like the insignia worn by the Magickers, dominated every scene. The low ceiling bulged with a full relief image of a cobra's body.

A dry, almost dusty perfume pervaded the passage. No one spoke as they quietly wended their way down the curving stairwell. They heard nothing but their own controlled breathing and the scuff of their feet on the gritty stone steps. Kane realized that the deeper they walked, the brighter it became. A waver glow from below, like a phosphorescent fog, lit their path.

The stairwell made another gentle turn, then ended abruptly in a corridor full of shadows and echoes. A blue-green glow shimmered from the end of the passageway, flickering in a rapid, almost hypnotic rhythm. Still hand-in-hand with Zhou Tzu and Nora, Kumudvati walked toward the throbbing radiance.

The corridor entered a vast chamber, and they all jolted to a halt, gazing around in speechless surprise. It was like a temple built beneath a temple, a shrine shaped somewhat like an amphitheater, with huge square pillars stretching up to a ceiling lost in darkness. The surfaces were carved into contorted shapes and coiling arabesques. Kane, Brigid and Philboyd blinked in amazement, trying to absorb the vision their eyes fed their minds.

The floor slanted downward at an ever increasing pitch, so the center of the chamber formed a huge, funnel-shaped hollow. Rising from the epicenter loomed a gleaming object twice the height of a man and three times that in width.

Light pulsed all around it, shifting, shimmering, strobing. At first Kane could make no sense of what he was looking at—four perfectly round rings, a concentric series of smaller wheels within wheels, all spinning and rotating in relation with one another. The largest outermost ring was mounted on a metal shaft atop a gimbal bearing. The alloy-sheathed shaft glowed as from within, streams of light playing all around the spinning rings like coiling and uncoiling snakes of blue-glowing fog.

The blaze of light seemed to pour up from the central shaft, as if it were a conduit. The strobing effect accentuated by the spinning rings was almost hypnotic. Luminous circles of silvery blue spread swiftly around the wheels and vanished, beams of light that laced and interlaced in fantastic yet ordered geometric forms. Glowing spirals sprang out from the outermost ring in a shimmering borealis.

Squinting away from the light, Kane finally got his voice and lungs working again. Dragging in a deep breath, he asked, "Is this the essence of the Naga?"

Kumudvati only nodded, as if she were too numb to speak. Then she leaned her head back and cried, *"Sudarshana!"*

The cavern walls threw her voice back, the echoes chasing one another throughout the gloom. Then the echoes were broken by a deep laugh from Brewster Philboyd. Kane glanced over his shoulder at the man. A slightly mocking grin creased his face, but in the pale blue radiance of the chamber, he looked like a drowned corpse.

"What's so funny?" Kane demanded.

"I don't know what a Sudarshana is supposed to be," Philboyd replied, his voice husky from repressing a chuckle. "But I damn well know a gyroscope when I see one."

"What?" Kane demanded raggedly, his one-word exclamation echoing repeatedly.

Brewster Philboyd nodded toward the spinning rings. "I'm an astrophysicist, remember? I worked with gyroscopes all the time. That thing may be one of the biggest I've ever seen, but it's still a gyroscope."

Brigid said doubtfully, "Are you sure? What would a gyroscope have to do with earth energies?"

With all eyes trained upon him, Philboyd stepped the very edge of the funnel-slanting depression and gestured. "Look at it. A rigid central mass spinning around a central axis in balance. The same properties apply to Earth…our planet acts like a giant gyroscope as it orbits the Sun, right?"

Brigid's eyes roved over the glinting, rotating wheels. "You've got a point," she said musingly. "According to Einstein's general theory of relativity, if most of the matter in the Universe happens to be spinning, most of the free energy particles will be pulled around with it. So if the gyroscope here is a tap conduit over a nexus of geomantic energy, it might act as both a governor for the flow and a vent for the excess build-up."

Nora suddenly spoke in such an emphatic fashion that everyone jumped. "The Naga, the Annunaki or whatever you want to call them, installed that here as a way to bleed off the build-up of electromagnetic energy generated by the ley lines. The gyroscope maintained the wavelength balance, kept it harmony so the radiation interacted with the people in a cause-and-effect relationship."

"What do you mean by that?" Javalara asked, brow deeply creased in consternation. Kane received the impression that Magicker already knew what Nora meant.

She swung on the man, her eyes narrowed in accusation. "Like my colleague Dr. Philboyd, I'm an astrophysicist, but my field of study was subatomic particles. We used something very much like a gyroscope to generate them, what we called a particle accelerator. One of the things I learned about particles and gyroscopes is that they will resist the axis of their spin being altered. For example, if you apply torque in one direction it will respond with motion in a different direction. It's called gyroscopic precession."

She waved an arm toward it, stating flatly, "I think the spin is powered by the electromagnetic flux. There's no way for gyroscopic precession to occur without a causal effect. So you did more than alter the spin, Javalara—you torqued it into reverse. When you reversed the spin direction, you reversed the wavelength of the geomagnetic radiation. What had once been neutral became harmful."

Nora shot a look over at Brigid, Kane, Zhou Tzu and Kumudvati. "How are you feeling?"

The question surprised Kane, but only because he had become aware of feeling unwell. His chest ached when he breathed, and intermittent sharp pains stabbed through his head, starting from his sinuses and seeming to completely pierce his skull. But rather than list his symptoms, he said simply, "Not so good, thanks for asking."

"I don't feel so good, either," Brigid said. "Pain in my head and joints…of course that last could be a carryover to spending half the day on the back of an elephant."

Nora didn't laugh. "When I studied energy particles I read reports of how some wavelengths of electromagnetic radiation affected biological matter."

Tapping the side of her head, she said, "Nerve cell loci, located on the walls of the cerebral aqueducts of the brain, and the choroid plexus of the brain are affected, which causes secretion of cytokines into the bloodstream. The number-one major symptom of that is psychological depression and chronic stress, which in turn lead to dissociative disorders."

"Like overwhelming ambition," Zhou Tzu stated grimly. He flicked his gaze toward Javalara. "The desire to gain power…and to rule."

The Magicker licked his lips nervously. "Colonel Puyang was an ambitious man long before the balance of the essence was altered."

"Yes," Kumudvati agreed darkly. "And according to my mother, you were a manipulative man. You brought the idea of changing the balance to Puyang, didn't you? You hoped if he agreed to help you do so, you would be able to control him and through him, control the Devi-Naga."

"Is that true?" Brigid challenged. "Were you in collusion with Colonel Puyang?"

The man forced a sickly, derisive grin to his face as if the notion was too ridiculous to seriously consider. Then his shoulders slumped in resignation, in defeat. In a flat, dead voice he admitted, "Yes. But I had only the best interests of the empire at heart."

"I've heard that before," Kane intoned ominously. "I ended up having to kill most of the people who said it."

Javalara shook his head sadly. "I did not understand the nature of the phenomena. The direction of the spin and thus the energy flow were designed for a specific purpose, to essentially maintain the life force here in Angkor. I did not realize what would happen when I reversed it."

"What do you think happened?" Brigid asked.

Zhou Tzu took it upon himself to answer the question. "Antilife, for all intents and purposes."

Philboyd regarded the man speculatively. "That's a little metaphorical...and very unscientific."

"I don't think so," Nora said. "The frequency, the wavelength of the radiation, was turned in the opposite direction so it became the antithesis of life as we understand it. The discord here is proof of that."

Mind racing, Kane said, "The Cerberus recon satellite was blinded by an energy surge discharged by the towers of this complex. My aircraft's electronics were inhibited when I made a flyover. Are you saying that Angkor Wat has always acted as a vent for the geomagnetic energy, but when the particle flow was reversed it generated a dampening field?"

Nora nodded. "I believe so. When the nexus was in balance, the discharge of neutral energy would not have adversely affected biological or other matter."

"How come nobody ever discovered this chamber before?"

Kumudvati shrugged as if the matter was of little importance. "Angkor Wat is honeycombed with hidden passages, secret doors disguised as frescoes. If the existence of the essence was restricted to a priesthood, then that knowledge would not be widely disseminated."

"The question still remains," Brigid declared, turning to face Javalara, "how do we reverse the reversal?"

Javalara edged back toward the door. "I've given that much thought. I fear it will require an intense exposure to the geomantic energy. And that could be fatal."

Kane took a step toward him. "Why do I get the feeling you won't be the first to volunteer?"

Javalara swallowed hard, then squared his shoulders. "I won't deny I'm frightened, but if I have to sacrifice myself to undo what I—"

The staccato crackling of a subgun on full-auto rang out. Wads of lead gouged dust-spurting furrows in the edge of the doorway. Javalara cried out, his back arching as if he had received a powerful kick between his shoulder blades. The fabric of his robe burst open and blood bloomed on his chest. Staggering forward, he pitched into Kane's arms.

Kane wrestled him to one side. "Take cover!" he barked.

Everyone did as he said, except for Zhou Tzu, who gazed without expression into the corridor. Distorted shadows crawled along the floor and walls. Calmly he said, "Colonel Puyang has stepped onto the game board. The warlord's gambit draws to a close."

Chapter 28

Kane placed Javalara in a half-prone position against the wall. The man's face twisted in pain but he said nothing, not even when he coughed up the pink froth from a punctured lung.

Sin Eater in hand, Kane darted behind the nearest pillar, barely avoiding a short burst of bullets that stitched pockmarks in its ornately carven surface. Peering around the edge, he saw nothing in the corridor beyond but a hulking shadow. He threw a swift glance toward Brigid, who crouched behind the column opposite him, her TP-9 held in a double-handed grip.

Although Nora and Kumudvati had rushed to cover, Zhou Tzu hadn't moved. The blaze of geofire behind him formed a shimmering halo around his body. He called out in Khmer and after a moment, a man's harsh voice responded, full of fury and thick with hatred. Zhou Tzu responded in a calm, slightly contemptuous tone, then stated in English, "Colonel Puyang would take up where we left off ten years ago. He would fight me and one or the other of us would kill the other. I have not the time nor the inclination to grant him his wish. Besides, I think he is injured."

"Is he alone?" Brigid asked.

"I believe so."

"Then it might be easier to reason with him if you tell him he's outnumbered."

"Perhaps," Zhou Tzu replied. "But words of reason are wasted on him. I can tarry no longer."

"Tarry?" Kane echoed. "We're not going anywhere, are we?"

Zhou Tzu favored him with a slight smile, almost pitying in nature. "*I* am, Mr. Kane. I will finally discharge the karmic debt incurred by Jayavarma the Seventh a thousand years ago. Only I can restore the balance of the essence of the Naga, and in doing so, return harmony to the empire of the Khmers."

Kane stared at him in confusion, feeling both compassion and anger welling up in him. "We've got a fused-out maniac ready to blast his way in here…fooling around with that whirligig contraption can wait until we take care of him."

"I expect you, Mr. Kane and Miss Baptiste to, as you say, take care of Colonel Puyang and to keep him from interfering with what I have to do. Furthermore, I charge you with protecting the Devi-Naga and her guardian from him."

"Her guardian?" Philboyd demanded, flattened against the wall. "Who the hell is that?"

"That would be me," Nora said quietly as she enfolded Kumudvati protectively in her arms.

Half rising in an angry incredulity, Kane turned toward her. "What are you talking about? You can't—"

Automatic fire hammered and Kane sank down again. Two of the little subguns blasted in a drumming syncopation. Double streams of slugs chipped flinders from the pillars, rock dust sifting down in a haze. Twisting, Kane squeezed off two shots through the door and the gunfire stopped abruptly.

"As I told you earlier today, Mr. Kane," Zhou Tzu said unperturbed, "Miss Pennick is no longer your concern."

"You can't make that decision," Brigid snapped. "You can't force her into this role."

"No one forced me, Brigid," Nora declared matter-of-factly. "The role I was forced into was that of an exile in Cerberus. Here an offer was made to me and I accepted. It was meant to be."

"*What* was?" Philboyd exploded in disbelief. "You think you were predestined to be offered the job of nanny to the little serpent princess? Come *on,* Nora! You're a scientist, you can't honestly believe—"

The jackhammering thunder of submachine-gun fire overwhelmed the man's words. Chunks of stone burst from the pillars, ricochets keening wildly throughout the vast vault. Kumudvati cried out in fear and buried her face in Nora's shoulder as a bouncing slug showered them with gravel.

Kane returned the fire with a three-round burst from his Sin Eater. Midway through the full-auto fusillade, he realized only one gun was firing. Brigid realized it, too, and swung around the base of column and squeezed off two shots. Neither of them had any idea if their bullets found targets. They saw only shadows crawling across the floor and walls of the corridor but the gun fell silent.

Zhou Tzu shouted in Khmer, a demand or a question. After several seconds, Puyang responded, his voice tight and wheezing.

"I believe he has been wounded," the general said. "But not mortally."

Kane glanced toward Zhou Tzu, looked away, then his head swiveled back so swiftly his neck tendons twinged in protest. The general still stood ramrod straight, but he clutched at his right rib cage, hand cupped as if to catch the pain and the blood. His fingers glistened red and wet and his shirtfront was sodden.

Kane started to rise but Zhou Tzu checked the movement with an imperious gesture of his free hand. "As you were, Mr. Kane. You, too, Miss Baptiste. I have informed the colonel of my intentions regarding the essence of the Naga. He will try to stop me. You in turn will stop him."

"General—" Kane began, but the man cut him off with another sharp gesture.

"Do you remember what I said to you about duty, Mr. Kane?" Zhou Tzu's face was calm and composed, his bearing still dignified.

Kane answered quietly, "You said that a soldier does what is needed to fulfill a duty or to discharge an obligation, or he is no more important to the cycle of life than a grain of sand in the Gobi."

Zhou Tzu nodded approvingly. "I also said that as soldiers you and I can make common cause and fulfill our respective duties. You are a fine soldier, Mr. Kane. Honor me and yourself by helping me to fulfill *my* duty and leave a legacy more important than a grain of sand."

Kane did not speak, but he met the general's gaze unblinkingly. The image of Ayn Thoraldson, mourning for the husband he had been duped into killing, flashed into the forefront of his mind. Bitterly he said, "I won't be your pawn, general."

"No, you *will* be a soldier…but I will not issue an

order in this instance. I can only make a request." He paused and in a voice pitched barely above a whisper, Zhou Tzu said, "Do not let a thousand years of karma go for nothing, Mr. Kane."

Feeling Brigid's eyes on him as well as those of Nora and Kumudvati, Kane could say only, "No, sir. I will not."

Zhou Tzu inclined his head in a respectful, grateful bow. "Thank you, Mr. Kane."

Struggling to keep the sadness welling up within him from registering in his face or voice, Kane replied softly, "Goodbye, sir."

Zhou Tzu turned smartly on his heel and with almost military precision, stroked the tear-streaked faces of Nora and Kumudvati, a brief farewell caress. Then he stepped down in the funnel-shaped depression and slid down the incline, out of Kane's range of vision.

Another hard-edged, hate-filled tirade in Khmer bawled out of the corridor. Kane looked expectantly over at Brigid. "What'd he say this time?"

In a flat tone she translated, "He says all of us in here will die, even the Devi-Naga."

"If we don't do what?"

"There is no 'if,'" she answered darkly. "He's going to do his damnedest to kill us all."

As if on cue, flame and lead poured into the vault, and Kane pulled back as a storm of slugs chiseled more fragments out of the pillar. Ricochets twanged like multiple guitar strings. Howling like a blood-mad berserker, Colonel Puyang charged out of the corridor and into the vault, weapon blazing in a left to right arc. The man was more than willing to risk death so he could deal death.

Crimson flowed from a laceration on the right side of his head, and his uniform tunic bore two wet, red stains.

Brigid huddled down, not daring to move during the barrage. Kane leaned around the base of the column, finger crooked over the Sin Eater's trigger stud. A ricochet caught him a glancing blow on the right forearm, numbing his limb from fingertip to elbow.

Puyang whirled toward him, leading with his flame-spitting subgun. Then the firing pin clicked dryly on an empty magazine, and for an instant the expression of baffled rage that crossed his face was so comical Kane almost laughed. All humor in the situation vanished when Puyang hurled his weapon directly at Kane, the butt smashing against his forehead.

Multicolored spirals pinwheeled behind Kane's eyes as a bomb of stars seemed to detonate inside his skull. Moving incredibly fast for such a heavyset man, Colonel Puyang jumped forward and kicked him in the chest with his heavy boot. Kane took the kick rather than risk a fractured wrist trying to block it. The blow knocked almost all the wind from his lungs, slamming the back of his head hard against the stone snout of a cobra that projected from the column.

Puyang bulled on past him, hands outstretched to grasp Nora and Kumudvati. They cringed away, but their expressions of defiance didn't alter, even when his hand closed around the slender column of Nora's throat.

Brigid Baptiste bounded at him, gauging the distance between him and the women as too narrow to risk using her pistol. She landed on his broad back like a pouncing wildcat, the fingers of her left hand curving around to gouge at his eyes.

Puyang snarled, releasing Nora so his arms could reach over and back to clutch Brigid. She chopped with the steel barrel of the TP-9 once, twice, three times at the back of his groping right hand. She heard the crunch of metacarpal bones.

Bellowing in a mad fury, Colonel Puyang kicked himself back to crush her against the unyielding rock of the vault's wall. Throwing herself clear, Brigid landed in a crouch and when Puyang heeled around to face her, she squeezed off a single shot. The round took the scar-faced man high in the chest.

Puyang staggered blindly, an animal whimper issuing from his blood-and-saliva flecked lips. Teetering on the edge of the incline, he touched the blood pumping from the hole in his chest, looked quizzically at Brigid and vomited vermilion. Arms windmilling, he toppled backward like a felled tree.

Breath rasping in and out of her straining lungs, Brigid exchanged a long look with Nora and Kumudvati. "Are you all right?"

Nora gingerly fingered her throat and nodded. Kumudvati clung to her but remained silent.

Then the reaction hit her. She began shivering, her mind recoiling in horror from what she had done and from what might have been, had she not done it. At the scuff of feet behind her, Brigid turned to see Philboyd dragging Kane forward. He squinted through the streaks of blood that trickled from the cut at his hairline. She went to him, asking, "Are you all right?"

"Hell, no, I'm not all right," he bit out. "But I'm better off than Puyang and that's something."

"At this juncture," Philboyd panted, "I'd say that's pretty much everything."

They moved to the edge of the depression, squinting against the dazzling light that pulsed and swam around the spinning, rotating rings. Kane sluiced blood away from his eyes, barely able to make out the figure of Zhou Tzu standing at the base of the support column. The general grasped it with both hands, his forehead pressed against the metal, his lips moving as if in silent prayer.

The body of Colonel Puyang had not slid completely down the funnel-shaped walls. A smear of blood marked his passage, and a ribbon of scarlet crawled down the incline where it intersected with the shaft at the point where it sprouted from the floor. As the blood touched it, the light shifted, shimmering, the color wavering from blue to green to yellow to orange to red.

Kumudvati and Nora joined them at the edge. Closing her eyes, the girl steepled her fingers beneath her chin and began a ghostly, singsong chant. Zhou Tzu intoned the same words in cadence with her, words more ancient than even Brigid had known existed.

Kane experienced the shuddery sensation that they weren't just words, but sounds whose roots stretched far, far back into a dim time before humans had a language of their own. Perhaps the warlord and the serpent princess spoke the same tongue as the Annunaki and the Naga.

The light wavered, losing its red hue, strobing back down to a green-blue. Incandescent tentacles uncoiled from the outermost wheel, sliding down around Zhou Tzu's shoulders, slipping over his body, embracing him and sheathing him in a cocoon of phosphorescence.

Kumudvati's chant reached crescendo, a shrill, eerie wail. A humming pressed against their eardrums, as of a disturbed gigantic beehive. The dark outline of Zhou Tzu's body became a flickering shadow, then a gray mist. The mist flowed up, drawn into and absorbed by the glimmering aurora of geomantic energy channeled through the spinning rings. Its blue tint deepened, changing to a rich, verdant green, a luminous reflection of the jungle colors.

The hum slowly subsided and as it did so, the pain and physical discomfort of the people standing before the essence of the Naga ebbed. Wonderingly, Philboyd probed up under the bandage wrapped around his head and his fingers came away dry. He touched his bruised face and announced hoarsely, "I don't hurt anymore."

In hushed whisper, Nora said, "The general did it."

Then she and Kumudvati sank down on the edge of the incline and wept in each other's arms.

Brigid turned Kane's face toward her and eyed the laceration on his forehead. The cut was still there but no longer trickling blood. "Amazing," she said falteringly.

Although Kane no longer felt pain, he didn't feel much of anything at all. He felt drained, an empty man, bereft of emotion and thought. He, Brigid and Philboyd turned away, to leave the two women to share their grief. Nora called out to him, "Kane...wait."

Philboyd and Brigid walked to the doorway of the vaulted chamber as Kane stepped beside Nora Pennick. In a voice choked by sobs, she said, "This wasn't our doing, you know...but something else entirely. We were both caught up in the wheel of the general's karma. I think it might have been my destiny from the very beginning... Another will than mine brought me here."

"Like a puppet," he said in a flat, dead voice. "A tool. A pawn in the warlord's gambit."

Nora shook her head. "No, not a game or gambit at all. It was preordained."

Kumudvati gazed up at Kane, her eyes glimmering with tears but also with an emotion he could not—or would not—identify. "You were an agent of that fate, Mr. Kane, and Zhou Tzu knew that. You are much like him, but in this incarnation you were the general's lieutenant whose own devotion to service allowed him to discharge his duty. You should be proud."

Kane took a long last look at the essence of the Naga and murmured, "No more important than a grain of sand."

Then he turned and strode across the chamber to where Brigid waited for him.

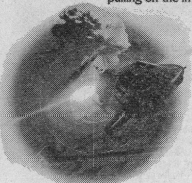

THE
DESTROYER
DREAM THING

DEMONIC GOD—OR FISH STORY?

A strange seismic disturbance in the south Pacific has put the world in a fighting mood. Violence is especially high among the peaceniks, as spiritualists morph into savage mobs. Scientists acknowledge that the oceans are shrinking, but nobody can explain why.

Steam vents as big as volcanoes burst open around the world. But is it free geothermal power...or a death knell? A typhoon smashes Hawaii; the Amazon is a killer sauna; Rocky Mountain skiers are steamed like clams. Is the world succumbing to a theoretical Tectonic Hollow...or the will of a giant squid? Either way, it just won a date with Remo, who's ready to fry some calamari.

Available April 2005 at your favorite retail outlet.

GECCGEN05MM